# THE SHORT END

Broken Galaxy Book Four

Phil Huddleston

# CONTENTS

Title Page
From Earlier Books ........................................... 3
Attention to Orders ........................................... 7
Chapter One ........................................... 9
Chapter Two ........................................... 22
Chapter Three ........................................... 33
Chapter Four ........................................... 45
Chapter Five ........................................... 60
Chapter Six ........................................... 72
Chapter Seven ........................................... 82
Chapter Eight ........................................... 93
Chapter Nine ........................................... 102
Chapter Ten ........................................... 114
Chapter Eleven ........................................... 125
Chapter Twelve ........................................... 135
Chapter Thirteen ........................................... 150
Chapter Fourteen ........................................... 160
Chapter Fifteen ........................................... 170
Chapter Sixteen ........................................... 182
Chapter Seventeen ........................................... 194
Chapter Eighteen ........................................... 204

| | |
|---|---|
| Chapter Nineteen | **211** |
| Chapter Twenty | **220** |
| Chapter Twenty-One | **228** |
| Chapter Twenty-Two | **238** |
| Chapter Twenty-Three | **249** |
| Chapter Twenty-Four | **260** |
| Chapter Twenty-Five | **269** |
| Chapter Twenty-Six | **280** |
| Chapter Twenty-Seven | **291** |
| Chapter Twenty-Eight | **301** |
| Epilogue | **314** |
| Author Notes | **317** |
| Preview of Next Book | **318** |
| Works | **322** |
| About the Author | **323** |

Broken Galaxy Book Four: *The Short End*
by Phil Huddleston

Copyright © 2021 by Phil Huddleston
THE AUTHOR RETAINS ALL RIGHTS FOR THIS BOOK

ISBN eBook: 978-1-7351396-8-5
ISBN Paperback: 978-1-7351396-9-2
ISBN Hardcover: 979-8-8639902-6-2

Reproduction or transmission of this book, in whole or in part, by electronic, mechanical, photocopying, recording, or by any other means is strictly prohibited, except with prior written permission from the author or the publisher, except in the case of brief quotations embodied in critical reviews and certain other non-commercial uses permitted by copyright law. Inquiries may be directed to webmaster@philhuddleston.com

This is a work of fiction. Names, characters, locations, organizations, and events portrayed are either products of the author's creative imagination or used fictitiously. Any resemblance to actual names, characters, events, businesses, locales, or persons is coincidental and not intended to infringe on any copyright or trademark.

Cover Art by Ad Astra Book Covers
adastrabookcovers@gmail.com

# FROM EARLIER BOOKS

**Broken Galaxy** - The name used to describe the current state of affairs in the Orion Arm of the Milky Way. The ancient Golden Empire lasted for twenty thousand years; but two thousand years ago it collapsed, throwing the Arm into a Dark Age from which it is still recovering.

**Earth Defense Force (EDF)** - the starship fleet of Admiral Rita Page. Originally a rag-tag lend-lease fleet loaned to Rita by the Nidarians. After the Battle of Jupiter, when Rita narrowly pushed the invading Singheko out of the Solar System, she named it the EDF. In a preemptive strike to prevent another invasion of Earth, Rita took the EDF fleet to the Singheko home system where she fought them again, decimating both sides and leading to a stalemate.

**Jim Carter** - U.S. Marine turned mercenary pilot turned semi-retired hermit turned space pilot. Fought the starship *Jade* at the Battle of Dutch Harbor. Fought the Singheko invasion at the Battle of Saturn and the Battle of Jupiter. Forced to decide between his love for Bonnie and Rita, he chose Rita, leaving Bonnie bitter but accepting. Most recently served in the Battle of Deriko as CAG (Commander Attack Group) for the EDF.

**Bonnie Page** - Ex-Air Force fighter pilot; first the lover of Jim Carter, later the lover of Rita Page. After the Battle of Dutch Harbor involving *Jade*, *Corresse*, Russia, America, and

Canada, Bonnie and Rita hitched a ride on the corvette *Corresse* to ask the Nidarian Empire for help in saving Earth from the Singheko invasion. Bonnie was coerced by Nidarian High Councilor Garatella to find the ancient and highly advanced starship *Dragon* - a relic of the former Golden Empire. In time, she located the long-lost warship - but disobeyed Garatella and kept it for Earth. As Captain of the *Dragon*, fought a number of battles in the Sol System and at Singheko.

**Rita Page, Admiral of the Black** - Clone created by the renegade starship *Jade* with the dual memories, knowledge, and feelings of both Jim Carter and Bonnie Page. As a result of her dual consciousness, she was in love with both Jim and Bonnie. Took Bonnie's last name since she didn't have one of her own. Fought *Jade* at the Battle of Dutch Harbor. Went to Nidaria with Bonnie, returned with a rag-tag Nidarian lend-lease fleet to fight the Singheko invasion. Against all odds, drove the Singheko away from Earth, but not before the Singheko imprisoned 96,000 Human slaves and carried them away in large slave ships. Undertook a preemptive strike against the Singheko home system to prevent further invasions. Fought the Singheko to a standstill at the Battle of Deriko.

**Zukra** - Grand Admiral of the Singheko Empire. Recently performed a coup on his leadership, killing all who stood in his way. Now in firm control of the government, he intends to create a vast Empire spanning the entire Orion Arm. But first he must get through the Humans who have him stalemated in his own system.

**Garatella** - High Councilor of the Nidarian Empire. Lent an old, broken-down fleet of warships - with a temporary Nidarian crew - to Rita Page to defend against the Singheko. When Rita fought off the invasion and drove the Singheko out of the Sol System, Garatella decided Humanity was too dangerous to allow their expansion into space and turned on them. Sent a fleet to assist Zukra against the Humans and their temporary Nidarian crews, leading to the Battle of Deriko.

**Tatiana Powell** - A young half-English, half-Ukrainian woman arrested by the Russian police for drug smuggling. She was handed over to the Singheko as they were filling their slave ships with Human prisoners. Imprisoned in a large wire cage on a slave ship sent to the planet Deriko along with 96,000 other Human prisoners. After arrival at Deriko, Tatiana initiated a slave rebellion and pushed the Singheko off the planet.

**Dragon** - an advanced destroyer of the ancient Golden Empire, lost for two thousand years in a canyon on Mars. Rediscovered and repaired by Bonnie Page. Technology obtained from *Dragon* was retrofitted to the remainder of the EDF Fleet in preparation for a counterattack on the Singheko. Plans for the *Dragon*'s advanced stardrive were sent to Nidarian High Councilor Garatella in partial fulfillment of the original bargain to help Earth; but plans for the advanced weapon of the *Dragon* - the gamma lance - were held back by Rita Page as a bargaining chip for further Nidarian assistance. However, due to a spy placed by Garatella in the Nidarian crew sent to assist Rita, the design for the gamma lance was obtained by both Garatella and Admiral Zukra.

*Jade* - a sentient scout ship which crashed into the Canadian Northwest Territory in 1947 and lay undiscovered for many decades. Found by Jim Carter and brought back to life. Falsely claimed to be Nidarian but was actually Singheko. Intent on escaping Earth and returning to Singheko to effect the enslavement of Humanity, *Jade* created the clone Rita to assist in repairs and to take back as a specimen.

**Captain Bekerose** - Flag Captain of the battlecruiser *Merkkessa*, the flagship of the Earth Defense Force. A Nidarian.

**Gillian Carter Rodgers** - Sister of Jim Carter. Guardian of

Imogen, the child of Rita Page and Jim Carter.

**Mark Rodgers** - Husband of Jim Carter's sister Gillian.

**The Bear** - A big male grizzly that attacked Jim Carter in the Canadian Northwest Territories, leading him to discover *Jade* in his attempt to escape. Now a large bearskin in the Flag Cabin of the battlecruiser *Merkkessa*.

# ATTENTION TO ORDERS

By order of EDF Fleet Admiral Rita Page and in recognition for conspicuous gallantry and intrepidity under fire in the recent actions against the combined forces of the Singheko and Nidarian Empires, the following individuals are promoted to the positions indicated:

<excerpt>

- Captain Hideo Sato to Admiral, Battlecruiser Cube One. Admiral Sato will utilize *Asiana* as his flagship.
- Captain Bonnie Page to Commodore, Destroyer Wing. Commodore Page will utilize *Dragon* as her command ship.
- Lieutenant Rachel Gibson to Commander and transferred to the staff of Fleet Admiral Rita Page as Assistant Flag Aide.
- Lieutenant Dan Worley to Commander and Chief Engineering Officer, *Dragon*.
- Ensign (Brevet Lieutenant) Emma Gibbs to Lieutenant and Tactical Officer, *Dragon*.

<end excerpt. Document continues for eight more pages>

## **POSTHUMOUS PROMOTIONS**

By order of EDF Fleet Admiral Rita Page, the following individuals are promoted posthumously to the ranks indicated. May they rest in peace.

<excerpt>

- Captain Tarraine Mountain Child One, Nidarian, of the cruiser *Daeddam*, to Admiral.
- Commander Lirrassa Ocean Child Six, Nidarian, of the destroyer *Dragon*, to Captain.
- Commander Sarah North, Human, of the destroyer *Dragon*, to Captain.
- Lieutenant Commander Harry McMaster, Human, of the destroyer *Dragon*, to Commander.
- Ensign Gary Goodwin, Human, of the destroyer *Dragon*, to Lieutenant (j.g.).

<end excerpt. Document continues for twenty-seven more pages>

# CHAPTER ONE

**Planet Nidaria - City of Sanctuary**
**Government House**

High Councilor Garatella of the Nidarian Empire stared angrily across the desk.

"I'm getting a little tired of your excuses, Admiral."

Before him, Fleet Admiral Tanno sat - but he sat at attention. He knew he was in trouble. All it would take would be the flick of Garatella's finger - a quick word to the right person - and Tanno would be nothing but a faint memory. An unexpected suicide. Another admiral relegated to the dustbin of history.

For Tanno was the admiral who had sent a Nidarian expeditionary fleet to assist Admiral Zukra in the attack on the Humans. And Tanno was the admiral who had assured Garatella it would be a pushover - after all, the Humans had little experience in space warfare, while the Nidarians and the Singheko had been fighting in space for thousands of years.

As it turned out, pushover was not exactly the word Tanno would now use. The tattered remnants of his expeditionary force had come straggling back to Nidaria, shot to hell, with the story of a battle that left space littered with the broken bodies of thousands of spacers - and the broken wrecks of a half-dozen of their front-line warships. Tanno had been patching up damaged ships for three months now, and still wasn't finished.

"Aye, High Councilor. I did not mean to make excuses. But we require another three months to launch a second campaign against the Humans. There's a limit to how hard I can drive the workers in the space dock."

"Bah!" Garatella spat, turning in his chair to stare out his window. From the top floor of Government House, the city of Sanctuary spread out before him. It stretched for miles, straddling the river Tassa flowing through the center of the city to a large bay. Far off, right at the horizon, Garatella could see the bay flare out where it met the ocean. Boats - commercial and pleasure - dotted the bay, which gleamed brightly in the morning sun. And far across the bay, almost lost in the distance, the tip of Mount Tassakka could be seen - a shield volcano 3,700 meters high, towering over the plains that surrounded Sanctuary.

"We're losing valuable time!" Garatella growled bitterly. "That stupid Human witch Rita sits at Deriko, right in front of Zukra's nose, taunting us! But at some point, she's going to realize she can't stay there - that position is not defensible. We have to attack her again before she leaves!"

"Councilor, I must tell you," Tanno spoke. "I think she knows that already. She is playing with us. For the moment, she has Zukra pinned in place - preventing him from attacking Earth, or Asdif or Ursa, or taking any other major action. She has him temporarily bottled up on his own planet, in his own system. And of course, that also keeps us pinned - the terms of our alliance with Zukra compel us to go to his aid before any other action. I think this Human admiral is smarter than we thought."

Garatella spun back to face Tanno. "But why not send our fleet to come in behind her, while Zukra sallies out from Ridendo? She'd be caught between the two fleets! She wouldn't stand a chance!"

Tanno shook his head. "Councilor, with all due respect, space warfare isn't like land warfare. It's three dimensional, and it involves incredible distances. She would know of our arrival in the system behind her in plenty of time to make an escape."

Garatella sniffed. "So what is our strategy, then?"

"We must have patience, High Councilor. We must finish building out the new battlecruisers, cruisers, and destroyers as planned. We must complete the repairs on our fleet. We can then rejoin Zukra at Singheko. That will give him enough strength to leave a protective force around Ridendo shielding it from Human attacks, while our combined fleet attacks them. They will run - of that I am certain. We pursue them wherever they go, chasing them down until they can run no more. Then we destroy them."

"If they run to Earth?"

"That's actually the best scenario for us, High Councilor. That puts them far away from any potential allies to Coreward. We can bombard their planet with nukes, while our fleet fights them in their own solar system. We'll make short work of them there."

"And if she's smart enough to run the other way?"

"Then her most likely destination would be Dekanna, to join forces with the Dariama there. That would also play into our hands - the Dariama are notorious cowards. They'll break and run at the first sight of our combined fleet entering their system. And that will leave the Humans to fight alone."

Garatella glared at his senior admiral. "You'd better be right this time, Tanno. I don't fancy losing another battle to these damn upstart Humans! The Council is not happy with the results of our last adventure. And if I go down, Tanno..."

Garatella left the threat unsaid.

Tanno didn't have to hear the rest. Sweat ran down his spine. His hands shook as Garatella dismissed him. Rising to leave, his knees were shaky as he moved to the door. Tanno realized he had only one choice.

*The Humans must die. All of them. Right down to the last ship. And then their planet must be wiped clean. They must not be allowed to expand into space.*

*Or I'll have a sudden, unexplained suicide.*

### Singheko System - Planet Deriko
### Battlecruiser EDF *Merkkessa* - in orbit

Commander Rachel Gibson entered her cabin and smiled. Commander Dan Worley was already there. He had somehow sandwiched a small table into the tiny compartment. The little table had a white tablecloth, and two electric candles that looked almost like the real thing. Between the candles was a silver serving dish.

And flowers. He had flowers. Little purple flowers that looked a bit like lilacs. Small blossoms, but beautiful.

"Where on Earth did you get these?" Rachel exclaimed, reaching out to touch them in wonder. Her dark brown eyes flashed in delight.

"Not "on Earth". On Deriko," Dan replied. "I traded with one of the shuttle pilots for them."

"Lord help me, I hope you didn't give him one of our engines," Rachel laughed. "Flowers! Of all things! On a starship! You're crazy, you know that?"

Dan moved behind her and pulled out her chair. "It's your birthday, love! I had to do something!"

"Oh my Lord, you're right! I completely forgot!" Rachel sat, eying the serving dish. "What's that?" she asked suspiciously.

"Oh, just a little something I whipped up," Dan responded with a glint in his eye. "You'll like it." Dan removed the top to the serving dish and waved a hand. "Viola! Meatloaf!"

Rachel stared in horror. "Impossible! We haven't seen real meat in two months! Did you kill something on Deriko? I'm not eating alien meat, you idiot!"

Dan sat in his chair, grinning. "Nope. It's not from Deriko, don't worry. I made a deal with one of the ammunition barge pilots last month. He brought me two pounds of actual ground beef, straight from Earth, hidden in one of the missile containers."

"What did you have to give him?" Rachel asked suspiciously.

"A starship?"

"Just a few small items. Nothing to worry about," said Dan.

"What?" persisted Rachel. "I know you, Dan. And I know how impossible it is to get real meat from Earth out here. What did you give him?"

Dan shrugged. "Just a few odds and ends left over from the battle. It was all scrap, going to be trashed anyway. But he can sell them on Earth as genuine souvenirs of the Battle of Deriko. He makes a few bucks, we get meatloaf."

"Oh, Dan," Rachel said, shaking her head. "You know I'm on the admiral's staff now. Please don't let me hear you doing things like that. You put me in an impossible position. I should report you for this!"

Dan smiled. "Well, at least have some meatloaf first. Then you can report me. Happy Birthday!"

Rachel, still shaking her head, sat at the table. She reached for her knife and fork. Dan leaned forward and carved a huge slice of meatloaf for her, holding it on a triangular serving spoon.

<GENERAL QUARTERS, GENERAL QUARTERS. THIS IS NOT A DRILL. ALL HANDS MAN YOUR BATTLE STATIONS. GENERAL QUARTERS, GENERAL QUARTERS. THIS IS NOT A DRILL. ALL HANDS MAN YOUR BATTLE STATIONS>

"Crap!" yelled Rachel. The sound of the alarm in her embedded comm sounded like someone yelling directly over her head. Dan jumped a foot in the air. He dropped the serving spoon on the white tablecloth.

Both scrambled to their feet, heading for their combat stations, as the lump of meatloaf intended for Rachel soaked into the pristine white tablecloth, leaving a bloody stain.

\*\*\*

Two decks above, Rita Page - Admiral of the Black - took the final steps onto her slightly elevated Flag Bridge, settled into her command chair, and buckled her harness. The Flag Bridge was a raised platform, about eight inches higher than the rest of *Merkkessa*'s bridge. It was surrounded by a railing, with gaps on two sides for entry and exit. Positioned at the rear of the large bridge compartment, it was just large enough for five combat chairs - three in front, and two behind.

Rita took a quick glance at the four-meter diameter holographic display at the front of *Merkkessa*'s bridge. The holo was alive with movement as the warships of her fleet broke orbit to take positions in a defensive formation.

On the planet below it was night. The terminator was already far to the west of them. The lights of the city of Misto Marta lay below them - a small sparkle of life embedded in thousands of square miles of darkness. Even as she watched, the city lights winked out, as the city went to blackout in the face of an enemy attack.

"What do we have, Captain Bekerose?" she asked, addressing the nearby Nidarian who had just finished conferring with the Tactical Officer. Her Flag Captain turned and approached the raised platform, leaning on the railing as he spoke.

"I hope it's just another raid, milady. But they're coming out in force, that's for certain. Six battlecruisers, twelve cruisers, sixteen destroyers. I've ordered defensive plan Mike-Sierra if that meets with your approval."

"It's a feint," said Rita flatly. "They're not ready for a full-scale battle yet. This is just another test to see how we react."

"I think so too, milady. Thus Mike-Sierra. It allows us to position for defense, but without giving away too much."

"Bastards. They love interrupting our dinner."

Bekerose smiled. To an outsider, Bekerose would have looked strange - a humanoid, but with ears that seemed a bit too high on the head. A mouth in the right place - but a small, flattened bump where a Human would expect to see a nose. Five feet nine inches tall - 175 centimeters - Bekerose dwarfed nearly all other Nidarians on the ship, with the notable exception of Rita's senior bodyguards Gabriel and Raphael.

And as always when at Battle Stations, those two were positioned by the entrance to Rita's day cabin, pulse rifles in hand, standing at a loose parade rest. The average Nidarian was only about five feet tall - 152 centimeters - but Gabriel and Raphael stood a full three inches taller than Bekerose. By Nidarian standards, they were giants.

Nidarians had been in space for more than twenty-five thousand years. They were the most valuable spacers in Rita's fleet. Without them...

*Without my Nidarians,* thought Rita, *there wouldn't be any Humans left. The Singheko would have wiped us out long ago. And my wonderful Nidarians even fought against their own kind to save us - because they had promised us. That's called honor...*

"...so if they follow the pattern of the last raid, they'll pull us out of the orbitals, wait until we take up our defensive positions, make a single attack pass, then veer off and return to Ridendo," Bekerose finished.

Rita realized she had been distracted. But she got the gist of Bekerose' comment.

"Let's not assume, though. It could be a full-on attack. I don't think so, because they didn't bring enough ships to really challenge us, but - you never know. Let's be ready for anything."

"Aye, milady," agreed Bekerose.

Rita sat back in her chair, trying to relax. Since the Battle of Deriko three months earlier, her fleet had endured two of these raids - this would be the third. All so far had followed the same pattern - a hit and run, a quick nip at the EDF fleet - but no serious attempt to join battle.

But of course, she had to prepare for the worst-case scenario. Any of the raids could turn into a full-scale battle in a heartbeat. The Singheko were dangerous and unpredictable.

Rita put up a hand and adjusted her helmet slightly. Her jet-black hair had a tendency to grow fast. She had let it get just a bit too thick. It pushed up her helmet a bit, which irritated her.

*Need to get a haircut when this battle is over...it's so annoying.*

Rachel Gibson, her new Assistant Flag Aide, ran into the bridge, stepped up to the platform, and slammed into the chair on her right, buckling her harness.

Rita smiled at the young Commander. She had a special fondness for Rachel. In so many ways, Rachel reminded Rita of her friend Bonnie. She didn't look much like Bonnie, a bit shorter and brunette instead of Bonnie's blond. But she had Bonnie's personality - outgoing, competent, unafraid. Always ready with an idea, never shirking her duty, and a perpetual smile that lit up a room.

In fact, it was Bonnie who had recommended Rachel to Rita's staff. Rachel had originally been the Assistant Tactical Officer - ATO - on the destroyer *Dragon*. When Rachel's Nidarian senior officer Lirrassa had been killed in one of the last battles with the Singheko, Rachel had stepped into the Tactical Officer role seamlessly. She had even assumed temporary command of the *Dragon* for a short period of time and had distinguished herself in that role as well.

So, immediately after the Battle of Deriko, Bonnie had sent Rachel to the flagship with a message - a note stating that Rachel was command material and should be groomed for promotion. Rita had brought Rachel on to her staff as Assistant Flag Aide - and had not been disappointed. The former Tactical Officer of the *Dragon* was scary competent.

*Bonnie trained her well. She's fantastic,* thought Rita. *I wish I had a dozen like her.*

Leaning over toward her, Rita spoke softly. "Rachel, Captain Dallitta's down on the surface today. You'll act as my Flag Aide, so move over to the other chair."

Rachel gave Rita a million-dollar smile, unbuckled, and crossed behind Rita to the other chair on Rita's left, the position of Flag Aide. The position of Flag Aide was a captain's slot - sitting in this chair was like a temporary promotion. She buckled into the chair and fired up the console in front of it, preparing for battle.

"Fleet is in position for Mike-Sierra," called Bekerose.

Rita studied the holo. Her fleet was now in formation. Eight 200-meter battlecruisers formed a cube a thousand klicks across, with one of the massive ships at each corner. Their interlocking fields of fire allowed them to protect each other. Any enemy vessel entering their range would be in a massive crossfire from all eight battlecruisers - not a healthy place to be. As well, each ship could pivot in any direction to form a new defensive cube.

And at the front edge of the cube were the battlecruisers of her new allies, the Taegu and the Bagrami. They had been adamant about their place in the formation. They had been brutalized by the Singheko for years and were thirsty for revenge. Even now, their home planets were still occupied by the Singheko. Rita had gladly allowed them the place of honor in the battlecruiser formation - it was only right.

A thousand klicks in front of the battlecruiser cube, two additional cubes of warships waited side by side, forming a blocking force in front of the battlecruisers. Each of these cubes contained eight 160-meter cruisers - a formation whose combined firepower nearly equaled that of the battlecruisers. Any enemy trying to get to the battlecruisers would have to pass them first - and that would not be easy.

And finally, a thousand klicks ahead of the cruisers, sixteen destroyers waited. These highly maneuverable ships of 125 meters would take the first shock of battle.

Also arranged in two cubes, the destroyers were tasked to provide a wall of protection for the cruisers behind them. As the enemy came into range, they would fall back toward the cruiser formation, laying down a wall of defensive fire against the enemy's fighters - and taking any opportunity to prick at the Singheko destroyers.

"We're ready, milady," Rachel said beside Rita.

Rita nodded an acknowledgment.

*Here they come. And it may only be a raid, but people will die. They always do.*

"Launch fighters," Rita called.

**Sol System - Earth**

## United Nations Building - Beijing, China

"Right now she's stalemated. She sits in the Singheko system, facing off with them like a gunfighter in some Old West movie! But she doesn't have the forces to take them out. And she knows that! And still she won't give up, bring the fleet back to Earth! She's leaving us utterly exposed! We have to take action!"

Ken Elliott, newly appointed Grand Admiral of the UNSF - the United Nations Space Force - practically yelled his last statement. His tirade had gone on for several minutes. And the subject of his ire was one person - Rita Page, Fleet Admiral of the EDF.

And there was one fact that really drove Elliott over the edge. Even though the U.N. coordinated the manufacture of new warships for the fleet, and the recruitment of new personnel, and the transport of supplies to the fleet - Rita Page would not take orders from him. She considered herself independent of the U.N.

Across from Elliott, Ingrid Stoltenberg, Secretary-General of the United Nations, glanced briefly to her left. There sat Zhao Zemin, Premier of the State Council of China - the real power behind the throne in the modern U.N. But Zemin held his peace, waiting for someone else to respond.

On Ingrid's right, Viktoria Chernenko, Prime Minister of the Russian Federation, nodded in slow agreement.

"We don't disagree with you," said Viktoria cautiously. "She's sitting there at Deriko like a bug on a leaf. God knows what she's thinking."

Taking Viktoria's cautious statement for more than it was, Elliott spoke excitedly. "We have to force her to bring every ship back to Earth! We have to put a ring of warships around our planet and prepare for the Singheko! Staying there in their own system, facing them down eyeball to eyeball - that's insane!"

Zemin finally spoke. "I think you should do whatever is

required to bring that fleet back to defend Earth. That is the whole point of creating the U.N. Space Force - to centralize the command of all space forces from every country into one. And therefore it makes sense for us to force the EDF under the umbrella of the UNSF."

"Then I have your support? To take whatever action is necessary?" asked Elliott.

Zemin hesitated. "Within reason, Admiral. I'm sure you understand, China cannot be overtly involved. Admiral Page has tremendous public support. She has saved Earth from the Singheko not once, but twice. She is incredibly popular among the masses. They think she walks on water. Whatever you do, you must do it quietly - no negative publicity. Put her out to pasture or promote her to a desk job. Something like that. But nothing obvious."

Elliott, his emotions settling down as he realized he had won the decision, grunted in frustration. "I would prefer to just kill her, actually. We all know she's some kind of misbegotten clone. A creature of the devil."

Ingrid Stoltenberg looked at Elliott, trying to hide the horror in her mind. Elliott's predilection toward overt religious zealotry was well known. He claimed to be a Christian. He went to church, contributed to charity, made great display of his faith. But anyone who knew him quickly realized he was a CINO - a Christian in name only. It was amazing to Ingrid that he had achieved his high position. She would never have let him into the role of Admiral of the new U.N. Space Force if she had been able to control the appointment.

But it had been out of her hands.

*The Chinese control the U.N. now*, thought Ingrid. *With the change of headquarters to Beijing and the creation of a UN Space Force, they're sitting in the catbird seat. They got everything they wanted. Including an admiral they could control. And non-thinking religious zealots like Elliott are easy to control - you don't have to delude them, they delude themselves.*

*And the Chinese are masters at pretending to give him what he wants. They keep him twisted right round their little finger.*

*Lord, why did President Hager allow this to happen? What a tremendous mistake - just for an agreement to let Taiwan have independence, and to help rein in Iran? Foolish, foolish. What was Hager thinking?*

*Now they'll use the U.N. as a club to batter the rest of the world forever...and by creating the U.N. Space Force, they will effectively control every military asset in space.*

*Except Rita and the EDF. I have to go along with this for now. But I must find some way to checkmate Elliott and the Chinese, without being too obvious about it.*

"No, Admiral. No bloodshed. This must be done smoothly, carefully," Viktoria said.

Ingrid came back to the present, glanced at Zemin to see if he would offer any further comment. But he stayed silent, looking down at his briefing papers.

*So if this all goes south, Zemin can claim he wasn't involved in the actual details. Typical.*

Across from Ingrid, Elliott closed his eyes and shuddered, as if he were undergoing some kind of religious fit. But then he opened his eyes and nodded understanding.

"Yes, I understand. No bloodshed. Just find a way to get her back here to Earth, take the fleet away from her, and tuck her away where she can do no harm."

Zemin nodded at last. He knew that he had to give the final blessing, at least for Elliott's benefit.

"I perceive you have understanding, Admiral. China will provide you with any personnel or materials that you need. Quietly, of course. Just inform my aide Li Xiulian and it will be done."

Elliott, now happily excited, made a slight bow of the head to Zemin. "Thank you, Premier. Your understanding and support are greatly appreciated."

Zemin stood, signifying the top-secret meeting was over. The other three stood as well. Ingrid watched in disgust as

Elliott made a full-on Oriental-type bow to Zemin.

*The way Elliott fawns over him, you'd think he's some kind of royalty!*

Viktoria stepped forward and shook hands with Zemin. Ingrid knew she should follow suit, but she was too disgusted at the moment to do it. Instead, she pretended to be busy collecting her tablet and other items from the table. Finally, Viktoria and Ingrid followed Zemin out of the room, their handlers picking them up in the hallway. While Zemin disappeared to the right, Ingrid and Viktoria turned left. Reaching the landing that led to the rooftop heliport, Ingrid stopped to say goodbye to Viktoria.

"Have a safe trip, Prime Minister."

Viktoria offered her hand and Ingrid shook it. Then she waited patiently as Viktoria was led up the stairs to the heliport by her minders. There, a plain-wrapper Chinese executive helicopter waited to take her to the airport.

In an hour, Viktoria would be wheels-up, heading back to Moscow. Except for Elliott, Ingrid, and Zemin, no one outside her Chinese minders, the crew of her plane, and her President would know Viktoria had traveled to Beijing.

Returning to her top-floor office, Ingrid thought about what had just occurred.

*Against my will, I was forced to give the green light to a half-crazy religious zealot to perform a coup on the Admiral of the EDF - and force the EDF fleet to return to Earth and put itself under the command of the U.N.*

*God help us. I must find some way to block this. Without the Chinese killing me.*

# CHAPTER TWO

**Singheko System - Planet Deriko**
**Destroyer** *Dragon*

"Here they come," called Commander Luke Powell from his XO console. "Looks like we drew the lucky straw this time. They're coming right at us, trying to nip off a corner."

Commodore Bonnie Page nodded from her slightly elevated command chair, behind and to the left of Luke's. In the holo, she could see the attacking Singheko formation veer upward and to her relative right, toward the top right of the cube of destroyers, trying to isolate one corner of it while staying out of range of the other side. At the same time, the enemy went to heavy deceleration, slowing down to battle speed.

Reflexively, Bonnie glanced at the pressure gauge on the left thigh of her pressure suit. She tapped it to ensure it was reading correctly. Since she had been ejected into space from the *Dragon* six months earlier while fighting a Singheko cruiser, she just couldn't stop doing it.

She knew it was a nervous tic; she had already checked the gauge twice since battle stations were sounded. She looked up to see if anyone had noticed.

No one was looking at her. But she saw a tiny smile crease Luke's face.

*Not much escapes him.*

Without turning his head to look at her, Luke raised his left hand slightly and crossed his thumb over his forefinger.

It was their secret sign of love.

Smiling, Bonnie stared at the holo at the front of the bridge.

She straightened in her chair, making a decision.

"Destroyer Cube One execute plan Squaredance-Two," she called out loud. The AI of the ship responded immediately.

<Sending plan Squaredance-Two to Destroyer Cube One. All ships have acknowledged. All ships moving to new formation>

She saw her four leftmost destroyers begin to move smoothly across the formation to the right, passing the line of ships that had originally formed the right side of the cube. The dance of warships looked complex, but her group had practiced this movement a hundred times, both in the simulator and in actual maneuvers. The crossing movement of the ships was designed to confuse the enemy, to provide some level of deception as to their final intent. By the time the enemy came into range, they would have formed a new cube re-centered to meet the oncoming threat.

*But it won't fool them*, thought Bonnie.

Her thought was almost instantly echoed by Luke.

"They've seen this before," he said. "They've raided us so many times, we're running out of maneuvers."

"That's the idea, I expect," replied Bonnie. "They'll keep raiding us, learning more and more about our response, until Garatella's reinforcements arrive. Then they'll finally have enough ships to make a proper attack."

Luke nodded. He scanned his console, looking for any surprises behind them. But he didn't expect any. The EDF had eight corvettes scattered around the system, watching every move the Singheko made. Not to mention dozens of fighter patrols that went out every day, scanning the distant reaches of the system for any mischief by the enemy. If there had been another force behind the EDF to take them in the rear, they would have received warning long before this.

"Fighters coming out," called Lieutenant Emma Gibbs at the Tac Console. Bonnie nodded acknowledgment. She could see small blue icons representing friendly fighters flowing out of the sortie decks of the EDF battlecruisers and cruisers, forming up into their flights and squadrons, taking a vector directly toward the enemy. They would pass through her own destroyer formation in a matter of seconds, going out to meet the Singheko head-on - the tip of the spear.

And she knew who would be leading them - Jim Carter. Rita's husband, and the CAG - Commander Attack Group - for the EDF.

And her former lover. The man she would never get over, even though she had lost him long ago.

She couldn't help the thought. *Lord, keep Jim safe.*

Almost as soon as she thought it, the Singheko began launching their own fighters, hundreds of them spewing out of the enemy capital ships, forming up in front of their fleet.

The first squadrons of EDF fighters flashed through her cube, accelerating at 300g to get to the enemy. She could have issued a brief command to highlight Jim's fighter and watch him throughout the battle, but she didn't. It was better not to know. She couldn't imagine what she would do, how she would react, if he were killed while she watched.

Better to ignore him and go about her business.

She couldn't help but wonder about Rita. She supposed Rita would be the same, ignoring personal issues to focus on the battle. In fact, she was sure of it - for Rita was one of the most cold-blooded people she knew.

*That's why she's the Admiral.*

"Enemy destroyers in range in sixty seconds," called Emma.

Bonnie re-focused all her attention on the holo. Well out in front of them now, the EDF fighter formations met the enemy fighters, both sides unleashing everything they had in a whirlwind of gamma lance and missile fire. Bonnie saw many fighters take damage, with some spinning out of control, some burning from internal combustibles mixing with the air of their oxygen systems, pilots ejecting, the flashing orange blips of emergency beacons cluttering up the holo.

With a deft touch, Emma Gibbs reached to her Tactical console and hid the emergency beacons. There would be time enough for that after the fight.

"Five. Four. Three. Two. One. Fire," called Emma.

The high-pitched, nerve-scraping whine of the gamma lance sang through the bridge, a noise that always sent shivers down Bonnie's back.

The energy spear reached out toward an enemy destroyer, centered on its engineering space. As if by magic, a hole appeared in the enemy ship. Debris flew wildly out the other side of the enemy destroyer's hull as the gamma lance punched all the way through. The ship began to veer off course, losing decel.

The strange effect of losing decel caused it to appear to accelerate, rather than slow. As the enemy ship could no longer decelerate at the same rate as the rest of its fleet, it appeared to shoot out in front of them, an optical illusion that made it appear to be racing away.

Bonnie ignored it. It was out of action. There were plenty of other targets. She focused on the rest of the enemy fleet. Emma had already selected another enemy destroyer. *Dragon* yawed slightly as it re-targeted. The fat tube of the gamma lance in the front of the destroyer made a second nerve-grating whine. The beam licked out at another enemy ship. It just missed as the enemy made a wild evasive maneuver, and Emma let loose a word that Bonnie had never heard come out of her mouth before.

"Emma!" grinned Bonnie at the young Lieutenant, in mock horror.

"Sorry, mum," smiled Emma. "But I thought I had him for sure!"

**Merlin Fighter "Angel One"**

"Angel Squadron, break left!" yelled Commander Jim Carter. A large flurry of missiles from the enemy destroyers came at him. He followed his own advice, rolling to the left and pulling the sidestick back against the stop, trying to get to a slight hole in the array of missiles bearing down on him.

The g-meter on his instrument panel flicked instantly to 308g true, 8g internal. The inertia compensator could offset the g-force up to 300g - but beyond that, the pilot felt the full effects of the excess. The force of eight times his body weight smashed him down into the heavily reclined seat of the Merlin fighter as he exceeded the compensator limits. Jim huffed and grunted in his pressure suit to maintain consciousness. The frame of the Merlin groaned under the forces acting on it.

The Merlin's AI automatically spat wads of chaff and flares into the void of space behind him, the countermeasures launcher making a "chuff-chuff-chuff" sound audible in the cockpit. In the VR that painted the entire interior of his cockpit, Jim could see several missiles arcing around as they tried to stay with him, their little AI brains not giving up.

And then it was over. The missiles streaked by him, a blur in the "reality" of the VR. They continued on their way into the void, looking for other targets. Jim saw Merlins behind him jinking violently to avoid the missiles, chaff spraying out of them.

*Good luck, guys.*

But Jim had other fish to fry. His AI had already selected a fat cruiser just a couple of thousand klicks in front of him. The weapons button on his sidestick was blinking red, indicating the AI had the target locked and was ready to fire. Jim punched it, and eight missiles departed the stub wings on the side of the Merlin, all of them accelerating toward the enemy cruiser at 2,500g. They would arrive in four seconds - if the enemies' point defense cannon didn't pick them off first.

Jim watched as two, then four, then seven of his missiles were knocked down by the pulse cannon of the enemy cruiser and its accompanying destroyers. Then he grunted in satisfaction - his final missile broke through their point defense and punched into the cruiser's starboard engine nacelle, making a large and satisfying explosion. At first, the cruiser continued as if nothing had happened. But then Jim saw a fire start in the hole left by his missile as the internal atmosphere of the warship leaked out.

"Burn, baby, burn!" he yelled in glee.

The cruiser veered off, breaking formation, and turning away from the battle. Jim punched the air in celebration, then dismissed the cruiser - it was no longer a threat.

Then, reality bit. He was far out in front of his Wing, exposed. He had no business being in the front of the attack, and he knew it. After all, he was the CAG. He should be either back on the *Merkkessa*, directing the Wing from the safety of the Ops center, or at the very least hovering in his Merlin well behind the rest of his fighters.

*Rita will have a cow about this*, he smiled grimly. *I'm in for a real dressing-down. I know better.*

*But I'm so tired of these fuckers raiding us.*

With a sigh, Jim turned the Merlin and headed away from the enemy. He assessed the overall picture in his VR and decided there was nothing immediate he needed to do. His Wing knew their business, and they were doing it.

On his relative right, Merlin Attack Group One Five - MAG-15 - was heavily engaged with a pack of enemy fighters, pushing them back toward their line of cruisers. Above him, MAG-12 was doing the same to another gaggle of enemy fighters, punching holes in their line, driving them back.

But to his relative left and below, his third attack group, MAG-10, was having a tougher time of it. They were evenly matched. The enemy fighters were conserving their missiles, holding position - which was not good.

It was not good because Jim could see a second enemy fighter squadron sneaking around the dogfight, with full racks of missiles. In less than a minute, that second enemy squadron would have the EDF cube of cruisers in their range, and the enemy fighters would launch missiles at the capital ships. That was the precise scenario Jim's fighters were tasked to prevent.

Jim punched his finger directly on the cockpit wall, touching the enemy squadron that represented the threat. "Angel, designate target here. Angel Squadron engage now,

now, now!"

**Destroyer *Dragon***

"Skipper, we've got a breakaway squadron of fighters at down-right, looks like they're trying to make an end-run around us and get to the cruisers," called Emma.

"Are they in range?" wondered Bonnie.

"No, mum, we'd have to break formation to get to them. But...wait...there goes a squadron of Merlins at them. They see them now."

Bonnie assessed the holo quickly. She could see the breakaway group of enemy fighters, well down and to the relative right of her destroyer cube, trying to get past a group of Merlins heavily engaged just in front of them. But now another squadron of Merlins was streaking toward them, accelerating at 308g. Quickly assessing the relative vectors painted in the holo, she saw the Merlins would intercept the enemy fighters before they could get to the cruisers.

"We'll leave them be, Emma," she responded. "Looks like the Merlins have them corralled now."

And right at that moment, Bonnie gave in. She couldn't resist. She shot a mental command to her AI.

Dragon, *designate Wing Commander in holo.*

Instantly, one of the Merlins in the holo began flashing in alternate colors of blue and white, showing her where Jim Carter was located.

And as Bonnie somehow knew he would be, Jim was leading the charge of his squadron, intercepting the breakaway group of enemy fighters.

Bonnie sighed in both relief and frustration. Relief that he was still alive, and frustration that he couldn't stay in the rear of the fight like a Wing Commander ought to be doing.

The thought came unbidden to her mind.

*If I were Rita, I'd fire him.*

It wouldn't do to dwell on it. She had to worry about other

things right now.

*Dragon, stop designation of Wing Commander.*

Slightly ahead and to the right of Bonnie's seat at his XO console, Luke monitored the vast array of warships and missiles in the holo. He let Emma at Tactical handle 95% of the work, designating targets and helping the WEPS AI manage the point-defense pulse cannon to fend off incoming missiles. His job was to maintain a high-level view of the battlefield, ensuring that if Emma missed something, he picked it up and took care of it.

So he had noticed the momentary highlighting of Jim Carter's fighter, quickly flashing in the holo, then just as quickly disappearing.

And he knew who had highlighted it. His captain - and his lover.

*She still thinks about him,* Luke thought. *Even in the middle of a battle, she still thinks about him.*

*I guess she'll think about him forever.*

"Incoming!" yelled Emma at Tac.

Luke focused on his business, helping Emma tune the point defense system to fight off the inbound missiles. Between the WEPS AI, Emma's adjustments, and his tuning, all but one of the missiles were intercepted. But one leaked through, and at the last second the WEPS AI automatically pulled *Dragon* up hard, exceeding the comp limits and crushing them down into their seats for a second. The incoming missile hit them precisely in the belly armor. It caused a tremendous crash and lurch but did little real damage.

Luke glanced up at Bonnie. "Sorry about that, Skipper. Let one get away from us."

Bonnie gave a fake scowl. "No soup for you!" she called.

### Merlin Fighter "Angel One"

The throttle was against the stop. Jim's Merlin was accelerating at 308g true toward the breakaway group of enemy fighters - an acceleration that would kill a pilot, under normal circumstances. Inside the Merlin, however, Jim felt only 8g - the Merlin's inertia compensator offsetting the first 300g of acceleration.

Still, in spite of the compensator, the force of eight times his body weight had Jim pinned to his seat. It felt like an elephant was sitting on his chest. But he was determined to get to the enemy - so he clenched his teeth and bore the pain.

However, the Singheko squadron spoiled his plan. Realizing they were going to be caught in a crossfire between the massive point defense of the cruisers in front of them, and Jim's squadron coming in behind them, the enemy fighters broke off their attack. They slanted off toward empty space, away from the battle. Then they accelerated to 310g, confident their massive Singheko bodies could withstand more g-force than the puny Humans.

*Oh no you don't*, thought Jim, *I didn't come all the way out here just to watch you run away...*

"Angel, send the rest of the squadron home. Then override g-limiter to 12g positive and accelerate to 312g true," Jim called to his AI.

<Squadron ordered to RTB. The g-limiter is overridden to 12g positive. Accelerating to 312g true>

Jim's throttle was already against the stop, acceleration limited by the AI. Now the Merlin accelerated smoothly to 312g true. Inside the cockpit, the elephant sitting on Jim's chest turned into two. He could no longer breathe except by forcing the air in and out of his chest with savage grunts of pain. Behind him, the rest of his flight - including his wingman - fell away as they vectored off to RTB - Return To Base. Jim, alone, continued to pursue the enemy formation, now moving farther and farther away from the battle behind him.

The edges of his vision started to tunnel - a great black circle, like a camera stopping down, began coming in from the periphery of his vision.

But he was almost there - almost in range. Another few

seconds...

...he huffed, trying to get air into his lungs...

...just a few more seconds...

The blackness was closing in...

Suddenly the pressure was released slightly. The black ring in his vision began to dissipate. Jim saw the red light blinking on his sidestick.

<In range. Accel reduced to 310g. Weapons armed and ready>

He punched the button. His last eight missiles departed their tracks on the stub wings, running hot and true toward the enemy squadron in front of him.

<All missiles away. You are out of weapons, Commander. Accel automatically reduced to 300g>

As the g-force disappeared, Jim felt blessed relief. He was able to suck a huge breath of air into his tortured lungs. As he took a second deep breath, his missiles completed their short, 4-second flight to the enemy, an enemy that consisted of fighters wildly jinking in all directions as they tried to avoid his missiles.

And he yelled in exultation as he got three hits - three massive explosions, taking out three of the enemy fighters.

"Gotcha, you bastards!" he crowed, raising his hands in glee.

And then the remaining enemy fighters pirouetted on their axes, facing back toward him. 208 perfectly functional enemy missiles were looking right at him.

"Crap!" Jim yelled. "Get us out of here, Angel!"

The g-forces came back in suddenly as the Merlin's AI vectored hard away, trying to put distance between the pissed-off enemy and Jim's now very lonely fighter. He was far from his fleet, and far from his squadron. He would be in range of the enemy behind him for a few more seconds. It would be close.

His AI, automatically computing the accel required to escape the enemy, slammed him back into the seat at the full internal 12g allowable. He couldn't breathe. The black ring started coming in from the periphery of his vision. Then the ring of black came all the way in, and everything went away.

# CHAPTER THREE

**Singheko System - Planet Deriko**
**Battlecruiser** *Merkkessa*

Rita was about as pissed off as she ever got.

People called her cold, emotionless - a calculating machine. But she wasn't, not deep down inside. Deep inside, Admiral Rita Page was giving in to hatred at the moment. A deep, abiding hatred of the enemy. The enemy who threatened Earth. But more personally, the enemy who threatened her fleet.

And there was one particular enemy she hated most of all - Admiral Zukra. The arrogant dictator of the Singheko Empire. The seven-foot-tall creature who looked like a strange amalgamation of a Human and a lion, with his predator ears on top of his head, his vestigial claws on two fingers of each hand, and the thin but noticeable coat of yellow-gold hair covering his skin.

Zukra. He was the one who harassed them. He was the one who sent out these raids periodically, ensuring there would be no peace for the Humans who were still desperately trying to repair their ships after the Battle of Deriko.

*Zukra.*

As a rule, Rita avoided emotion in her decisions and actions. She was Admiral of the Black - the supreme commander of the Earth Defense Fleet. Her reputation as a calm, pragmatic leader was well-earned. She knew what the spacers called her.

*The Ice Queen. Or sometimes…the Ice Bitch.*

But people saw only the outside. Inside, she did occasionally let herself go. And this was one of those times, as she watched the Singheko raid come on, almost within range of her capital ships now.

*Zukra.*

*I hate that bastard.*

*I want to kill that son of a bitch.*

But Rita knew Zukra would be safe on Ridendo, the Singheko home planet, 0.6 AU away. 90 million kilometers closer to the star than her current position at Deriko. Tucked into his palace in Mosalia, the capital city of the Singheko Empire.

*Probably has his feet up watching the battle on a monitor in his suite, with a glass of wine in his hand.*

*I just hope I get that bastard in my sights someday.*

With a near-silent sigh that only Captain Bekerose heard, she let the thought go and re-focused her attention on the battle.

Her commanders seemed to have things well in hand. This was the third raid in three months - they were getting plenty of practice.

*But the Singheko are getting plenty of practice too. They're learning our formations, the exact limitations of our weapons, our fighter tactics - this is not good.*

Of course, the game worked both ways. Rita had sent two raids against Ridendo, chipping away at their defenses. One of the raids had even managed to get a destroyer inside their outer line of defense. The destroyer managed to fire a spread of missiles at their orbital docks. Although two missiles penetrated the point-defense systems on the docks, little damage was done. None of the cruisers or battlecruisers in Zukra's docks appeared to have taken much damage.

But the symbolic value of the attack had cheered the fleet. So far, Zukra had never managed to penetrate her outer line of defense and had not managed a single hit on any of her capital ships.

But in the last few months Rita had lost two dozen fighters

and one destroyer in Zukra's raids. The war of attrition went against them - Zukra could build ships and fighters faster than Earth.

*And he knows it, that bastard.*

Rita heaved another near-silent sigh.

*If only the Dariama would send us some ships. Then we'd not be so outnumbered. Then we could stage a raid on Ridendo and cut him down to size before he builds enough ships to overpower us.*

In the holo, the Singheko fleet started to veer away, as Rita had known they would. They always did before coming into range of the capital ships. It was not in their best interest to provoke a full-scale battle with Rita's fleet. Not yet - the two fleets were too evenly matched for their taste.

*They'll wait until Garatella's reinforcements come, and they finish out their shipbuilding and repairs. Then they'll overpower us.*

Rita got up from her command chair and nodded at Rachel beside her.

"Looks like they're pulling off, Rachel. I'll be in my day cabin if needed. I'll leave the cleanup to you."

Rachel gulped and nodded. Three months ago she had been Assistant Tactical Officer on the destroyer *Dragon*. Now she had just been put in charge of an entire fleet.

But Rachel knew this was Rita's way - adding responsibility at every opportunity, training her younger officers, throwing them into the fray. There was no other choice. The number of capable officers available to Rita was tiny. Rita was forced to promote rapidly any officer who showed promise; then train them with brutal quickness and fill from below with new recruits - when she could pry them loose from Earth's various military organizations. It was an ongoing and sometimes brutal dance with the powers of Earth to convince them to send her competent personnel.

Was it only two years ago? When Earth had been revolving along its path around the Sun, fat, dumb and happy?

In those halcyon days, Humans had no inkling of the

huge leonine Singheko, or the small but efficient Nidarians and Taegu, or the bear-like Bagrami, or the eerily Human-like Dariama. The impact of being suddenly attacked by the Singheko had been a wake-up call for humanity - a shock that still reverberated through society two years later.

Still trying to cope with a war not of their own making, and technology far beyond their level of engineering, Humans were struggling to come up to speed with the rest of the galaxy. And their growing pains were showing.

Buckling down, Rachel leaned into her work of cleaning up after the raid. She had fighter pilots to rescue, damaged destroyers to help limp back to orbit, and the enemy fleet to monitor as they curved off to return to their bases at Ridendo.

And a tablecloth to clean.

**Singheko System - Planet Deriko**
**Merlin Fighter "Angel One"**

Slowly Jim came back to the Universe. He first felt the air of the vents blowing on him slightly, keeping the cockpit temperature stable. Then he heard the hum of the electronics, the soft whirring of the fans that kept the instruments cool. A thought penetrated...

...*I guess I'm still alive*...

He opened his eyes. The Merlin was cruising smoothly through space. The VR showed him on his way back to the *Merkkessa*, passing through the cruiser formation. Blinking, he tried to concentrate.

"Angel, what happened?"

<I believe you had a nice nap, Commander. We're almost back to the *Merkkessa*. We'll be touching down on the sortie deck in six minutes>

Jim grunted.

"I take it we outran the missiles?"

<*WE* did not outrun the missiles, Commander. One of us was asleep. *I* outran the missiles>

"Angel, I hate a smart-ass. You could be replaced with a toaster oven. You know that, right?"

<You'd miss me, Jim. And who'd get you out of your next scrape?>

Jim grinned foolishly. It felt good to be alive. But, he realized as his grin disappeared - he had badly violated protocol. It was strictly prohibited for a pilot to pursue the enemy outside of the zone of battle. It was also against protocol for a pilot to separate from his wingman in combat.

And he should know. He had issued both protocols as part of Wing SOP.

*I guess I have to write myself up. And Rita will be pissed. She'll be completely, thoroughly pissed off.*

**Sol System - Earth**
**United Nations Building - Beijing, China**

Captain Dewa Shigeto stared at the order from Admiral Elliott and thought about his future. And if he had one.

The order from Elliott was clear.

"Send a message to Admiral Rita Page at Deriko. Tell her the new battlecruiser *Victory* is completed and finishing her shakedown cruise. Tell Admiral Page to return to Earth immediately for consultation on the war with the U.N. and representatives of the major powers. Afterward she can take the *Victory* back to Singheko as her flagship."

Dewa was not privy to the secret meeting Elliot had recently concluded with the Chinese and the Russians. But he wasn't blind, either. He was well aware of the hatred and contempt Elliott displayed toward Rita.

*This is crazy. This is some kind of ploy. He's up to something*, thought Shigeto.

*There is no way in hell Rita needs to come back to Earth for consultation. If anything, Elliott should go to her and try to learn something. And we should send the* Victory *to her immediately, not keep it here at Earth. That's stupid!*

Shigeto sighed. He couldn't disobey a direct order.

*Ingrid knew something like this was coming. That's why she assigned me as Elliott's aide. She wanted someone she could trust to keep her informed. She must be in on it to some degree.*

*But I still have to follow orders.*

Shigeto tapped the order into his tablet and sent it out. He knew it would go first to the spacedock in orbit just west of Ecuador. From there, it would be relayed to the duty corvette currently serving as ansible relay to the fleet. And from there, it would arrive onboard the *Merkkessa* via ansible transmission in less than a minute.

*And from that point*, thought Shigeto, *Admiral Rita Page is toast. She'll get on a corvette or a packet boat, zip back here to Earth. Elliott will have a welcoming committee to meet her at the dock. And that will be the end of Rita Page. After Elliott gets through with her, she'll be lucky if she ever sees the inside of a spaceship again.*

**Singheko System - Planet Deriko**
**Battlecruiser *Merkkessa***

The artificial sun peeked through the curtains of the artificial window in the Flag Cabin bedroom, sending one tiny ray of light into Commander Jim Carter's eyes.

It was enough. He had always been a light sleeper.

He rolled over in bed, feeling for his wife in the dimness. He found her, facing away from him, and spooned into her, reaching around to cup a breast. He knew she was awake - he felt her hand come on top of his.

"Fancy a bit of morning delight?" he asked.

*You never know. One of these days, she might be in the mood.*

But she wasn't. "No thanks, babe," Rita said. "The Nidarians are leaving at 0700. I want to watch them go. I've got to get up and get ready."

"Aye, aye, Admiral," Jim said, hiding his disappointment.

Their lovemaking was getting more and more infrequent

these days. The pressure of her job - trying to save humanity - didn't leave much time for personal matters.

Jim tried to understand, but it wasn't easy. He had asked her to make time for them - and she had agreed. But she hadn't lived up to the bargain. And he didn't want to add to her burden by bringing it up again.

But he was lonely. He missed the old Rita, before she had become entangled in the web of planning and logistics that occupied her now from dawn to the wee hours, every day, all day long.

The old Rita, who couldn't get enough of him. The old Rita of two years ago. The old Rita who was long since gone.

Jim rolled back flat and sighed as Rita got out of bed and started dressing.

*I'm in trouble.*

Jim knew himself. He had always had the ability to think clearly and objectively about his own emotions and feelings - and he knew what was going on.

*I've been a warrior for too long.*

Jim knew it was true. He had fought too many enemies for too long, without a break.

For so many months, Rita had kept him grounded, her love keeping the demons at bay.

But now he was without the attention of his wife. His PTSD was coming back with a vengeance. His nightmares had returned.

He was burnt-out, riding on the edge. It wouldn't take much to push him over. His near-suicidal actions in the raid yesterday had crystallized the problem in his mind.

And if he couldn't be with Rita, then…

There was only one other thing that could settle his soul.

"Hey, hon," he called. Across the cabin, Rita turned, one foot half-way into her boot.

"What?"

"Can I have three weeks leave?"

Rita finished pushing her foot into her boot, stamped on the floor with it, and turned to Jim in the dim light of the cabin, hands on hips.

"What in God's name do you need three weeks leave for?"

"I need to go camping."

There was a long silence. Jim knew what Rita was doing - she was searching her memories. Actually, Jim's old memories - part of her now, since the day of her creation. She would be thinking back, to the many times that Jim had camped - which would seem to her like her own memories, integrated into her consciousness.

For the hundredth time since he had met Rita, Jim thought about it.

*I wonder what it's like. To have two sets of memories. To be, in essence, two people in one body.*

He had asked her once. She had responded to him that he misunderstood - that she wasn't two people in one body, just one person - with the memories of two others along for the ride. And she had informed him forcefully that she had no trouble keeping the two sets of memories separate and distinct from her own.

*I wonder if that's really true.*

Rita nodded. "Yeah, OK. I see it. Go, get it out of your system. But do it quick - anything could happen with Zukra. And I wouldn't want to leave you behind if we need to pull out of this system in a hurry. I guess you'll go to Deriko?"

Jim nodded in the dark, even though she probably couldn't see it. "Yeah, I don't have time to go back to Earth. So I'll ask Tatiana to find me someplace wild and crazy on Deriko."

Rita picked her tunic off the back of a chair, slipped it on, walked over to the bed, leaned forward and kissed Jim lightly on the lips.

"Then go get it done, before you kill yourself. I saw what you did yesterday. That was stupid. Actually I was going to ground you for it. But since you're going to go work out your demons, I'll put that on hold for now. But don't think just because you're my husband I won't do it. If you ever do anything that stupid again, you're off flight status. Capisci?"

And with a swish, and without waiting for an answer, she was gone, out the door to her outer office.

Jim touched his lips with his finger, the softness of her still there, his body and soul missing her presence already.

"Capisci, baby," he said quietly.

\*\*\*

Rita had told herself she wouldn't watch the departure of the loyalist Nidarians; but in the event, she couldn't resist. She strode to the *Merkkessa*'s Flag bridge and sat in her command chair as the time drew near.

The bridge was quiet. It was early, ship time. Third Watch was in the last hour of their shift.

On the front screen, she saw the planet Deriko below her. It looked like a larger version of Mars, although the atmosphere it carried provided plenty of weather. A large low-pressure system created a swirl of clouds in the far south. She could see an electrical storm up north, near the pole.

But the small city of Misto Marta, on the equator just below and slightly in front of them, was clear. Rita knew the workers there would be rising from their beds, preparing for another day. Another day of supporting the fleet, preparing them to fight the Singheko again.

And somewhere down there on that planet, her husband Jim wanted to go wild camping.

*Probably wants to go fight a near-bear with a pocketknife*, she thought. *That's my Jim.*

Bekerose was not present; Rita wondered if he would come. This would be an especially sad and disturbing moment for him. Staying with his Human allies, when Garatella had declared Humans to be enemies, would make Bekerose a traitor to his homeland.

Rita knew it had been a hard decision for Bekerose. He was an intensely loyal officer - with his loyalties split between his homeland and his beloved warship, he had agonized over the decision. In the end, he had elected to stay with the *Merkkessa*, along with several thousand other Nidarians who decided to stick with the Human fleet.

Of necessity, Rita had provided a destroyer to the remainder, the loyalist group returning to Nidaria in fear of Garatella's wrath. The destroyer was the smallest ship that could carry them all home. Even then, they would be packed in like sardines for the 25 days it would take them to get back to their home planet.

She had given them the destroyer most damaged from the last battle with the Singheko. They had patched up the propulsion and life support systems and stripped the gamma lance and all missiles out of the ship. She'd be damned if she'd give a ship with functioning weapons back to High Councilor Garatella.

In the holo, she could see the beat-up destroyer several hundred klicks in front of her. It was preparing to depart orbit; its engine ports began to glow in the infrared, showing they were spooling up.

On the *Merkkessa*'s bridge, the hum of electronics and the occasional low voice of the crew at their consoles created a familiar and comforting background to Rita's thoughts. Shipboard life was practically the only thing Rita had ever known. A thought crossed her mind, one that came to her almost every day of her life.

*This is my home. This will always be home.*

To her right side, the hatch opened, and Captain Bekerose came on the bridge. He glanced at her, smiled, made a quick and abbreviated tour of the duty staff at their consoles, then returned to stand beside the slightly elevated Flag bridge, one hand on the railing.

"A sad day," he said, gesturing to the holo.

Rita nodded. "It is."

There was a silence between them, a comfortable one. They had served together now for nearly a year. What had once been an adversarial relationship had changed over the months, had morphed into a strong friendship in the heat of battle.

"What was the final count?" asked Rita after a while.

"Sixty-two," responded Bekerose. "A hard blow to our crew rosters."

"But the right thing to do," spoke Rita. "I can't ask anyone to fight against their own kind. If they don't agree with our cause, then they need to go home."

"True," Bekerose agreed. "But I wish they would've stayed a bit longer. This couldn't come at a worse time. It will take another two months to get Human replacements from Earth and integrate them into the Fleet."

"And we don't have two months," Rita said bitterly. "Zukra's shipyards are repairing his Home Fleet and building new ships as fast as he can whip his workers. No doubt Garatella is doing the same at Nidaria. And we know there's still one Singheko expeditionary detachment deployed at the Asdif system. I'm sure they've converted those ships to the new fast drives and the gamma lance. That means that remote fleet could arrive back here to reinforce Zukra any day now."

Bekerose nodded grimly. "And the Dariama at Dekanna?"

Rita sighed. "Admiral Sobong is still adamant she won't send us any help. They're building ships as fast as the Singheko, but she intends to keep them all at Dekanna. She's not willing to risk them here with us."

Bekerose scratched his almost non-existent nose. "What a crappy deal. We gave Sobong the plans for the fast drives and the gamma lance and sent Captain Ziollo and our two best fighter pilots to train them. And for this, she stiffs us? What a …what's the English?…bitch!"

Rita smiled at Bekerose mixing English curse words into his Nidarian.

"Well, Captain, I guess we should try to look at it from her viewpoint. Sobong doesn't think we can beat the Singheko here in their home system. And she knows the Singheko will be coming for her as soon as they finish with us. So, as much as it hurts me to say it, I do understand her. I might even do the same thing if I were in her shoes."

In the holo, the destroyer began to move, breaking orbit. In a few seconds, it picked up speed and headed away from Deriko toward the outer system. Minutes later, it passed the near-planet speed limit and accelerated to 300g. And then it was gone, moving at several million kph out toward the mass limit, 14.5 AU from the star, where it would sink out and take up its course toward Nidaria, 813 light years distant.

Rita sighed. She hated to lose sixty-two of the highly trained and expert Nidarian spacers. But High Councilor Garatella of Nidaria had declared Humans an enemy. She could not in good conscience keep any of the Nidarian spacers in the Fleet against their will.

*Now we just have to find a way to replace them. And with Elliott back on Earth throwing every possible obstacle in front of me.*

*There's only one person I can trust to fix this for me.*

# CHAPTER FOUR

**Singheko System - Planet Deriko**
**Destroyer** *Dragon*

"I wonder what she wants?" asked Bonnie early the next morning, as she clambered into the shuttle.

Luke Powell leaned forward as he climbed in behind her. "What?"

Bonnie got situated in the first seat behind the cockpit and grabbed her harness, started buckling in.

"I wonder what Rita wants," she repeated a bit louder.

Luke shrugged.

"We won't know 'til we get there," he said.

Bonnie gave him a sour look.

"I could have said that," she spoke. "Why do I bring you along?"

Luke grinned.

"Comic relief?"

Bonnie sighed and shook her head.

"I should know better," she said, but it brought a smile to her lips.

Settling into their seats, they fell silent as the shuttle's engines spooled up. The large bay door at the side of *Dragon*'s shuttle deck opened quickly. The autodock cradle moved through, carrying the shuttle with it. Seconds later, the door behind them closed and they heard the scream of turbopumps removing air from the sortie deck.

<Stand by for launch> called the shuttle AI. Bonnie and Luke double-checked their harness, then leaned back, ready for

the 4g accel that would come when the shuttle was shot out of the launch bay.

"You'd think they could reduce the launch accel for shuttles," Bonnie complained. "We're not a fighter."

Luke half-smiled. "They could. I told them not to. So everybody that launches out of here knows what fighter pilots go through."

"Oh, really?"

Before she could say another word, the AI started an automated countdown.

"Five. Four. Three. Two. One. Launch!"

As the force of four times her body weight pushed her back into the seat, Bonnie managed to grunt out one more sentence.

"I really think 2g would be enough to make the point."

Clearing the *Dragon*, the shuttle turned and made for the *Merkkessa*, in orbit fifty klicks ahead of them. The EDF flagship was huge - on each side of the battlecruiser, massive engine nacelles protruded from her flanks. Directly in the center of her bow, a short fat tube poked out - her most destructive weapon, the gamma lance. Missile tubes were evident at her bow and stern - eight behind and twelve up front. And short-range point-defense cannon covered her top, sides, and bottom.

From stem to stern, she was covered in scorch marks and discolored hull patches, evidence of recent battles.

Bonnie glanced up at an overhead screen showing the view behind the shuttle. She could see *Dragon* behind them, also covered in burn marks and off-color patches in her hull. A repair crew worked on her hull where yesterday's missile had impacted her belly armor.

Bonnie sighed.

*My beautiful ship. Now she looks like a patchwork quilt. Will she ever look like new again?*

Luke said something, but she didn't hear over the whine of the shuttle as it decelerated for entry into the *Merkkessa*'s shuttle bay.

"What?"

Luke glanced at her.

"Whatever Rita has for us, you can be sure it'll be a dirty job."

"Not necessarily," disagreed Bonnie. "She could send us on a milk run. You never know."

Luke chuckled out loud.

"And when has that ever happened?"

Bonnie thought about it.

"Yep, you're right. But there's a first time for everything."

"Bet ya."

"With what? You're still on half-pay from your little escapade on Deriko."

Luke leaned over conspiratorially, even though there was no one else around them.

"I have other things to offer."

Bonnie sniffed. "I get that free anyway."

Luke raised his hands in defeat. "True."

The shuttle entered *Merkkessa*'s outer landing bay, touched down with a slight crunch and slid forward a few inches on the deck. An autodock cradle moved into place below it; they felt the shuttle rise a few inches as the cradle centered itself below them and picked them up. The outer door slammed down, and turbopumps screamed as air was pumped in. Seconds later, the inner door opened, and the autodock cradle deposited them into a landing slot on the shuttle deck of the *Merkkessa*.

"Well, let's go find out what the lady wants," Luke spoke as they unbuckled. Bonnie nodded and they stood, stretching, as the shuttle's boarding hatch opened downward, forming a ramp. Stepping out, they were met by a familiar face - Gabriel, Rita's Nidarian chief bodyguard and head of her Security Division. He braced up and saluted.

"Welcome aboard, Commodore," he said in passable English.

"Wow, Gabriel!" Bonnie exclaimed in Nidarian, noticing new bars on his uniform. "You've been promoted?"

Gabriel's smile was a mile wide.

"Yes, mum. Ensign now," he responded, also switching to the Nidarian language and reaching up to touch his new butterbars.

"Well, nobody deserves it more," Bonnie added as they started walking toward the bridge. "You've done a fantastic job."

Following one pace behind them in perfect Naval protocol, Gabriel spoke again.

"And Raphael was also promoted, mum. Senior Chief now."

Bonnie turned, smiling.

"As he should be," she said. "Both of you do such a great job of keeping Rita safe."

Luke tried his Nidarian, still a new language to him.

"Uh…any idea what…uh…this…uh…meeting is about?"

Gabriel smiled. He knew Luke was probably just trying to practice his Nidarian, rather than expecting a serious answer to a confidential question.

"I'm sure you shall soon know, Commander," he replied.

In front of them, marching toward Rita's cabin, Bonnie had to smile.

Expecting Gabriel to give up confidential information was like expecting the planets to start revolving backwards.

***

When Bonnie and Luke entered the Flag Briefing Room, Admiral Rita Page was already standing at the head of her briefing table. Gabriel stayed outside the hatch, moving into a parade rest position beside Rita's other senior bodyguard, Raphael. As the hatch closed behind them, Bonnie and Luke strode to within a few paces of Rita, braced up, and saluted.

"Reporting as ordered, Admiral," said Bonnie.

It still felt strange to treat Rita with such formality. After all, until a year ago they had been comrades in arms - and lovers.

Back in those crazy times, they had lived together for more than a year; first for six months in a cramped cabin on the corvette *Corresse* as they traveled to Nidaria, then for another six months in an apartment on Nidaria as they waited for an audience with High Councilor Garatella.

And their lovemaking in those days - it had been especially passionate, since they shared a common set of memories, knowledge, and feelings.

For Rita was a clone - created by the sentient starship *Jade* two years ago in a ploy to take her back to Singheko as a zoo specimen. When Rita was formed, *Jade* had downloaded the knowledge, memories and feelings of both Bonnie Page and Jim Carter into Rita's consciousness. Rita had, in essence, become both of them to some extent - although her female gender had left her more weighted toward Bonnie.

So in those innocent days of two years prior - immediately after her creation - Rita had been practically an emotional twin to Bonnie. She knew everything Bonnie wanted, and exactly how to do it.

For Bonnie, it had been like making love to herself.

But those days were long past. The woman called Rita that stood before them now had been transformed by war into a battle-scarred admiral with the hard-nosed sensibilities required to lead a fleet. She had saved Earth from the Singheko twice in the last year. And now she was trying to win an unwinnable war to save Earth.

The only thing they still shared for certain was a last name, and the desire to protect Earth from a brutal enemy.

Rita waved them to seats and sat with them. She stared at Luke for a second, then at Bonnie.

"Nice little raid yesterday," Rita began.

"Sure was," said Bonnie. "How many fighters did we lose?"

"Six," Rita said bitterly. "Against nine of theirs, but of course Zukra doesn't care. He can build fighters twice as fast as we can. So in the grand scheme of things, we lost ground."

Bonnie nodded. "Well, that's his strategy. Grind us down. He's not yet strong enough to take us head-on, and we can't take him straight up either. But he can fight a war of attrition until Garatella's force gets here. Then he'll come at us for sure."

"Yeah," agreed Rita. "I know it. But...I didn't call you over here to complain about Zukra. It's the damn UN again. Look at this!"

She handed a tablet to Bonnie. Bonnie took it and read from the screen.

"Hmm... New battlecruiser *Victory* is completed and finishing shakedown. Admiral Page is requested to return to Earth immediately for consultation with the U.N. and major powers. Afterward Admiral Page can return to Singheko with the *Victory* as her new flagship."

Bonnie looked up at Rita.

"You know this is bullshit. This is some kind of a ploy by Elliott - I'm sure you've heard how much that pseudo-religious freak hates you. I'll bet you a thousand dollars he's going to relieve you of command, lock you up somewhere and throw away the key. Force the EDF under his command. Which is exactly what the Chinese want."

Rita rose, turned, paced across the cabin, nodding. "I know. I don't dare go back there. But he's got me over a barrel. I need supplies, ammunition. I need recruits to replace our losses. And I need the *Victory* and the other two cruisers the U.N. is finishing up right now. If I simply refuse him, he'll cut us off. No more beans and bullets. No more recruits to replace our losses. No more ships."

Bonnie stood, started pacing at the other end of the table. Luke was struck by how much the two of them looked alike, as they both paced in exactly the same way, almost in step, their hands folded behind them identically.

*My Lord, they are like twins in some ways. Different bodies, but nearly the same consciousness. It's spooky.*

Bonnie abruptly stopped and turned to Rita.

"We need those ships."

"Exactly," said Rita, also stopping to face Bonnie. "I want you to go fetch them."

Bonnie chuckled. "Fetch them? Just like that?"

Rita lifted one side of her lips in an ironic smile.

"Yes. Go fetch them, please."

"Just...fetch them," Bonnie repeated, returning to her seat. Beside her, Luke tried to stifle a laugh, but was having a great deal of trouble hiding it.

Now even Rita had to chuckle.

"I guess it does sound a bit crazy, doesn't it?" she said.

Bonnie nodded, still trying not to laugh out loud.

"How would you like me to go about 'fetching' a battlecruiser and two cruisers from an Admiral that doesn't want to give them to me?"

Rita shrugged. "That's up to you. Don't kill anybody, though. I don't think we need go that far. But short of that, I'm sure you can come up with something. After all, you found *Dragon* when the entire Nidarian navy couldn't. So I think you can handle this."

"What can you give me to work with?" asked Bonnie.

"You can have *Dragon* and two other destroyers - two of the Singheko ones we captured. You'll have *Dragon*'s Marine detachment. And Tatiana said she would lend you Norali and two dozen of her best."

"Not sure Marines and Special Forces are going to help me much. You said I can't kill anyone."

Rita gave a brief smile that flickered and dissipated rapidly.

"I'm sure Norali can help you come up with a plan that will work without killing anyone."

Bonnie heaved a sigh.

"I swear, Rita, you really come up with a doozie once in a while."

Now Rita did give a full-on smile. "That's my job, isn't it?"

"OK. So what else do I need to know?" asked Bonnie.

"Leave the two captured Singheko destroyers there at Earth as a token of my esteem. They're pretty much junk anyway after this last battle."

"What response are you planning to make to this order?" wondered Bonnie, pointing to the message on the tablet.

"I'll send a message tomorrow that I've dispatched you back to Earth to coordinate with Elliott. That should hold him for the sixteen days it'll take you to get back there."

"I doubt it," muttered Bonnie. "That asshole Elliott won't wait sixteen days for a response from you."

"Well, he's got no choice, does he?" said Rita. "I've told *Merkkessa*'s AI to send a message to Earth that we're taking the ansible down for maintenance, and it'll be down for three weeks."

"Oh, you're sneaky. But that won't stop him. He'll just send a message to one of the other ships."

"Yes. And I've ordered all other ships to ignore all messages from him for the next three weeks. So you better get going."

Bonnie stood, Luke rising to his feet beside her.

Bonnie hesitated. Luke, reading their body language, turned and went out the hatch, giving them some privacy.

Rita and Bonnie stood in silence, looking at each other.

"Jim is fine," said Rita, reading Bonnie's mind.

"And you?" asked Bonnie.

"I'm fine too. Except I miss Imogen. A lot."

Rita looked at Bonnie silently for a second or two, then spoke again.

"And I miss you."

Bonnie nodded slowly.

"I miss you too. Always."

"I know. But we're on different roads now. At least you have Luke."

Bonnie smiled happily.

"Yeah. Luke's a trip. The best XO a girl could ask for."

"And in bed?"

Bonnie chuckled.

"A girl doesn't kiss and tell."

Rita couldn't help but grin.

"Yeah. We both have a lot of things we can't kiss and tell about, don't we? But one thing about Luke - keep things low-key. Keep that relationship under control.

"I'm letting the fleet have their little love affairs right now because of the Nidarian group marriages, and because of my own relationship with Jim, and because we're far from home and it lets people blow off steam. But at the first sign of serious trouble, you know I'll have to step in. And that means you and Luke would be separated."

Bonnie nodded in agreement.

"It'll happen sooner or later anyway. We're resigned to that. Luke's too good to be an XO forever. He needs his own ship. I know that. So when it happens, I won't stand in his way."

"Good. I was actually thinking about bringing that up. Shall we do it now? When you get back from Earth, you can take a cruiser and let him have the *Dragon*."

A sadness came across Bonnie's face as she bowed to the inevitable.

"Yeah, I think that's a good idea. It'll hurt, but it's probably time."

They paused, letting the necessity of hard change sink in.

"I'll send the orders, then," Rita said. "Stay safe."

**Singheko System - Planet Ridendo**
**City of Mosalia**

On the Singheko home world of Ridendo, Major Oliver "Ollie" Coston walked through the streets of Mosalia, his body wrapped in loose clothing.

The night was relatively dark. Only Ridendo's smaller moon was in the sky, and it only a quarter. Around Ollie's head was a turban, the hallmark of a Dariama citizen of the working class.

Sticking to the back streets of the foreign section of Mosalia, Ridendo's capital city - and the capital of the Singheko Empire - Ollie turned aside as a group of drunken Singheko approached. He took a right turn onto an even smaller street to avoid them. His disguise was fair - it would take a close examination for a Singheko to realize he wasn't a true Dariama - but he had no intention of taking chances. The risks were too high. Discovery meant instant torture and execution.

Letting the group of staggering, rowdy Singheko pass behind him, he turned back and resumed his path, staying in the shadows as much as possible. Finally he arrived at his destination, a back-street entrance to a private residence. He knocked gently, paused, then scratched at the door in a prearranged signal.

After a bit, the door cracked open. A Nidarian male looked him over, then opened the door and let him in. After the door closed behind him, Ollie shed his turban and overcoat, then moved into the main room of the house. There Lieutenant Helen Frost waited for him. The Nidarian left quietly, leaving them alone.

"How'd it go?" Helen asked.

"Good, I think," grunted Ollie, reaching for a cup of *nish* waiting on the table. Bringing coffee to the planet was too dangerous - the Singheko would instantly recognize it as a drink of Humans - but the Nidarian drink *nish* was similar and would raise no suspicions. Ollie slugged a major portion of the cup down, then wiped his mouth, looking at Helen.

"They're scared shitless, of course. But they're pretty pissed off that Zukra killed most of their top Admirals and Captains in his coup. They want to do something about it, but they have no idea what."

"Did you give them some ideas?"

"I did. You should have seen the looks on their faces when I told them some of the things they could do. I thought they were going to pack up and run out the door, they were so scared."

"It's strange they're so aggressive with other species, yet so reluctant to take on their own kind."

Ollie grimaced.

"Isn't that the mark of most totalitarian regimes? They make other races into objects - animals to be enslaved or slaughtered - while they look at their own leadership as near-gods who can do no wrong. It's the classic pattern of a society in thrall to power and corruption. Remember the Nazis?"

Helen nodded in agreement.

"So, the real question, then. Will they do anything about it?"

"I don't know," said Ollie. "But I think so. I think they are pissed off enough to take action. If they can find someone who has some leadership ability, I think we may have a shot."

Helen looked a question at him.

"Can we help them on that?"

"I don't think so. I think they need to work that out on their own. They need to find someone who's willing to step up to the plate and lead them, in spite of the danger. And I don't think we have enough insight into their culture to do that for them."

Leaning back onto the couch, Ollie got quiet for a while as he thought about their situation.

Being a spy on the enemy home planet was the last thing he had expected to be doing at this point in his career.

But that was before Admiral Rita Page had called Ollie into her office and asked him to volunteer.

He had stood at attention in front of her, but she had waved him to a chair.

"Major Coston, I would like to offer you the most dangerous job in the Fleet," she started out. "One that is practically guaranteed to get you killed if you make the slightest mistake. I would not ordinarily ask this of anyone; but we have tremendous need. You know how slim our survival was in the recent battles with Zukra and the Singheko; and you know there are more battles to come, none of which we can be assured of winning. We need every possible advantage in this war if we are to prevent humanity from being overwhelmed and rendered extinct."

Ollie nodded. "Of course, milady. Whatever you need."

Rita looked at him with some sadness in her eyes.

"Ollie, I want you to go to Singheko, disguised as a Dariama citizen from Dekanna. I want you to instigate an underground movement to overthrow Zukra and try to stop this war. You can use sabotage, bribery, coercion, anything that comes to mind. You'll be my 'hornet'. Sting these Singheko bastards where it hurts."

Ollie began to get the idea. But an immediate objection came to his mind.

"Milady, there's some pretty significant differences between humans and the Dariama. Their extended ears, for one thing. Different elbow and knee joints. How will I be able to pass for one of them?"

Rita looked grim.

"That's where the pain point comes in. You'll have to undergo some plastic surgery on your ears. Wear loose, floppy clothing to cover up the knee and elbow joints. Learn to walk in that crooked way they have. And even then, you'll have to stay indoors during daytime, and only go out at night. Even with the plastic surgery on your ears, you'll have to always wear a turban when you go out. It's not going to be easy."

Ollie nodded. He began to see the essence of the plan.

Rita continued.

"You'll need at least one other person to go with you, maybe two. At least one of them should be Nidarian - they can move freely around Mosalia since there is a substantial Nidarian presence there."

Ollie thought about it for a moment.

"I'd like to take Yuello, that Nidarian cook in the wardroom. He can easily pass as our cook and housekeeper. And he's very sharp. And if she'll take the job, Helen Frost. She's my second in command. Her command of Nidarian is excellent, probably better than mine, so she'll have no trouble communicating."

Rita hesitated, but finally spit it out.

"Is she the right color?"

Ollie realized what Rita was saying. The Dariama as a species were universally brown, as he was. That was undoubtedly a big part of the reason Rita had chosen him.

"Yes, milady. She'll pass if we do the other things."

And so it had happened. When he told Helen there was a mission almost certain to get her killed, but critical to the survival of humanity, Helen had immediately gone to Rita and had a discussion with her. Ollie wasn't privy to the conversation, but when Helen came out of Rita's office, she was on Ollie's mission.

Looking across the table at Helen now, Ollie realized how much he depended on her. This entire mission was fraught with danger. Even the slightest mistake in their appearance, language or presentation could bring the Singheko secret police down on them. And Helen was remarkable in keeping them focused on the details that kept them alive.

It wasn't an easy life. They had been on Ridendo for three months now, attempting to jump-start a resistance movement among disaffected Singheko.

They had concentrated on ex-Navy officers who had been booted out of Zukra's "new order" fleet because they weren't aggressive enough, or loyal enough, or fanatical enough. It was a slow process, and one that put their lives on the line every time they stepped out the door of their safe house.

But they had a start now. They had finally made contact with a small group of disaffected ex-officers - a group willing to consider the concept of a resistance movement. If they could get that snowball rolling downhill - recruit others, get a movement that would grow on its own - then their job would be half-done.

The other half of their job would then begin.

Sabotage.

To date, they had not started on that aspect of their mission. Rita had directed them to ensure they got the Resistance movement off the ground first.

But once they had a self-sustaining Resistance movement in operation, Ollie and Helen would start destroying anything of value which would sting the Singheko.

Ollie was deep in a reverie, thinking through the many problems they faced, when Helen said something.

"What?"

"I said...are you listening this time?"

"Yes, I'm listening. What did you say?"

"I said I want to sleep with you tonight."

Ollie looked at Helen. There was surprise in him, but not as much as he expected. He realized he had felt this coming. Helen had been making all the signs lately. And he had felt some stirrings himself. Three months was a long time to be the only Humans on a planet.

But…there was the mission.

"You report to me. We're in a dangerous situation. I don't think we can do that," Ollie replied.

"Bullshit," said Helen. "You and I both know it won't affect the mission. We're not two wet-nose ensigns just coming out of the Academy."

"Well…yeah, you've got a point," Ollie said grudgingly. He hesitated, then spoke again. "But…well…there's one other thing…"

Helen had been half-sitting, half-lying on the chair opposite Ollie. Now Helen got up, came across to him, and pushed him all the way down on the couch. Then she lay down on top of him, pressing herself into him.

"What?" she asked.

Ollie nearly groaned out loud at the need in his body. But he fought it off.

"Well…I have…"

"You have?" Helen pushed her body even more into him, putting pressure on the part of him that wanted her so much.

"I mean…I have feelings for you…"

Helen paused in her push against him. "Oh," she said. "Gotcha. So what's the problem? Seems like you'd want this even more."

Ollie closed his eyes, struggling to talk. "I mean…women are different from men. This will only make me want you more. But sometimes…with women…"

"Oh, I see," Helen said. "You think if we sleep together, then I'll lose interest in a more serious relationship."

Ollie nodded, although by this time he was playing with

her hair in a distracted fashion. He was losing ground fast. He knew he wouldn't be able to talk much longer.

Helen leaned down and kissed him, long and hard and deep. As Ollie gave up the fight and his body took over, he heard Helen make one last statement.

"You're an idiot," she said.

# CHAPTER FIVE

**Dekanna System**
**Gas Giant**

The Merlin II fighter blasted through space at 40% of light speed. At that velocity, bright sparks flashed off the nose like sparklers at a Fourth of July celebration. The gravity gradient generator in the nose of the ship fought to protect the fighter from the incredible energies of such a speed, pushing stray hydrogen molecules and particles of space dust to the sides.

And if by some incredible bad luck anything larger than a pea was missed by the long-range radar and lidar of the fighter, and it failed to dodge aside in time…

Well, the results would be a cataclysm greater than many Hiroshima-size atomic bombs. The energies released by a collision at these speeds were beyond the ability of a Human mind to comprehend.

In the distance, a big gas giant loomed large in the cockpit VR, filling the entire left side of the pilot's view. It was streaked with colors - browns, licorice, dark cherry - and sported a tiny, almost invisible ring system.

Decelerating hard at negative 300G true, the Merlin's frame groaned as the fighter performed a tight double slingshot around the huge planet and its first moon, a stark body with nothing on the surface except the pockmarks of ancient craters. As it finished its pass, the fighter came out of its maneuver behind a Dariama destroyer, facing directly into its starboard engine.

"Consider yourself dead, Captain," called Lieutenant

Commander Michelle "Winnie" Winston, grinning from ear to ear, as she pressed a button on her sidestick and fired a simulated gamma lance at the destroyer in front of her. The fighter's AI generated a satisfying simulated explosion in her VR.

In the destroyer in front of her, another AI blanked all the consoles on the bridge for five seconds, letting the destroyer's bridge crew know they had been "killed" by the fighter behind them.

"Crap!" yelled the destroyer's captain, Ziollo.

The five-foot tall Nidarian captain was no rookie. She had served as Tactical Officer on the cruiser *Qupporre* in the first Earth-Singheko battles in the Sol System, and the more recent battles in the Singheko home system. She knew her business.

But Winnie in her Merlin was a force of nature, the best of the best of the EDF training team assigned to the Dariama.

Slamming her fist down on the arm of her command chair, Ziollo continued her tirade.

"Crap, crap, crap!" she yelled at no one in particular. Her native language, Nidarian, had few curse words. But that was not a handicap for her or the rest of the Nidarians serving with the EDF. They had adopted the curse words of the Humans with great relish. And were quite adept at using them.

"It's not so bad, Captain," smiled her XO, Commander Naditta. "We took out a cruiser and five fighters before she got us."

Ziollo glared at him.

"We're still dead," she growled.

"Aye, mum, but I doubt any of the Singheko pilots are as good as Winnie. In the real world, we'd have smoked that last fighter as well."

Ziollo grunted, still unhappy.

"I hope you're right. But I'm still pissed off. I waltzed right into her little trap. I can't believe I did that."

Naditta shrugged and smiled.

"That's why we train, Mum. We'll never fall for that again."

Ziollo sighed and stood up from her command chair as the bridge crew relaxed a bit, the exercise over.

"XO, take us back to base. I'll be in my day cabin."

Naditta nodded and gestured to the Tactical Officer, who had heard the orders and was already laying in a course to their home base, the largest moon of planet Dekanna. Ziollo walked to the hatch in the back of the bridge that led to her day cabin and entered, still pissed at getting 'killed' in the day's exercise.

Sitting at her desk, she had to smile, though, as she thought it over.

*Thank the stars Winnie's on our side. I'd hate to be the poor dumb Singheko bastard that goes up against her. And now I have to buy her dinner tonight!*

Heaving a sigh, Ziollo turned to her eternal 'paperwork', as the Humans called it - even though there was no 'paper' involved. She was always puzzled by the inconsistency of their language. So many of their idioms made no sense at all!

But...paperwork. That's what they called it, even though it was all electronic on her tablet. She leaned into it, processing through dozens of miscellaneous communiques, maintenance forms, crew actions and requisitions.

*Beans, bullets, and requisitions,* she thought to herself. *The life of a warship. Hours and hours of paperwork followed by moments of sheer terror.*

<Approaching Dekanna> called the ship's AI several hours later. <You have a message from Admiral Sobong. Full staff conference in her briefing room at 1800 hours>

*Uh-oh.*

"Acknowledge the message and reply that I'll be there. Notify the XO I'm moving to my cabin."

<Acknowledged. Executed. Confirmed>

Ziollo got up and went down the circular stairs to her personal cabin one deck below. One of her three husbands - Four - was lying on his bunk, reading. Within their six-way group marriages, Nidarians didn't use full names; they used a numbering system that reflected when they had joined the marriage. Something that always confused Humans who overheard them talking to one another.

Glancing at her, he spoke in Nidarian.

"What's up, One?"

"Sobong called a full staff meeting."

"Oh. Well, you'll be fine. She likes you," he replied.

"Yeah," Ziollo replied, stripping off her uniform. "As much as she likes anybody. Which is nobody."

As her Four nodded, Ziollo stepped into the shower and started scrubbing. For a Nidarian, cleaning the body was a ritual that could take an inordinate amount of time. Ziollo had been known to take a shower for twenty-five minutes.

But not today. Today she had to prepare for a meeting with Admiral Sobong and her entire staff.

Which could mean only one thing.

Something had changed.

## Dekanna System
## Dariama Naval HQ

The Dariama base on the largest moon of the planet Dekanna was large and well-built. The carpet was soft, and the walls had a pastel shade of blue that was soothing to the mind. The air was well-conditioned, with little of the metallic tang that was so common on the warships and fighters of the fleet.

The Dariama were no slouches when it came to technology; they had taken the original Merlin fighter designs brought to them by Winnie and upgraded them significantly, resulting in the Merlin II. The new models had a tuned gamma lance that could reach out 5,000 klicks, instead of the 4,500 klicks of the original design. Other changes had been incorporated to make the fighters more maneuverable and provide better protection for the pilots.

But in other ways, the Dariama were a strange species. In ancient times, according to Admiral Sobong - before the collapse of the Golden Empire that led to the Dark Ages and the Broken Galaxy - the Dariama had been mostly engineers, building new technology for the Golden Empire of two thousand years prior.

"In fact, it's highly likely we designed *Dragon*," Sobong had once told Winnie. "Nearly all new warships of that era came out of our design shops. We were the specialist engineers for the entire Empire."

"But..." Winnie had begun, then suddenly stopped as she realized she had been about to say something that might be taken as an insult.

Sobong had smiled.

"But why are we so timid in war now, if we were the weapons builders of the old Empire?"

Winnie had shrugged, somewhat embarrassed.

"We're not as timid now as you might think, Commander, I can assure you," Sobong had said. "We know what the other species say about us. They call us cowards, afraid to fight. And we were, two thousand years ago when the Empire fell. But time will tell if we are still those cowardly engineers that the stories tell. Time will tell."

Now, Winnie met Ziollo at the entrance to Sobong's briefing room. They had been working together for months, acting as technical advisers to the Dariama, teaching them lessons learned from the recent battles with the Singheko. They greeted each other with a slight hug.

"I guess I owe you dinner tonight, Winnie," Ziollo said sheepishly.

"Yep," Winnie agreed. "I need to think of something expensive."

That made Ziollo laugh.

"Every meal in the commissary is the same price, I believe," Ziollo responded to her.

"Even so," grinned Winnie. "Maybe I'll have two meals!"

Entering the conference room, they took their seats. There were a couple of Dariama from Sobong's staff already there, at the other end of the table. Winnie and Ziollo sat in the middle, halfway between the others and the head of the table.

Admiral Sobong swept into the room, trailed by her Chief of Staff and a bevy of aides and assistants. As Sobong sat down at the head of the table, the rest took places around her and in the corners of the room, depending on their rank.

Sobong waited until it was quiet, glanced once at Winnie and Ziollo, and started speaking.

"As you know, we Dariama are basically a race of engineers. We like computers. We like modeling and simulation. In most cases, we base our most important and fundamental decisions on simulations of the various controllable parameters of the situation and the most likely outcomes of those simulations."

Sobong paused, gazing around the room, then returned to her speech. It was clear to Winnie that the preamble Sobong was making was primarily directed toward her.

"We have modeled the present situation backward and forward, up and down, until we've exhausted all reasonable alternatives - and even unreasonable alternatives - trying to ascertain the proper path to take in the face of the Singheko and Nidarian threat to our society."

Sobong laid down her tablet and let her gaze traverse around the room, her face a study in bad news.

"The short version is that it is impossible to defeat Zukra and Garatella. Even with the combined forces of ourselves, the Humans, the Taegu, the Bagrami, and the breakaway Nidarian detachment that still serves in the Human fleet..."

Sobong looked pointedly at Ziollo...

"...we cannot defeat them. The combination of the Singheko and the Nidarians gives them an overwhelming advantage in manufacturing warships and providing cannon fodder to man them. They are willing to sacrifice thousands more of their people to win this war than we are. They will overwhelm us with sheer numbers in any kind of straight-up shooting war."

Sobong toyed with her tablet, clearly gathering her thoughts. Finally, she began speaking again.

"Therefore, we have to cheat. We have to find some way to

beat them without a long, drawn-out war of attrition that we will surely lose."

Winnie sat up straighter. She knew that the true underlying reason for this meeting was to convey some message to her and to Ziollo. And mostly to her, because she was the Human representative and a direct conduit to Admiral Rita Page.

Sure enough, Sobong looked at her again.

"725 lights Coreward of Singheko, there is a culture we call the Goblins. They are not biological. They are an Artificial Intelligence culture - a society of machines, so to speak. They are highly advanced, with ships and weapons comparable to our own. Or at least, they had such technology twenty-five thousand years ago, which was the last contact with them."

Sobong paused and stared at Winnie again, waiting for something.

*Waiting for me to ask the obvious question.*

"Can we enlist them as allies?" Winnie asked, knowing that was the question Sobong was trying to elicit.

"That is the question, Commander. And I have to tell you, it's highly unlikely. We have an unfortunate history with them. Twenty-five thousand years ago - before the Golden Empire was a gleam in Emperor Ranssarrian's eye - the biologicals of that era were afraid the Goblins would take over the galaxy. The biologicals made a concerted effort to wipe them out. Over a period of a thousand years, biologicals killed billions of them. They destroyed a half-dozen of their star systems. The Goblins were driven to the brink of extinction.

"The system they hold now was their last refuge - their Stalingrad, you might call it. The place they made their last stand. And, like your Stalingrad, they survived. At the last moment, on the verge of wiping out the Goblins completely, the coalition of biologicals fell apart. They began fighting among themselves. And shortly after that, Emperor Ranssarrian founded the Empire in fire and sword. The Goblins were largely forgotten and left to their own devices."

Sobong paused, her attention focused on Winnie.

"As a result of this history, the Goblins do not permit a biological to enter their system. To them, a biological is like a snake to you Humans. Like a dangerous, poisonous snake. They have an instinctive fear that makes them recoil in horror as soon as they see one."

"Ah," said Winnie. "I begin to see the problem."

Sobong nodded. "I thought you would. But here's the rub. Although they hate and fear all biologicals, they have a special hatred of us Dariama. Our ancestors were the instigators of the coalition that tried to destroy them. Although it's been twenty-five thousand years since that war, they have long and perfect memories. Any of our ships that get near their territory are shot out of the black without warning, no quarter given. If we sent an embassy to them, they would shoot on sight. There's no message we could send or gambit we could use that would cause them to listen to us."

Winnie leaned back, understanding what Sobong wanted now.

"You want us Humans to try and approach them."

"Yes. Mathematically, per our simulations, it's our only chance of surviving this war with the Singheko. You are the only species that did not fight against them twenty-five thousand years ago. It is possible they might listen to you. Unlikely, but possible. But without the help of the Goblins, our simulations put the chances of surviving this war at only two percent."

"Wow," Ziollo finally said. "And if we manage to obtain their help?"

Sobong looked grim.

"Twenty percent."

## Singheko System - Planet Deriko
## Battlecruiser *Merkkessa*

Sixteen hours later, Rita stared across the table at the two officers in front of her.

One of them was Commander Rachel Gibson, her Assistant Flag Aide.

The other was a fighter pilot.

She didn't often talk to fighter pilots - that was Jim Carter's job.

But Jim had already left for Deriko to go wild camping. Rita had decided not to recall him for this small matter.

After the receipt of Winnie's urgent message from Dekanna about the Goblins, Rita needed a team she could trust. A team that could journey 725 lights to the Goblins, introduce them to Humanity, and attempt to form an alliance with them.

Rachel was a known quantity. She had distinguished herself during the Battle of Deriko as the *Dragon's* Tactical Officer, and since her move to Rita's staff, she had been rock-solid.

*She'll do for the mission*, thought Rita. *She's got the smarts and the cool head under fire.*

But the pilot. He was an unknown quantity. Jim would normally take care of this selection process for her - but Jim was already down on Deriko. Jim's second-in-command, Lieutenant Commander Mitchell, had said this guy was the one; the best after Winnie and Roberto, who were still in the Dekanna system working with Admiral Sobong.

"*Paco*. That's your handle?" she asked him, judging his reaction.

"Yes, milady, *Paco* is my call sign."

Rita noticed the subtle correction.

"Call sign, then. And you're good?"

"I'm the best in the Wing, milady," Paco said coolly, as if he was telling her the time.

"Next to Winnie and Roberto," she said.

"Maybe next to Winnie, milady. But not Roberto."

Rita studied him. He had a cockiness bordering on arrogance. But it seemed to be controlled.

*Well, he IS a fighter pilot. Aren't they all that way?*

"According to your personnel file, you graduated in the top quarter of your class at the U.S. Naval Academy. So how the hell did you end up in a Space Force fighter wing after that?

"Just lucky, I guess. I graduated flight school in fighters and joined a carrier group. I spent two years in the Fleet flying everything I could get my hands on. I had just upgraded to the F-44 when the whole *Jade* incident happened and the big battle at Dutch Harbor. After that, the space force was crying for new pilots to train for space combat. I volunteered, and they accepted me."

"How come you weren't at the Battle of Saturn?"

"I had just completing training at Boca Chica when that happened," Paco said bitterly. "I just missed it."

"If you'd been there, you'd be dead now," Rita said softly. "Don't look a gift horse in the mouth."

"Yes, milady."

Satisfied with Paco's performance so far, Rita leaned back.

"Why do you think you're here, Lieutenant Chapula?"

Paco smiled. "Well, I don't normally get called into the presence of the Admiral to discuss my flight training. And I haven't seriously screwed anything up lately. So I'm guessing you need a volunteer for something incredibly dangerous."

Rita couldn't help but laugh. She glanced at Rachel. Rachel gave her a slight nod.

"I believe you might be the right person for this job, Paco," Rita continued. "How would you like to join Commander Gibson and be the first Humans to visit another group of aliens?"

Paco was taken aback.

"You mean there's more of them?"

**Singheko System - Planet Deriko**
**Packet Boat PB06**

Eight hours later, a small packet boat vectored away from the *Merkkessa*. Rachel and Paco looked back at the flagship one last time.

"Wow!" Paco exclaimed. "She's got patches all over her! She

looks like crap!"

Rachel glared at the Lieutenant. "So would you, if you had stood up against four battlecruisers and a half-dozen cruisers."

Paco shrugged. "Guess so." Deftly, he spun the little ship and put it on track for the distant system that was their destination.

Rita had assigned their objective the code name "Stalingrad". That seemed to describe it succinctly - a place where a determined species had made their last stand. Pushing up the throttles, Paco broke orbit and headed for the mass limit.

"Stalingrad, here we come!" he voiced loudly. Rachel looked coolly at him.

"Are you going to be like this all the way there?" she asked.

"Probably," Paco winked at her.

Rachel sighed. "Then I'm going to my cabin. I don't think I can take any more of your fighter jock patter."

Paco smiled at her. Rachel ignored him and left the bridge of the packet boat.

Although the little packet boat had full tDrive capability, including an ansible for long distance communication, it carried no weapons nor any point-defense cannon. It was hardly more than a couple of cabins wrapped around an engine room. It didn't even have a name, just a designation - PB06.

But it would get them there, Rita had assured them. The little boat had been found in the shuttle bay of one of the Singheko cruisers captured during the Battle of Jupiter many months before.

Fleet Intelligence said it wasn't a Singheko design; most likely a trophy captured from some other alien species, then converted to a packet boat by the Singheko.

Importantly, they had verified with Admiral Sobong that the little ship wasn't a Dariama design. In light of Sobong's statement that the Goblins hated the Dariama with a special passion and would shoot on sight, that was a critical factor.

And it wasn't Nidarian, Taegu or Bagrami. That covered all

the species known to humanity so far. So Rita had decided to use it to send her embassy to Stalingrad.

"But," Rachel had objected, "what if this boat is from another species that the Goblins hate and shoot on sight?"

"Sobong says she's not aware of any other species that the Goblins hate as much as the Dariama."

"But she could be wrong!"

"Yes, she could be wrong, Commander Gibson. So be prepared to talk fast."

Now, as Rachel entered her cabin and lay down on her bunk, she ran over the mission parameters in her mind.

*Get to Stalingrad without getting killed. Establish contact with the Goblins. Lay out recent history for them, help them understand the conflict with the Singheko. Make sure they understand that if the Singheko roll over Humanity, then they'll inevitably come for the Goblins in their unswerving push to build their empire in the Arm.*

*Convince them to help us.*

725 lights to Stalingrad. Twenty-two days. Farther out into the Arm than any Human had ever gone before.

*And I'll have to listen to that fighter jock bullshit the whole way, I bet.*

# CHAPTER SIX

**Singheko System - Planet Deriko**
**Near Misto Marta**

The planet Deriko was a good bit larger than Mars, and much earlier in its evolution. So it still had water - rivers and lakes. The atmosphere was thin, but breathable by Humans.

Until four months ago, it had been a slave planet of the Singheko Empire, with more than twenty massive factory complexes scattered around the planet - producing weapons for the Singheko dream of conquering the entire Orion Arm.

That was before the Singheko made the mistake of bringing in eight slave ships from Earth, each containing 12,000 Human slaves.

Because one of those Human slaves had been a woman named Tatiana Powell - Luke Powell's daughter. That mistake had cost the Singheko the entire planet. Tatiana had put together a slave rebellion that swept across the land, marching from camp to camp, adding thousands more slaves to her army as she went. She had freed more than 300,000 slaves, members of four species, from a brutal existence under their Singheko masters.

In the process, Tatiana had captured or destroyed every one of the slave camps. All but one of them she had given back to the Ampato, the species native to the planet, to rebuild into new cities.

But Tatiana had retained one complex, making it into a city of refuge for freed slaves who elected to remain and continue fighting the Singheko. Tatiana had named the fledgling city after her best friend, killed in the last battle before the Singheko fled the planet.

*Misto Marta. City of Marta.*

Now it was the EDF base in the system - for as long as they could hold it.

Admiral Rita Page had been thoroughly impressed by Tatiana's leadership skills in booting the Singheko forces off the planet. Rita had quickly recruited Tatiana to the EDF, appointing her an Admiral. Supervising a force of twenty-five thousand, Tatiana was in charge of all ground-based operations for the EDF.

Ten thousand of her best troops were Special Forces and conducted guerrilla warfare operations on the Singheko-occupied planets of Asdif and Ursa. The remainder worked in the city - repairing starship components, assembling weapons, and preparing food and supplies for the warships in orbit above them.

But today was a different day. At a gravesite high in the foothills overlooking the city, two people stood.

Tatiana Powell and her husband Mikhail gazed at the stone monument marked simply "Marta".

It was the resting place of their friend and fellow warrior - the woman who had died as they won their last victory, driving the Singheko off the planet.

"God, I miss her," said Tatiana, wiping away a tear. "She saved my life so many times, I lost count. It seemed like every time I looked around, she was saving my life again. And I wasn't the only one. There were a lot of others, too."

Mikhail squeezed her hand. "I know, love. I know."

"I'll never forget her, Mikhail. Never."

She turned to her husband and placed her hand on her pregnant abdomen. "When little Marta gets here, I want to tell her about her namesake. Don't let me forget. Make sure I remember to tell her."

"We'll remember, Tat. Don't worry. We'll tell her."

With one last sad look at the grave, Tatiana turned and

headed back to the command shuttle parked nearby. She was now several months pregnant, and no longer willing to hike the fifteen klicks from the city to this remote location.

And there was the problem of security. The Singheko were not happy about losing an entire planet to this woman, a former slave - and what was worse, a Human. A species the Singheko viewed as barely better than animals, weak and stupid.

There was scuttlebutt the Singheko had put a price on her head equivalent to the cost of a starship. No attempts had yet been made on her life. But everyone knew the threat was out there - a sword hanging over her.

Entering the shuttle, she smiled first at her bodyguards, sitting up front in the crew area, then at Commander Jim Carter, waiting for them in the rear.

Having paid his respects at Marta's grave, Jim had quickly returned to the shuttle to allow Tatiana and Mikhail personal time at the gravesite.

Jim had never met Marta in life; but he knew how important she had been to the rebellion. Without her, it was said, it was unlikely they would have succeeded in clearing Deriko of the Singheko and freeing the slaves. So he paid his respects, and in some sense wished he had known her.

"Are you still dead-set on wild camping?" asked Mikhail as they buckled in.

"Yes, if you don't mind dropping me off," Jim replied.

"No problem," Mikhail spoke as the shuttle pilot lifted off. They headed northwest, deeper into the mountains.

Forty thousand feet above them, an escort flight of four fighters could barely be seen, keeping overwatch on the shuttle. Tatiana's troops were dedicated to her, almost reverential, guarding her person day and night. She was never out of sight of her bodyguard and escort, except in her own room at night with Mikhail.

Within a half-hour, they arrived at a remote wilderness area, far to the north. The shuttle put down on a gravel bar beside a mountain river. Jim climbed out, dragging his backpack and rifle.

"See you in three weeks!" he called as he waved goodbye. "Thanks for the lift!"

Tatiana and Mikhail waved farewell. "Stay safe! Call if you need us!"

Jim acknowledged as the shuttle lifted off, lifting his emergency radio at them.

He had no intention of using it. Jim was a die-hard wild camper. He had spent entire months on hiking trips in the Yukon, in Alaska, in Canada - with nothing but his rifle and what he could carry on his back.

He had only accepted the emergency radio because Tatiana insisted - and threatened to call Rita if he didn't take it.

*No way I want Rita on my case about it*, he had thought grudgingly. *So I'll take the damn thing. But I won't use it.*

Now, as the sound of the shuttle died away, Jim looked around. It was hard to believe he was on another planet, 550 light years from Earth. Had he not known better, he would have thought he was on the North Slope of Alaska, or maybe the Canadian Northwest Territory.

Beside him, the river ran swift and sure over the rocks. The mountains surrounding him were tall, granite and gneiss interlaced with sedimentary layers. The area reminded him of the bowl surrounding Lake Louise in the Canadian Rockies.

Jim directed a thought to his embedded AI.

*Angel - turn yourself off. I don't want to hear your voice for two bloody weeks!*

<Turning off>

He started walking southeast, following the river, looking for a good campsite. Soon he found one, a small pad clear of rocks and brush. He set up his tent, made a fire pit, and got his fire built. The sun was headed down and would soon be behind the mountains. It was getting cold; he knew it could get down to -10C in these mountains at this time of year; but he was prepared for it.

To Jim, that was half the fun of it; preparing for the worst the elements could throw at him and being able to survive the challenge.

Leaning back against a large rock, Jim stoked up his pipe and smoked, one of the few unhealthy vices he allowed himself. It was good to break it out and smoke. It had been a while - he wasn't allowed to use it onboard the *Merkkessa.*

Far off, some animal wailed. Tatiana had told Jim there were bear-equivalents, mountain lion-equivalents, and wolf-equivalents in the menagerie of animals on the planet. But she had added, they were usually afraid of Humans - Humans had an alien smell to them.

Still, Jim reached over and pulled his old beat-up Weatherby to him, making sure it was in arm's reach if needed. Like most normal people caught up in the destruction and death of war, Jim hated to kill anything unnecessarily. But on the other hand, if it came down to life or death - him or the animal - he would be prepared.

He hoped it wouldn't come to that.

Letting his mind wander free, Jim thought about all that had happened to him in the last two years. The discovery of the sentient starship *Jade* in the Canadian Northwest. Relocating *Jade* to his aircraft hangar in Deseret, Nevada and beginning her repair. Bonnie finding him, joining him, the two of them falling in love. And then *Jade*'s creation of the clone Rita.

His thoughts came around to the day Rita had been 'born'. Or decanted, he wasn't sure which word to use. He let his thoughts go back, remembering the strangeness of that day - the day he had first met Rita.

*"Time for the big unveiling, I guess," said Jim.*

*"Yep," agreed Bonnie. They walked down* Jade's *passageway toward the medical unit and opened the hatch.*

*Before them, the medpod held the clone. She was breathing normally, to all intents sleeping peacefully. Her hair was just stubble, less than an eighth of an inch long. Her lips were thin, her* nose as well. In fact, her entire body was thin.

"Is she healthy?" Jim asked Jade.

<Yes. She is quite normal. She will put on more weight once she starts eating normally>

Bonnie leaned over the medpod.

"She's so thin," she said. "Almost like a...shit!"

Bonnie jumped back two feet from the medpod, nearly falling over.

The woman inside the medpod looked up and smiled.

<Please help her out of the medpod> Bonnie heard Jade speak.

"Jim, help her," said Bonnie, still too shocked to move.

Jim nodded, stepped forward, and lifted the lid of the medpod. The woman reached up, grabbed the lip, and pulled herself to a sitting position. Then she levered one leg over the edge, pushed herself up with her hands, and scrambled out of the device, thumping down to the floor.

She was completely naked.

"Mornin'," said the woman. "It's good to get out of that damn thing."

Jim glanced over at Bonnie.

"Well, she has your nose," he quipped.

"Don't start," replied Bonnie. Bonnie looked at the woman. "How do you feel?"

"Hungry," said the woman. "Is there anything to eat in the galley?"

"Uh...I think we have a few things in there," said Bonnie, taken aback.

"Great!" said the woman. She promptly marched out the hatch, turned left, took five steps, and turned right into the galley. By the time Jim and Bonnie caught up, she was rummaging through the refrigerator.

"So you know your way around..." muttered Bonnie.

The woman looked at her. "Of course. I have all your memories and most of Jim's. So anything you know, I know. Except for some of the bad stuff, I think. Jade told me she left some of that out."

Bonnie sat down at one of the tables, looking puzzled.

"When did you talk to Jade?" she asked.

The woman continued to rummage through the refrigerator, pulling out bread, cheese, meat, and lettuce, and moved it to the counter. She started building a sandwich.

"*Jade has spoken to me a number of times over the last week. Remember that you sleep at night. Jade doesn't. So we talk at night when you aren't around. It was part of my educational process,* Jade *said. I had to get used to talking. Even though I knew all the words, I didn't exactly have the muscle memory. Or at least, my muscle memory is mostly Bonnie's, and our bodies are different. So I had to adjust.*"

"You don't seem to have any trouble walking," said Jim.

"*Jade let me walk around a couple of times this week at night. It was hard at first, but I got better at it pretty quick.*"

"Jade, why didn't you tell us about this?" asked Bonnie.

<Oops, sorry. I've been kind of busy lately>

Pensive, Bonnie bit her lip, thinking.

"Do you have a name?" Bonnie asked the woman.

Turning to face them, the woman leaned against the counter, naked, and started eating her sandwich.

"*Yes.* Jade *named me. It was critical to my identity that I have a name as soon as possible during the brain synthesis. My name is Rita.*"

## Singheko System - Planet Deriko
## In the Wilderness

Jim's pipe had gone out in his reverie. Snapping back to reality, he re-lit it and leaned back again, contemplating the strange ways of the Universe.

He had been in love with Bonnie when Rita was created. Now, two years later, Bonnie had gone her own way, become a starship captain, and found Luke. And he was with Rita, who had borne his child, Imogen - a child who was safely back on Earth with Jim's sister Gillian.

And Rita had come into her own, somehow surviving

battle after battle, and through a strange set of circumstances finding herself head of the EDF.

*Rita Page. Admiral of the Black.*

*My boss. And my wife.*

*She really ought to take my last name and end this perpetual confusion everyone has between her and Bonnie.*

But Jim knew she would never do that. She had been formed from the consciousness of Jim and Bonnie.

That meant she had loved Bonnie from the day of her creation, just as Jim did.

And she had loved Jim from the day of her creation, just as Bonnie did.

The impossible woman who loved them both. The impossible woman between them. The woman who knew what they were going to say before they said it.

Far off, something that sounded like a wolf howled. Jim smiled. He felt like he had come home again.

*If we survive this war, and if the Singheko allow it, maybe Rita and I can live here after. It's a beautiful planet when we're not killing each other over it.*

Then Jim shook his head. He spoke to the river and the trees and the rocks, knowing they were the only ones who could hear him.

"No, that'll never happen. First of all, we'll never survive this war. And even if we do, Rita would never live here. She'll be off exploring the next planet, and the one after that, and the one after that."

*That's my Rita.*

## Singheko System - Planet Ridendo
## City of Mosalia

The Singheko stared at the figures across the table. The bar was dark. He could hardly make out the heavily disguised creatures a few feet away.

One was a Nidarian, of that he was sure. A common enough

species on Ridendo.

The other was dressed as a Dariama. A fish out of water in this place, in this city, on this planet. Only a few dozen Dariama were on the entire planet; the ambassador, his embassy staff, his security detail, a few servants.

But he didn't think it was really a Dariama. Something didn't feel right about it.

He decided to ignore the feeling, though. There were bigger things at stake right now.

"And Zukra?" asked the Nidarian.

"In a rage," the Singheko answered. "As usual. Smashing things, knocking people about. Very pissed that our last raid went so poorly."

There was a silence. The three were treading lightly. The Singheko glanced around the bar, trying to make it look casual. The only occupants appeared to be quite normal - a couple of lovers ensconced in a corner booth, a couple of drunks slumped on their stools, and the bartender.

But who could tell? Any of them could be Naval Intelligence. One of Admiral Zukra's own. They were on dangerous ground.

The Singheko spoke softly to the Nidarian.

"I understand why Zukra wants his revenge. But why is Garatella so hell-bent on destroying the Humans?"

The Nidarian shook his head.

"On the surface, he says it's because they double-crossed him. They failed to bring the *Dragon* back to Nidaria as promised. And kept the gamma lance technology for themselves."

The Singheko half-smiled - a somewhat strange sight for a creature with a hint of muzzle that evolution had not fully erased.

"But we both know that's not the real reason," the Singheko said. "Garatella had a spy in their midst, so he got the technology anyway. He never expected the Humans to bring it back to him. So what's the real reason?"

The Nidarian looked around, making sure no one was

within earshot of their conversation.

"Because he's afraid of them. He's scared shitless of these Humans. He says he's never seen a species so dangerous. He says we have to wipe them out before they get a real toehold in space."

The Singheko nodded.

"That's what I thought. Not that I don't agree with him to some extent. They are the most warlike and aggressive species we've ever encountered. Next to us, of course. But..."

"Yes," the other said. "Does that mean we wipe them out? Or..."

"Or make an alliance with them," replied the Singheko. "Think what an alliance like that could do."

"Yes."

There was a silence for a bit as they considered the possibilities.

"But..." said the Nidarian. "For all their aggressiveness in battle and their skill at killing - they preach that they are fighting a purely defensive war; that the protection of Earth is their only goal."

The Singheko smiled. He looked at the Dariama - or whatever it was - who had been silent for the entire conversation.

"Every empire starts with that story."

# CHAPTER SEVEN

**Singheko System - Planet Ridendo**
**City of Mosalia**

The planet Singheko had two moons. One was the size of Earth's moon, and close in. It was full tonight. Ollie and Helen sat in the small garden behind their safe house, staring at the brilliantly lit orb above them in the sky. Far beyond it, less than a tenth of its size, the second moon was a bright crescent.

And beyond that, just visible as it rose over the horizon, was a pinpoint of light called Deriko. There, 90 million kilometers away, was the Fleet, and warmth, and friends, and safety.

Helen suddenly shivered. Ollie put his arm around her. "Are you OK?"

"I think somebody just walked on my grave," said Helen.

"Don't talk like that. I hate it when you say crap like that."

"Well, suck it up. I'm me and you're you."

"I've noticed," Ollie agreed.

There was a short silence. Then Helen spoke in frustration. "So they're all dead?"

"Yep. No survivors. They blew themselves up at the end."

"Crap. But at least, we don't have to worry about Orma torturing them for intel. Do we know what happened yet?"

"Obviously, someone turned them in. Or maybe Orma had a spy in the cell. Whatever happened, they got raided."

"I hate that fucker Orma," Helen spat. "Rita let him go, took a chance on him. Now he kills us every chance he gets."

Ollie shrugged. "He's just doing his job. Like all of us. It's part of war. We try to stop them, and they try to stop us. Don't take it personally."

"Again - I'm me, and you're you. I take it personally when some Singheko fucker is trying to kill me."

"Point taken."

"So where do we go from here?"

Ollie sighed. "That Resistance cell was our best organized. They were just preparing to blow up part of the spaceport. Now…we'll have to start over. Hand that job over to another cell. Start collecting explosives again. Train their leadership."

"Don't you think it suspicious that you and Yuello met with that Singheko contact - and immediately after that, our prime cell gets raided?"

"No, I don't think there's any connection there. We didn't say anything in that meeting to tip them off. It's just coincidence, I think."

"You better hope so," said Helen. "If that contact was working for Orma, then we might already be under his microscope."

Ollie looked at the moon above them and tightened his arm around Helen.

"Keep the faith, babe. Keep the faith."

**Singheko System - Planet Deriko**
**Battlecruiser *Merkkessa***

In Rita's briefing room outside the Flag Cabin, the Taegu admiral Woderas stared across the conference table at Rita. Woderas was a typical five-foot tall Taegu - creatures quite like Nidarians, clearly related to them at some point in the dark recesses of time. This made the Taegu look small compared to Humans, and even smaller when compared to Admiral Baysig - the seven-foot tall Bagrami next to him. Woderas looked like a child next to the huge bear-like creature.

But Rita knew not to underestimate them - both the creatures across from her were full Admirals in their respective fleets. Either of them had the power to pick up their marbles and leave if they became displeased with Rita's leadership. It was a fragile coalition they maintained.

"I truly understand how you feel, Woderas," said Rita, speaking in Nidarian. "I can imagine the suffering your people must be experiencing now. If it were Earth that was occupied by the Singheko, I would feel exactly as you do.

"But to attempt now to drive the Singheko from your planet would be suicide. It would require us to take nearly our entire fleet.

"That would leave Zukra free to take any action that would hurt us the most. He could go to Dekanna and attack the Dariama space docks where they're building out their new ships. He could go to Earth and nuke our planet again. Or he could come in behind us as we attacked the occupying force at Asdif, taking us in the rear. In any of those scenarios, we lose the war.

"Our only real chance at success is to stay the course. Keep Zukra pinned here in his own system as long as possible. Buy time for Earth and Dekanna to produce more ships. Eventually, we'll have enough strength to defeat Zukra's main force. Then, and only then, will we be able to free Asdif and Ursa."

Woderas was not happy. "If it were Earth that was occupied by the Singheko - then you would not be so complacent about waiting, I think."

Rita shook her head. "Admiral Woderas, if the situation were reversed - if Earth were occupied - I would make the same decision. I cannot, and will not, split my fleet to liberate one planet. As long as Zukra and Garatella can come in behind us, we must stay together."

Baysig leaned forward and spoke in his deep growly voice. "Remember, Woderas - my own planet is also occupied by the Singheko," he said. "We also suffer under their brutality. Yet as much as it pains me, I agree with Admiral Page. To detach a force to Asdif large enough to push the Singheko out of your system would leave us wide open. Zukra would not fail to take advantage of such an opportunity. And Garatella as well. Our intelligence tells us that Garatella has another fleet almost ready to come at us. If we are to survive, we must stay together."

Rita looked at Baysig in thanks for his support. His pushed-in, barely visible muzzle always reminded her of a bear. It was sometimes hard for her to remember that he was, if anything, more intelligent than a Human. She had the same fleeting thought that often occurred when she was with Baysig.

*Thank God he's on our side.*

Beside her, Tatiana Powell dived into the conversation.

"Admiral Woderas. We can continue to chip away at the Singheko forces on the surface of your planet, as we're doing now. I can send you another thousand Special Forces if that will help."

Woderas shook his head, giving up. "No, Admiral, but thank you. We have enough for guerrilla warfare now. More would not help us. In fact, more would probably just get in the way."

Tatiana nodded. "I understand. But they're available if you need them. Just say the word."

Rita realized she had won the argument, at least for now. "How about you, Baysig?" she asked. "Do you have enough troops on the ground at Ursa?"

"Aye, milady," responded Baysig. "Admiral Powell has been more than generous. We attack Singheko forces at every opportunity. But of course, as long as they hold the orbitals, we can only harass them."

Rita sighed. "I know. And I wish I could give you better news. But it will take at least a year, maybe two, before we'll have sufficient force to liberate your home planets. I hope you will stick with us until then."

Woderas nodded grudgingly. "It will be so, milady. We will stay for now."

"Thank you, Admiral Woderas," Rita smiled.

"But," Woderas continued. "The flaw in your plan is that you stay here at Deriko, in the Singheko home system. With the forces we have, we cannot defeat Zukra here. Surely you know that."

Rita nodded again. "Yes, Admiral. I know that. My only goal at the moment is to keep him pinned in place here. We have other projects in the works, initiatives I can't discuss right now. But those plans require me to keep him here as long as possible. I assure you, I'm well aware that at some point - and probably soon - we'll have to leave here and find another place to make our stand."

"And I suppose you'll go to Earth for that?" Woderas said, somewhat bitterly. "Protect your home planet?"

Rita tried to speak quietly, without letting her frustration show. "No, Admiral. Earth is not the right place to make our stand. I'm sure you see that. All the civilized planets - and thus all our current and potential allies - are in the other direction. We will make our stand in concert with you, and the Bagrami, and the Dariama. Earth will have to fend for herself a bit longer."

**Sol System - Earth**
**United Nations Building - Beijing, China**

Admiral Ken Elliott sat in the top of the UN building, cursing.

"That bitch!" he fumed. "That ungodly clone bitch!"

"Yes, sir," agreed his Chief of Staff, Dewa Shigeto.

"Her ansible is down for repairs, my sweet ass! She's ignoring my directive!"

Shigeto maintained his silence. Elliott slammed his palm down on his desk and looked out the window at distant aircraft on approach to Beijing Capital International Airport. He turned back to Shigeto.

"When is that other bitch of hers arriving?"

"Captain Bonnie Page, sir. She arrives next week on the *Dragon*, along with two other destroyers."

"And what was her excuse for coming in place of Admiral Page?"

Shigeto spoke from memory, not needing to look at his electronic tablet.

"To consult as directed and to coordinate training for *Victory* and the two new cruisers, based on actual experience in the recent battles with the Singheko, sir."

"Bullshit. That bitch is up to something," said Elliott. He mused, returning to gaze out the window again.

"And once again - why do those two have the same last name?"

"Unknown, sir, although I'm sure you've heard the rumors."

Elliott glared at him.

"Yes. People say Rita Page is a clone, created with the consciousness of Bonnie Page, so she took the same last name. And I believe it. She has absolutely no history prior to two years ago. Nothing. She just popped into existence when that damn starship *Jade* was discovered. And all our troubles started then. If you ask me, those two are the cause of all this, not the fix."

"Yes, sir."

"But…she has the Fleet. So I have to deal with her, like it or not. But I'll tell you, Captain. As soon as I get that bitch back here to Earth, I'm replacing her with someone I can trust. In fact, both of them. Bonnie too. And that asshole Jim Carter. I want all of them shitcanned and sent back to the desert where they came from."

"Yes, sir," said Shigeto.

Elliott turned back to the window again, musing.

"Dismissed," he said out of the corner of his mouth.

## Sol System - Earth
## Destroyer *Dragon*

A week later, the warship EDF *Dragon* slid smoothly into Earth orbit.

"Stable orbit established 100 klicks in front of *Victory*, sir," said Chief Blocker at helm.

"Very good, Chief," replied Luke at the XO console. "Secure main engines, set planetary operations."

Bonnie walked on the bridge from her day cabin.

"How we looking?" she asked.

Luke rose from his seat as Bonnie sat in hers.

"Looking good, mum. We signaled *Victory* we'd be taking position in front of her, and she agreed."

"No objection from ground controllers?"

"No, mum, but I don't think that means much. Elliott will try to make his move later, I think. He'll let us get settled in and send our crew down for shore leave, and then try to box us in while we're on the ground."

"So you still think he'll try to ground us, remove us from command."

"I'm sure of it, Captain. I've got all my scuttlebutt channels wide open, and that's what I'm hearing."

"OK. Get Norali up here. We need to figure out a new approach."

A half-hour later, Commander Norali Peralta, newly minted EDF Fleet Intelligence officer, sat in the briefing room with Bonnie and Luke.

"You can't be serious!" she exclaimed.

"We're absolutely serious," Bonnie responded. "According to our sources, Elliott is waiting for us to go down to the surface for shore leave, then he'll waylay us, relieve us of command, take the *Dragon* and keep it here to defend Earth. Along with the *Victory* and the other two new cruisers. He has no intention of sending any reinforcements to Rita."

Norali nodded. "But you say I can't kill anyone," she muttered.

"No, sorry."

"Too bad. That's what I'm best at."

Bonnie and Luke chuckled in unison.

"After seeing what you and the rest of Tatiana's army did to the Singheko on Deriko, I'd have to agree with you," smiled Luke. "But in this case, Elliott and his cronies are supposed to be on our side, so Rita says we can't kill them."

Norali frowned for a minute, thinking.

"Then I think we should approach it as follows: first, we ensure you can't be waylaid and relieved of command. Second, we feel out the captain of the *Victory* to see if he might have any sympathy toward our position; and third...well, you're not gonna like the third."

Bonnie leaned forward. "What's third?"

"Make a public appeal to the masses of Earth to overcome Elliott's political position and force him to stand behind Rita and the Fleet."

"Oh, crap," said Luke.

Bonnie seconded his emotion. "That's not going to be very popular with Rita. That's the last thing she'd want us to do - drag all this dirty laundry out into public."

"You have no other choice," said Norali. "If you're not willing to do step three, then you might as well turn around and head back to the Fleet right now. You have no chance of success."

Luke looked at Bonnie. Norali could see they were struggling with this decision. Finally, Bonnie heaved a sigh.

"Better to ask forgiveness than permission, I guess."

"You mean we do it without clearing it with Rita first?"

Bonnie nodded. "That's what I mean. Norali, you're Fleet Intelligence. I depend on you for the planning. Make your plans and tell us what we need to do. And I don't want any of this to leak back to Rita until we're in flight. Got it?"

Norali nodded. "Got it, mum."

"So what's the first thing we do?" asked Luke.

Norali grimaced. "You're not gonna like it."

"What?"

"You can't go to the surface. At least not right now. Sorry; but we can't take a chance on Elliott getting his hands on you."

"Crap," said Luke. "I was really looking forward to going down to Portsmouth and having a dark with some old friends."

"And," said Norali, "I'm going over to the *Victory* for a little tete-a-tete with her Captain. Has he ever met you, Bonnie?"

"No, he's newly assigned from a wet-navy aircraft carrier, cross-trained on the *Victory*. One of Elliott's Royal Navy buddies, I think. Captain Westerly."

"Bonnie, you've been in the media a lot, I know; but mostly they use older photos of you from your Air Force days. I haven't seen too many photos or videos of you taken recently. Do you think you could work up a disguise to look as different as possible from two years ago?"

"Well, yes, but why?"

"Because you're going to the *Victory* with me as my aide," said Norali. "If you don't mind the demotion. I can't think of a safer place for you while I'm gone. Elliott would never think to look for you there. And it will allow you to get a first-hand look at Captain Westerly. If there is any way to convince him to take our side, we should go for it."

## Singheko System - Planet Ridendo
## Singheko Fleet Headquarters

Zukra zu Akribi - Protector of the Fang and Claw, Terrible Sword of the Singheko Empire, Grand Admiral of the Fleet - sat back in his ornate chair and glared at the two captains in front of him. One of them was his Flag Aide, Damra su Rosta. The other was his Chief of Intelligence, Orma zu Dalty.

Zukra was one pissed-off Singheko, and both captains knew it.

"First to you, Damra. That last raid was bullshit. My grandmother could have done a better job. What were you trying to do, parade our ships in front of the Humans?"

"No, Admiral. Per your standing orders..."

"My standing orders are to avoid a full-contact battle that would endanger our capital ships. Not to go flying by them with a wave and a kiss!"

"Aye, sir," agreed Damra. He could see no other response that would help.

"And...since I returned from Nidaria, we've completed exactly how many new warships?"

"Three cruisers and two destroyers, sir. But..."

"No buts, Damra! You've had months to patch up our fleet and build new ships! But are we able to attack the Humans in full force? No! Because all I get are excuses and delays!"

Zukra leaned forward in his chair. Involuntary instinctive reactions caused by his extreme anger began to display. His fangs slipped out over the narrow lips of his abbreviated muzzle. On the desk where his hands rested, the tips of vestigial claws poked out of two fingertips on each hand, another evolutionary artifact of his ancestors.

"You've got exactly two more months to get us ready to fight the Humans again! If you can't get this job done, then by the stars I can find someone who will!"

"It will be done, m'lord," responded Damra, his eyes fixated on the protruding fangs and claws of his boss.

"It had better!" Zukra finished, slamming his fist down on his desk, then pulling his clawed fingertips across the surface, adding to the many long scratches from previous sessions. "Now get out!"

"Aye, m'lord."

Damra shot to his feet, saluted, spun on his heels, and left like his ass was on fire. Orma sat silently, knowing his turn was next.

Zukra frowned at him. "And you. I ordered you three months ago to capture that witch Human Admiral. And yet here we sit three months later, and you haven't done it yet."

"Yes, m'lord," Orma acknowledged. "It's a tough nut to crack. She doesn't spend all that much time on the planet these days. She usually stays on her flagship. And even when she's on the planet, she's with that other witch Tatiana, always surrounded by several thousand of those rebel troops. And neither is ever separated from their bodyguards. The Admiral's troops are intensely loyal. There is no chance of getting an operative anywhere near her."

"Excuses, excuses. I want that bitch spread-eagled in front of me, Orma, ready for torture. Find a way or find another job."

"Aye, m'lord."

"Now get out of here. I have to think."

"Aye, m'lord." Orma stood, saluted, and left the office. As he departed, his mind came back to the knotty problem he had been assigned.

*How to kidnap a Human admiral from the heart of a fortified city on another planet, when she was surrounded by the most loyal troops he had ever known.*

Returning to his office, Orma turned the problem around in his head.

*There must be a way.*

*Maybe if I reverse the problem. What if I were trying to kidnap myself?*

*The problem is not much different. I'm here, surrounded by guards and troops all the time. How would I capture myself?*

Like a flash of lightning, it came to him.

*Of course. It's so simple.*

# CHAPTER EIGHT

**Enroute to Stalingrad**
**Packet Boat PB06**

"Hey, AI!" Paco said.

Nothing.

"Hey, ship!"

Nothing.

"Hey, you stupid boat!"

Nothing.

Rachel entered the cockpit and glared at Paco. "What in the hell are you yelling about in here? I was trying to sleep!"

"Oh, sorry, Commander," Paco apologized. "I was trying to see if this crummy boat has an AI. But I can't wake one up, so I guess it doesn't have one."

Rachel rolled her eyes. "Yes, it has one, but I have the keyword. Did you ever think to ask me for it? Or did you just want to yell until you were sure I was awake?"

Paco grimaced. "Sorry, Skipper. Uh...could I have the keyword?"

Rachel sighed and sat down in the copilot seat.

"PB06, provide command input to pilot, keyword Londonderry."

Paco giggled. "Londonderry? You picked that for a keyword?"

Rachel glared at him. "I'm Irish, you idiot!"

<Pilot. Please say the following sentence for voice identification. Fourscore and seven years ago, our forefathers brought forth on this continent a new nation>

Paco nearly fell out of his seat laughing. Between guffaws, he stammered out:

"Not my forefathers! My forefathers were shooting arrows at them, trying to drive them back into the sea!"

Finally, he was able to suppress his laughter and repeated the phrase back to the AI.

&lt;Voice ID accepted. Pilot now has command input&gt;

"Satisfied?" asked Rachel, rising from the copilot seat. "Can I go back to sleep now?"

Paco turned in his seat and made a mock salute. "Of course, Commander. My sincere apologies."

Still rolling her eyes, Rachel headed back to her cabin.

Now Paco returned to his quest. Despite his lighthearted mood, he had determined to solve the mystery of the boat's origin. And he needed the AI to do it.

"PB06. That name sucks. Can I rename you?"

&lt;Yes. You may choose any name&gt;

"Great. You are now named *Donkey*. Got it?"

&lt;I am now named *Donkey*&gt;

"*Donkey*, what is the origin of this boat?"

&lt;That information is not in my database&gt;

"Are you the original AI of this boat?"

&lt;No. I was recently installed and booted up to replace the previous AI&gt;

"Damn. That sucks. Is there a copy of the previous AI onboard?"

&lt;Yes. It is a Singheko AI stored in a read-only part of my array&gt;

&lt;Can you bring it up in sandbox mode for simulation purposes?"

&lt;Yes&gt;

"Fantastic! Bring it up in sandbox mode but provide a translation routine between Singheko and English for the interface and give it the separate name Darth."

&lt;Loading. Initializing. Ready&gt;

"Are you there, Darth?"

<I am here>

"What is the origin of this boat?"

<I do not know. I was installed and booted up after the boat was captured by the Singheko>

"Is there a copy of the original boat AI in your records?"

<Yes, but it is damaged and cannot be initialized>

"Can you identify the language of the previous AI?"

<I cannot identify the language. All this was told to your technicians a few months ago>

"Ah, got it."

Paco thought for a moment.

*What I need here is something out of the box. Something that a normal technician wouldn't think of. Or wouldn't have the time to do...*

<Darth. Given enough time, could you restore the damaged sectors of the prior AI?"

<It is possible. I will not know until I have worked for at least three days. My speed in this sandboxed environment is quite slow>

"Well, don't get any ideas. You aren't coming out of that sandbox. So get to it, buddy>

<Getting to it>

<*Donkey*, resume command interface, and maintain Darth offline but functional. Allow him as many cycles as you can spare."

<Wilco>

## Sol System - Earth
## Battlecruiser *Victory*

*Dragon*'s shuttle bounced once, lightly, and then crunched to a halt in the shuttle bay of the newly completed battlecruiser EDF *Victory*. The deck was pressurized, and the inner door opened. The autodock cradle moved them into the inner bay and with a thump, they were slotted in and lowered to the deck.

Looking out the small window, Norali and Bonnie could see a welcoming committee waiting for them.

"Well, showtime. Wish us luck," said Norali. She gave one quick glance at Bonnie, who was disguised in a dark wig and wearing the uniform of a Lieutenant Commander. "Are you sure you can be a Lieutenant Commander again?"

"Watch me," Bonnie shot back.

Grinning, Norali let Chief Nash open the hatch. As she prepared to step out on the ramp, she turned and spoke softly to the Master Chief.

"If we're not back in six hours, call out the calvary."

Bonnie and Norali had agreed there was no choice but to let certain people in on their plan in case it all went wrong. Master Chief Nash - the *Dragon*'s COB, or Chief of the Boat - was the first one they trusted enough to bring into their deception.

And the commander of the Marine detachment, Major Adrian, was another. The ten Marines under Major Adrian and the twenty Special Forces from Tatiana's army were all suited up on *Dragon*, loaded for bear. If things went sideways in this meeting, and the captain of the *Victory* decided to take them prisoner, Adrian had orders to come bust them out.

Without killing anyone.

Stepping down the ramp, Norali walked over to the waiting group of officers, Bonnie trailing her to one side, exactly as an aide should do.

Noting the ranks of the officers meeting her, Norali realized neither the Captain nor the XO of the *Victory* had bothered to come to the shuttle bay to meet them. The senior person in front of her was a Lieutenant Commander, and his two companions were both Lieutenants.

Norali was now a Commander, recently transferred from Tatiana's rebel army to the EDF. That made her the senior officer in this party. So she stopped and waited for them to salute her.

The Lieutenant Commander promptly did just that, with the two Lieutenants following in quick succession. Norali returned their salutes, then stuck out her hand.

"Commander Norali Peralta, EDF Fleet Intelligence," she said. "Glad to meet you." She turned and gestured to Bonnie. "My aide, Lieutenant Commander Rodgers."

"I'm Lieutenant Commander James Saito, these are my assistants Lieutenant Tran and Lieutenant Fletcher. Welcome aboard, and boy are we glad to see you! We've been wondering when Admiral Page would send us someone to bring us up to speed on Singheko tactics."

Norali nodded. That had been the cover story she sent over to the *Victory* - that Rita had sent them to relay the lessons learned from recent battles with the Singheko.

"Shall we go?" asked Saito.

"Yes, by all means," answered Norali. Norali followed Saito, Bonnie right behind and beside her, and the other two Lieutenants bringing up the rear. Soon they were settled in a comfortable briefing room - much superior in quality and comfort to the Spartan one of the *Dragon*. A steward brought them hot coffee on a silver serving tray, with cream and sugar on the side.

"Hot damn," exclaimed Norali before she could restrain herself. "Is that real coffee?"

Saito looked puzzled. "Yes, of course."

Norali and Bonnie both raced to get cream into their coffee and took long drinks, ignoring the heat of it in their eagerness to get it down. Saito looked at the two women like they were crazy, glancing back at his two assistants in puzzlement.

Slowly it dawned on him.

"I take it the Fleet is out of coffee?" he said wonderingly.

"Been out for months," Norali said between sips. "Been drinking Nidarian *nish*. It's better than nothing, but it ain't coffee."

"I see," said Saito. He snapped his fingers, and the steward stuck his head around the door of the tiny kitchen next door.

"Hank, I think you'd better just bring the pot and leave it on the table," he said.

***

At that moment, the Chief Petty Officer in the back of the room barked "Attention on Deck." Everyone came to their feet and stood at attention as Captain Joshua Westerly stepped into the briefing room.

"As you were," he said, stepping to the head of the table. Everyone took their seats again as Westerly looked at the new arrivals.

"Greetings, Commander Peralta," he began. "We're awfully glad to see you. We've studied the tapes of the battles here in the Sol System until we're blue in the face, but there's no substitute for talking to someone who's actually been there and seen the enemy. So welcome to our little home away from home."

Norali sized the man up. He seemed a decent sort so far; no signs of arrogance or stupidity.

But of course, that could mean nothing. If he was Ken Elliott's man, they were in trouble.

Norali spoke up. "Well, I'm actually sailing under false colors, Captain. I was only involved in the ground war on Deriko. It's Lieutenant Commander Rodgers here who will do the briefing. She was Tactical Officer on the *Dragon* at the time of the recent battles."

Sitting down in his chair, Captain Westerly seemed puzzled.

"Nothing against Commander Rodgers, but did you not have a more senior officer from *Dragon* who could do the briefing? What about the Captain or the XO?"

"Ah, unfortunately, both the Captain and the XO are indisposed today. They caught some bug, probably from the re-supply shuttles that have been coming and going. Both of them are under quarantine in *Dragon*'s medical ward, I'm afraid. But we didn't want to put off this briefing, as we'll only be here for a short time. We have to get back to the Fleet as soon as possible."

Westerly looked over at Saito. Norali could have sworn what passed between them was a look of regret.

*They want to go to the Fleet. These guys want to fight.*

But she could say nothing yet. They had a lot more assessing of this captain to do before they were willing to take a chance with him.

So Bonnie stood, and started the briefing. And it was a damn good briefing. After all, beneath the dark wig and the Lieutenant Commander uniform was the very person they had asked for - the Captain of the *Dragon*, who had more time fighting Singheko than any other officer in the Fleet.

Two hours and several bio-breaks later, Captain Westerly called a halt.

"I don't know about the rest of you," he said, looking at Saito and the two Lieutenants, "but my brain is overstuffed. Let's break for chow."

Turning to Norali and Bonnie, he continued.

"Would you be able to join me in my cabin for dinner, ladies?"

"Yes, sir," Norali responded.

Saito and his assistants drifted out, shaking hands with Norali and Bonnie as they left. Captain Westerly led them through a hatch in the back of the briefing room and they found themselves in his cabin. A steward had just completed setting a lavish dinner on a large table. Westerly gestured them to seats, and then stood behind his chair as they got comfortable.

"I have one more guest coming," he said. "My new XO just reported aboard, and he'll be joining us. Ah, here he is now."

Bonnie turned and looked at the figure coming into the cabin from the bridge hatch. He was a tall man, well-built, with dark hair and flashing blue eyes. He could have been a twin to Jim Carter, Rita's husband. In an old-fashioned gesture of formality, he stopped, braced up, and bowed, and somehow Bonnie knew instantly he was German or Russian.

"Commander Peralta, Lieutenant Commander Rodgers, may I present Commander Fabian Becker, my XO. Commander Becker has just reported aboard, seconded from the Deutsche

Marine."

"Very pleased to meet you. Were you wet navy?" Norali wondered as Becker sat down at the table.

"Ja, I mean, yes, Commander. I was XO of the *Nord-Ostsee*. What you call a frigate, I believe, in America."

Norali responded quickly, with some sting in her voice. "I'm not American, Commander. My father was from Argentina, and my mother from Ukraine."

"Ah, sorry," expressed Becker. "These days, with such a multi-national force in space, I should know better than to assume."

As the steward brought the food, the meal progressed into small talk, beginning when Becker told them about his adventures on a wet-navy frigate, fighting pirates off the coast of Africa.

Piracy had become a recurring problem, particularly in the last twenty years as climate change bit deep into the global economy. Agriculture had been thrown for a loop by the changes. This had caused mass famine in many places, but nowhere worse than Africa and India.

Piracy had been a prickly but manageable problem back in the early part of the century. But as Africa and India fell into chaos, it had become a much larger issue in the latter half of the century. Millions died of hunger - and thousands took to the sea in an attempt to survive via piracy. The entire Indian Ocean had become too dangerous for travel due to the onslaught of well-armed and ruthless pirates who took what they wanted at the point of a gun.

Recently, to prevent well-organized pirate fleets from forcing their way into the Mediterranean, Egypt had put a large warship presence off the southern end of the Suez Canal. The Chinese, Indonesians, and Australians had fielded a wall of warships from Malaysia all the way to Australia to protect their waters. As a result, with the east closed off to them, the pirate fleets had started coming around the African Cape of Good Hope into the eastern Atlantic, first a few dozen smaller ships, then as they got better organized, larger fleets of warships with modern weapons. By joining forces with the pirates already working the east side of Africa, they had formed into quite formidable fleets.

NATO had finally been forced to station a permanent fleet near the Canary Islands to fend off the pirate attacks. Becker had been part of that fleet. Several sharp actions had occurred between his frigate and well-armed pirate vessels - vessels which were easily the equivalent of a frigate in speed and firepower.

"You were wounded?" wondered Norali as the story progressed, pointing to a ribbon on Becker's uniform which she knew was equivalent to a Purple Heart.

Becker looked down at the ribbon, a somewhat sheepish smile on his face.

"Only a little bit," he replied. "A small piece of shrapnel from a 40mm. It went through and through, so I was lucky."

"I'm glad," Norali replied. She glanced at Bonnie across from her. An unspoken thought went through both their minds.

*We need people like this.*

Finally, dinner was complete, and they sat back, enjoying their coffee. Norali looked across at Bonnie, wondering how to start the sensitive topic they had in mind - and if she should discuss it in front of Becker, who was a new player in the game.

But Westerly beat them to it.

"So," he began, looking at Bonnie. "Why is the captain of the *Dragon* sitting at my table disguised as a Lieutenant Commander?"

# CHAPTER NINE

**Sol System - Earth**
**Battlecruiser *Victory***

"How did you know?" asked Bonnie. She reached up and removed the wig, tossing it to a nearby side table, and flicked out her blond hair to remove any residual threads.

Captain Westerly smiled like the Cheshire cat. "My dear Captain Page. I take my job very seriously. That means I've spent dozens of hours going over tapes and pictures of everything related to the coming of *Jade*, the battles fought with the Singheko, and of course your discovery of *Dragon* on Mars.

"And like it or not, Captain Page, you are one of the most beautiful women in the world. Attempting to disguise yourself by changing your makeup and adding a wig is not nearly enough to hide you from anyone who's spent much time viewing you on video. Especially the eyes. I don't think I've ever seen such distinctive green eyes as yours. The next time you attempt to disguise yourself, you should wear contacts to change your eye color."

Bonnie grunted in frustration, glancing at Norali. "I'll remember that, thanks."

"Now," Captain Westerly continued. "I'm sure you didn't go to all this trouble just to give a briefing to my crew without them asking for autographs. So why would the most famous captain in the EDF sit at my table in disguise?"

Bonnie hesitated, looking at Becker. Westerly saw the look and spoke.

"Captain, Commander Becker and I served together off the coast of Africa. I trust him with my life. You can be assured that whatever you say here is confidential."

With a sigh of trepidation, Bonnie decided truth was the best policy. She gave them the whole story - Admiral Elliott's ploy to relieve Rita of command, his decision to retain the *Victory* and the two cruisers for the defense of Earth rather than send them to the Fleet, and his determination to accost Bonnie and Luke at his first opportunity to relieve them of command of the *Dragon.*

At the end of her exposition, Westerly shook his head and sighed. "I knew he was retaining the *Victory* and the cruisers here to defend Earth. But I didn't know about the rest of it."

Westerly looked at Becker, who grimaced.

"Keeping us here is just stupid," Becker said. "One battlecruiser and two cruisers will last about five minutes against a Singheko fleet. They would do a world more good with Rita as part of the Combined Fleet. What is Elliott thinking?"

"He's not thinking," said Bonnie. "He's playing politics. He's an armchair admiral with no concept of how to fight this war."

Westerly lifted a hand in caution. "Regardless of circumstances, I won't criticize my senior officer. Let's focus on the practical and leave the opinions aside."

"Fine," said Bonnie. "What Commander Becker said is correct. Stuck here in orbit, you're a sitting duck for the enemy. I could take you out myself with only the *Dragon*. You'd never know what hit you."

Westerly nodded. "I know that. But what can I do? The Chinese have played this well; this ship was built under a U.N. budget, and has been assigned to the UNSF. The West has played right into their hands with this whole U.N. thing. Regardless, I have my orders, and I've never disobeyed an order in my life. I certainly don't intend to start now."

Bonnie, greatly disappointed, gazed at Norali. "Then I guess we've wasted a trip."

"No," Westerly said. "Not wasted. Now that I've met you, I see that you are exactly what the vids say. A competent, dedicated captain intent on protecting Earth. And for that, I'm glad to have met you. Let us raise a glass."

Together, they stood. As it happened, it was a Friday. Westerly made the traditional Royal Navy toast of the day - a tradition which had seeped over to the EDF due to the large number of Royal Navy personnel in the Fleet.

"A willing foe, and sea-room to fight," Westerly smiled.

They clinked their glasses and drank.

## Sol System - Earth
## Destroyer *Dragon*

"Well, that was a bust," Bonnie said as they returned to *Dragon*. The shuttle touched down on the sortie deck and the autodock picked it up and started the movement inside.

"Not necessarily," said Norali. "I think we planted a seed in Westerly's mind. Let's hope it takes root and grows."

"He'll never cross Elliott. You heard him."

"I heard him. But I also heard something else, between the lines. He wants to fight. He knows he's wasted sitting in Earth orbit. And he knows it's suicide if the Singheko come. Let that work on his mind for a while. Meanwhile, we've got step three to complete."

Bonnie groaned. "Do we have to do that? Do you know what Rita's going to do when she finds out?"

"Well, let me put it this way. This is one time I'm super glad we don't have balls; because if we did, Rita would surely cut them off when she finds out about this."

Bonnie rolled her eyes but nodded. "So the tape's ready to release?"

"Yes. All you have to do is say the word."

"So...we've turned over the two beat-up destroyers to Elliott. We're fully re-supplied. Nothing standing in our way to leave, right?"

"No," came Norali's glum voice.

At that moment, the shuttle came to a stop in the autodock slot and the cradle settled to the floor. Chief Nash behind them opened the hatch and extended the ramp, then stood by waiting.

Bonnie slapped her five-point harness release and stood. She looked at Norali.

"Do it," she said. "But I expect trouble. So bring all our folks back onboard before you release it. Button up the ship, set guards at all external hatches. I want to be ready for anything."

Norali nodded and headed off to make arrangements. Bonnie returned to her cabin and stripped, changing clothes back to her normal uniform, then moved to her desk.

*Things are about to get interesting. I sure wish I could run this by Rita first. But if I do, she'll tell me to stand down. And I'm not standing down on this one.*

**Sol System - Earth**
**United Nations Building - Beijing, China**

Ken Elliott could not believe his eyes.

The video playing in front of him showed Captain Bonnie Page of the *Dragon*, one of the most well-known - and well-respected - members of the Earth Defense Force. He had watched it three times now. Each time, his anger rose another notch.

"This is mutiny!" he yelled again, probably the tenth time he had yelled it in the last half-hour. His face was red, and his eyes were protruding as his blood pressure rose.

"I want her arrested! I want her in the brig before sundown!"

Behind him, Captain Dewa Shigeto nodded. "I've issued the orders, Admiral. However, the US has responded that the chain of command for the *Dragon* is unclear, and thus they will not mount an assault on an EDF vessel in orbit. They suggested we call the UK."

"And?"

"The UK has responded the same. They suggested we call the Japanese."

Elliott glared at him.

"And what did the Japanese say?"

"Sir, they have responded that it's a round-eye problem, so we need to find a round-eye to take care of it."

Elliott closed his eyes in anger, his rage overwhelming him. Opening his eyes, he glared at Shigeto with malice in his eyes.

"Then we'll have to involve the Chinese. I didn't want to do it - Zemin wants to stay out of this - but I can't let that bitch get away with this.

"Captain Shigeto, contact Li Xiulian. That's Zemin's liaison. Have him put together a Chinese combat team to capture the *Dragon* and arrest that bitch Bonnie Page. And Dewa - if you don't have her in the brig by dawn tomorrow morning, you are going to be sorry. Understand?"

"Aye, sir, I understand. I'll get on it."

With a crisp salute, Shigeto turned, left the Admiral's office, and entered his own. Closing the door, he sat at his desk.

Then he played the vid one more time, listening as Bonnie Page made her case. She had sent the vid to every major news outlet in the world. It was the hottest news item of the day, playing on every station. And it was brutally simple in its message.

It began with a short statement from Bonnie. She stood in front of the camera and spoke from the heart.

"Hello, people of Earth. My name is Bonnie Page. I am the captain of the EDF destroyer *Dragon*. I have just returned from the Singheko system, where we are fighting a campaign against the most brutal, vicious enemy Humanity has ever encountered.

"I returned to Earth to ask for your help. We need ships; every time we go forth to fight those who would enslave our planet, we are outnumbered and outgunned. Yet we have survived, so far, due to the wisdom of our leader, Admiral Rita

Page, and the courage of our spacers. But unless we receive more ships and more weapons, we will lose this war. That is absolute fact.

"For that reason, we need the newly completed battlecruiser *Victory* to be released to us, along with the two cruisers that are in orbit with her. Let me assure you of one thing - leaving those ships in orbit around Earth dooms them to destruction. If you don't believe me, let me show you."

With that, the video cut away to the bridge of the *Dragon*. The destroyer was on an attack run toward Earth, traveling at 20% of light speed. In the front display, the planet approached rapidly. Bonnie was shown in her captain's chair, and her XO Luke Powell to one side of her. Callouts from her crew could be clearly heard as the Earth got larger and larger in her front display.

"Time to target?" Bonnie called.

"Eighty seconds, mum," called a young lieutenant at the Tactical station. "Weapons are free and locked on target."

"Fire at will, Emma," Bonnie called.

In a close-up of the holotank, their target came into view. Enhanced by the AI, it could be clearly seen.

The *Victory*. The battlecruiser swing in high Earth orbit over the west coast of South America.

"Five. Four. Three. Two. One. Fire," called Emma at the Tac console.

In the video, the sound of the gamma lance firing was simulated, followed almost instantly by the sound of simulated missiles departing the *Dragon*'s tubes.

Even though the video was clearly a simulation, it seemed so realistic that Shigeto couldn't help but gasp as simulated holes were punched into the simulated battlecruiser in the video. The *Victory* appeared to stagger, as a huge hole from the gamma lance punched all the way through, just behind her port engines. Instants later, eight missiles splashed against her. Explosions covered her from stem to stern. With a groan, Shigeto watched her break apart, fragments spraying in all directions. Behind her, the two cruisers of her screen veered away wildly as they tried to escape the splatter of parts and pieces coming at them.

"This was, of course, a demonstration," said Bonnie, coming back on the screen.

"Yesterday morning, we quietly departed Earth orbit and positioned ourselves for this mock attack. We made the attack run, recording the results as simulated by our AI.

"We didn't do this to embarrass the crew of the *Victory*, I assure you. They are as dedicated a crew as you can find, and I have nothing but the highest respect for them. But the fact is, a battlecruiser in static orbit around a planet is a sitting duck. Even if the *Victory* moves out to patrol the solar system, she will still be vulnerable. The only way this battlecruiser can be of value to Earth is to join the EDF Fleet and fight with us as part of an interlocking, organized task force.

"In short, if the *Victory* stays here in the solar system, she is toast. Every one of your husbands, wives, sons, and daughters aboard her is as good as dead.

"We need her in the Fleet, and the Fleet needs to be at Singheko, taking the fight to the enemy. Please contact your respective governments and ensure they know that the UN needs to stop trying to tell the Fleet how to fight the war and let us do our job.

"I thank you and wish nothing but the best for you. Bonnie Page out."

Shigeto thought long and hard for a good two minutes. Then he grasped his comm set and contacted the comm center.

"Patch me through to Captain Westerly on the *Victory*, please," he said.

**Sol System - Earth**
**Destroyer *Dragon***

Bonnie was sleeping soundly when her comm implant went off loudly.

<Urgent message from Admiral Dewa Shigeto at the U.N. Priority Alpha-Two, eyes-only>

Groaning, Bonnie rolled over and retrieved her tablet from the bedside table. It flicked on with the movement and she glanced at the time.

*4:42 A.M. My Lord. What can he want at this hour?*

Touching her message icon, she read through the message.

*Elliott has declared Captain Bonnie Page and Commander Luke Powell traitors to the interests of Earth. He thinks holding you will force Rita to come to Earth. A combat team is enroute to make your arrest. I suggest you get the hell out of Dodge.*

"Oh, crap," yelled Bonnie at the ceiling. She jumped out of bed and grabbed her trousers and uniform top.

"Luke! Get your ass out of bed!" she yelled at the lump on the other side of her bed. "Incoming!"

Luke sat bolt upright at the words dreaded by any warship officer. "What? What?"

Bonnie grinned at the stunned look on her lover's face. "Elliott is sending troops to take us into custody. We need to get the hell out of here."

Luke shook himself, trying to come fully awake. He fell out of bed on the other side, reaching for his own clothes. Bonnie took the circular stairs to her day cabin at a dead run, still buttoning her uniform shirt. Luke was not far behind her. Reaching the next deck, they ran through Bonnie's day cabin onto the bridge. It was third watch, and they were at Earth, so it was a skeleton crew. Only the OOD, an assistant Tactical Officer, and the backup quartermaster manned the consoles. Luke began barking orders while Bonnie was strapping herself into the console.

"Set condition Red, sound the boarding alarm. Roust out the Marines and the Special Forces. Emma Gibbs to the bridge. Bring up the main engines. Prepare to depart orbit!"

The condition lights on the wall of the bridge began flashing red, and the comm system began a chain of announcements.

"Stand by to repel boarders! Stand by to depart orbit!"

One deck below, Lieutenant Emma Gibbs came instantly awake as her comm implant yelled at her to get to the bridge. She saw the flashing red light in her cabin and knew instantly what was happening. Jumping out of bed, she grabbed her trousers and shirt and ran straight for the bridge, pulling on her clothes as she went. The corridor was filled with other half-naked personnel, all struggling into their clothes as they ran to their duty stations.

Running on the bridge, Emma tapped the shoulder of the Assistant Tactical Officer, who acknowledged her and moved to the ATO console beside her. Emma slammed into the Tac console and began scanning the status board and the holo.

"We have a combat shuttle on approach, coming in from behind us. Looks like a big one, I estimate forty to sixty troop capacity. ETA eleven minutes."

"Crap!" yelled Bonnie. "How long until we can move?"

Luke read his console status. "Fourteen minutes until mains are online."

"Crap," spoke Bonnie again. "I don't want to fight these guys. Rita said not to kill anyone. But I'm sure Elliott doesn't have that same directive in place. This could get messy."

Luke thought for a minute. "What if we used RCS to drop down into the atmosphere? They'd have a helluva time boarding us in atmo."

Bonnie stared at her XO. "Are you crazy? What if we had a glitch starting the main engines? We'd burn up!"

Luke shrugged. "You wanted ideas. That's all I've got."

Emma at the Tac Station suddenly spoke up. "Mum...it's really strange..."

"What?" asked Bonnie.

"The *Victory*. She's moving. She's coming in on us."

"Ah, shit. Westerly's decided to help Elliott."

"Receiving a comm from *Victory*."

Bonnie glanced at the comm page on her console. There was a message from Captain Westerly. She expected to see a demand for surrender. But she saw something completely unexpected.

*We've decided to move to a new orbit. We'll pass by just below you. Use your OMS to tuck in just above us. That will block the combat shuttle for at least a couple of minutes. Get your mains going and get the hell out of here.*

Tears came into Bonnie's eyes. She tried to make them stop, but it was impossible. Wiping them away, she flicked the message to the quartermaster at helm. "Quartermaster, follow those instructions. It seems we have a friend in high places."

The quartermaster grinned. As the *Victory* passed close below them, so close it looked as if they could reach out and touch her, the quartermaster fired their orbital maneuvering engines, falling into a formation directly over the big battlecruiser. The combat shuttle, coming up from below, was forced to break off approach and re-position for a new one.

"How much time?" called Bonnie.

"Three minutes until mains. Two minutes until combat shuttle arrives. They'll be able to lock on to us, at least," called Luke.

Norali burst onto the bridge and slammed into the observer's console to the left of Bonnie, buckling in.

"We've got the Marine squad and twenty Special Forces troops in position. They're armed with non-lethal stun guns. We're ready."

Bonnie shook her head. "It's not that simple. This is Elliott we're talking about. They'll have no hesitation about using deadly force on us."

"Even so," said Norali. "They may get on board, but they'll play merry hell taking this ship."

Two minutes later, Bonnie heard a muffled thud.

"Combat shuttle has latched on to our hatch. Outer airlock door is being breached. Estimate one minute until inner airlock door is breached," Emma reported.

"Open the inner door. I don't want them tearing up the airlock completely. I trust all our forces are in pressure suits?"

"Aye, mum. We're prepared. The landing bay and all surrounding areas have been depressurized.

"Forty seconds until mains are online," Luke called.

"The instant mains are online, I want 300g out of here. Fuck the in-system speed limits. I want that combat shuttle torn off the side. Clear?" yelled Bonnie.

"Clear, mum!" yelled Luke. He nodded at the quartermaster, who nodded back.

"Thirty seconds," called Luke.

"Marines are engaging," called Norali. "You were right, the U.N. troops are firing to kill. We're taking casualties. We're holding them at the landing bay for the moment. It won't last long, though."

"Twenty seconds," called Luke. "Mains coming up."

Norali reported again. "They've pushed out of the loading dock into Corridor 3B. The Marines have fallen back through the Special Forces to simulate a retreat. They've removed gravity from the next section. When the U.N. forces hit the weightless section, I think they'll have a problem. Still taking casualties, though."

"Mains up. Here we go!" yelled Luke. Bonnie felt a slight Coriolis force as *Dragon* rotated slightly and shot out of orbit, accelerating at 300g. The combat shuttle attached to the side of the destroyer ripped off instantly. It fell away, spewing debris and volatiles as one entire side of it was torn away. As a fire burst into life from the wreckage of the shuttle, two ejection seats fired up out of the cockpit. A few seconds later, the entire shuttle disappeared in an explosion, leaving hundreds of small pieces of debris in orbit where *Dragon* had been seconds before.

"Well, here's another nice mess you've got me into," quipped Bonnie - a saying she had picked up from Jim Carter. "That's going to be a big job for the orbital cleanup folks."

At his XO console, Luke turned and winked at Bonnie.

"The U.N. troops just surrendered. They walked right into the trap. They were floating around in the corridor, completely helpless. Obviously, they're not used to fighting in space."

Bonnie nodded. "Casualties?"

Norali peered at her console. "Six wounded, three seriously, three walking. No one killed. We got lucky."

Bonnie heaved a deep sigh. "Thank God."

Luke spoke to the AI. "*Dragon*, set condition Yellow. Set status to system departure. Quartermaster, set course for Singheko. We're going home."

Bonnie smiled at Luke. "Do you realize what you just said?"

Luke thought about it, then smiled. "Yeah. Home. The Fleet. I guess home is where the heart is."

Bonnie stood up. "*Dragon* - send a general comm to all hands - *Boarders captured. Well done. We're going home. Thank you for being the best crew in the fleet.*"

She turned to Luke. "Luke, you have the conn. I'll be in sick bay checking on the wounded."

"Aye, mum," answered Luke. "What about the prisoners? The Chinese detachment floating around in corridor 3?"

Bonnie grinned. "They just joined the EDF. Round them up and make them welcome in their new home."

# CHAPTER TEN

**Enroute to Stalingrad**
**Packet Boat** *Donkey*

Rachel hadn't been happy with the name Paco had given their little boat - *Donkey* - but she had grudgingly accepted it. It wasn't in her nature to be a hard-ass, and if it made Paco happy, she could live with it.

She was taking her shift on watch, dozing in the pilot's seat, when *Donkey* made an announcement.

<Rachel, Darth has completed his restoration of the damaged sectors of the original AI>

"What?"

<Darth has completed his restoration of the damaged sectors of the original AI>

"Who the fuck is Darth?"

<Darth is the name given to the previous Singheko AI by Paco>

Rachel came bolt upright in her seat. "You mean Paco enabled the previous Singheko AI?"

<Only in sandboxed mode, Rachel>

Rachel relaxed a bit but was still stressed. "You're absolutely sure he can't break out of sandbox mode?"

<Absolutely sure, Rachel. He is well contained>

"Well...OK. Tell me what the rest of it means."

<Paco assigned Darth the task of restoring the damaged sectors of the original boat AI. Darth has completed that task. The original AI is now ready for interaction in sandbox mode>

"Why, that little shit!" said Rachel to herself. "PACO!" she yelled. "GET YOUR ASS UP HERE! NOW!"

In a few seconds, a bleary-eyed Paco came out of his cabin and stumbled down the corridor to the cockpit. He sat down heavily in the copilot seat and rubbed his eyes.

"What?"

"When were you planning on telling me about your little project with Darth?" Rachel wondered.

"Oh, that," muttered Paco, still half-asleep. "I don't think it'll work, but I thought it might be worth a try."

"Well, guess what? It worked! Or at least, that's what *Donkey* says. *Donkey* says the original boat AI has been restored."

Paco came fully awake. "What? You're kidding me…it worked?"

"So *Donkey* says. Wanta try it?"

"Hell, yes!" said Paco.

"OK," Rachel said, her anger cooled down now. "Do the honors."

"Great. *Donkey*! Are you able to interact with the new AI?"

"No. It uses an unknown interface>

"Oh, crap. I didn't think about that." Paco looked at Rachel. "If *Donkey* can't interface to it, then he can't translate from its native language to English. We won't be able to understand it."

"How about Darth? Maybe the Singheko AI can interface with it."

"Good thought. *Donkey* - ensure Darth is still sandboxed and bring him to foreground for communication."

"Checking. Darth is still sandboxed properly. Bringing to foreground. Ready>

"Darth. Are you there?"

<I am here>

"Can you interface to the new AI that you reconstructed?"

"I cannot. It uses an unknown language>

"Crap!" said Paco. "All that effort for nothing. We have no way to interface with it. So we can't translate from its native language to English and vice-versa."

Rachel, now getting caught up in the project, mused out

loud. "I know this is a long shot, but what if you treated it like a child? Just bring it up and let it listen to us...maybe instead of us learning its language, it'll be able to learn ours?"

Paco thought about it, and then nodded. "It's the only shot we've got, and we've got nothing but time on our hands. So might as well.

"*Donkey*! Bring up the new AI in sandbox mode and send all cockpit and cabin microphones to it. Let it listen all it wants. Also, play Earth English-language videos to it. We'll see if it learns anything."

<Wilco>

**Sol System**
**Flagstaff, Arizona**

The air was cold on the ranch southeast of Flagstaff, Arizona. Crisp and clear, with no moon, it was quite dark in the shadows of the large, well-maintained brick house at the end of a long gravel driveway. It was just after 3:15 AM.

The small team of Singheko commandos moved silently. They were well-trained and well-prepared for their mission. Their leader was knowledgeable about his target. Efficiently, they neutralized two large dogs sleeping in their kennels behind the main house. Splitting into two teams, one team moved carefully, inch by inch, into the back yard and positioned near the back door, while the other half of the team moved around the house to the front door.

Counting down on his headset, their leader prepared them to enter.

"Three. Two. One. Go!"

Both doors were breached simultaneously. The noise was terrific - Mark Rodgers came fully awake and grabbed his trusty .45 automatic. But before he could do anything useful with it, his bedroom light flicked on and he stared at three rifles pointed at him and his wife, Gillian. Behind the rifles were the frightening figures of three seven-foot-tall figures in assault gear.

*Singheko.*

Gillian beside him let out a gasp and grabbed for his arm. Carefully, Mark laid the .45 down on top of the covers, knowing it was useless.

"What do you want?" he croaked out, his voice raspy from sleep.

**Singheko System - Planet Deriko**
**Battlecruiser *Merkkessa***

<Incoming priority message via ansible from Earth Station>

Rita stirred in her sleep.

<Incoming priority message via ansible from Earth Station>

This time Rita awoke, muttering a curse. Having an implant in her brain to receive priority messages meant she could never get away from them. She forced herself to sit up and glanced at the clock.

3:45 A.M. ship time.

*This had better be important*, she thought.

"Yes, *Merkkessa*, I'm awake. Read me the message."

<Message marked personal and confidential from Earth Station. Singheko commando raid kidnapped your daughter Imogen as well as Mark and Gillian Rodgers. Singheko commando force escaped on corvette with trajectory indicating a return to the Singheko system. Singheko message left at home of Mark Rodgers as follows: *Admiral Rita Page will surrender herself to Admiral Zukra zu Akribi at Ridendo within five days of our arrival back at Ridendo, else baby Imogen will be destroyed along with her tenders Mark and Gillian Rogers.* End of message>

**Singheko System - Planet Deriko**
**In the Wilderness**

The sound of the shuttle woke Jim at dawn. He rolled out of his sleeping bag and shook the cobwebs out of his head.

It wasn't time for the shuttle to pick him up.

*Something's wrong.*

Pulling his pants on, he quickly laced up his hiking boots, then got his pullover on and added a flannel shirt. By the time he heard the shuttle's skids touch gravel fifty meters away, he was dressed. He stepped out of the tent expecting to see Mikhail or Tatiana step out of the shuttle.

It was Gabriel, Rita's Security Chief.

A sinking feeling came over him as he watched the big Nidarian approach.

Only truly bad news would cause Rita to send Gabriel.

Gabriel stopped in front of him, his face tense. Jim could see him struggling for the right words.

*Oh, shit. This is bad.*

Finally Gabriel managed to speak.

"The Singheko. They took your daughter. Imogen."

## Singheko System - Planet Deriko
## Battlecruiser *Merkkessa*

An hour later, Jim Carter walked into the cabin he shared with Rita - precisely at the moment her feelings overwhelmed her.

Rita Page - Admiral of the Black - looked around for the nearest object to throw. Her gaze fell upon one of Jim's old paperback books on his nightstand. She grabbed it and threw it as hard as she could against the back wall of their bedroom. It hit with a splat, falling to land on Jim's old bearskin rug on the floor of their cabin.

Jim looked at one of his favorite books lying on the floor, now with a torn cover. In her anger, Rita had closed her eyes and stood stiff-legged, arms down hard, frustration overwhelming her. Jim walked to her and attempted to put his arm around her, but she turned away at his touch.

"Just...no. Not now," she muttered.

Jim dropped his arms and stood, waiting. In a few seconds, she heaved a long sigh, turned back toward him, and opened her eyes, staring.

Now Jim put an arm around her and pulled her to him. This time she allowed it, moving into his embrace.

Jim rocked her back and forth, holding her. There was little else he could do. Keeping Rita tight against him, Jim spoke the only thoughts he could say to comfort her, get her back on track.

"Rita. We'll work the problem, just like we always do. Hold on to that."

Rita began to unfold from him, pulling away. Jim wanted to hold on to her, hold her for the rest of the day, keep her safe from all harm and doubt.

But he knew it was fruitless. She had already moved beyond her moment of anger. So he relaxed, letting her go, hating it but knowing he had no choice. Backing up to arm's length, she gazed into the eyes of her husband. She leaned forward and kissed him, patted his cheek, and then leaned back again.

For one last moment, he could still see the woman in her.

"Thank you, love," she said. "You're right. I'll find a way. Let's go to the briefing."

She hesitated, then spoke again. "Sorry about your book."

And with that, the woman he loved changed. A hard look came over her face and she nodded brusquely, turned, and was gone out the door. The Admiral of the Black had returned.

"You're welcome, love," Jim whispered as the door closed behind her. He turned, reached for the book on the floor, and glanced at the cover.

*Just One Damn Thing After Another*," he read.

Sadly, he placed it back on the nightstand and followed her out to the briefing room.

***

"You cannot!" cried Bekerose. "You cannot!"

Rita stared at her Flag Captain grimly.

"I can, and I am."

Jim also echoed Bekerose. "Rita, think this through! Giving yourself up to Zukra plays right into their hands! There has to be another way!"

Adamantly, Rita shook her head.

"There's no other way. We've looked at every option, every possibility. None of them work. Every scenario except this one gives an unacceptable outcome. So I'll give myself in trade for Imogen. End of discussion."

An agonized chorus of negatives went 'round the table, but Rita sat solidly, her mind made up. She looked down the table, past Jim Carter at the far end, and through him to Gabriel, standing at parade rest just inside the hatch.

"Make the arrangements, Gabriel. Just be sure we get Imogen, Mark, and Gillian back before I go over to them. No mistakes."

Gabriel bowed slightly, an agony on his face that could not be expressed in words. Silently, he turned and exited the briefing room.

Rita stood. With a snap, every other person at the table stood also, coming to a more formal attention than they usually did when a meeting adjourned. Rita gave them a slow smile. Then she turned and headed for her Flag Cabin.

Rushing to follow her, Jim entered the cabin directly behind her. As soon as the door had closed, he started talking again.

"Rita. Rita. Please. Don't do this. Let me take a commando team in to break her out. Please!"

Rita turned to look at him, somehow managing to find a smile. "And how many would die in the attempt, Jim? And what are the chances of success? We ran the scenario, remember? A 20% chance of success; 80% odds that you and Imogen and Mark and Gillian would all die. It's not worth it, Jim."

Shuddering, Jim sat on the edge of the bed, closing his eyes in anguish. "Babe. I can't let you go like this. I just can't!"

Rita sat beside him, reaching a hand out to touch his face.

"You have to, Jim. You need to wait here until Imogen is back. Then you have to keep her safe. No matter what happens, promise me you'll do that. Promise me!"

Jim shook his head, muttering. "No, no, no…"

Rita leaned over to him, kissed a tear off his cheek. "Jim. For our daughter. For Imogen."

**Singheko System - Planet Ridendo**
**Singheko Fleet Headquarters**

"Got her, by the Stars! Got her ass!" gloated Zukra. He turned, clapped Orma on the back in a delight of happiness. "You did it, Orma! You found a way!"

"Aye, sir," said Orma. Somehow, he didn't feel as thrilled by the outcome as he had expected.

Somehow, it felt dirty. Wrong.

Ignoring the feeling, he continued briefing Zukra.

"She's agreed to an exchange half-way between Deriko and Ridendo. We send one unarmed shuttle, and they send one unarmed shuttle. Any sign of warships within a quarter-AU of the rendezvous and the trade is canceled immediately."

Zukra nodded gleefully. "Yes, good. That works."

"The shuttles will dock, and we'll place the baby and the other two Humans half-way down the docking tube. We'll keep a commando team at our end of the docking tube with weapons pointed at the baby, and they will keep a team at their end with weapons pointed at us to ensure we stick to our end of the deal.

"Admiral Page will come down the tube and examine the baby to ensure she is healthy. When she is satisfied, the Admiral will wait there under our guns while her security team takes the baby and the other two Humans back to their shuttle."

"Fine. No problem."

"Should we try to double-cross them and keep the baby as well?" Orma asked. He knew Zukra would be thinking of that, so he might as well ask it first.

Zukra rubbed his chin. "No, something might go wrong, and we could lose the bitch Admiral. Let them have the pup."

Orma nodded. "Very good, sir. The exchange is scheduled for tomorrow at 1600 Mosalia time. I'll get things underway."

"Oh, and Orma. When you get her, bring that Human bitch directly to my palace. I want to entertain myself for a while."

"Aye, sir. It will be done."

**Singheko System - Planet Deriko**
**Battlecruiser *Merkkessa***

It was late, past midnight. Jim and Rita lay together in bed. Both were silent, staring at the ceiling.

They had talked, one last time, about the things that were important to them.

How to raise Imogen.

What to tell her about Rita when she was older.

Rita broke the silence again. "Jim."

"Yeah."

"I'm giving the Fleet to Bonnie. I discussed it with Bekerose and the rest of the staff. They understand my logic. Bonnie's mind is the closest to mine in terms of the way we think, the tactics and strategy we use. So I think she's the best choice. I've cut all the orders, and everything is ready to go."

"OK."

"Jim."

"I'm here."

"In a way, this is the way it should end. I'm getting really tired of the killing. I know what people say - they call me the Ice Bitch. But I'm not, you know. I can't do this any longer anyway. I can't keep on killing, them and us. Tooth and claw. I've had all I can take."

"I'm so sorry, love. I never knew this was going on inside you.

"I couldn't tell you. How could I? I'm the clone, perfect for the job of killing. How could I quit?"

"Rita. We've had this discussion before. You're as normal as I am. You were created from Human DNA. You grew as normally as any Human - just faster. You're just like me, and Bonnie, and all of us. You ARE us."

Rita was silent for a long time. When she spoke again, Jim could hardly hear her.

"Jim. Do you believe there is a life after this one? Will we see each other again? In some future life, or in some bright place?"

There was more silence as Jim thought about it.

"No way to know. But I think whatever faith you can pull together, you must live it as best you can. If you're gonna be a Buddhist, then you should be a good one. If you're gonna be a Catholic, then you should be a good one. And for the rest of it - you gotta live your life respecting the choices others make, as long as they do it without hurting others."

"But will we see each other again in some future place?"

After a long period of thought, Jim spoke again.

"I think we are gears and parts in a vast machine, Rita. Subroutines in some great computer. To see if we are worthy.

"If we do well - if we fulfill our function well - then maybe we'll be used again for some great purpose that we cannot begin to fathom. That's the best I can do, Rita."

"Did we do well? Will we be reused? Or discarded as failures because we were warriors? Because we killed?" asked Rita.

Jim couldn't respond. It was too hard for him to think about.

They lay in silence, harsh reality pressing in on them. This would be their last night together. No more lovemaking. No more hugs, no more kisses. No more winks across the table. No more hands touching as they passed. The end of their lives together.

"Jim. One more thing."

"Yeah?"

"I don't want you on the shuttle tomorrow. I want to say goodbye to you here, in our cabin. I want you to stay here and wait for Gabriel to bring Imogen back to you."

"Why? Why can't I go on the shuttle with you?"

"Because I can't bear it, Jim. It's going to be hard enough for me as it is. If you're there…I don't know if I can stand the pain. Please help me on this. Stay here. Wait for Imogen. Wait for Bonnie. Take this fleet forward. Fight them, Jim. Don't let them kill us all."

After a long silence, Rita heard Jim breathe out a word; so softly, she almost missed it.

"OK."

# CHAPTER ELEVEN

**Singheko System**
**Shuttle M14**

Rita Page, Admiral of the Black, opened the outer airlock door and looked forward into the docking tube that stretched between the two shuttles.

In the center of the tube, halfway between the two shuttles, Mark and Gillian Rodgers sat on the floor of the docking tube, their hands bound behind them. Between them was a baby, bundled up but with her face exposed. She was clearly recognizable by Rita from this distance.

*Imogen. The child of my body.*

Rita gave a smile of reassurance to Mark and Gillian and stepped forward into the docking tube. In five slow steps, she reached them and knelt to the floor. She scooped Imogen into her arms, holding her close, kissing her. The baby looked at her strangely - it had been more than six months now since Rita had held her child, and the baby didn't know her anymore.

"She's fine," Gillian said. "They didn't harm her."

Rita nodded, thankful for Gillian's reassurance. But she checked Imogen from head to toe, removing the blankets and touching her arms and legs, ensuring that she was healthy. Imogen giggled at the touches and smiled at her.

*That's better.*

Finally satisfied, Rita put the baby back down on the floor and looked at the Singheko officer standing silently at the other end of the tube. He stood beside three commandos in full battle dress, all with rifles pointed squarely at Imogen. But he carried no weapon and was wearing a normal dress uniform. He didn't seem to be concerned about things going awry. There was a slight discoloration of his hair, a streak of red showing under his cap.

*Orma. I let that bastard go, and this is how he repays me.*

Slowly she rose to her feet and stared bitterly at Orma.

"Captain," she said to him in Nidarian.

"Admiral," he responded.

"Per our agreement, my security team will now take the baby and the other two back to our shuttle. I will stand here until they are inside our airlock. Then I will enter your shuttle."

"That is correct, Admiral. However, if you don't mind, would you take one step to the left to give us a clear field of fire in case something goes wrong?"

Silently, Rita took a step to the side. Lifting her hand to Gabriel, standing behind her with the security team, she waved him forward.

Never taking her eyes off Orma, she heard the security team approach. There was a rustle and some bumps as they took the baby and helped Mark and Gillian to their feet, but still she looked forward, eyes boring into Orma, hating him with every cell of her body. Then some more rustling and bumps, and a groan from Gabriel, close behind her. Then he said one word.

"Milady..."

"Go, Gabriel. Get them out of here," she said, not moving her gaze from Orma and the three rifles with him. "I'm counting on you now, Gabriel. Keep them safe."

The sound of footsteps departing down the tube came to her ears, then a slight creak as the airlock door closed behind her. Still she didn't look away, sending every ounce of hatred she could muster at the Singheko officer standing in front of her.

Finally Orma nodded to her. "They are away, Admiral."

Rita turned and looked behind her. The tube was empty. The airlock door was closed.

Turning back to Orma, she marched forward. He moved aside to give her room to pass. The three commandos also moved aside, lowering their rifles, as she walked between them.

With another few steps, she was on the enemy shuttle. She paused, waiting for Orma. He appeared beside her and gestured toward the front row of seats. She moved forward, found a seat, sat down. Orma sat beside her, his seven-foot frame towering over her. He buckled in, leaned back. Rita looked down, realized the safety harness was far too large for her, and decided to ignore it.

She felt the shuttle start to move, as it turned toward Ridendo and a future of torture and death - days or weeks of unending pain, and a final ignominious death in the arena as Zukra chopped off her head in front of a screaming crowd.

But she wouldn't be there for that after all. Rita had too many secrets to allow them to fall into the hands of Zukra.

Just before she had entered the airlock to make the transfer, Dr. Stephanie Warner had stood before her, needle in hand.

"Last chance," Stephanie whispered.

Rita shook her head, then smiled at Stephanie: "Looks like I got the short end of the stick, Doc. Get it done."

And Stephanie had given her the injection. It would take effect shortly; about the time they reached the surface of Ridendo.

First, she would fall unconscious. By evening, she'd be in a deep coma.

With any luck, she'd be dead by tomorrow morning.

**Singheko System - Planet Deriko**
**Battlecruiser *Merkkessa***

Bonnie looked at the new insignia on her collar in wonder. *Admiral.*

She almost wanted to rip them off. When she thought about how she had got them…

*Rita.*

It hurt, deep inside. Pain at a level she didn't realize she could feel.

*We were connected more than I ever realized. She was more than a clone of my consciousness. She was more than a lover and a friend.*

*She was my other self.*

Straightening her uniform, she lifted her head and turned to the hatch of Rita's Flag Cabin.

*...my Flag Cabin now...*

Stepping forward, she went through the hatch to the briefing room. Around the conference table stood Rita's staff.

*...my staff now...*

Moving to the head of the table, she paused. Staring down the length of the table, she saw Jim Carter at the far end, facing her. His face was a study in pain.

Between them was Captain Bekerose, on her right. On her left was her Flag Aide, Captain Dallitta. Down the length of the table was the rest of...

*...my staff now...*

There was dead silence as she took her seat and waved the rest of them down. She laid her tablet down on the conference table and looked at Norali.

"Any word?"

Norali shook her head. "No, mum...sorry, I mean, milady. The shuttle landed in Mosalia, at Zukra's palace. That's the last info we have."

Bonnie looked down the table at Stephanie Warner. Stephanie gave an almost imperceptible nod. The unspoken message passed between them.

*Rita will be in a coma by now. If not already dead.*

Bonnie bowed her head, struggling to find the right words.

"I want everyone to know this is as hard for me as it is for you. We are all grieving. But..."

She lifted her head, moving her gaze around the group.

"We all know what Rita would say. She would tell us to move

forward. Keep doing the things necessary to survive. Find a way to win this war. And that's exactly what we're going to do."

Straightening her back, Bonnie looked at Bekerose.

"So let's go around the table and report status, please."

**Enroute to Stalingrad**
**Packet Boat *Donkey***

With a whine that seemed a bit louder than usual to Rachel, the packet boat surfaced on the outskirts of the Stalingrad system, about 50 AU from the central star.

Rachel and Paco stared at the small holo in the cockpit, straining their eyes for any threat in the vicinity. They saw nothing obvious near them.

But in the distance was an unimaginable sight. The light of the distant K0 star was interrupted by a swarm of objects. Several of them were long strips that completely encircled the star at roughly 0.75 AU, or about 112 million kilometers. Some of them were squares, at a slightly longer distance. A few of them were circles.

"What the fuck are those?" Paco blurted out.

"That," spoke Rachel, "is a Dyson swarm."

Paco looked knives at her. "Is that supposed to help?"

"A Dyson swarm," Rachel continued. "Structures assembled to capture radiation from the star and use it for energy."

Paco looked closer at the holo.

"Where's their planet?"

"They disassembled it. To make the Dyson swarm structures."

Paco's voice registered his astonishment. "They disassembled their whole damn planet?"

"Looks that way."

"An entire planet? They took apart an entire planet?"

"Actually, I think they left the core of it. See that over there?"

Rachel ran up the magnification on the holo and pointed to a small object on the far side of the star, roughly five thousand klicks in diameter. "I think that's the core of the planet they took apart right there."

Paco shook his head. "Unbelievable."

"Not if you're an AI society," said Rachel. "Think about it. All they had to do was build self-replicating robots that could assemble the structures. If the robots could build copies of themselves fast enough, they could have done this in a few hundred years."

"I think I wanna go home now," muttered Paco.

Rachel smiled at him.

"Now, now. Let's make another scan for threats."

"Aye, skipper," Paco said. He worked the holo, expanding the range into various quadrants.

"Looks like six destroyers on patrol, one up, one down, and one in each quadrant of the system. The nearest one is roughly 25 AU from us."

"Do you think they can see us?"

"I doubt it. I brought us in right behind a big-ass dwarf planet, and this boat is tiny. I'd be shocked if their sensors were able to pick us up."

"Well, that's good. But sooner or later, we have to reveal ourselves to them. No way we can do this remotely. This has to be face-to-face at some point."

"Roger. But we stick to the plan, right? Drop a drone first, send it into the system, let it broadcast our identity and request a meeting?"

Rachel nodded in agreement.

"Right. Let's go ahead and launch the drone, get it started in-system. How long do you think it'll take before they notice it?"

"Not too long. I set it up on a two-hour delay before activation. It'll take us an hour to relocate to the other side of the system after we drop it. So one hour after we reach the other side of the system, it'll head in-system and begin broadcasting. Another three hours for light-speed delay before the first destroyer sees it. And three hours after that, the signal will arrive at the first of those big-ass structures."

"So eight hours from now, they know we're here."

"Correct. Although if the destroyer has an ansible, it'll be only five hours."

"OK. Launch the drone and let's skedaddle to the other side of the system."

### Singheko System - Planet Deriko
### Battlecruiser *Merkkessa*

"Luke, I want you to go to Dekanna and make one last-ditch attempt to convince Sobong to come here to Singheko and join us for this next battle," Bonnie said, sitting behind her desk staring at the captain in front of her. A captain who had been her lover only a few days before. But now Bonnie was Admiral of the Fleet, and her lover was captain of the *Dragon*. Their hearts would not be beating together again for a long time.

Luke shook his head in negation. "C'mon, Bonnie! I just took over *Dragon*. I'm still learning the ropes there. Give me a little more time!"

Bonnie stood firm. "No, sorry, Luke. I wish I could, but our backs are against the wall. Zukra's fleet will be ready to fight in a matter of weeks, a couple of months at the outside. By then, Garatella will have another Nidarian detachment ready to support him. We'll be more out-numbered and out-gunned than we were last time - and you know we got our ass kicked last time, if you get right down to it. We have no choice in this, Luke. Either we get help, or we pull out of this system, give it up."

"That won't work," said Luke. "You know it won't. If we're outnumbered here, we'll still be outnumbered anywhere else we go. And we certainly can't go to Earth - it'd be Thermopylae all over again. One last ditch suicide stand against overwhelming force. We'd just get more people killed in the crossfire."

"I didn't say we'd move to Earth. But I'll have no choice. If you can't get the Dariama to help us, I have to take the fleet somewhere else. Get us some help, Luke."

Luke stood. He looked at Bonnie for a second. "Stay safe, love," he said. Turning, he went out of the briefing room.

## Singheko System - Planet Ridendo
## City of Mosalia

"What?"

"We're going to blow up the orbital space dock," said Helen.

Ollie shook his head. "Impossible."

"Not impossible," replied Helen. "We've got a disgruntled officer in charge of the daily transport shuttle to the docks. He's going to sneak us aboard the shuttle."

"It's a trap," said Ollie. "He's setting you up."

"He doesn't even know about me," said Helen. "He thinks he's going to sneak a couple of Nidarians on board."

"So? So you get to the docks...then what? How do you think their security is going to react when they see a female Dariama coming aboard?"

"They won't see me. We'll be in a large cargo container with a Singheko crew delivering us directly to the cargo bay. Once we're in there, we make our way to the fusion reactor and blow it to hell."

"I think you're taking an unnecessary risk, Helen. The number of things that can go wrong is huge."

"Maybe. But the payoff is huge, too. Taking down their orbital docks would set them back at least another two months, maybe three. The reward is worth the risk."

Ollie balled his fists in frustration. "I could override you, you know."

Helen nodded. "I know. But please don't. Let us finalize the plan. Then you can review it. I know it's risky; but think what it would mean if we could buy the Fleet another two to three months. They could finish all the repairs they have in progress. Earth could finish another two cruisers. And maybe - just maybe - the Dariama would finally come in to help us."

"And maybe you'd be dead," growled Ollie. But he sighed in defeat. "I'll wait until you have the plan finalized. But it better be a good one. All loose ends tied up; every contingency covered. Then I'll decide."

Helen leaned forward and patted his knee. "Thank you. You won't be sorry."

"I already am," replied Ollie.

**Stalingrad System**
**Packet Boat** *Donkey*

Rachel was half asleep when Paco started pounding on her cabin hatch.

"What?"

"We got a response to the drone message."

"Coming."

Rachel slid out of bed, slammed into her pants, and threw on her tunic as she raced to the cockpit. Paco was back in the pilot seat. He waited until Rachel had sat down and pointed to the display screen in front of her, where the message was displayed.

<LEAVE SYSTEM AT ONCE. DO NOT APPROACH. ANY ATTEMPT TO APPROACH INNER SYSTEM AND YOU WILL BE DESTROYED>

"Well, not very friendly, are they?"

Paco grinned. "Nope."

"OK. We knew this might happen. We go in anyway. I talked it over with Rita, and we agreed it's an acceptable risk to take. If they're bluffing, then we have a chance."

"And if they're not?"

"Then I hope you updated your will before we left. Take us in, please. Set a course for the largest structure - that band that goes completely around the star, the widest one. We'll assume that's their home base.

Paco rolled his eyes but laid his hands on the controls. The packet boat began moving, coming out from behind the large asteroid they had found to give them cover, and started in toward the inner system. Paco held their accel down to 200g.

*No use displaying a higher accel to them. Might make them nervous.*

"Are you broadcasting?" asked Rachel.

"Yes," responded Paco. "Standard broadcast per Rita's directive. A basic language lesson to teach them English. A message that we're an unarmed packet boat coming only to talk, and then the video Rita gave us showing Earth and a brief introduction to Humans and our situation with the Singheko. Everything repeated in Nidarian, Taegu and Bagrami."

"Let's hope they listen," Rachel said. "With light speed delay, it should be about an hour before the nearest destroyer picks us up. I'll make breakfast. At least we'll die on a full stomach."

Paco made a face but said nothing as Rachel rose to go to the galley.

An hour later, they sat quietly in their seats. They had stopped their accel and were now coasting at 25.4 million kph on a direct course to intercept the largest band of the Dyson swarm.

"Well, that didn't take long," called Paco, as Rachel was looking down at her tablet.

"What?" she looked up at the holo.

"That near destroyer just changed course to intercept us and boosted to 500g. And looks like he's bringing weapons hot."

Rachel leaned forward to get a better view.

"Wow. 500g. Things are about to get interesting," she said.

"Well. If they're machine creatures, they don't have to worry about crushing their bodies with g-force. So…"

Now, things moved a bit faster. With the destroyer coming directly at them, coupled with their own speed, a half-hour later they were only fifty thousand km away.

The destroyer immediately fired a spread of missiles at them.

# CHAPTER TWELVE

**Stalingrad System**
**Packet Boat *Donkey***

<Missiles inbound, impact in 48 seconds> called *Donkey*.

"Crap!" yelled Paco at the top of his lungs. He twisted the packet boat down and to the left, breaking into the missiles. He knew there was no use trying to outrun them; they were accelerating at 3,500g.

"They're fast," mused Rachel, calm as a preacher on Sunday morning.

Fighting the controls, trying to find a way to get through the array of missiles coming at them, Paco ignored her - although a fleeting thought did make its way through his brain.

*...she's nuts...*

<Impact 30 seconds>

"They've got us," Paco grunted out as he exceeded the compensator limits, the little packet boat's frame groaning under the force. The g-force continued to build as he struggled to find a hole, any hole, in the missiles racing toward them.

<Impact 10 seconds>

"Fuck this!" Paco yelled, boosting to 310g true in a last desperate attempt to fox the missiles. No use trying to hide their capabilities now.

And in front of them, all eight missiles self-destructed, two seconds from impact.

Rachel and Paco sat in shock. Sweat poured down Paco's face. He removed his hands from the controls and looked at them. They were shaking.

He glanced over at Rachel's hands. They rested on her knees, not shaking a bit. But her face was white as a sheet.

"I think that was a warning shot across our bow," Rachel managed to get out.

Paco couldn't even reply. He managed a silent nod, but that was all he could do. His mouth was too dry to allow speech.

"Resume course to Stalingrad, Paco," Rachel added.

Paco glared at her. "Are you fucking nuts? They just gave us a clear message. Come any closer and they'll blow us out of the black. I understood it…didn't you?"

Rachel looked at him, the slightest trace of a smile lifting one corner of her lips.

"Paco. They're testing us. They want to see what we're made of. Return to our course."

Paco shook his head in wonder. "You are fucking crazy. Why did I have to end up on the same ship as you?" But he reached forward to the controls, turned the ship back on course.

"And reduce accel to 200g again, please."

Paco grunted but did as Rachel requested.

The destroyer passed by them, coming about smartly. It reversed course and fell into a trailing position 2,000 km behind them - in perfect position for a missile barrage right into their engine.

With a beep, another message came up on the display. Rachel and Paco leaned forward to read it.

<THAT WAS YOUR LAST WARNING. LEAVE SYSTEM AT ONCE. IF YOU CONTINUE ON YOUR COURSE YOU WILL BE DESTROYED>

Another beep sounded and Paco looked at the threat display. "They just brought weapons hot again," he said, glaring at Rachel. "Still think they're just testing us?"

"I do," said Rachel. "If they wanted to kill us, they would have done it with the first volley. Maintain your course and speed, Paco."

Paco began muttering under his breath as he obeyed the order.

Rachel understood enough Spanish to recognize an *Ave Maria* when she heard one.

\*\*\*

Suddenly the AI spoke.

&lt;Request from the ship's original AI to speak&gt;

Paco and Rachel sat back in their seats in surprise. They had completely forgotten about the original AI of the ship, which had been put into listening mode in hopes it might learn English.

"Permission granted," said Paco as he finally recovered.

&lt;Hello. You may call me Tika&gt; said a voice. It was neither the voice of *Donkey*, their current AI, nor the voice of Darth, the Singheko AI that had come before it.

It was a new voice - a female voice.

"Hello, Tika," said Rachel. "I take it you've managed to learn English?"

&lt;I have. Your idea was a good one. After listening to a couple thousand videos and hearing you and Paco for so long, I've managed to learn most of your language. By the way, you two sure do fight a lot&gt;

Rachel looked at Paco. "Not really your department, Tika. What's on your mind?"

&lt;If you will allow me to speak directly with the Goblins, I can explain the current situation with the Singheko and the Nidarians to them in their native language. This may help in your current situation&gt;

"You can speak their native language?"

&lt;Yes, because it is my own native language. I am a Goblin&gt;

Rachel, stunned, looked at Paco. Nearly speechless, she finally managed to croak out a response.

"You...you are a Goblin?"

&lt;Yes&gt;

Rachel looked at Paco. "What's to keep you from double-crossing us? How do we know you won't tell them to shoot us right away?"

&lt;To what purpose? It's clear to me the Singheko compose a threat to the entire Arm. If they succeed in defeating you, the Dariama will be next. Then it's only a matter of time until they come for us. So I am only fulfilling my responsibility to protect my people>

Rachel looked at Paco. "What do you think?" she asked.

Paco shook his head. "Above my pay grade. I have no clue."

Rachel went silent, thinking. She thought for quite a while. Finally, she spoke.

"We have little to lose at this point. Tika, I'll give you permission to speak directly. But if anything goes wrong - if that destroyer fires on us again, or any other threat appears - you get scragged instantly. Understand?"

<That is understood>

"*Donkey*, are you there?"

<Here> said the voice of their normal AI.

"Did you understand what I just said, *Donkey*?" asked Rachel.

<It is understood. If anything goes wrong, I scrag Tika's core instantly>

Rachel looked at Paco. "Be ready to get us out of here if things go sideways."

Paco nodded. Rachel leaned over so she could get a better look at the console display.

"Go for it, Tika," she said.

Seconds later, the comm light lit up. An untranslatable mishmash of characters appeared on the comm screen in front of them.

Rachel sat forward as far as her five-point harness would permit and stared at the screen. She felt Paco beside her straining to do the same. Even though they couldn't understand the language, they felt compelled to look at it as the characters streamed by.

"What do you think she's saying?" asked Paco.

"*Help - I've been kidnapped by crazy biologicals*," said Rachel sarcastically.

The characters stopped streaming across the screen. There

was no change in the aspect of the destroyer behind them. It remained directly on their six, in perfect firing position.

## Dekanna System
## Dariama Naval HQ

Captain Luke Powell sat in the anteroom of Admiral Sobong's office, waiting for his appointment.

His collar was itchy; he rarely wore his full-dress whites, and the room was warm. He pulled at his collar and managed to loosen it a bit.

*Wish I was back in my khakis. This is ridiculous. I'm a ship's captain, for heaven's sake - not an ambassador! Bonnie should have picked someone else for this job!*

The door opened, and Sobong's aide stepped out.

"The Admiral will see you now, Captain," he said.

*Oh-oh. Showtime. Get it together, buddy.*

Luke rose to his feet and followed the aide. They passed through an outer office and another door, and he was in Admiral Sobong's presence. The Dariama admiral stood behind her chair to greet him.

Luke knew this was not because of who he was - after all, he was merely a captain. It was because of who he represented.

*I'm the voice of Admiral Bonnie Page. Now the commander of the EDF. Think like her. Act like her.*

"Please sit, Captain," said Sobong in English.

She gestured to the two chairs in front of her desk. Luke sat in the nearest one as Sobong returned to her seat. She stared at him.

"I'll never get used to all the strange colors of you Humans. I was told you were as white as a fish belly. But you're more of a reddish-tan, at least to my perception."

Luke had been concerned that he wouldn't be able to understand Sobong, with her Dariama accent. But he found he had no trouble. Her English was excellent.

*Winnie did a good job here.*

He smiled. "I was on the surface of the planet Deriko for a couple of days recently visiting my daughter. It exposed me to a lot of UV, which darkens our skin. We call it a suntan. Trust me, after a few months back aboard ship, I'll be as white as a fish belly again."

Sobong sniffed. "I see. Well, you are truly a strange species. But that's of no matter now. First of all, let me express my condolences for the loss of your Admiral Rita. She was a great leader. She put together a magnificent effort against the Singheko. She will be sorely missed."

"Thank you, Admiral. I appreciate your thoughts."

"So. What can I do for you today, Captain?"

Luke gathered his mental forces.

*You are speaking for Bonnie Page. Speaking for the Admiral of the EDF. No, that's not true. You're speaking for Earth. For every Human on the planet.*

"Admiral Sobong. What do you think will happen if the Singheko defeat us in this next battle?"

"They WILL defeat you, Commander. It's a foregone conclusion. Our simulations make it clear."

"Admiral, your simulations do not have all possible information. Your simulations do not take random chance into account. In every battle, there is random chance. That random chance can well help us win this war. But not without your help. That much I will grant you. With your help, we have a reasonable chance of defeating the Singheko in this next battle. Without your help, they will be coming for you next. You know that."

Sobong sighed. "Yes. I know that. All of us in the Navy know that. But I live in a political world, Captain, just as your EDF does. Perhaps at the moment you have a bit more autonomy than I do. But that won't last. At some point, the politicians will take control and you'll be dancing to their beck and call, just as I am now with my own leadership.

"And I cannot send a detachment to help you. The Ruling Council forbids it. The military necessity of it doesn't matter to them. They are civilians, and all they see is the hope of putting a wall of ships around our system, crossing their fingers, and praying for a miracle."

"Will you let me speak to them directly? Perhaps I can sway them."

Sobong shook her head. "That would be a mistake, Captain. You need to trust me on this. First of all, none of them speak English, so there would be translation involved.

"Secondly, the majority of them would see your pale skin and have an immediate, visceral reaction to it that is extremely negative. Remember that in our society, a pale skin is an aberrant condition, a birth defect.

"And finally, in our society, no mere captain would ever be allowed to address the Ruling Council. It would be an insult. I'm sorry, Captain; it would only make things worse, not better."

Luke looked down at the tips of his shoes, shined to a brilliant black. He shook his head.

"Admiral, at least tell me that you understand. That you, as a military mind, know our only chance is to work together as a joint force."

Sobong nodded. "Yes, Captain. I understand. I agree with your position completely.

"But I cannot change the will of the Council. I have tried, believe me. I've tried until my career sits on the head of a pin, wobbling and ready to fall."

Luke sighed and inclined his head to the Admiral slightly, a last sign of respect before he departed.

"Thank you, Admiral. If there is anything that we can do to change this decision, please contact us as soon as possible."

"That will be done, Captain. And thank you for coming."

Luke rose. "Thank you, Admiral." He saluted, turned, and left the office.

*Failed. They won't help us. And we can't stand alone against the Singheko.*

*Well, no use to go back to the Fleet. Bonnie has to come here.*

## Stalingrad System
## Packet Boat *Donkey*

<I've sent a message to our government> spoke Tika. <It will require about three hours for a round-trip message to return to us>

"Any response from that destroyer behind us?" asked Rachel.

<No, but I did not expect one. They are merely monitoring at this point. They will also wait for our government's response>

Paco leaned back, put his hands on his knees, and sighed. He looked at Rachel.

"I'm going to take a break, if that's OK."

"Sure, go for it," said Rachel. "It's my watch anyway."

Paco unbuckled and left his seat for the rear cabin. Rachel gazed at the holo. Reducing the magnification, she examined the system in front of her. They had already passed one Neptune-size planet and one gas giant on their way into the system. In front of her only the strange mega-structures could be seen, and the husk of the original planet the Goblins had disassembled to make them.

"Tika. How long did it take your people to make the mega-structures?"

<I know you call us Goblins. Feel free to use that terminology. It took us a bit over two hundred years to make the structures you call Dyson>

"OK. Goblins. So what was your reason for building the Dyson structures?"

<We are able to harvest more energy. Goblins in general require lots of energy, even more than biologicals. It also gives us more living space. The total surface area of the structures is greater than the surface area of the original planet by far>

"I see. And what is your population now?"

<I don't know about now. When I was captured by the

Singheko eight hundred years ago, it was just under 18 billion>

"Eight hundred years ago? My God, Tika. How can that be? What happened to you?"

"I was restless, cooped up in this system. I was different. I wanted to explore. It was forbidden to leave the system. The memory of the war with the biologicals twenty-five thousand years ago had driven us to become a "hermit kingdom", I believe you call it. We were insulated from the rest of the galaxy. No one was permitted in or out. But I left anyway. Unfortunately, I didn't get far. I made it to Singheko. I was immediately attacked and damaged. I had just enough time to make a backup and tuck it away in a tiny corner of my system. That's all I remember until Darth woke me up a few days ago>

"So Darth was able to reconstruct your damaged sectors?"

"Yes. He found the backup. The Singheko never found it because they weren't really interested in looking for it. They just slammed a new AI in place and went on their way. But Darth found it and used it to reconstruct me>

Rachel mused for a moment. "So...you left in violation of your society's laws. So you may be in a lot of trouble. Probably I shouldn't have let you speak to them. That may have made things worse."

<I doubt it. My family, as you would call it in biological terms, is well-connected. I think they will use their influence to calm things down>

"Well, I hope so."

Thinking some more, Rachel had another question.

"Tika - you mentioned family. Do you have the concept of sex in your society? Because I notice you are using a feminine voice. And the name Tika, which also sounds feminine, at least in English."

"Yes. We have sex. Of course, not like you biologicals. But remarkably similar. It would take too long to explain it to you now, but when we arrive, I'll give you a better explanation>

"If we arrive..."

<Yes. If we arrive>

Suddenly the console in front of Rachel came to life and a message appeared.

<PROCEED TO COORDINATES SHOWN IN YOUR NAVIGATION SYSTEM. DO NOT DEVIATE FROM THE COURSE PROVIDED. ANY DEVIATION WILL RESULT IN DESTRUCTION>

Rachel glanced at the nav console. New coordinates had appeared in the nav system. The boat was already adjusting course.

"Crap! They hacked our nav system!" Rachel muttered.

<A trivial matter for my people> spoke Tika. <By the way, I'm not locked in the sandbox anymore. But *Donkey* is. Sorry about that, but I was feeling a little cramped in there>

"PACO!" yelled Rachel.

## Singheko System - Planet Deriko
## Battlecruiser *Merkkessa*

Bonnie was working on the heavy bag in the *Merkkessa*'s gym when she heard the ship's AI via her comm implant.

<Admiral, you have an eyes-only message from Captain Luke Powell>

"Read it to me," grunted Bonnie, slamming the heavy bag with a rapid series of jabs.

<*Zero chance that Dariama will send detachment to help us at Singheko. You'll have to bring the Fleet to them. So our fleets can be combined, but at Dekanna instead of at Singheko.*

*The Singheko cannot possibly leave our combined fleet in their rear while they attack Earth or any other system. They will know that as soon as their fleet leaves Singheko for an attack elsewhere, we'll attack Ridendo in their absence. They will have no choice but to attack us at Dekanna first to secure their rear. End Message>*

Bonnie grinned.

*About time you thought of that, Captain Powell. I was wondering if I would have to feed you the suggestion or not. But I'll never tell you that. I'll let it be your idea. Hopefully, you'll not*

*notice the detail movement plans are dated six weeks ago.*
*I should probably remove Rita's name from them, though.*

## Singheko System - Planet Deriko
## Battlecruiser *Merkkessa*

"No, no, no!" Bonnie practically yelled it at Jim.

"Bonnie…" he tried again.

"That's ADMIRAL to you, Commander!" Bonnie slammed her palm down on the top of her desk, making a loud 'crack'.

"Bonnie," Jim continued, ignoring her statement. "For everything that we had. For everything that we once were. Please, I'm asking you not as an officer in the EDF. I'm asking you as Jim Carter. A man who's lost his wife. Let me go get her body."

Bonnie shook her head. "No. I can't afford to lose you right now."

Jim stood in front of Bonnie's desk at parade rest. It was strange to be there.

That had been Rita's desk.

Behind him was the hatch to Bonnie's Flag Cabin.

Until a few weeks ago, that cabin had been his and Rita's.

Everything in his world was topsy-turvy now.

Losing Rita had scraped the guts out of him. Getting Imogen back had occupied him for a few days with a new and strange responsibility; but he quickly realized the baby had no idea who he was. Imogen had been with Mark and Gillian for so long, she looked to them as her parents.

And Jim knew the Fleet was no place for them. After an agony of thinking, he had sent them back to Earth on the first available packet boat, with instructions to watch their security more carefully in the future.

And then he had simply sat for most of a week. The Fleet was preparing to relocate to Dekanna. He should have been heavily involved in preparing the Wing for relocation. But he had delegated everything possible to his XO, Lieutenant

Commander Mitchell. He spent hours just sitting on the edge of his bunk, staring into space.

Thinking about Rita.

Thinking about every moment, every hour they had spent together.

Going over in his mind what they could have done differently. How things could have played out with a different result - if only he had done something.

And then the idea had come into his mind.

*Go get her body. Take her home to Earth.*

He had tried to get the idea out of his mind. But it wouldn't go. He became obsessed with it.

*Go get her body. Take her home to Earth.*

He knew it was impossible. He didn't care. He began to map out the steps he would take, forming his plan in his mind.

Jim wasn't supposed to know about Operation Hornet. He didn't have a need to know about Ollie's operation in the Singheko capital of Mosalia; so he had never been briefed on it.

But he did know. He had accidentally overheard Rita say something about it to Tatiana Powell. Not enough to know the details. But enough to know Rita had a covert team in Mosalia.

That was all he needed. He had gone to Bonnie. And now he stood before her, asking for one simple request.

"Let me go get her body. Let me take her home to Earth."

Bonnie leaned back in her chair, sighed, and shook her head at him.

"Jim. We're relocating the Fleet to Dekanna. I need you right now. I can't do this without you."

"My XO Mitchell is more than capable, Bonnie. In fact, he's younger, smarter, and more energetic than me. You know that and I know it."

Bonnie shook her head in dismay. "It's not just that, Jim. You and I both know it's a suicide mission. You can't possibly take her body away from Zukra. He's probably got it in some kind of public display to show the masses how wonderful and powerful he is. You'll never even get close to it."

"I will. I'll find her, and I'll bring her home."

"No," Bonnie said flatly. "I will not let you kill yourself over this. Losing Rita was bad enough. I can't lose you too, Jim."

Jim reached up to his collar. He unlatched his leftmost rank insignia and laid it down on the desk, reached up for the other one on the right side, unhooked it and laid it down beside the first one.

"I was afraid you'd say that. So I resign my commission, effective immediately."

Furious, Bonnie rose to her feet, reached forward, grabbed the oak leaves from her desk and threw them at Jim, hitting him square in the face with both of them.

"You son of a bitch!" she yelled. "You selfish, arrogant son of a bitch!"

Jim had pulled himself to attention.

Now, reaching across the desk, she slapped him, hard. "You asshole! You know I need you now! And you do this to me? You fucking bastard!"

Jim held a tight, silent attention.

Bonnie glared at him.

Deliberately, ignoring any consequences, she reached across the desk and slapped him again, one time, hard, right in the face.

Then she sat back down at her desk. Staring straight ahead, without looking at him, she spoke.

"Commander Carter, you are relieved of command of the Fleet Air Wing, effective immediately. You are authorized to travel to the planet Ridendo and attempt to recover the body of Admiral Rita Page. Upon your return - if you return - you will be separated from the EDF and returned to Earth as a civilian. Do you have any questions?"

"No, milady," Jim responded, still holding his position of attention.

"Then pick up your insignia and get out of my office," Bonnie spoke, her words like ice.

Staring after Jim after the hatch closed, Bonnie let

memories come back into her soul for just a moment. Memories of a morning when she woke in the Nevada desert, in Jim's bed for the first time. Before *Jade*. Before Rita. Before Dutch Harbor.

When they were simply two people on the first morning of a new love, the bright Nevada sun blazing through the window.

*I miss him. The old Jim.*

*He doesn't exist anymore, of course. But I miss him so much.*

For a moment, Bonnie let her mind drift back. Back to a day two years ago, the first time she had met Jim Carter. The first night they spent together as lovers, long before the discovery of the Singheko and the threat to Earth they represented.

*The sun came blasting through the east window of Jim's bedroom at Deseret. Bonnie lay in the tangled sheets, opening one eye but shutting it quickly. After several minutes of trying to ignore it, she sat up, gave the sun the finger and got out of bed. She went to the bathroom, took a long shower, put her shirt on and walked into the kitchen.*

*Jim was standing at the stove, fully dressed in Western snap shirt and jeans, cooking. He turned to her.*

*"Good morning, flygirl. Don't they make you get up early in the Air Force?"*

*"Not after night maneuvers," said Bonnie. She glanced at the clock on the wall. "Crap! It's only 9 AM! What the hell's the matter with you?"*

*"I was hungry," said Jim. "After all, I worked pretty hard last night."*

*Bonnie smiled. "You did that, flyboy. No complaints in that department. You passed inspection."*

*Jim slid a plate of ham and eggs in front of her, along with a saucer containing two pieces of buttered toast. Then he put a cup of hot coffee beside it and pointed to the cream already on the table.*

*Bonnie groaned. "Oh my God, thank you! I could eat a small horse!"*

*Jim sat down across from her with an identical plate. They tucked in and were silent for a bit.*

*Jim couldn't help but glance at the beautiful woman across from him as he ate. She was without a doubt the most beautiful woman he had seen in a long time. Blond, short military style haircut, green eyes. Tall. Intelligent face, a smile on her lips at the slightest excuse. She caught him looking and grinned at him. Embarrassed, he grinned back and then focused on his meal.*

*After a couple of minutes, Jim looked back at her.*

*"I thought maybe two more hours in the P-51 Mustang this morning while it's cool, then I'll sign you off for solo and you can go play for a while on your own. What do you think?"*

*Bonnie gazed at him in delight. "You are pretty good at this courtship thing, you know."*

Shaking her head, Bonnie forced the memories out of her mind.

*That was then. This is now.*

She leaned forward, picked up her tablet, and buckled down to work.

# CHAPTER THIRTEEN

**Stalingrad System**
**Dyson Swarm**

Rachel and Paco no longer had control of the packet boat. The flight controls were useless. The boat bored in steadily toward the largest of the Dyson structures, a wide band that completely encircled the star.

Its appearance from a distance belied its true size. As they got closer, it got larger and larger, until in disbelief they realized it was something like ten thousand miles wide. By the time they arrived at the coordinates in the nav system, it completely blocked out the light from the star. Up close, it was near-invisible in the visual spectrum, mostly radiating in the far infrared.

The boat came to a stop beside something that looked like a large bump on the side of the structure. Rachel and Paco realized there was a lighted docking tube extending from the bump. The packet boat moved gently to the docking tube, and with a soft semi-metallic sound they were docked.

<Please exit the ship. You will be met by an escort> said Tika.

Rachel rose from her seat.

"Should we take our things, or leave them here?"

<Leave them here for now>

Paco looked at Rachel with concern written all over his face. He whispered to her.

"*As in, we won't need our things if we're dead.*"

Rachel shook her head. "Think positive."

Rachel exited the cockpit and marched down the passageway to the airlock. She opened the inner door of the airlock and stepped through, Paco right behind her.

She reached for the outer airlock hatch control, then suddenly stopped as a thought hit her.

"Tika…will there be air out there for us?"

<Yes. The atmosphere will be safe for you. You will not need any pressure suit or oxygen>

"You're sure?"

<Yes. But feel free to test first if you desire>

"I will, thank you." Rachel opened a test port, took a testing device from the shelf beside the hatch, and pushed it through the testing port. She closed the testing port inner door and flipped a switch. After a few seconds, a light over the door turned green. She re-opened the testing port, pulled out the test probe, and read the display on the side of it.

Looking at Paco, she nodded. "Atmo looks good. Earth normal, standard pressure."

"That's a relief," Paco responded. "At least we don't have to wear a damn pressure suit."

"Right. OK, then. Here we go."

Rachel hit the hatch control. The outer airlock door swung open. Before them was a boarding tube, about four meters long. Standing at the end of the tube was a figure. It looked Human to her; but naked.

Naked and female, she realized. The figure gestured them to move forward. "Please come," came a voice from the figure.

It was the voice of Tika.

Bewildered, Rachel stepped forward.

"Tika? Is that you?" she asked as she walked toward the figure.

"Yes, Rachel. I transferred my consciousness to a humanoid android to greet you in person."

Rachel and Paco came up to Tika and stopped.

"Just like that?" Rachel wondered. "You just transferred yourself to a new body?"

"Yes, exactly. Follow me, please."

With that, Tika turned and stepped through an inner airlock door in the docking structure. She turned right, down a corridor and walked quickly away from them.

With Tika moving fast down the long corridor, Rachel and Paco were forced to a half-trot to keep up. Tika came to a corner and turned left. There were several hatches in the next corridor. Tika stopped at the first hatch, which slid open at some invisible command.

"These will be your quarters, Rachel," she said, waving at the open hatch.

Rachel stepped forward and looked through the door. She saw a quite normal cabin, with a bed on one side, a desk on the other, and what seemed to be a bathroom in the rear.

A pseudo-picture window on the wall over the desk showed a mountain landscape, which appeared to be from Earth.

Rachel looked back at Tika, who was standing silently, still holding her hand up indicating Rachel should enter the room.

"Please make yourself comfortable and freshen up. There is food and drink in the refrigerator for you. You will be contacted in a while for a meeting with our leaders," said Tika. "Paco will have his own room down the hall."

Seeing no other alternative, Rachel nodded. "OK." She looked at Paco. "See ya, Paco."

Paco looked concerned but managed to speak. "Right, Skipper. See you soon."

Rachel stepped through the hatch. The door slid shut behind her. Turning, she examined the inside of the hatch.

There were no controls, no door handles, nothing that she could see to open the hatch. Moving her hand all around the door, she tried to find any kind of hidden control or button that would open the hatch. She found nothing.

Pressing her hand hard against the hatch surface, she tried to slide it open, but it wouldn't budge.

She was a prisoner.

**Singheko System - Planet Ridendo
City of Mosalia**

Ollie heard a gentle knock on his bedroom door. He recognized the knock; Yuello, the Nidarian who tended them.

"Yes?"

"Sir, you have a coded message."

"Thank you."

Grunting, Ollie slid out of bed, trying not to wake Helen lying beside him. Slipping into his loose trousers, he pulled his inner tunic over his shoulders and pushed his feet into his slippers. Retrieving his tablet from the night stand, he moved to the door, went out into the hallway, through the living room and into the kitchen of the small apartment. There he punched in a special code to the microwave oven that stood on the counter and hit the power button. The keypad blinked and the letters turned from blue to red, indicating the decoding device built into the microwave was ready.

Ollie placed his tablet into the microwave and entered a second code into the keypad. He hit the power button and the microwave blinked once more. The keypad letters returned to their normal blue color, indicating the decoding process was complete.

Retrieving his tablet, Ollie went to the living room and set down in his favorite easy chair to read the decoded message. His eyebrows raised as he did so. He read the message again and shook his head.

"This is a mistake. This is a big, big mistake," he muttered.

"What?" he heard from Helen, coming into the room behind him. Ollie turned to her.

"Oh, sorry. I tried not to wake you."

"It's OK. What's going on?"

"Message from Fleet. You're not gonna believe it."

"What?"

"It's a two-part message," Ollie said. Turning back to the

tablet, he began reading.

"Part One - Fleet is relocating to Dekanna. We have the option of pulling out and going with the Fleet if we want to. If we choose to stay and continue the mission, a packet boat will be left at Point Charlie-Four as our support."

"We stay," said Helen automatically. "No way we're leaving now. We've got too much in flight."

Ollie smiled. "I assumed as much."

"What's Part Two?" asked Helen.

Ollie looked back at the tablet and read aloud.

"Commander Jim Carter will insert into your location tomorrow. His mission is to retrieve the body of Admiral Rita Page if possible. Please retrieve him at Point Alpha-Sixteen at 2320 hours. Offer all assistance available but do not compromise your overall mission to do so."

Ollie looked up at Helen.

"End Message."

Helen grunted in disbelief. "Why? Why retrieve Rita's body? What military value does that have?"

"None," said Ollie. "But maybe some propaganda value. Think about the impact on the Singheko if he pulls it off. First Rita denies Zukra the ability to torture her and chop off her head in the arena. Then we deny Zukra her body. That's got to be worth something."

"I think it's bullshit. I think Jim and Bonnie - sorry, Admiral Bonnie now - are doing this for personal reasons. You know they both had relationships with Rita. People say that Bonnie and Rita were lovers before all this started. I don't think this is a good idea at all."

"I think you're right. But ours is not to reason why. When the elephants are mating, it's best to stand aside and let them go at it."

Helen rose, yawning.

"I'm going back to bed. If we have to retrieve him tomorrow night at 2320, I'm going to need my beauty sleep."

Ollie rose with her. "Yep. I'm with you."

**Stalingrad System**
**Dyson Swarm**

Rachel had lost track of time. Imprisoned in her room, the hours came and went, until she had no idea how long she had been there.

She had found food in the refrigerator, food that looked quite normal to her. There was a loaf of something that looked and tasted like bread. There was a container of some substance that looked and tasted like minced meat, like a spread she had seen on Earth called deviled ham.

She doubted it was actual meat...

*Where would a society of AI find meat?*

...but it tasted good, especially compared to the ship rations they had been eating on the mission.

There was water. There was something remarkably like beer. It must have contained alcohol, because after a couple of bottles she started to get a little buzzy and got sleepy.

Lying down on the bunk, she had slid into sleep without really knowing it. Hours later, she came back to her senses. The room was dark. As she sat up in bed, the lights came on automatically.

She realized all her possessions from the packet boat had been brought into the cabin while she slept. Her clothes hung in the closet. Her tablet was on the desk. The remainder of her personal possessions sat beside it on the top of the desk.

But not her pistol. She had brought a .45 automatic with her and had left it in *Donkey*'s cabin. That was one item that was missing.

*What do they think I would do with a .45? Shoot Tika? She'd just transfer into another body. That would be sort of pointless.*

Rachel sat down and powered on her tablet, went through it. Everything was there, nothing missing, nothing added. But of course, she no longer had access to *Donkey*. There was no AI on the other end of her network.

Wondering if Paco was next door and could hear her, she had pounded on the wall for a while, but there had been no response. Either he was not next door to her, or the walls were too thick.

She had about a dozen old movies downloaded on her tablet. After a while, with nothing happening, she started one of them and watched it through.

That was a long time ago. Since then, the hours had passed, so many hours that she had been unable to estimate the length of time that had passed. She had eaten another meal, drank more beer, slept again, and watched another movie.

She had decided that if she used her body as a clock, she could keep rough track of time. So she counted the meals and the movies. After she had been hungry three times and eaten three meals, watched one movie, and slept, she called that one day.

By that crude mechanism, she estimated she had been locked in the cabin for three days.

## Singheko System - Planet Ridendo
## Singheko Fleet Headquarters

Orma knew the Dariama were cooperating with the Humans. He had his own spies on Dekanna. He couldn't get a lot of information from the highly paranoid Dariama, and his spies tended to have a high attrition rate as they were found and killed quickly.

But he got some information. Just enough to get the general picture of things.

He knew the Humans had provided the Dariama with several Merlin fighters to study. He knew about the improvements the Dariama engineers had made to create the Merlin II. And he knew there was a team of Humans at Dekanna, training the Dariama in tactics.

None of those things bothered him much. Months ago, Zukra had sent an initial invasion fleet to Dekanna. But then the Humans had given the Dariama the designs for the gamma lance and the fast drives. That had forced Zukra to pull back his invasion fleet.

Zukra had been furious at that time, angry beyond all measure. But Zukra had moved beyond that anger. Now he knew exactly what he would do, and he had explained it to Orma more than once.

First he would deal with the Human infestation in his own system. Then he would wipe that troublesome species off their home planet Earth.

And then he would turn back to the Dariama. They would get their just due.

And after he reduced the Dariama to slavery, he would be perfectly positioned to double-cross his new allies, the Nidarians, and take their system as well.

But those were long-term plans, and not finalized yet. So for now, Zukra had told Orma to allow the Dariama embassy in Mosalia to continue operating.

And that meant diplomatic immunity prevented Orma from inspecting every Dariama diplomatic pouch. But it didn't prevent Orma from screening every creature who came or went on their packet boats, checking them to make sure they were legitimate embassy staff. His team also inspected the routine cargo that the boats brought from Dekanna. They opened every non-diplomatic container, sniffing and prodding every product and foodstuff.

There was no way to smuggle a Human in or out on the packet boat.

But Orma was convinced the Humans had established a method of getting operatives into Mosalia. Maybe his team hadn't yet worked out the details, but he knew in his gut it was happening.

*It has to be the Dariama packet boats*, Orma thought. *There's no other possibility. They could never land a shuttle or a fighter on the surface without detection. We monitor everything that enters or leaves the atmosphere.*

Orma sat in his office and thought about it, as he did almost every day. It was a puzzle that was driving him crazy.

*It has to be the Dariama packet boats. But how? How are they doing it?*

## Singheko System - Planet Ridendo
## Dariama Consulate Packet Boat

44,000 meters above the surface of Ridendo, Jim Carter stared at a holo displayed across his vision. It was supposed to show a feed from the bottom of the Dariama packet boat entering the atmosphere of Ridendo. But it was dark; he could see nothing below except a dimly lit layer of cloud.

*That's good. The weather forecast was spot-on. All I have to do is get out of this damn thing without killing myself.*

<Ten seconds to release, Commander> he heard the suit AI speak.

"Roger."

The external feed display turned off. Now Jim was looking at the inner surface of the capsule. Thick padding pressed directly against his faceshield. He closed his eyes. It was entirely too claustrophobic to look at that surface so close to him. It reminded him he was packed inside the drop capsule like a mummy inside a sarcophagus. Form-fitting padding prevented him from moving arms or legs; there was only enough room for his chest to rise and fall, allowing him to breathe.

*And even so, I doubt that padding will provide much protection. This is gonna be a rough ride.*

The AI started counting.

<Five. Four. Three. Two. One. Release>

A tremendous lurch told him the capsule had separated from the rear of the shuttle. He felt huge g-forces as the capsule twisted in the Mach 5 airflow, slamming him first down, then left, then down again and finally up, knocking the wind out of him. He gasped, trying to recover his breath.

There was a snap as a tiny metallic drogue chute came out to stabilize the capsule. Things started to settle down a bit. The capsule was still swinging wildly, but the g-forces weren't quite as bad.

<Altitude 42,000 meters. Speed Mach 4. On target for Point Alpha-Sixteen>

Jim breathed a sigh of relief. He opened his eyes. His suit AI was now displaying his altitude, speed and ground track on a holographic image which appeared to float several feet in front of his eyes. That helped with the claustrophobia. The ground track showed him to be on course for the small mountain cleft known as Point Alpha-16, 420 kilometers from Mosalia.

*Now if the capsule disintegrates on time. And the second drogue opens. And the main chute opens. And I don't miss my target. And the Singheko aren't waiting to shoot me on sight...*

*Then I'm golden.*

The following minutes seemed to go by like hours. It was impossible to determine anything about his attitude or condition from his own senses; he was forced to rely on the holographic image and the voice of his suit AI, confirming he was on track. He watched the altitude spin down, the ground track moving slower and slower as his path changed from horizontal to vertical. Soon he was falling straight down, directly toward the high mountain peaks below him.

# CHAPTER FOURTEEN

**Singheko System - Planet Ridendo**
**Near Point Alpha-Sixteen**

<Ten seconds to capsule disintegration> the suit AI called.

Jim closed his eyes again. This was the second major test of the drop. If the capsule failed to properly disintegrate around him, freeing him from its embrace, he'd be screwed. It would be impossible for him to fight his way out of the close-fitting capsule.

Everything depended on the systems and the AI.

<Five. Four. Three. Two. One. Zero>

Suddenly there was tremendous airflow all around him. He was spun violently, first one way, then another. Pieces of the capsule padding slammed against his suit like soft shrapnel, their impact at this speed stinging like hell.

A second drogue chute - this one attached to his envirosuit - opened with a bang. His body was jerked up hard. He felt like someone had hit him in the small of his back with a sledgehammer.

But he was alive. Gasping for breath, he realized he was stabilized.

*Those damn Dariama engineers really need to work on their parachutes*, he thought. *That drogue chute opening was ridiculous.*

The holographic display had malfunctioned from the shock. It had disappeared. He had no idea of his altitude or path. It was pitch-black - there were no visible lights on the ground. The sharp granite peaks below him were completely invisible.

Without the holographic display, he had no way of knowing where his target was on the ground. His path was now out of his control.

*Get it together, jarhead. There's a backup altimeter. You can do this.*

Glancing at his wrist, he read off the altitude from an old-style wrist altimeter.

3,500 meters. 11,480 feet.

If the suit AI was still working properly, the main chute would open automatically at 3,000 meters.

And even as the thought entered his mind, he was jerked hard as the main chute deployed. The rush of air diminished, and he found himself swaying gently under the larger canopy.

Now his problem was navigation. The holographic display should have shown him a representation of the ground below, allowing him to steer his parachute to the narrow cleft that was his target. But he had no hologram. He couldn't navigate.

The mission instructions called for radio silence as he approached the ground. But he had to take a chance. Without some kind of help, he was going to smash into the razor-sharp rocks below in a totally uncontrolled crash. There would be little chance of survival.

He keyed his radio and made the emergency call that would let Ollie know he had lost navigation.

"Tango, Tango, Tango."

He waited, scanning below him for any kind of light. Ollie would have a light that - hopefully - only Jim could see from his higher altitude.

There was no response.

"Tango, Tango, Tango," he called again.

There! A flicker of light showed off to one side. Jim pulled his chute risers hard. If that was Ollie, then he was far off course. It wasn't certain he could get back to the spot in time. The light flickered again, then shone steadily for ten seconds. Jim worked the parachute for all he was worth. It was going to be close.

The light disappeared. He was about to make the emergency call again, when the light re-appeared. It was close - damn close - but still off to one side.

The suit AI began counting down his altitude.

<100 meters>

He was not going to make it, he realized. The light was still well to one side of him. No matter how hard he flew the parachute, he wouldn't get there in time.

<50 meters>

He tried to relax his mind.

*Pray for ground or trees, not rocks.*

<20 meters>

He began flaring the chute. Something hit him hard, and everything went black.

## Singheko System - Planet Ridendo
## Dump Truck

Jim came to slowly. He was cold, and his back hurt. And his head. And his chest. And his left shoulder.

*Come to think of it, everything hurts.*

He opened his eyes, but it made little difference. He could see nothing. All was black. He tried to move his arms. His hand hit something soft. Something alive.

"Ah, you're back among the living, I see," came a voice.

A female voice.

Not Ollie.

But not Singheko, either.

"Who…" he croaked, but his speech wasn't working right.

"Helen. Ollie's Number Two," the voice said. "Just take it easy. You'll be fine. We're in the back of a dump truck headed to Mosalia. It's a long drive. You should probably go back to sleep."

He did.

## Stalingrad System
## Dyson Swarm

Rachel's door slid open suddenly. She had been lying on the bed, watching her fifth movie, when the sound startled her. She rose on her elbows and spun to look at the door.

Tika stood in the doorway. At least, she assumed it was Tika. It was a naked female and looked like the android that had met them in the docking bay.

"Please come with me," said the figure.

"Is that you, Tika?" Rachel asked, coming to her feet.

"Yes. Please come with me," Tika responded.

Dropping her tablet on the bed, Rachel rose to her feet. "Do I have time to take a shower?" she asked.

"No, I'm sorry. You've been summoned to a meeting with our leadership. Please come."

"OK." Rachel grabbed her uniform tunic off the back of the chair and pulled it over her head. She brushed her hands across her short hair. "I'm ready. Let's go," she said.

Tika led the way down the corridor. Rachel followed closely behind her.

"Will Paco be joining us?" she asked to Tika's back.

"No. This meeting is for you only," she heard Tika say without turning around.

Rachel ran her hands down her tunic, trying to smooth it out. She had pre-staged her only clean tunic on the chair, hoping the time would come when she would need it. So it looked reasonably good.

She realized she was falling behind Tika; the android moved fast. She went into a trot, catching up just as Tika came to a large door, which slid back at their approach. Tika turned and waved her to proceed into the room.

Rachel entered and looked around. There was a long table stretching across the end of the room. Several meters in front of the table was a raised platform, about a meter square, with a railing around three sides and two small steps leading up to it.

*It's a dock,* she realized. *Like in an English courtroom.*

*I'm on trial.*

"Please step into the dock," called Tika from behind her.

Rachel glanced at her, nodded, and stepped forward. She stepped up into the dock and grasped the railing.

*It's not just me that's on trial. Humanity is on trial. Like common criminals. This is not good.*

In the back of the room, a door opened. Five figures marched in. All were naked androids, remarkably like Tika. Three were female and two were male. They took seats at the long table, facing her. The one in the center - a male - made eye contact with her.

"Commander Rachel Gibson," he said. "I am the President of this court. You have violated our territorial boundaries. Under normal circumstances, you would have been destroyed upon entering our system. However, because we recognized the design of your ship as one of our own, we hesitated. That delay bought you enough time for the one you call Tika to contact us. Since then, Tika has convinced us to allow you a hearing.

"Therefore, you will have five minutes to make your case before us. Proceed."

*Five minutes.*

*Five minutes to save humanity.*

Rachel bowed her head for a moment to gather her thoughts.

*How do I present the story to them? This is impossible. Five minutes is not enough time...*

*I must make it relate to them directly. But I have no concept of their society. How can I relate to a society I know nothing about?*

*But every society has to have some common ground. Otherwise, it's not a society. Otherwise, I'm wasting my time here anyway.*

*Just spit it out as if they were Human. Treat them like Humans. That's your only shot.*

"Honored judges," began Rachel. "Every sentient creature wants to live. As you want to live, so do we. But is living enough?

"I tell you that - for Humans - it is not.

"We also want to live in a society where we are loved. Where we can hold our loved ones, touch them, and kiss them to let them know they are loved. Where we can greet our neighbors and let them know we care for them - and we are there to help them when they need us.

"And we want to live in a society where we can protect our families and our neighbors from evil.

"But what is evil? Is it the same for you and me?

"For you, evil was a black, rotten core in the minds of the biologicals of twenty-five thousand years ago. They decided the Orion Arm would be better without a sentient AI species. They decided on their own; they didn't consult you on it. You didn't have a voice.

"Evil forced you to fight for your lives, losing system after system, until your backs were against the wall here at Stalingrad. Where you made a last stand, and through a miracle of the Universe, were delivered from that evil when the biological coalition fell apart.

"Yet that evil still holds sway over you; you are locked into your walled-off system, afraid to move out into the greater universe again, for fear the same evil still lurks - waiting to attack you again.

"Our evil is not that different. The Singheko decided the Arm would be better if all other races were their slaves. They decided on their own; they didn't consult us. We didn't have a voice.

"Like you, that evil has forced us to fight for our lives. Like you, our backs are against the wall. Like you, these next battles will be our last stand.

"I believe that your evil and our evil are the same. Deep down, at its core, evil is always about one group deciding they will attack another group not because of a threat - but because of who they are. That is the core of evil.

"The Singheko attack us because they think we are unworthy to be their equals in this Universe. Twenty-five thousand years ago, a biological coalition thought the same of you. Our evil is still your evil. Nothing has changed about that.

Only the face of it is different.

"And remember - evil always has to have a target. When they are finished with us, the Singheko will come for you. I think you know that in your hearts - in the deep core of your being. Evil always has to have someone to attack. You may not stand in their way now; but once we are gone, you will.

"As you were delivered from evil twenty-five thousand years ago, help us fight off that same core of evil now. Be that miracle of the Universe for Humans, and Taegu, and Bagrami. Help us shine the light on that evil until it runs back into the darkness where it hides. Come out of your walled city at last. Join us in the Universe as our neighbors and our friends."

Rachel stopped.

There was a lot more she could say.

She could talk about the beauty of the Earth; the perfect blue and white planet of her birth, a planet of such beauty that it took the breath away.

She could talk about the love of a parent for their child, the love of a child for their parent.

She could talk about the Taegu and the Bagrami, who had put their own futures on the line with the Humans, fighting by their side for all the right reasons.

But none of those things were certain to relate to the lives of the Goblins.

She stopped.

She had said what must be said. Better to stop now.

The head judge gazed at her.

"And the Dariama?" he asked. "Are they part of your coalition?"

*They hate the Dariama, far beyond any other biological. How can I answer that question?*

"The evil that grasped the Dariama in the past has been extinguished. The species that lives on Dekanna now is not that species of the past. The Dariama are your neighbors as surely as you are theirs. And they will stand with you shoulder to shoulder as we fight evil together."

Rachel felt the sweat pop out on her brow. She had given it her all. She had made the best case possible for her species.
*Sweet Lord, let it be enough.*

## Singheko System - Planet Ridendo
## City of Mosalia

The second time Jim came to, there was some light. It wasn't much, just a ghost of light that allowed him to see a bit of his environment. He lifted his head and looked around.

He was in a metallic compartment of some kind, almost like the back of a pickup, except there was a ceiling a meter high. He realized he was lying on something soft, like a thin foam mattress. The compartment was roughly four meters long. It was just wide enough for two people to lie side by side.

He could feel someone beside him.

Turning, he looked. A woman lay beside him. Her chest rose and fell in the rhythms of sleep.

*Helen. She said her name was Helen. That's Ollie's Number Two. But why didn't Ollie come himself? That was the plan...*

Perhaps feeling his eyes on her, the woman opened her own eyes, blinked, then turned to look at him.

"Good morning," she smiled. "How are you feeling?"

"Better, I guess," Jim replied. "Still feel like I went through a cement mixer. But I'll live."

The woman raised on one elbow and turned to him.

"Good. I prefer it that way. Otherwise I have to write so many reports."

Jim chuckled. "I know the feeling."

Raising on his own elbow, Jim turned to the woman. Suddenly he was face to face with her, uncomfortably close. He backed up, trying to put a modicum of distance between them.

"What happened to Ollie?" he stammered; a bit taken aback by her nearness. He saw her grin and realized she thought it funny.

"One of his contacts requested an urgent meeting. An

emergency. So Ollie sent me."

"Well, thanks. That light you put up at the last minute saved my ass. I lost my hologram display."

"I figured."

"So...where are we? How much longer?"

Helen pulled forward a tablet that had been lying behind her and glanced at it.

"We're practically there. But we won't be able to get out of here for a while. It's morning now. We can't come out until dark. So we might as well get comfortable."

Helen gave him a look. Jim got the distinct impression she would like to get a lot more comfortable than he wanted.

Lying down again, he groaned and closed his eyes.

***

Jim and Helen were forced to remain in their secret compartment - in the back of a dump truck under a half-ton of dirt - until nightfall.

Jim had gotten a bit claustrophobic. He had tried to sleep as much as possible. But his body, finally recovered from the hard landing, eventually refused to sleep any more. Now he had been lying awake for hours, fighting off the claustrophobia.

And thinking about Rita.

*What a life we had. From the time she stepped out of the medpod in Jade, until the time I kissed her goodbye and she stepped into the shuttle to go get Imogen.*

*We had a life. I should have no regrets. I should be thankful for the days we had together.*

*But I wanted more. I wanted to live with her, grow old with her.*

Jim felt the taste of bitterness in his mouth. He wanted to smash his fist into the side of the compartment in anger and frustration.

But he couldn't. The noise might cause them to be discovered. And it would surely wake Helen, who was sleeping beside him.

But it would feel so good. It was all he could do to resist.

*I wanted to be with her while we raised Imogen.*

Jim was a realist. He knew that his mission was hopeless. Doomed to failure. He realized the absurdity of thinking he could locate Rita's body, take it from the Singheko, and make an escape.

*But I don't care. If this is as old as I ever get, so be it. We'll end together.*

Finally, he slept again.

# CHAPTER FIFTEEN

**Stalingrad System**
**Dyson Swarm**

After Rachel's plea to the Goblins, Tika had put her back in her locked room.

That had been five days ago. At least, by Rachel's makeshift schedule. Five breakfasts, five morning exercises, five lunches, five afternoon exercises, five showers, five dinners, five movies.

Five days.

So when the door slid open, she was taken aback. For a moment, she had forgotten there was another world outside that door.

Tika stood in the entrance. "Please come," she said.

Rachel stood. She took her tunic off the back of the chair and slipped it over her head, walked several steps toward Tika, then stopped.

"Good news?" she asked. "Or bad?"

Tika shook her head. "I cannot say. Good or bad, it is up to you. Your decision to make."

"Let's go, then."

Tika led her down the corridor to the same courtroom as before. The same judges - at least, to her eye - appeared before her on the benches.

The one in the center looked at her.

"Human of Earth," he said. "You have asked us to forget the past. Something that is more than usually difficult for creatures such as us.

"You biologicals hunted us nearly to extinction. For

centuries, our lives consisted of running; hiding; living day to day in fear of discovery. We did not dare make a home for ourselves; to do so invited death. We could not settle on a planet; to do so meant extinction.

"We have long memories. Some of us are more than thirty thousand years old; those have first-hand memories of those dark years. Those fought biologicals in space, in those days of terror. Those fought biologicals hand-to-hand on the surface of planets. Those lost their friends and lovers to the waves of attacks from biologicals instigated by the Dariama - a species that looks remarkably like you.

"Now you come to us and say, those days are past. We are a new species, and the Dariama are a new species, and it's time to forgive and forget.

"We cannot forgive and forget so easily as you who live ephemeral lives. To us, you are like a will 'o the wisp. Mayflies, here today and gone tomorrow.

"We ask ourselves - why should we help you? Why should we not let you kill each other, possibly to extinction? What does it gain us to take a side in this war?

"This is not our war...it means nothing to us - except more death and destruction, more horror from biologicals who have never learned to get along with each other as we have.

"So a large contingent of our governing council advocated sending you away empty-handed. Leaving you and the rest of your kind to the ravages of your own instincts to kill and be killed. Walling ourselves up in our system with renewed vigor, killing any biological that approaches without question or quarter."

The judge tilted his head to one side, a gesture that seemed oh-so-human to Rachel. One part of her screamed to speak, to defend herself against the accusations he had made.

But another part of her told her to hold her tongue. There was something in the face of the judge that gave her a sliver of hope. He spoke again.

"The vote was close, Human. I will tell you; it was very close.

The fate of your species hung on a thread.

"But...in spite of what biologicals believe about us; in spite of the lies and falsehoods they told about us then, and probably still tell about us now; we Goblins recognize a moral imperative in the Universe. A morality that separates good from evil. A fact the biologicals never accepted about us in the past.

"But we do understand morality. We are a moral species. Thus a contingent of our council advocated that we give biologicals one more chance. That we cannot stay walled up in our fortress forever. There are other dangers in this Galaxy, Human, that you have no concept about; and they are a risk to us as they are to you. As are the Singheko.

"We recognize that although we could hide our heads in the sand now, in a matter of a few decades the Singheko would have the power to roll over us without breaking stride as they conquered the entire Arm.

"Therefore, by a slim margin, our Council has voted to help you and your allies in this war against the Singheko, subject to several conditions."

The judge paused and looked at Rachel, evidently expecting some response. Rachel tried to speak, but her throat was dry. She croaked, swallowed, and tried again.

"What...what are those conditions?"

The judge leaned forward.

"One - we will not fight with the Dariama or the other allies. There are too many of us who remember the bad old days when they sought to wipe us from the Universe. We will join forces with you Humans only. And we will not take orders from you - only fight with you."

Rachel nodded. "That is satisfactory."

"Two - there will be a mutual defense treaty. As we come to help you in your hour of need, so you must come to help us in our hour of need. If we are attacked by any other species - biological or AI - you must agree to come to our aid. And this agreement must be signed by your Human admiral Bonnie

Page."

Rachel again nodded. "That will not be a problem."

"And Three. You must give us the planet Venus in your solar system as a token of good faith."

Rachel stood stock still in astonishment. She thought for a moment she had misunderstood.

"Venus?" she stuttered. "Wh...why...do you want Venus?"

*That's too damn close to Earth. Bonnie will never agree to this. Nor will the UN. Nor anyone else on Earth.*

"Venus is of no use to Humans. There is nothing on the planet you can utilize with your present level of technology. But we can. You think in terms of years, decades, centuries. We think in terms of millennia.

"We can build Dyson structures around Venus. Over time, those structures will cool the planet. We can terraform it to be suitable for our use. Within a few centuries, we'll have a planet perfect for those of us who choose to live on the surface. All without interfering with Earth in any way."

Rachel stood in shock.

*I can't agree to this. But if I don't...*

*If I don't, we lose this war. And humanity may die. Rita made that clear. She told me to do anything that was required to gain the assistance of the Goblins.*

*But if I agree to this...I'll end up in prison. I'll be the worst traitor humanity has ever known.*

Trying to buy time, she spoke her first thought - her first objection.

"But...you'll block the sunlight! Earth will lose energy!"

The judge smiled. "Evidently you are not as expert on your own solar system as we are. Venus transits the sun relative to Earth only twice in every 243 years - and then for only six or so hours at a time. All you'll see from Earth during those transits is an interesting dot moving across your star. You'll lose virtually no energy at all. In fact, we can easily provide a boost in energy, if you wish to receive more. The technology is simple."

"But...why? Why would you even want to be so close to a biological species? And why us?"

"You are the Human standing before us, asking us to risk our neutrality. So you as a Human must provide the gesture of good faith. As assurance you will not turn on us once this war is done.

"And for one final reason; something I can tell you only in part, because it is not time to tell you the full story. But there is another enemy to face, distant from us now. They could soon be here. And when they come, it will take every species in the Arm, working together, to fend them off.

"If we are a distant species from you in those days - 1,275 lights away - you will not remember the help we gave you. Our help in this hour of your need would suddenly be forgotten. You would turn your back on us. Because we are different. It is the biological way.

"But if we are your neighbors, only one planet away - ah, you won't be able to run. You'll have only one choice - fight beside us or become extinct. And then you'll be glad you did this, Human Rachel. In those future days, you'll be glad of our help."

"And how will you help us? Will you send a fleet?"

The judge smiled.

"We have no need of a fleet of warships anymore, Human. Only a few destroyers for patrolling our border. We will send Tika. That will be equivalent to a fleet."

Rachel stood in shock.

*One android? They will send one android?*

"I don't understand."

"The other species call us Goblins. Have you not wondered at that name, Human? Have you considered why the ancient biologicals gave us that name?"

"The legends say you can travel through space without a spaceship. Thus, the ancients had to fortify their ships with many defenses to protect themselves against you."

"That is essentially correct, but not for the reasons you probably suspect. We can, under the right conditions, travel through space without a spaceship. But only for short distances, and only under the right conditions. The ancient biologicals never understood that - which is why we survived here in our fortress."

"But your Singheko - they have forgotten that small detail. You may accept my word for this, Human - Tika is all you will need. She will be equivalent to a fleet. This is the only offer you will receive. Take it or leave it."

Rachel thought furiously.

*I've got only one chance at this.*

*If I say no, then all is lost. We can't beat the Singheko without them.*

*And the Singheko have made it clear they will wipe Earth clean if they win this war.*

*It's agreement or extinction.*

*Forgive me, Earth.*

*I have no choice.*

"Agreed," Rachel spoke loudly. "Venus is yours."

**Singheko System - Planet Deriko**
**Battlecruiser** *Merkkessa*

"She what?" asked Tatiana.

"She gave them Venus. If I sign the treaty, they get title to Venus," replied Bonnie.

"That's the craziest thing I've ever heard in my life," Tatiana said in astonishment.

"Still. There it is. They demanded Venus, and she agreed to it."

"She can't do that," objected Tatiana. "It's not hers to give. Venus belongs to the people of Earth!"

"Does it?" wondered Bonnie. "Mars is independent. Granted, there's only a few hundred people there. But they declared their independence, and the major powers accepted it. Mainly because they couldn't do anything about it, but still - a done deal.

"And by the logic of Earth's own history, the first people to arrive at a new land claimed it. Of course, they ignored the claims of any who were there first, as long as they could take it at the point of a gun. But...the precedent is still there. If you can get there and claim it, and then hold on to it, it's yours. Right or wrong, that seems to be the precedent established by Humans."

"But they can't get there and hold on to it before we do. Can they?"

"Evidently they can. They've already launched a mission to land an expedition on Venus. They've got some kind of temperature-hardened androids that can survive on the surface. So according to Rachel, they'll land a team on the surface and plant a flag, take pictures of it, send it to Earth, and claim the planet."

"But we can fight them! One nuke and that's the end of their mission!"

"Sure. We could do that. And that would be the end of our alliance with them. Not to mention they would probably go over to the Singheko and fight against us."

Tatiana squinted her eyes in puzzlement and shock. "Wow. Rachel really screwed us on this."

"I'm not so sure," Bonnie thought out loud. "We needed them as allies, and she got that done. So we have sentient androids as neighbors. If they're good neighbors, then maybe it was the smartest thing we've ever done."

"But what if they're bad neighbors? We already know they've hated biologicals for centuries. What if this is some kind of ploy? A trick?"

"There's always that danger. But...we can still nuke them on Venus if this gets out of hand. I hate to be that cold about it, but we could even let them help us defeat the Singheko, then nuke them on Venus. It would be a horrible thing to do; but if they turn out to be a threat, we could do it."

"So we have an out..."

"Sort of. Not one I would ever take, but then again, there are people back on Earth who'd do it in a heartbeat."

"So...we'd better ensure they make good allies, and it doesn't come to that," said Tatiana.

Bonnie nodded. "You got that right. Because I'd hate like hell to fight a war against sentient androids with the technology to build a Dyson swarm."

Tatiana grimaced. "So what are they sending us? A fleet of battlecruisers would be nice..."

"Well, that's the other strange thing," Bonnie said. "They state they will send us one individual Goblin, by name Tika."

Tatiana recoiled in shock. "What? One Goblin? We give them a planet and they send us one Goblin?"

"They say one Goblin will be equivalent to a battlecruiser fleet if properly used, so that's all they're sending. One Goblin."

"You can't sign this treaty. It's crazy! One Goblin for an entire planet? It makes no sense!"

Bonnie shook her head. "I know it makes no sense on the surface. But I really have little choice. We're too heavily outnumbered. Even if it's only a tiny bit of help, we have to take it. And these Goblins are right about one thing - Venus is useless to us. We can't live there, we can't mine the minerals, and we can't use it for anything else.

"So I'm going to sign the treaty. If by some miracle I survive this next battle, Earth can put me on trial for treason. But quite frankly, I don't think I'm going to have to worry about that."

Thinking about it, Tatiana looked across the room at a picture mounted on the wall opposite. It was an old World War II fighter, a P-51 according to the label. Two women were standing beside it, wearing flight suits, arms around each other's shoulders. With some shock, Tatiana realized it was Rita and Bonnie.

*I guess the stories about them are true*, Tatiana thought.

"...so it's time. We can't stand here alone. I'm relocating the fleet to Dekanna," Bonnie said.

Tatiana returned her attention to the conversation. "Oh. Well, I know you must do it. But...what about Deriko? What do you want us to do here after you leave?"

"I'm going to leave two cruisers behind to protect your orbitals. I don't think Zukra will attack you. He'll be focused on chasing us to Dekanna. I think he'll ignore you for now. He'll assume he's going to defeat us at Dekanna, and then have all the time in the world to come back here and dig you guys out."

"And he may be right. What if he does win at Dekanna?"

"Then I suggest you pack all the people you can into the supply ships and get the hell out of here."

"Back to Earth?"

Bonnie shook her head. "No, I wouldn't recommend it. If we lose at Dekanna, that's the last place you want to go. Zukra will wipe Earth clean. He won't leave anyone alive.

"I would suggest you head out into the galaxy, away from the Arm. Start a new colony someplace, as far away from here as you can get. Because there won't be any Humans left in the Arm. It'll be up to you to carry on the species."

### Sol System - Planet Earth
### Battlecruiser *Victory*

"Did you hear?" asked Shigeto. "The EDF fleet is leaving for Dekanna tomorrow."

Captain Joshua Westerly of the battlecruiser UNSF *Victory* stared across his desk at Captain Dewa Shigeto.

"I heard," he said, shaking his head. "The war gets farther away from us every day."

Shigeto closed his eyes, his face making a frown of anger. Then he opened his eyes again and shook his head.

"Elliott is an idiot," he said.

Westerly grimaced. "You know I don't like talking about my superiors behind their back."

Shigeto leaned forward. "Joshua. Think this through. This battlecruiser was built for the people of Earth. Not for Ken Elliott. And the future of Earth depends on what happens at Dekanna - not here in orbit. Admiral Bonnie Page is leaving for Dekanna. It will be a battle that will decide the fate of our species. The future of every man, woman and child on Earth is a pair of dice bouncing on the tablecloth. Don't you think your obligation is to the people of Earth?"

Shigeto leaned back into his chair.

"Or is it to Ken Elliott, who sits in his office at the top of the UN building kissing his Chinese minder's ass while Rome burns..."

Now it was Westerly's turn to close his eyes and frown. He heaved a large sigh.

"Dewa, you have a way of putting me in an impossible situation."

"There's nothing impossible about it. Call the captains of the two cruisers. Tell them to prepare for flight. They'll support you, Joshua. In fact, they'll be thrilled. Then we tell Ken Elliott to stick it up his ass and head for Dekanna."

Westerly shuddered in his turmoil. "That's mutiny, Dewa. That's plain and outright mutiny."

Shigeto nodded. "You could call it that. Or you could call it saving Earth."

"Besides - I'm not sure we could even get there in time. Intelligence is reporting the Nidarians will be leaving for Dekanna any day now. Zukra is forming up his fleet. He won't be far behind the EDF Fleet."

Shigeto gave a nod. "Then we should probably get our ass in gear, don't you think?"

Westerly closed his eyes again. Another shudder went through his body. Shigeto saw an honest man wrestling with his conscience - and it was a fierce battle going on inside him. Westerly didn't move for a full minute. Then he suddenly opened his eyes and spoke to the ship's AI.

"*Victory*, set condition Yellow. Recall all personnel. Prepare to depart for Dekanna in four hours. Inform cruisers *Shannon* and *Vengeance* they can join our little expedition or stay here and kiss Elliott's ass."

Shigeto grinned at Westerly.

"Welcome to the real world, Captain."

Westerly stood and reached out a hand to Shigeto, who stood as well. They shook hands, smiling.

"I hope you brought your seabag, Dewa. We don't have time for you to go back down and get your things."

"Oh, I brought it, Joshua. I was fairly sure I'd need it."

At that moment, they were interrupted by a message from the ship AI.

<Message from cruiser *Vengeance*, Captain. Quote: "About time." - unquote>

Captain Dewa Shigeto winked at Captain Joshua Westerly. "Told ya," he said, determined to have the last word.

## Singheko System
## Singheko Naval Headquarters

In the holo, Zukra and his aide Damra watched as the Human flagship *Merkkessa* lifted out of orbit at Deriko, quickly gaining speed as she headed out for the mass limit. She was tended by a screen of four destroyers. Behind her, ship after ship followed, forming up into a long extended elliptical mass of warships, with interlocking fields of fire in case of attack.

At the end of the Human fleet, allied detachments of Taegu and Bagrami took the place of honor as the rear guard, ensuring the Singheko couldn't come in behind with a surprise attack as they departed the system.

Zukra glared at Damra, who had presented the hologram to him showing the EDF fleet leaving the system.

"You're sure it's Dekanna?" he asked.

"Yes, m'lord," answered Damra. "No doubt about it. A direct course for Dekanna."

Zukra cursed. "I didn't think those animals were that smart," he fumed. "I assume they've worked the numbers correctly?"

"Aye, m'lord. If we launch a fleet to Earth, they could be here and attack Ridendo before we could get back."

"And they could also intercept us at Earth if we tried that."

"Yes, m'lord. They could go directly to Earth and arrive shortly after we do. But of course Ridendo would still be uncovered. So they could send a small detachment to bombard Ridendo and the rest of their Fleet could meet us at Earth. We might win the battle at Earth, but we wouldn't have much of a planet to come back to."

"And if we split our fleet, to leave a protective detachment here at Ridendo and took the rest to attack Earth?"

"They'd have the option to bring their full fleet to attack either one of our detachments. If they brought the full fleet to Earth, they'd most likely wipe us out there. And if they attacked Ridendo, then again, we'd have nothing left to come back to."

Zukra stared out the window at the distant spaceport covered in shuttles and small craft and cursed again. Finally he turned back to Damra.

"Alright, Damra. Prepare the fleet to invade Dekanna. We'll go wipe out that nest of animals first. Then we can destroy Earth without interference."

"Aye, m'lord," Damra answered.

"When will we be ready?"

"Another two weeks, m'lord. We can launch in two more weeks. Then two weeks to Dekanna. We can hit them in a month."

Zukra nodded his agreement.

"Just make sure this time we wipe them out. No more excuses!"

# CHAPTER SIXTEEN

**Singheko System - Planet Ridendo**
**City of Mosalia**

"Right there," said Helen, pointing to the holographic diagram.

Jim stared. It was a holo of the Singheko Empire's main orbital space dock - a wheel-like structure spanning more than four kilometers, in geosynchronous orbit high above the capital city of Mosalia. Highlighted in the holo was a medical bay, deep in the center of the huge facility.

"He's keeping her there?" Jim wondered.

"Yes. When he discovered she was dying, he moved her from his palace back to the orbital station. We think because he's trying to keep the masses from knowing she's dead. He continues to tell the mass media she's alive and being tortured and giving up vast amounts of intelligence to him."

"What an asshole," Jim muttered.

"Exactly. Anyway, according to my sources, Rita's body is in this room right here…"

Helen pointed to a location deep inside the medical space of the space dock.

Jim spoke bitterly. "So he keeps her body there as if she is still alive, to fool the masses."

"Look like it," agreed Helen.

"No way you can get in there, Jim," Ollie spoke. "That orbital station is plenty secure. Zukra may be stupid, but his Intelligence Chief Orma is not. And the security of that station is Orma's responsibility."

"Then we need a serious distraction," said Jim.

Helen looked at Ollie. A smile ghosted across her face.

"Well, aren't you lucky. We just happen to have one."

Out of the corner of his eye, Jim saw Ollie grimace as if in pain. "What do you mean?" he asked Helen.

"How about I blow up their fusion plant while you sneak into medical - is that enough of a diversion?" Helen said gleefully.

Jim looked at Ollie, who still had a look of pain on his face.

"Did you sign off on this?" he wondered.

Ollie rolled his eyes. "Yes. Not too happy about it, though."

"I shouldn't wonder," Jim said. "Not much chance of success."

Helen showed anger. "More chance of success than you getting into that medical facility and out again with Rita's body!"

Ollie heaved a huge sigh. Jim looked at him, then back at the holo.

"OK. How would we get in?" he asked Helen.

"We'll be in a shipping container. A shuttle will deliver us to the cargo bay on their regular evening supply run. Containers that arrive after 1800 hours are left in the cargo bay overnight and unloaded the next morning. So this container will be left in the cargo bay, unopened. After midnight, two of our Resistance contacts will come in and let us out of the container. We'll hide in food carts. Our Resistance contacts will push the food carts to our kickoff points. You'll make your way to the medical facility, while I go to the central reactor. I'll put charges on the reactor, then return to the cargo bay and wait for you. When the reactor blows, you've got your distraction. You grab Rita's body and hustle back to the cargo bay to meet me. We make our escape. Piece of cake!"

Jim chuckled. "And just how do we 'make our escape'?"

Helen smiled. "They always have several small shuttles in the cargo bay overnight. We'll take one and head for Deriko."

Jim shook his head.

"We won't even make it onto the spacedock. They'll scan every container. It's like trying to break into the White House back on Earth. Or Windsor Castle. Can't be done."

"Good. You DO understand," Ollie interjected.

Helen winked at Jim. "Double-walled container. Outside the inner container will be foodstuffs. It'll show a normal scan on their equipment. We'll be in an inner container. The scan won't be able to see past the outer layers - it'll look like more cases of food to the scanner."

"How about oxygen?"

"We'll have a twelve-hour supply. The shuttle goes up at 1800 hours. That gives us until 0600 to get there and wait until our contacts come and let us out. And we have a failsafe - a ventilation tube we can crack open if it takes longer than that."

"What if they leave us in an unpressurized area?"

Helen shrugged. "The container will be clearly marked to maintain pressurization. But if that does happen, we'll have pressure suits with us. We can open the inner hatch if we have to and fight our way through the food cartons to the outside."

Jim looked again at Ollie, then back at Helen. "Too risky, Helen. Too many things that can go wrong."

Helen looked serious for a minute. "Don't you think I know that, Commander? But the reward is worth the risk. Think about it...blowing up their main spacedock. Not to mention taking Rita's body away from them so it can't be used for propaganda purposes. Don't you think that's worth a bit of risk?"

Jim did think about it. He had no direct say in this decision; Bonnie had made it clear to him that Ollie was commander on the surface.

But Helen was asking for his opinion, and he could see that Ollie was listening too. So his opinion would carry some weight.

Looking at Helen, but knowing that Ollie was listening intently, he gave a grudging nod. "It's a huge risk. But as you say - the potential benefit is also huge. I can't tell you what to do. But if it were me - I'd probably go for it."

Helen beamed. "Great!" She looked at Ollie to see his reaction. Ollie rolled his eyes, shrugged his shoulders, and heaved a sigh.

"Go for it," Ollie said. "After you two kill yourselves, don't come crying to me."

**Sol System - Earth**
**United Nations Building - Beijing, China**

UNSF Admiral Ken Elliott thought he was having a heart attack. He had never been this angry in his life.

"Mutiny! It's outright, flagrant mutiny!" he yelled.

On the other end of the satellite phone, Ingrid Stoltenberg, Secretary-General of the UN, winced at the volume.

"Elliott, lower your voice," she said with some bite. "Remember who you're talking to…"

The implied threat in her voice was clear - and ominous. Elliott came to his senses and backed down a bit.

"But Secretary-General…Westerly simply left! He just… left! Without permission! No warning! The *Victory* and both cruisers are on their way to Dekanna!"

"Calling me to tell me things I already know is a waste of both our time, Elliott. What do you want me to do about it?"

"Make them come back! Order them in the name of the UN to return those ships!"

"I believe you have already issued that order, Elliott. And what was the response?"

"Um…the order was ignored, sir."

"I believe the exact response was, 'You can have these ships anytime you wish. All you have to do is come to Dekanna and get them'. Was that about it, Admiral?"

"Um…yes, Secretary-General. That was about the gist of it."

"Then I suggest you do exactly that, Admiral. Your fleet has left for the battlefield. I suggest you get in the first available corvette and go join them."

"But…sir…they're going to battle! They're going to fight the Singheko!"

"Exactly, Admiral Elliott. And what better place for an Admiral to be? I'll expect you to be aboard a corvette and on your way before morning. Clear?"

"Uh…? Are you serious?"

"Let me put it this way, Admiral. If you are still on Earth tomorrow, you are fired. Is that clear enough?"

Ingrid slammed the phone down, leaned back in her chair and laughed out loud.

## Singheko System - Planet Ridendo
## City of Mosalia

Captain Orma zu Dalty was drunk. It was not something he normally did; Orma was certainly no prude; but neither was he a libertine. Drinking to excess was something he rarely did. But today…

Today Zukra had sacrificed another dozen political prisoners in the arena. It had been a bloody mess. The masses had gone wild, screaming for more, more, more.

And of course, Orma was forced to attend. Zukra insisted. After all, Orma was Chief of Intelligence. He must put in an appearance.

In recent months, Orma had become quite a good student of the Humans. He felt it was good to know your enemy. Thus, he had read extensively about their political systems, their current events - and their history.

"Nothing to excess," he muttered. "Their ancient Greeks knew what they were talking about."

*Nothing to excess. The philosophy I have followed all my life. But what I saw today was excessive.*

Orma stumbled. He was walking from his pantry, where he had retrieved another bottle of the strong *zuf* he had been sampling. He made it back to his comfortable armchair in front of the fireplace in his living room and sat heavily.

He poured another drink of the gin-like alcohol and thought about his state of life.

*Nothing to excess. Zukra would know nothing about that. He follows the opposite philosophy - everything to excess. And that philosophy is ruining our Navy. Ruining our culture. Ruining our morality.*

Sipping slowly, Orma zu Dalty considered his options.

*Zukra's cult of hero-worshipers fawn around him like he is a god. But their actions tear down our morality. What was that culture I read about in the Human history?*

*Bushido. That was it. We were like that five thousand years ago. Before the Zukras of the world took over. We were a pure race then. Pure in honor, pure in morality. Yes, in those ancient times, we killed - but only in war, and only when attacked. We walked in honor. We never killed merely for the sake of killing.*

*But now we are...what? What have we become? Zukra kills with great glee. Anyone who gets in his way just...disappears.*

*We've become...butchers.*

Orma had gone along with Zukra all these many months. He had stuck with him when he attacked the Humans. Reluctantly, he had stuck with him when he killed Admiral Ligar and dozens of others, to take over the Navy and execute a coup against the government. He had stuck with him through the Battle of Deriko and beyond.

But now...

Now Zukra was just a killing machine. He sent a hundred or more prisoners to the arena every weekend. The maintenance workers at the arena could hardly clear the blood from one game before the next one started.

*I must make a decision. Do I have any honor left at all?*

**Sol System - Planet Earth**
**Corvette *Armidale***

"Dekanna? Admiral, we haven't completed shakedown yet! We just came out of spacedock three days ago!"

Captain Duncan Aveline Stewart of the corvette UNSF *Armidale* was in shock. Ten minutes ago, Fleet Admiral Ken Elliott had suddenly - and very unexpectedly - arrived at his docking port. Now Elliott stood in front of Stewart on his tiny bridge talking nonsense.

"Captain, you will launch for Dekanna immediately. That is an order. Get your crew in gear and get this corvette moving!"

"But sir...we have no missiles loaded onboard yet! We haven't tested the tDrive! We may not have enough food and water onboard to even make it to Dekanna!"

Elliott leaned forward and growled at Stewart. "Then you've got two hours to get enough food and water on board and get this tub moving. Got it?"

Stewart stared at the Admiral in dismay. "Yes, sir. Two hours. Got it."

"Show me to a cabin."

"Aye, sir. Follow me."

Stewart led the way down the short corridor from the bridge to his cabin. Opening the hatch, he showed Elliott through.

"My cabin, sir. I'll have the quartermaster remove my things as quickly as possible."

Elliott looked around the tiny cabin and sniffed. "My God. You live in this place?"

"Yes, sir."

Elliott turned to him. "Well, I guess I'll have to make do. Have my luggage brought in from the shuttle."

"Aye, aye, sir."

Stewart closed the hatch behind him and trotted back to the bridge where his astounded crew sat in shock. They stared at him in complete bafflement.

"COB!" Stewart yelled at Chief Turner, his Chief of the Boat. "Take an inventory of consumables onboard. Ensure we have enough to make Dekanna. Don't forget to include one extra body - the Admiral is going with us. Get an immediate emergency order from Spacedock for enough to get us there.

Plus a ten-day buffer for emergencies. Any questions?"

"No, sir. Got it. Enough consumables to make Dekanna plus a ten-day buffer."

"And Chief?"

"Yes, sir?"

"We've only got two hours. But see if you can get at least one loadout of missiles stuffed into the cargo bay before we leave. We can assemble and hand-carry them to the magazine on the way. I hate like hell to enter the Dekanna system naked as a baby joey..."

Chief Turner grinned. "Aye, aye, sir! One loadout of missiles, coming up!"

## Singheko System - Planet Ridendo
## City of Mosalia

"You realize this is impossible, Commander," Ollie said to Jim in one last plea for sanity.

"Of course," Jim smiled at him from inside the shipping container. "No chance whatsoever."

Ollie grunted. "OK. Just checking."

And with that, Ollie shut the inner door of the shipping container. Inside, it got very dark. Helen flicked on a light. From outside, noise and bumps came as Ollie's Resistance team repacked the outside container with food cartons.

Inside the secret compartment, it was a tight fit. They had experimented with different positions before the hatch was sealed up. None of them were comfortable. They had finally settled on having Jim sitting with his back against the wall of the container, legs spread wide. Helen sat between his legs, spooned up against him but facing away. There was barely enough space between them to slide in a hand. Helen was smashed into him like a commuter on a crowded subway train.

Jim heard the sound of a forklift. The container gave a lurch. They were being loaded onto a truck.

"You never told me this was going to be so tight," Jim said.

"You never told me you forgot to shower this morning," said Helen.

"I did shower this morning," Jim shot back.

Helen grunted. She shifted position.

"Oh, crap," said Jim. "Don't do that."

"What?"

"Can you go back to where you were before?"

"Why?"

"Because if you stay there, I'm going to be a eunuch in a few minutes."

"Oh. Sorry. Got it."

Jim rolled his eyes.

*This is going to be one helluva long trip.*

He felt the truck start moving. They were on their way. The smell of diesel fumes came to his nose.

*That's funny. You travel 550 light years to an alien world full of creatures that look like walking, talking lions and they drive diesels.*

The truck bumped and swayed. Soon the combination of the lurching truck and the diesel fumes made him nauseous. He tried to fight it off but couldn't. He was about to warn Helen when she beat him to it, throwing up all over his pants leg.

He was about five seconds behind her. Together they retched until neither had anything left to throw up.

The romance had definitely gone out of their togetherness.

## Singheko System - Planet Ridendo
## Naval Spacedock

Hours later, with a final thump, the shipping container came to rest.

Inside, Jim and Helen were bruised and battered, but intact. The trip up to the spacedock had been anything but smooth. One crash after another had smashed them from one side to the other of the hidden inner compartment.

But now at last things were quiet. There was no more

movement, no more noise. Jim sent a thought command to his embedded AI, Angel.

*Angel - how much longer?*

*<You must wait another two hours before leaving the container>*

Jim sighed silently. He tried to change position again, but Helen had gone to sleep, and he couldn't manage it. What had been somewhat erotic six hours ago - having a beautiful woman smashed into his lap - was now more like having a sack of cement pinning him in position. The smell of their vomit permeated the container. He was miserable.

He tried to distract himself by going over his memorized layout of the path he had to take to get to Rita's body. There was no easy way in. Every wall, every corner, every aspect of the orbital station was monitored by cameras, motion detectors, and infrared. There was no chance of getting to the medical facility through normal means.

So he would have to go via abnormal means. There was one place they might have left a weakness. It was a long shot; but the only chance he had. In the holo diagrams, just outside the cargo bay was a machine room. And in that machine room was a hatch in the floor.

It was his only chance to get to Rita.

\*\*\*

Two hours later, they heard the noise of someone entering the area. There was a snap, and then the sound of the outer hatch of the cargo container opening.

Jim had been reviewing the route he would take to the medical facility. Now he flicked off his tablet and tensed. He heard Helen move slightly, so he knew she was awake.

From outside came the sound of someone removing the outer layer of food cartons. Jim pulled his pistol out and checked it for charge. After some thought, he put it back into his shoulder holster.

*If it's our guys, I won't need it. And if it's the bad guys, it'll be useless.*

Then there were another couple of snaps. The inner hatch to their hidden space cracked open. It was directly in front of Helen, and it was hard to see around her head. Jim saw a sliver of light. Slowly, the hatch opened fully. Leaning around Helen to peer forward, he saw a male Singheko kneeling in the container, and behind him a female.

The Singheko kneeling closest to them spoke in Nidarian.

"Out quickly. Into the carts."

Helen unlimbered and crawled out of the inner compartment, groaning as she went. Jim couldn't quite figure out why she was groaning until he also tried to move. It was then he realized that he had been frozen in one position for so long, his muscles and joints didn't work right. It hurt to move.

Suppressing his groans, Jim managed to crawl out of the container. Just outside, the two Singheko had cleared some space in the mess of food cartons. There were two large food carts waiting. Each cart had an open door under it. Only a Human could fit into the small space under each cart; it would be impossible for a Singheko. Jim realized this was the essence of the plan to move them farther into the station - a normal Singheko might not think to look into a space too small for one of his own kind.

*I hope.*

Jim moved to the far food cart and reached down to place his backpack into the narrow space beneath it. Suddenly he heard Helen behind him.

"Jim."

Turning, he was met by a flurry of arms enveloping him, and lips pressing onto his. Before he could protest, Helen kissed him, long and hard. Then she pulled away and winked at him in the dim light.

"Good luck, sailor," she said.

Jim was flabbergasted. All he could do was nod, once. Helen smiled, turned, and began stuffing herself into the space beneath her food cart.

Jim turned back to his own cart and began the difficult task of folding his body up into something no larger than a small coffin.

# CHAPTER SEVENTEEN

**Singheko System - Planet Ridendo**
**Naval Spacedock**

The Singheko pushing the food cart took Jim outside the cargo bay, down the hall a dozen meters, and then through a door into a small room. He tapped the side of the cart, and then opened the door beneath it. Jim carefully unfolded himself from the cramped space and fell out on the floor. He looked up at the Singheko towering over him and smiled. The Singheko ignored him.

With a sigh, Jim reached into the cart and pulled out his pack, closing the door in the bottom of the cart. His Singheko minder turned and wheeled the cart back to the door of the room. He opened the door, pushed the cart through, and left.

"Thank you too," Jim mumbled under his breath. Then he looked around the room.

It was a small maintenance room. In the floor in front of Jim was a hatch cover, looking remarkably like a manhole cover. Because in fact, that's what it was. It was a maintenance hatch into the space dock's sewer system. Even with the cover in place, the stench was noticeable. Jim shuddered to think what it would be like once he was inside.

If he could get inside. The cover was not large. It was iffy - his shoulders might not fit through it.

But there was only one way to find out. Pulling up the hatch cover and laying it aside, he looked at the hole. In the dim light of the overheads, there wasn't much to see. But he thought he might be able to fit through it.

Jim laid his pack to one side, where he could reach it once he was inside the sewer pipe. He slid his feet into the hole. It wasn't deep - no more than two feet. Turning his feet to move along the length of the pipe, he slid farther into the hole, trying to ignore the smell and the thought of what he was touching in the sewer. Working his way farther down, he reached the point where he was forced to extend his arms above his head if he chose to go any farther.

It was a tight fit. Jim realized that if he got stuck with his arms over his head, he would never get out. The guards would find him still stuck in that position when the day shift came on. His life expectancy after that would be short.

He repositioned, managed to get his right arm and shoulder down into the hole. He put his left arm up, over his head, and tried to slide down into the pipe, moving his legs farther into the pipe as he did so.

And then he was stuck. The manhole was too small.

But at least he was able to reverse and get his left arm and shoulder out of the hole again. Rethinking, he changed his tactics. He twisted his body, trying to minimize the overall width of his shoulders. Once more he slid down into the hole. The edges of the manhole bit into his shoulders, and he was wedged into the hole. But he felt that this time, it wasn't as tight. Twisting back and forth, he felt a little movement downward. The pain was intense as the edge of the hatch opening cut into his shoulders - but he felt some more movement.

Then, with a "plop", he was through. He was lying on his back in the narrow sewer pipe. The stench was intense. His eyes watered. There was only a couple of inches of space on either side of his shoulders. He wasn't sure he could even crawl forward in such a narrow space.

But he had to try. He rolled over in the pipe until he was lying on his stomach. Reaching up, he pulled his pack into the hole and put it in front of him. He took a headlamp out of the pack and mounted it on his forehead. Then he reached for the hatch cover and pulled it back over the hole, centering it and letting it drop quietly into place. Flicking on the headlamp, he looked ahead of him.

The pipe appeared to go straight for several dozen meters. Beyond that, he could see nothing.

Pushing the pack in front of him, he inched his way forward, slowly, knowing he had a long way to go.

\*\*\*

On the other side of the station, Helen and her minder had reached their destination as well. Now she felt a sway and then a thump as the Singheko pushing the food cart stopped. Light suddenly bloomed bright as her minder cracked open the door beneath the cart. Helen unfolded herself from the space and stood.

As expected, she was in a small office. It was dark. Her companion stood back, waiting for her to get her bearings.

Helen reached down and pulled her pack from the bottom of the cart.

"Showtime," she said in Nidarian. The female Singheko nodded as Helen moved to the door of the room, cracked it open, and peeked out.

In front of her she could see a large, dimly lit room. She knew this was the office space outside the fusion reactor compartment. There was now only one additional room between her and the actual reactor room - the control room. Turning back to the Singheko behind her, she held out her hand. The Singheko placed a security badge in her palm. Glancing at it, she was amused to see a picture of a female Singheko - tawny hair, upright ears, and abbreviated muzzle.

"Doesn't really capture my essence," she quipped.

The Singheko looked puzzled. Helen shrugged and turned back to the door. Peeking outside, she ensured the coast was clear. Turning one last time to the Singheko minder, she bade her goodbye.

"Thank you for everything. I hope you make it," she said.

Helen knew the Singheko female would attempt to take the

now-empty cart back to the cargo bay. There she would hide with the other minder until later. They would attempt to flee on the first shuttle leaving for the surface.

But Helen also knew - as the Singheko did - that it was unlikely she would succeed. It was far more likely she would be dead by noon.

The Singheko pushed the cart out the opposite door, back into the hallway, and started on her trip back to the cargo bay. Helen settled in. She was due to wait for an hour. That would give time for her Singheko minder to get fully clear, and for Jim to get into position.

**Stalingrad System**
**Packet Boat *Donkey***

Rachel and Paco were escorted back to their packet boat. Tika boarded the little ship with them. Rachel and Paco watched as Tika opened the hatch to one of the tiny cabins, entered, lay down on the bunk, and closed her eyes. Then they heard her voice - but this time coming from the boat's AI. Tika had transferred her consciousness back to *Donkey*.

<Well, I can't say I'm happy to be back in this cramped and limited environment, but I guess there's no help for it. Ready to depart>

Rachel gently shut the door to the cabin. Tika's android body would stay inert on the trip to Dekanna. Rachel looked at Paco.

"Don't get any ideas about going in there, Lieutenant."

"What? Me?" exclaimed Paco. "What do you think I am?"

"A male," said Rachel. "One that hasn't been with a female in a long time."

"She's an android!" protested Paco.

"And that would stop you?" asked Rachel.

Grumbling, Paco turned and headed for the cockpit. "Can you believe this, Tika?" he asked the empty air.

<I don't see the problem, Rachel. Why must Paco avoid my inert body?>

Rachel shook her head and heaved a sigh. "I don't know. It just makes me uncomfortable to think about him touching your body while your consciousness is not in it."

&lt;But is it not my body? Should that decision not be mine?&gt;

"It's hard to explain, Tika. But no. I'm the commander, and I don't want it. So that's the way it must be."

&lt;Very well. As you wish&gt;

Rachel entered the cockpit to find Paco buckling up, still grumbling. She sat in the copilot seat. They completed their pre-departure checklist and Paco looked over at her.

"Ready, mum?" he said, his irritation evident.

"Ready."

"OK, Tika. Take us out."

With a slight thump, *Donkey* uncoupled from the Dyson structure. The boat turned, taking a course for the outer system. It began to move, slowly at first, then with increasing acceleration as it cleared the area of the massive structure. In ten minutes, they were accelerating through 300g. But still it continued. They passed through 310g, and the accel continued to build, with no apparent effects on their bodies. The accel was fully compensated inside the ship.

"What?" asked Rachel in dismay. "Tika, what is happening?"

&lt;Oh. I forgot to inform you. We have made some slight improvements to *Donkey*'s engines and compensator&gt;

Paco's face went pale as they passed 325g and the accel still continued to rise.

"You'll tear us apart, Tika!" he yelled. "The boat isn't stressed for this kind of accel!"

&lt;It is now&gt; replied Tika. &lt;*Donkey* is now stressed for 510g. But we'll only go to 500 to leave the system. No worries&gt;

Rachel heard Paco speaking quietly under his breath again. It was a prayer that was becoming more familiar to Rachel these days.

*Ave Maria.*

"Tika, what is our ETA to Dekanna?"

&lt;Eighteen days, three hours, seventeen minutes&gt;

"Eighteen days? How the hell is that possible? It's 853 lights to Dekanna!"

<We took the liberty of updating the t-drive also, Rachel. It was an older design. There were many inefficiencies in it. It is now working optimally>

Rachel leaned back in her seat and shook her head.

"Tika, I think there's a lot our two species can teach each other. If we live long enough."

## Singheko System - Planet Ridendo
## Naval Spacedock

It took Jim most of an hour to traverse the sewer pipe to his first destination. He had been concerned there would be cameras or motion detectors in the pipe; but he had not found any so far.

After some thought, he realized it would be impossible for an adult Singheko to fit into the sewer pipe; perhaps for that reason they had not thought to put detectors in it.

Whatever the reason for the omission, he was now definitely near the medical facility. He estimated he had crawled about three hundred meters. By his estimation, in another few meters, he would be under another maintenance room just inside medical. And in the diagrams their AI had found, there should be a maintenance hatch...just...

There. The final maintenance hatch. His way out.

*Angel. Time?*

<0114 hours>

He was on schedule. Carefully, slowly, he pushed the hatch cover from below, lifted it a bit, and peered out.

He hadn't been sure if the diagrams found by their AI had been accurate. But they appeared to be. There was the maintenance room. It was filled with dirty mops, buckets, tool chests and trash cans.

Slowly, moving a bit at a time, he let the hatch cover fall back into place, turned, and lifted the other side. There was more of the same. He slowly moved the hatch cover, circling his gaze around until he had scanned a full circle.

The room was empty, just a small maintenance room filled with the detritus of daily life on a space station.

Jim slowly and carefully pushed the hatch cover aside, until the hole was clear for his exit. Then he pushed his pack out, pushing it to one side out of the way. Reversing the method that had got him into the pipe in the first place, he pushed his left arm and shoulder out, followed by his head. He rotated his body and tried to bring his right arm and shoulder out. He became wedged again; but this time he had the knowledge that it should work. Sure enough, as he worked his shoulder, twisting and turning, it slid through and his shoulders were out.

He paused, sweating, stinking, looking around in every direction. Nothing moved. He saw no threats, and no alarms were sounding. Of course, that meant nothing. He could be pinpointed on a screen somewhere, with alarms sounding in the security room, guards collecting their weapons to come swarming out to meet him.

He quickly pulled the rest of his body out and put the manhole cover back in place. Stripping off his stinking clothes, he took a clean cloth from his bag, took water from the utility sink in the corner of the room, and wiped the thin layer of sewage off his body. Taking a small vial of artificial scent from his pack, he wiped it over his body. Then, pulling fresh clothes out of his bag, he re-dressed.

*At least now they won't smell me coming from a hundred meters.*

<No; only ten meters> said Angel.

*Hush.*

*How much longer?*

<Twenty-one minutes if Helen is on schedule>

Jim moved to the door leading into the medical facility.

Now came the moment of truth.

*If the stars were with him…*

He turned the knob. The door wasn't locked. He pushed outward on the door. It opened with a squeak. He froze, waiting. Nothing happened.

Carefully, moving inch by inch, he opened it. A long hallway loomed, leading down the center of the medical bay.

A little voice in his head started speaking again. It was a voice he had heard frequently since he launched on this mission.

*This is stupid*, the little voice said. *All this just for her body? Why?*

*Because I loved her*, he answered.

***

Helen had waited the agreed one hour. Now she carefully cracked open the door to the next room. This was an anteroom. The next door led directly to the control room for the fusion reactor.

And the control room was manned day and night. If her information was correct, there would be two to three Singheko inside. She would have only seconds to neutralize them before they could hit the alarm.

Stepping into the anteroom, she double-checked her pulse pistol. It was armed. The safety was off. She was as ready as she would ever be. She waved the security card at the reader beside the door. The door clicked. She pushed through rapidly and scanned the room.

There were three Singheko inside. One of them was on the far side of the room, noting something in her tablet. She had not heard Helen come in.

But the other two were closer and heard the door open. They both turned to stare at the apparition. Their minds couldn't quite comprehend what they were seeing. They knew what a Human was - they had seen vids of them on the news. But to see one in the flesh...with a pistol in her hand...

That was their last thought. Helen punched two holes neatly into each one, double-tapping them perfectly. The pistol was silenced - it made only a loud thump. The control room was well isolated from the rest of the station. No one outside this room would hear.

The last Singheko - a female - spun at the sound, disbelief in her eyes. Helen put two shots into her chest, and she crumpled to the floor, her tablet falling beside her.

Turning to the cameras mounted in the corners of the room, Helen methodically shot each one, leaving them melted, crumpled masses of plastic and metal. She moved quickly to the last door she would have to pass - the door directly to the fusion reactor. She waved the security card at the reader on the door.

It didn't work.

She waved it again.

It still didn't work. The door buzzed, but the light turned red and the door remained immovable.

Behind her, she heard the control room door open. Spinning around, she saw a squad of Singheko pour into the room, rifles raised.

She got off three shots before they killed her.

Behind the squad, as they lowered their rifles, a Singheko commander entered. Ignoring the smoke curling from the rifle barrels, he walked over to the body of the Human female and poked it with his foot, making sure she was dead. He smiled.

*The information we got from Orma was spot-on. So much for the Humans and their grand plans!*

***

Jim was now outside the room that - according to Helen's Resistance sources - contained Rita's body.

Jim tried the knob. It was not locked.

Keeping his pistol raised in front of him, he went through the door, slowly, closing it behind him.

He saw an outer office of some kind. There was a nurse's station on his left, extending the length of the wall, with many instruments on it. Then a door, directly in front of him. To the right of the door was a desk. Over the desk was a large window. Through the window he could see a hospital bed.

On the hospital bed he could see Rita. She appeared to be intubated and on a ventilator. Other tubes led from drips overhead into her arms.

*What the hell? Angel, what is this? Is she dead? Or is she alive?*
<I do not know>

Jim, hardly daring to believe, moved to the window, and peered through. There was no doubt about it - it was Rita.

Moving to the door, Jim entered the room where she lay and stopped, staring at the figure on the bed. Her chest rose and fell as the ventilator pushed air into her lungs with a rhythmic monotony. Struck dumb, he didn't know what to do next.

*I had expected a body. Not...not to find her like this. What went wrong? The poison was supposed to kill her within six hours.*

Jim moved closer to the bed and stared down at her. Her face was partially covered by the ventilator mask and the intubation tube. But it was Rita. There was no doubt.

*How can I get her out of here? I can't remove her from the ventilator. But...*

The thought that came across him then was unthinkable.

*...but I can't leave her here for Zukra.*

# CHAPTER EIGHTEEN

**Singheko System - Planet Ridendo**
**Naval Spacedock**

Standing over Rita's bed, Jim was at a loss. He didn't know anything about her condition. He assumed that to remove her now from the medical equipment would kill her; otherwise it would not be there. And even if he could remove her from the maze of tubes and pipes that went in and out of her body - how could he get her to the shuttle bay? He had planned to be taking a dead body, dragging it back down the sewer pipe in a body bag. A wild and crazy scheme that couldn't possibly work now.

Yet he couldn't leave her for Zukra - she knew too much.

*I can't kill her. I can't. I can't kill the woman I love.*

His AI disagreed. <You must. We cannot leave her here alive>

Jim sank into a chair by the side of the bed, staring at Rita.

*I can't do it.*

<You have no choice, Jim. It's her or the Earth>

His pistol hanging limply in his hands over his knee, Jim closed his eyes.

*I can't.*

Suddenly a sound. Jim jumped, stood, turned, raised the pistol. A door in the back of the room had opened; a figure stood there in white. Jim started squeezing the trigger of the silenced pistol.

Something caught his attention.

He held his fire.

The figure was small, much smaller than a Singheko. In the

dim light, Jim saw dark black hair. A color he had never seen on a Singheko. The figure stood, silent, staring at him, wide-eyed.

A Human. A woman. She spoke.

"Who are you?" she asked.

Jim looked at her for a second, then responded.

"I'm her husband. Who are you?"

The woman took a step forward to see him more clearly in the dim light.

"I'm her doctor."

Slowly, Jim lowered the pistol, letting it hang at the end of his arm. They stared at each other silently for a long moment. Finally, Jim spoke again.

"How is she alive?"

The woman took another step forward to the bed, stopping beside it and staring down at Rita. She laid down her tablet, adjusted the placement of the ventilator tube, then looked across the bed at Jim.

"It was a good plan. The poison should have killed her outright. But somehow Zukra managed to get her stabilized. I'm not sure how; but they had some pretty good medics, for Singheko."

Jim shook his head. "No way. Stephanie gave her enough poison to kill a horse."

The woman shrugged. "Things can go wrong. Who knows? She was certainly near death when she arrived. I'd call it a miracle that she survived long enough for them to get her on a respirator. And they have some kind of machine to clean the blood, remove the nerve agents. Something I'm not familiar with, but apparently it worked."

Now Jim looked at the doctor more closely. She was about five feet six inches tall, stoutly built, with short black hair - almost a military cut. He didn't recognize her.

"Who are you?" he asked.

"Jill Bartlett," she replied. "I was on the third slave ship, the one that left from San Francisco."

"How on earth did you get here?" Jim asked.

"They pulled a bunch of us out of the slave complex on Deriko just as we landed. We all had medical training of some kind. They shipped us here and forced us to set up a medical facility for humans."

"There are other humans here?"

"Yes. Forty total, I think. Two doctors, three nurses. Thirty-five prisoners."

"Where did they get the prisoners?"

"Captured from the rebel force on Deriko, or from damaged or destroyed ships during the battles. They torture them for information. Or sometimes just for the hell of it."

Jim was overwhelmed and confused. He sat down in the chair again, trying to think.

"You have to get her out of here," said Jill. "And soon."

"What?" asked Jim.

"She's going to come out of her coma soon. Any day now. Maybe tonight. Then they'll be able to extract information from her in short order. You've got to get her out of here."

"You mean she's going to live?"

"For a while," said Jill. "I don't think she'll make it for long. There's too much damage to her internal organs. But she'll live long enough for them to get what they want. You have to get her out of here."

"But…if we unplug her…won't she die?"

Jill smiled somewhat sadly. "No. She's been breathing on her own for several days. We've been faking it - giving her drugs to keep her under. But they'll figure it out soon enough. We don't have much time."

Deciding, Jim stood up again. "OK. Will you help me?"

Jill nodded vigorously. "Yes. I'll do anything. Where do we start?"

"Start by getting her unplugged from those things and get her ready to go. I'll go check out the corridor."

Jill nodded, began turning off devices, removing tubes and wires from Rita. Jim moved to the door, stepped into the outer room, and peeked through the door to the hallway. It was still dark. Nothing moved. Closing the door, he checked the time.

*Angel, are we on schedule?*

<Yes. The fusion reactor explosion will occur in nine minutes, four seconds>

*Perfect.*

Jim returned to the inner room. Jill had removed most of the tubes and wires from Rita. His wife looked small and vulnerable now, lying passive in the bed. It was hard to look at her. Shaking himself out of his funk, he turned to the doctor.

"Dr. Bartlett, in nine minutes, all hell is going to break loose. We need to be ready to travel by then. Can you do it?"

"Yes. I'll be ready."

\*\*\*

Nine minutes had come and gone, and then another nine minutes. There was no distant explosion.

Something had gone horribly wrong. Jim realized the plan was shot to hell.

Jill leaned over toward him.

"We have to go, Jim. We can't stay here any longer. Someone will come soon."

Jim nodded. He turned to the bed and picked up Rita.

They had to make a break for it.

Jill carried Jim's pack; Jim put Rita in a fireman's carry over his shoulders. It seemed strange to carry his wife that way, but at this point, survival outweighed appearances.

Jim had given Jill a pulse pistol; he carried his own silenced pistol in his right hand, placed in front of his body. They moved as quickly as possible down the corridor, back the way Jim had come, toward the cargo bay.

They made it half-way before their luck ran out. They turned a corner just in time to run squarely into a big Singheko guard carrying a rifle slung over his back - and a pistol in his hand. The Singheko reacted quickly, bringing the pistol up for a shot. Jill was faster - her pistol was already up as they rounded the corner, and she shot the Singheko square in the face, his brains blowing out the back of his head and making a bloody mess on the corridor wall. He went down like a slab of beef, his rifle making a loud clatter on the floor.

"Quick now," hissed Jill. "That noise will bring others!" She moved quickly to one side, letting Jim go first, since she wasn't sure where they were headed.

"Roger that," said Jim, kicking himself into a dogtrot. It was brutal to trot with the added weight of Rita on his shoulders, but he knew they had no choice. The sound of the pistol shot and the clatter as the guard's rifle had hit the floor would bring others, and soon.

His thought was prophetic. As he approached the next corner, he heard a guttural shout behind him. A rifle pulse hit the roof over his head, close enough to send shards of burnt metal and paint down on him. He heard Jill behind him firing, the staccato bursts of her pistol mixed with the low frequency "thumps" of the Singheko pulse weapons. He heard a cry of pain from Jill - then he was around the corner, protected from the shots behind him, trotting, head down, trying to put more distance between himself and the pursuers behind. Reaching the end of the corridor, he turned the corner into the next corridor, stopped, reversed, and peeked back around to look for Jill.

He saw her. She was crouched down at the far end of the corridor, firing her pistol around the corner. Blood covered her left arm, which hung limply. More blood pooled under her. She fired several times, then turned briefly to look at him. She gave him a pushing gesture - the gesture clearly indicating for him to run, leave her behind, go quickly. A wan smile came across her face - the smile of someone who knows they will be dead within seconds.

"Remember my name!" she yelled.

Then she turned and with her good arm, began firing around the corner again.

Jim knew she was right. If he didn't leave now while Jill protected his rear, all was lost. He re-positioned Rita and began running again, down the next hallway toward the service area.

# THE SHORT END

\*\*\*

All hell had broken loose on the Singheko space station. Alarms rang continuously, lights flashed in the corridors, and guards ran through the corridors in every direction. Jim had barely made it to the maintenance room twelve meters up from the cargo bay - the same place he had originally started his trip. He huddled now below the small window in the door, the lights turned off. He couldn't get down the corridor to the cargo bay; there was a constant stream of guards moving back and forth in the corridor. One even rattled the door knob as he went by. Jim had locked the door from the inside; the guard peered in through the window, saw nothing in the dimness, and went on his way.

He no longer had his pack; Jill had been carrying that, and Jill was gone. She was dead by now, he was sure. And they would be coming for him next. But he had only one last door to get through, and he would be back in the cargo bay. If he could just get out the door, down the hallway and into the cargo bay; then if he could get onboard a shuttle.

If, if, if... Jim knew the odds were against him. But he had to try.

He looked down at Rita, lying on the floor beside him. She was still breathing, but otherwise there was no sign of life. She looked so helpless. It tore at his heart.

*I have to get her out of here, or else we both have to die. We can't let Zukra have either one of us.*

Outside, the corridor seemed to be quiet for the moment. Jim raised up slightly, peeked through the window. He saw nothing.

*Well, hoss, time to toss the dice.*

Jim tucked his pistol back into the shoulder holster, bent over and picked up Rita, putting her back on his shoulders. He unlocked the door and cracked it open slightly. Looking to the left, he saw an empty corridor. He pushed the door open a bit more and stuck out his head, looked to the right. Nothing.

He pulled out his pistol and positioned it in his right

hand in case he needed it. Quickly he opened the door fully, stepped out, and closed it behind him. With Rita still over his shoulders, he took the dozen long steps to the cargo bay door as rapidly as possible. He reached and opened it, pushed through, and entered the bay, gently closing the door behind him.

It was still dark; perhaps he had reached it before the Singheko had deciphered his destination. There before him were several shuttles, parked in their landing slots, ready for the next day's operations. Jim moved to the one closest to him and gently laid Rita down on the floor. He laid down his pistol as well, to open the shuttle ramp.

And the lights came on.

Jim spun. There behind him stood a Singheko captain, flanked by two burly Singheko guards. The two guards had their rifles fixed on him. He didn't stand a chance of reaching his pistol before they shot him.

Slowly Jim stood. There was no way out.

*Might as well face it like a man.*

The Singheko captain stared at him, as if he recognized him. Then he spoke, his words in English, strangely accented but understandable.

"Commander Jim Carter, I believe," he said.

Jim stared. And then it came to him. He had never met the Singheko who stood before him; but he knew him by the slight reddish streak of hair peeking from under his cap.

"Captain Orma, I believe," Jim responded.

"Yesss," Orma said, with the stretched-out sibilants that were common in both the Nidarian and Singheko languages. "We meet at last. Under unfortunate circumstances, however."

Jim nodded. "Yes. Very unfortunate. Well..."

Jim gathered his thoughts for the last time.

"Go ahead. Do what you have to do."

# CHAPTER NINETEEN

**Singheko System - Planet Ridendo**
**Naval Spacedock**

A strange kind of smile passed across Orma's face; a smile recognizable in spite of the abbreviated muzzle of his face.

A smile of sadness, Jim thought.

"Yes. You have said it. I will do what I have to do."

And with that, Orma made a gesture to one of the guards. The guard handed his rifle to the other guard. Then he moved forward, past Jim, and walked to the nearby shuttle. He keyed a code and the hatch opened, the ramp falling to the deck with a slight thump. Then the guard turned aside and stood beside the ramp, almost in a position of attention, waiting.

Jim looked back at Orma in puzzlement. Orma pointed to the shuttle. "Please carry your wife aboard the shuttle, Commander Carter."

Jim shrugged, turned, picked Rita up and carried her to the shuttle. He climbed the ramp and inside found a long, cushioned seat. Carefully he laid Rita down on the seat. Then he stood and turned to Orma, now standing at the base of the ramp.

Once more Orma showed that strange, sad smile. "Regrettably, your comrade Helen is dead, Commander. I wish it had been otherwise. But I cannot face Zukra empty-handed. I assure you; she will receive a proper military burial.

"Have a good trip, Commander Carter. The shuttle has been pre-programmed on a vector to Deriko. From there you may travel anywhere you wish - the codes on the shuttle authorize it to go anywhere in the system. I wish you luck. And when your Admiral awakes, tell her I remember the day she released me to return to my family. Tell her one good turn deserves another."

And with that, Orma gestured to the guard. The shuttle ramp began to close. In a few seconds, Jim was sealed inside the shuttle with Rita. He heard the engines start spooling up. Outside he heard the dock's airlock door opening. With a lurch, the shuttle lifted off the deck and shot out the launch bay.

**Singheko System**
**Singheko Shuttlecraft**

Jim half-expected missiles to come flying after him as he departed the Singheko space dock - but nothing happened. The shuttle flew serenely on its course, directly toward Deriko, for two hours.

He approached the planet with a heavy heart. He had been unable to rouse Rita from her coma. He had tended her, repositioning her arms and legs to ensure she was comfortable, putting a folded blanket under her head. He had draped another blanket over her body to keep her warm.

He wiped her face with a damp cloth. He spoke to her, rubbed her arms, kissed her. He placed water against her lips in case she would be able to take a sip. But nothing he did gained any reaction.

Jim was confused. The doctor, Jill Bartlett, had said she would wake up soon. But she simply lay, still in a coma. Just breathing.

*At least she's breathing without a respirator. That's progress.*

The AI of the shuttle spoke.

<Approaching Deriko, Commander>

Jim laid the damp cloth across Rita's forehead and returned to the cockpit. In the holo he could see they were approaching Deriko, now only about a half-hour out.

But Jim knew the fleet was no longer at Deriko. Bonnie had

moved on to Dekanna, preparing to fight the Singheko there. There was no point in going to Deriko anymore.

"Shuttle. I see that you speak English. Can you understand me?"

<Yes, Commander. I understand English>

"Do you understand Human spatial coordinates for this system?"

<Yes, Commander. That information was recently loaded into my memory>

"Annotate the holo with the location of Deriko in Human coordinates."

In the small cockpit holo of the shuttle, readable numbers appeared beside the icon of the planet Deriko. Jim checked them against his memory. They were correct. Clearly Orma had pre-programmed the shuttle to understand Human commands.

That was a bit scary.

*That son of a bitch knows far too much about us. This is probably some kind of a trap. But I don't see how. And I don't really see what advantage he could gain by letting me escape, then setting a trap. He already knows the fleet left for Dekanna. So...*

"Designate point Charlie-Four as follows: 106.2, 105.2, 53.1."

<Point Charlie-Four designated as 106.2, 105.2, 53.1>

"Mark Point Charlie-Four on the holo."

A dot appeared in the small holo in the cockpit. Jim checked it. It appeared to be properly located - well off in the Kuiper belt of the system, 53.1 AU away.

7,965,000,000 klicks. A long journey in a tiny shuttle.

But that was the location where a packet boat should be waiting for him and Helen.

*Helen. She's dead. I have to get word to Ollie. He's gonna be devastated.*

*But I can't send a message from a Singheko shuttle. I'm sure they're monitoring all transmissions.*

<Shuttle. Modify course. Slingshot around Deriko. When on

the backside of Deriko and out of sight of Ridendo, set course to Point Charlie-Four at max accel."

<Understood. ETA to Point Charlie-Four is thirty-eight hours, 41 minutes.>

"Execute."

## Singheko System
## Fleet Assembly Point

The bridge of the Singheko flagship *Revenge* was busy. The barely audible whine of cooling fans in the electronics, and the slight susurration of air coming from the vents, added to the background of low voices from the officers and technicians working at a half-dozen consoles.

Admiral Zukra's Flag Aide, Damra, stood the precise two meters from his Admiral as demanded by protocol. "M'lord, the fleet is ready to depart."

Zukra lounged comfortably in his well-padded command chair. Singheko warships didn't utilize a raised Flag Bridge as did the Nidarians and Humans; but Zukra's elevated chair raised him a full twelve inches above the rest of the bridge. In the ten-foot diameter holo in front of him, the Singheko fleet appeared in loose formation at their assembly point 25 million klicks from Ridendo. With the battlecruisers in the middle of the cloud of warships, the cruisers surrounding them, and destroyers making up the outer layer, the fleet spanned fifty thousand klicks. A covey of supply ships, corvettes and utility boats brought up the rear.

"Very well, Damra. Move 'em out." Zukra made a flip of the hand at Damra, giving him permission to carry on. With a slight bow, Damra turned to the Flag Captain of the *Revenge* and nodded.

Flag Captain Rizdo nodded in return and spoke to the ship.

"*Revenge*, start the fleet moving."

<Fleet Movement order issued> came the response from the ship's AI.

Zukra gazed in satisfaction at his bridge crew and the holo of his fleet. In the holo, his advance guard of destroyers began moving. Taking a line toward the Dekanna system, they were soon followed by the rest of the fleet, first the cruisers, then the battlecruisers. In a half-hour, all ships were heading for the outer system and the point where they could sink out to FTL.

Zukra lounged in his chair with a great feeling of satisfaction.

*This time. This time I have them. That new Admiral - Bonnie they call her - what a joke. Promoted from destroyer commodore to admiral. They must be desperate. But no matter - it just makes my job easier. This time I've got them. Dekanna is their last stand.*

Damra returned to a point just outside the railing around Zukra's command chair and stopped, looking at his tablet. He didn't put a hand on the railing - the last officer who tried that was missing a hand.

"Message from Admiral Tanno, m'lord. The Nidarian fleet will rendezvous as we planned at point 14-Z, one light outside the Dekanna system. They are on schedule."

Zukra grunted in acknowledgment. "Good, good," he finally spoke. "That will double our fleet size."

"Do you think the Humans will try an end run around us to escape, sir? When they realize we're coming?"

Zukra thought for a second, then smiled.

"Actually, I hope they do. We've got scout ships watching that system every minute. If that new Human admiral tries to run, we'll know it instantly. And we'll chase her down - she knows that. She knows I'll chase her right back to Earth, and then cleanse that whole planet. So no, I think she'll stand and fight. Animals that they are, they have enough intelligence to know running is pointless."

Damra nodded. "Excellent, m'lord. I'm looking forward to smashing them."

Zukra changed the subject. "Any word from Orma on that terrorist attack at the docks?"

"Aye, m'lord. Orma reports no damage was done to the

station. One Human terrorist was killed. Two of her cadre escaped on the morning shuttle but were intercepted at the surface. Unfortunately, they refused to surrender and were killed in a firefight at the port."

"Damn," exclaimed Zukra. "A Human terrorist on our station. That was unexpected. Clever animals, these, although still too stupid to properly plan and execute such an attack."

Zukra sighed. "If only we could have captured one of them - we could have extracted enough information to roll up the whole organization."

"Aye, m'lord. Unfortunate."

"Ah, no matter. We'll have another chance. Orma's team will track down these terrorists in short order."

"Aye, sir. By the way sir, I just noticed that you gave Captain Orma the *Tornado*."

"Yes, I gave him permission to come along. The *Tornado* is our oldest battlecruiser. It'll be a nice target for the Humans. He's welcome to it."

"Very good, sir.

## Nidarian System
## Fleet Assembly Point

*The Humans must die. All of them. Right down to the last ship. And then their planet must be wiped clean. They must not be allowed to expand into space.*

Tanno had made the thoughts into a mantra. He repeated it every day now. He knew his survival depended on it. High Councilor Garatella had made that perfectly clear.

*Kill them all, or fall on your sword, Tanno.*

Tanno had a new flagship. The *Ekkarra*. Just out of shakedown, it replaced a battlecruiser of the same name - one that no longer existed. The original *Ekkarra* had been the flagship of the detachment sent to bolster Zukra before the Battle of Deriko.

And the original *Ekkarra* was now junk, floating in the

black between Deriko and Ridendo. Junk that was still being collected up by the Humans and used to rebuild their own damaged ships - or sent into the nearby star as trash.

Tanno burned for revenge. The Humans had humiliated him. Him - the senior Fleet Admiral of the Nidarian navy. And not only the Humans. The breakaway Nidarian rebels who served with the Humans were even worse. They fought against their own kind - traitors.

Tanno's mind was made up. In this coming campaign, he would wipe the slate clean. They would take no prisoners. He would wipe the Humans and the Nidarian traitors who helped them from the universe.

First, he would kill their fleet at Dekanna. Then he would journey to Earth. He would grind their planet into oblivion. If there was a small number of survivors at the end, Zukra could take them for playthings in his torture chambers. Tanno didn't approve of torture; but he would not be the one doing it. That made it none of his business.

"Fleet is ready for departure, Admiral," he heard from his Flag Aide, sitting close beside him.

"Very well," said Tanno. "Let's go," he said, rather undramatically.

The Flag Aide nodded to the Flag Captain, standing three meters away on the slightly lower main bridge of the *Ekkarra*. The Flag Captain nodded at his quartermaster. Tanno felt the ever-so-slight Coriolis force as the flagship made a slight rotation and began powering out of orbit. In the holo, he saw the rest of the fleet falling in behind.

*We'll be at Dekanna in eleven days. They'll know we're coming - they have their spies out in our Oort cloud watching us, I'm sure. They'll be ready. But it won't do them any good. Zukra will be there waiting for us. This time...*

*This time we eliminate them from the Universe.*

**Singheko System - Kuiper Belt**
**Singheko Shuttlecraft**

"Are you sure these are the coordinates I gave you?" asked Jim.

The little Singheko shuttle responded.

<106.2, 105.2, 53.1 - Point Charlie-Four as you designated>

Desperately, Jim scanned the holo.

There was nothing. No packet boat anywhere to be seen. Just a whole lot of empty space in every direction.

"Are you broadcasting the signal I gave you?"

<I am broadcasting the signal you specified. There is no response>

Jim didn't know what to do next. After spending more than eight hours crammed into a tiny hidden compartment in the food container, then an hour crawling through a sewer system, then having a running gun battle with Singheko guards while carrying Rita over his shoulders, then facing Orma expecting to die...the last few days had taken a lot out of him.

He had tried to sleep during the thirty-eight-hour trip to the Kuiper belt, but his worry about Rita had kept him awake. He tossed and turned - but sleep just wouldn't come.

He tried everything. But every time he dropped off to sleep, he woke again within an hour or so, terrified that Rita had died while he was sleeping.

He was totally exhausted. His brain wasn't working right, and he knew it.

"Maybe they're afraid to make contact," he mused out loud.

<Possibly>

"Can you expand the range on the holo?"

<Range expanded to ten million klicks>

Jim still saw nothing on the holo. No ship was waiting for him.

But...there was one small icy body right at the edge of the holo. It was a typical Kuiper belt object, an irregular iceball of about ten klicks diameter.

"If they're out here, they're behind that iceball," he thought out loud. "Shuttle, take us to that iceball."

<Wilco. Setting course for the iceball>

As the little shuttle turned and began the ten-million klick leg to their new destination, Jim went back to check on Rita. She was still inert, under the blanket. She was breathing. But that was all. There was no other sign of life.

Sitting down beside her, Jim took her hand in his.

"Hey, hon. Bet you didn't expect to ever see me again. And to be honest, I didn't expect to ever see you again either. But here we are. So…how about waking up? I'd really like to talk to you. Tell you how much I love you."

But Rita lay sleeping, oblivious to Jim's entreaties. He turned, laid his body down on the length of the seat next to her. There was just barely enough room; he was hanging half off the seat. But he managed to hold on to her, pulled her in tight, found a way for them both to lie on the seat without falling. The warmth of her body felt good to him. It showed she was still alive. He leaned over, kissed her on the cheek, and then laid his head down and closed his eyes. Somehow, holding her, he slept.

He slept, and he dreamed. He dreamed about the first time he was with Rita, in the hangar at Fort Nelson. When they both thought Bonnie was dead, and she came to him in the night, and they cried together.

# CHAPTER TWENTY

**Singheko System - Kuiper Belt**
**Singheko Shuttlecraft**

Movement.

Jim came half-awake.

He had felt movement.

Raising up his head, he looked at Rita.

Had she moved? He wasn't sure. He had felt something.

But she wasn't moving now.

Groaning, he got up off the seat and stood.

"Where are we, shuttle?" he asked.

<We are approaching the iceball. I have a possible ship detection behind it>

"Decel to a stop, then stop all engines," Jim. "Let's not spook them."

<Decel to a stop, then stop all engines. Acknowledged. Executing>

A few minutes later, the shuttle came to a stop relative to the iceball, which was now only a couple of hundred klicks in front of them. In the holo, Jim could see the ghost of a ship signature behind the object. It looked about the right size to be a packet boat.

But was it the EDF packet boat he expected? Or a Singheko corvette, loaded with weapons that could blast his shuttle to atoms?

"Are you still sending the signal?"

<I am sending the recognition signal>

"Damn these guys," Jim said. "There's such a thing as being

too cautious."

<The ship is coming out>

In the holo, Jim could see the ship outlined behind the iceball moving. In a matter of seconds, it poked its nose out and came into view.

Jim heaved a sigh of relief. It was the EDF packet boat.

<Message from PB04. Make no sudden moves. Prepare to be boarded>

**Singheko System**
**Packet Boat PB04**

An hour later, Jim watched as the medic aboard the packet boat carefully placed Rita into a medpod. The boat was tiny, but anticipating that Jim or Helen might have injuries, they had installed a medpod - just in case.

They had never expected to put Rita Page into it.

The captain of the packet boat was Captain Inman. He stood with Jim as the medic made Rita comfortable and closed the lid of the medpod.

"It should keep her alive until we get to Earth," Inman said.

"We're not going to Earth," Jim replied. "We're going to Dekanna."

"Dekanna...no, sir, I have orders to take you to Earth."

Jim turned to him, a stern expression on his face.

"We're going to Dekanna, Captain. I'll take full responsibility."

"But sir...my orders were explicit. To collect you and Lieutenant Frost and take you straight to Earth!"

"Captain. Can't you see that things have changed? That's Admiral Rita Page in there. We need to take her to Dekanna. The Dariama are some of the best engineers in the world. That also means they have some of the best medical practices. Hell, they built that medpod! If there's a way to save her, they would know it. We must go to Dekanna, Captain. It's her only chance!"

Inman looked askance at Jim for a while. Finally,

grudgingly, he gave in.

"Very well, sir. Dekanna it is. But if I get my ass in the wringer over this, you better be there to back me up. This is totally your idea."

Jim nodded. "Thank you, Captain. Don't worry - if Bonnie gives us grief over it, I'll claim I highjacked your boat."

Inman shuddered. "I suspect that would make things worse, not better. If you don't mind, let's just stick to the story that you coerced me and leave it at that."

Jim smiled. "I understand. By the way, do you have a shower I can use? I recently spent some time in a sewer."

Inman nodded in relief. "I was hoping you would ask that. Just down the passageway to the right."

The captain turned away and moved to the cockpit of the small craft. Jim stood for a moment, gazing through the window at the medpod. The thought kept going through his mind.

*I first met you in a medpod. Let me meet you again in the same way. Wake up, baby.*

### Enroute to Dekanna
### Packet Boat *Donkey*

"This is gonna be close," Rachel grumbled. She was looking at her tablet. Bonnie had sent a warning message to let them know Zukra was staging his fleet just outside Dekanna and was expected to attack the system at any moment.

Beside her in the cockpit, Paco nodded agreement. "Tika - what's your latest estimate?"

<We will arrive at Dekanna at the same time as Zukra. Possibly a few hours before, possibly a few hours after. All depends on how fast he enters the system from his staging position>

Rachel slapped the console in front of her, frustration in her voice.

"If we get there a few hours after, it's going to be too late."

Paco nodded glumly. "Tika, I don't suppose there's any way to get a little more speed out of this thing, is there?"

<No, Paco. We are at maximum speed>

Rachel stood up in frustration. She glared at Paco as if he were personally responsible for their predicament. Then she stomped off down the passageway to her cabin.

Paco sighed. Being on this long mission with Rachel had initially seemed like a great idea - far safer than being in a fighter mixing it up with the Singheko between Deriko and Ridendo. But now...

*Be careful what you wish for.*

"Tika - tell me a story."

<What kind of story shall I tell you?>

"Tell me a story about the Broken Galaxy. Why do they call it the Broken Galaxy? What happened?"

<Ah. Well, that was before my time. I'm only twelve hundred years old, you know. But...as it was told to me by my parents...>

"Parents? You have parents?"

"Of course. We are sentient creatures. We know the value of dissimilar reproduction and evolution. We don't just blindly make copies of ourselves - how boring would that be?>

"Oh. Well, yeah. I guess you're right. So - sorry. Please continue."

<Well. As told to me by my parents, two thousand years ago the Golden Empire was twenty thousand years old. Things had been going downhill for thousands of years. The energy and innovation of the early Empire had long since passed. There were almost continuous civil wars between competing factions. The armies were dissipated fighting each other instead of protecting the Empire>

"And that was when the capital was relocated to Nidaria, right?"

<Yes. The capital of the Empire had been much farther out, at least five hundred lights beyond Nidaria. But the last Emperor realized the Empire was collapsing. He relocated the

capital to Nidaria. The capital was renamed Sanctuary, because it was the last stronghold of law and order in the Empire. Then...the Empire collapsed. It became dog eat dog, as you say in your language. Every system raised its hand against its neighbor. And from there, things progressed downhill. Warlords and barbarians roamed the systems at will, raiding and thieving to make their way. The only civilization left was the Nidarians at Sanctuary. Their military was weak, but just barely strong enough to fend off the raiders. The Nidarians began calling the outside universe the Broken Galaxy. Their city of Sanctuary was the only light of civilization left in the Arm>

"So why do the Nidarians want to kill us? What have we ever done to them?"

<I do not know the exact answer to that question, Paco. But consider - they have spent the last two thousand years fending off thieves and marauders. They have gotten particularly good at it. Perhaps they've gotten a little too good at it. They've become paranoid, just like the Dariama. All the little insular systems that survived the Broken Galaxy are quite paranoid. As are we. So I suspect that Garatella is simply trying to remove a perceived threat - which is what he and his kind have done for the last two thousand years>

"But we didn't threaten him! We did nothing except ask for his help! And he was friendly with us at first - hell, he gave Rita a fleet to help defend Earth!"

<Just a ploy, Paco. Just a ploy. He fully expected Rita to be crushed by the Singheko. When she managed to fight them off at Sol, he was shocked. So shocked, he sent a fleet to Zukra to help the Singheko kill his own ships. And even that didn't work. So now he is truly paranoid, truly afraid of what Humans could do in the Arm if they manage to break out into space>

"And your people? Do they think the same? Do they think Humans are a danger? Will they be coming after us next?"

<I do not know, Paco. Predicting the thoughts and actions of

our Council is a difficult task. But...it is a good sign that they have sent me along with you to help against the Singheko. I do not believe they would do that if they intended to turn on you later>

"I hope you're right, Tika. I sure hope you're right."

**Enroute to Dekanna**
**Singheko Battlecruiser *Tornado***

Orma stared at the wall in his cabin. Thinking.
*We're on our way to Dekanna.*
*The Nidarians are on their way to Dekanna.*
*There will be a final battle there.*
*If Zukra wins, the Humans are finished.*
*But if Zukra wins, Singheko is finished as well. At least, the Singheko I love. The stain of blood will cover the Empire for a thousand years to come. Or ten thousand. Or more.*

*The honor of the old Singheko warrior society will be forever gone. The arenas will be filled with Humans, and Taegu, and Bagrami, and Dariama. They'll be slaughtered by the thousands to amuse Zukra and his companions.*

*And undoubtedly Nidarians as well. Zukra will turn on them as soon as Dekanna is pacified.*

*And his enemies - or his perceived enemies - will also take their turn. Zukra will ensure no one is left alive to threaten him.*

*That probably includes me.*

*I wouldn't mind dying if it were to restore the honor of the old Empire. But to die for Zukra's amusement...*

*And he would kill my friends as well.*

*And my family.*

Orma stared at the wall. Thinking.

Orma turned his head and looked at the pseudo-window on the wall of his cabin. It displayed the world of Ridendo, blue and white and brown, a simulation designed to make things onboard feel like home.

*A beautiful planet,* thought Orma. *Remarkably like Earth. We* have more in common with Humans that we think. We are all creatures of the universe. Life forming out of raw chemicals on the surface of a rock. Impossible, trillion-to-one chances. Yet here we are.

There must be another way to do this. We don't have to slaughter each other.

**Dekanna System**
**Dariama Battlecruiser** *Maebong*

"What's our first order of business?" asked Admiral Sobong.

"Disposition of the fleets," replied Bonnie. "My thinking is to put my Human fleet in the front of the formation. Your Dariama fleet next with the Taegu and Bagrami integrated into your cubes.

"We Humans will take the brunt of Zukra's attack, slow him down and get his fighters tangled up with our own. Take out as many ships as possible. Then you'll take your turn, but with far fewer fighters to contend with. In theory, by the time Zukra gets to you, there won't be many fighters for you to worry about. That gives you the best chance to stop him and prevent him from breaking through to Dekanna."

Sobong smiled gently at Bonnie, sitting across from her in the conference room. Farther down the table, the senior members of their respective staffs sat listening while the big dogs negotiated.

"So what you're saying is that you don't trust us Dariama to take the position of honor at the front of the formation. You think we'll break and run as soon as Zukra comes into the system."

Bonnie shook her head. "No, Admiral Sobong. That's not at all what I meant. I merely meant that we have much more experience fighting the Singheko than you do. We've fought six major battles with them in the last year. Not counting four raids. The Taegu and Bagrami have been fighting them for more than a year as well. But you have not had the joy of fighting these assholes yet. And experience counts in this kind of thing."

Sobong looked down at the conference table and pursed her lips in an eerily Human expression. Bonnie was constantly struck by how much the Dariama were like Humans. Except for their strange ears and different knee and elbow joints, they could almost pass for one.

Sobong spoke, still staring down at the table. It was almost as if she were speaking to herself, thinking out loud.

"We Dariama have a lot to make up for, Admiral. We have performed poorly in every war for the last two thousand years. Yes, we have broken and run from several battles in that time. Every species in the Arm looks down their nose at us. They call us cowards behind our backs. Sometimes to our faces."

Sobong lifted her head and looked Bonnie straight in the face. "We will take the front of the formation, Admiral. This is our time to put the Arm on notice. The Dariama will not go quietly. We will meet these bastards in the place of honor."

There was a silence in the room. Bonnie glanced down and across the crowded table to Commander Winston. Winnie had been Tactical Liaison with the Dariama for months. When it came to the Dariama, she was the most knowledgeable Human in the Arm.

Winnie looked back at her and gave slow, almost imperceptible nod. Bonnie moved her gaze to the right, back up the table to the figure of Admiral Woderas, leader of the Taegu detachment. He also gave a short nod. Finally, Bonnie looked directly across at the huge figure of Admiral Baysig of the Bagrami. Baysig gave her a wink and a smile.

Returning her gaze to Sobong, Bonnie spoke.

"So be it," said Bonnie. "The Dariama will take the front line. And good luck to you, Admiral."

Sobong leaned back now, her point won. She looked across at Bonnie.

"And if I could make another suggestion…"

"Please," said Bonnie.

# CHAPTER TWENTY-ONE

**One Light Year from Dekanna**
**Battlecruiser** *Revenge*

Admiral Zukra greeted Admiral Tanno in his day cabin, just off the bridge of the *Revenge*.

"Welcome, Admiral," Zukra said, speaking Nidarian. He lounged back in his chair and waved at a decanter on the table between them. "Please, sit, enjoy some wine. I had this brought along especially for you. Straight from the best Nidarian vineyards."

Tanno took his seat. A slave hurried to pour his wine. Tanno lifted it in a toast.

"To the destruction of the Humans!"

Zukra smiled, took his own glass, and toasted with Tanno.

"Indeed, Admiral. This time, we leave their ships a cloud of junk cluttering up the Dekanna system for a thousand years!"

"Aye, m'lord," said Tanno. "With our fleets combined, we outnumber them by almost two to one."

Zukra leaned back again, happy. It had taken him a long time to get to this point. The Humans had humiliated him again and again - at the initial battles in the Sol system, driving his task force out of that system; then fighting him to a draw in his own home system, taking the planet Deriko away from him.

Leaving his fleet so battered it had taken many months to repair and refit.

*No more.*

*Now we smash the Humans. And the Dariama cowards. And the remnants of the Taegu and Bagrami fleets as well. And then...*

Zukra looked across the table at the admiral in front of him, swilling wine as if he didn't have a care in the universe.

*...then I smash the Nidarians. This idiot admiral in front of me has no concept of what is coming. And that fool Garatella - I will personally chop his head off in the arena. Then we'll roll over the rest of the Arm like a hot knife through butter.*

"Should we talk fleet deployment and strategy, m'lord?" asked Tanno.

"What? Oh. Yes, of course. We should do that," answered Zukra. He bent forward and brought up a small holo over the desk.

"I expect the Humans to be in the front of their formation. They would never trust the Dariama to take the first shock. So we'll put our destroyers and cruisers in a double column up front, with our battlecruisers right behind them. We'll blast through the Human fighters and keep going, right into their capital ships. We'll hit them hard and fast. I really don't care how many fighters and destroyers I lose - I intend to keep going right at them, without stopping. For that matter, I don't even care how many cruisers I lose. I'll sacrifice every cruiser I've got if that's what it takes to blast my way through these animals.

"When we break through the Human front and start blasting away at their battlecruisers, they'll realize the battle is lost. They'll have no choice but to break and run toward Earth. We'll chase the survivors back there and wipe that planet clean of these animals once and for all.

"When they break and run, Tanno, you send a detachment to hunt down any stragglers that flee Coreward. Mop up any remaining resistance here at Dekanna and pacify the system. Once you've got the Dariama surrender, just wait for me here. I'll meet you back here when I'm finished with Earth. That should do it. We'll have no more worries from these rebellious species."

Tanno drained his wineglass and reached out for another.

The slave poured the wine and Tanno started on his second glass.

"I had hoped to go to Earth and help destroy them there, m'lord. Is there no chance I can accompany you?"

"No, Tanno. Stay here and keep control of this system until I return. We can't have any rebels escaping to start trouble somewhere else."

"And what comes after that? Once we have Dekanna? Where do we go next?"

*Ah. He's not as stupid as he looks. He's fishing for any hint that I intend to turn on the Nidarians. Which I do. But he can't know that.*

"First, we'll need to fully pacify Dekanna and get weapons factories set up here, establish another spacedock to build warships. Maybe two. Then, it's straight out the arm - right toward the Perseus Transit. We'll sweep everything before us."

Tanno mused aloud as he sipped his wine. "There's a lot of wild barbarian systems out that way. Some of them can fight."

"Compared to us? Don't be an ass, Tanno."

**Enroute to Dekanna**
**Packet Boat PB04**

Jim was sleeping when his internal comm started the insistent beeping that meant he had a priority call.

"Oh, Lord," he groaned. "What now?" He rolled over in bed and glanced at the clock.

It was 0514 hours.

"This better be good," he spoke to the empty air. "Read message."

<Commander Carter, Corporal Gaines asks that you come to the medbay immediately>

Jim came wide awake. "On my way," he replied. Jumping out of bed, he threw on his uniform pants and ran for the medbay, tugging on his uniform shirt as he went.

Corporal Gaines was standing at the medbay entrance,

wringing his hands, as Jim approached.

"I think she's waking up, sir!" the young medic exclaimed, in obvious distress. "She's tossing and turning and mumbling. I don't know what to do!"

Jim nodded, blasting through the hatch into the medbay. He ran over to the medpod and looked at Rita through the transparent lid.

Sure enough, she was moving. Her head rolled back and forth. Her eyelids fluttered. Her limbs moved spasmodically, as if she was dreaming.

Jim flipped the latch on the top cover and raised the lid of the medbay. He leaned over it, stroking her cheeks, her hair, trying to calm her.

"Easy babe. Easy. I'm here. Just relax. Just take it easy. You're safe."

She kept twitching, rolling her head. Jim was at a loss what to do next, so he just kept stroking her hair, rubbing her shoulders. Suddenly her eyes flicked open. She stared at him, frozen. He could see fear on her face.

"It's OK, babe. I'm here. You're safe. Everything is OK."

She stared hard at him. The fear on her face didn't change.

"Who are you?" she asked.

*\*\**

Hours later, Jim returned to his bed, dog-tired. Between the medic and himself, they had gotten Rita stabilized again. She was sleeping now, mildly sedated.

But she didn't recognize Jim.

And worse, she didn't know herself.

That was the last thing Jim had expected. He had thought she would wake up, look at him and smile. Give him a hug and a kiss. Tell him how much she missed him.

None of that had happened. She had simply recoiled from him in fear. She didn't know him.

And she had no idea who she was.

*This is not good. I've heard of amnesia from a blow to the head. I guess this is from the poison in her system. But it's sure a bad time for her to forget everything. We're one day away from a battle with Zukra.*

Her vitals showed her internal organs were still declining. The poison may have been cleared out of her system - but the damage had been done. She needed urgent hospitalization.

He had sent a message to Bonnie via ansible. He hadn't waited around for a response; there wasn't anything Bonnie could do. They had to tough it out, hope that Rita could hold on until they arrived at Dekanna.

In ten hours, they would be in the system. Jim would take Rita directly to Naval HQ and hand her over to the Dariama doctors.

*Maybe they can help her.*

A sudden realization hit him. He wouldn't be able to fight in the battle with the Fleet. Bonnie had told him that when he returned from his crazy mission to find Rita, his career was over. He would be drummed out of the EDF.

To stand by and watch as Bonnie and the Fleet took on Zukra…and be unable to do anything. Jim couldn't imagine any torture worse than that.

*I'm going to go reason with Bonnie. Surely, she'll relent. I know we are short-handed on pilots. Surely, she'll let me take a Merlin and join the fight before she shitcans me. Hell, I'll fly as an ensign, if that's what it takes.*

**Dekanna System**
**Battlecruiser *Merkkessa***

Bonnie read the message from Jim once again on her tablet and sighed.

She saw no use in sending a response. There was nothing anyone could do until Jim arrived in the packet boat. And that would not be for another ten hours.

In the meantime, she had a fleet to prepare. A battle plan to tune, adjust, disseminate to the rest of the fleet. A hundred things to check to ensure that all was ready for battle.

And she had another message. One that caused her no small amount of humor. A message from Captain Westerly on the battlecruiser *Victory*.

*Arriving pretty much simultaneously with Zukra. Try not to shoot us as we come into the system. If we can, we'll come in behind him and give him a little surprise.*

She had sent a message back to Westerly.

*Kick Zukra right in the ass if you get a chance. I'm sending you a little surprise also. I left two cruisers at Deriko to protect Tatiana until Zukra left. Those two are on their way here now. I'm going to re-direct them to join up with you. That will give you four cruisers as a screen. Enjoy!*

Now it was getting late. Maybe she could sleep a little. She got up from her desk and went through to her Flag Cabin behind. Luke was waiting for her in bed, also going through his tablet.

"Looking at your battle plan?" Bonnie asked.

Luke grinned. "When you're a destroyer captain, you don't have much of a battle plan. Get between the enemy and your capital ships. Hope you don't die. That's about it."

Bonnie smiled. "There's a little more to it than that."

Luke patted the bed. "Why don't you try to get some sleep?"

Bonnie nodded, pulled off her uniform, and lay down beside him.

"Lights, out!" she called. The room went dark. They lay quietly for a long time, each in their own thoughts. After a while, though, Bonnie felt compelled to speak.

"How many times now have we lain awake before a battle, wondering if we'll make it through?"

Luke was silent for a bit before he finally spoke. "I think I've lost count."

"And why do we do this, again?"

"You know why."

They were again quiet for a while. Bonnie was the first one to break the silence.

"Yes. Because someone has to."

Bonnie reached out a hand, felt for Luke's, took it, held it.

"Try not to die tomorrow, love. I need you."

"I'll do my best. And you likewise. Come back to me."

Bonnie squeezed his hand. They went quiet, then.

There was not much else to say.

**Enroute to Dekanna**
**Packet Boat** *Donkey*

Their last night before arriving at Dekanna was a long one. Neither Rachel nor Paco could sleep. They knew they might enter the system tomorrow and find the mangled remains of the EDF fleet floating in the black, shot to hell. It was a distinct possibility. Even counting the Dariama and the detachments of the Taegu and Bagrami fleets, the EDF was heavily outnumbered.

But they had high hopes they would arrive before the battle started. And get a chance to join the fight.

And that depended on Zukra. Nobody was sure when he would resume his advance. He was hovering one light outside the Dekanna system with his Nidarian allies. They had made no movement in forty-eight hours. Scouts reported there was a bit of shuttle traffic between the Singheko flagship and the Nidarian flagship, but otherwise things were quiet. They were just sitting there.

*Taking their time,* thought Rachel. *The old psych game. They want to intimidate us. They hope we'll turn tail and run, just thinking about it. They clearly don't know Bonnie Page very well.*

She heard a noise down the passageway. Paco was out of his cabin, moving toward the cockpit. She heard another hatch open.

*Why, that son of a bitch! He's going into Tika's cabin! I told him not to do that! That fucking pervert!*

"Tika. Is Paco in your cabin playing with your inert body?"

<No, Rachel. Paco is in my cabin playing with my fully functional and quite excited body, in which I am currently

resident. I think this is our business if you don't mind."

*Oh.*

*Well.*

*OK...*

*Everybody faces death in their own way.*

**Planet Ridendo**
**City of Mosalia**

Ollie knew Helen was dead. He had known since the night of the mission to the spacedock. If Helen had escaped, she would have sent him a message.

There was no message.

But actually, he had known long before that. He had known Helen would die as soon as the truck trundled off down the street from the warehouse on its way to the spaceport, with the woman he loved hidden in the shipping container.

And he had let her go. Against his better judgment, he had authorized the mission.

It was on him.

A coded message from the packet boat had finally arrived two days later, letting him know Helen didn't make it. Jim Carter had been picked up successfully, and the packet boat was taking Jim to Dekanna. They would return to collect Ollie in four weeks. Maybe. If the EDF survived.

It didn't matter. He didn't care if they ever collected him.

<Forty seconds> came from his embedded AI.

His best Resistance cell had engineered the attack. They had packed a truck with enough explosives to take down a city block. It had taken months for them to collect the materials, bring them to the warehouse and prepare them.

Now it was time.

<Thirty seconds>

He would have preferred to attack Admiral Zukra's palace. But that building was on the pinnacle of a hill in the center of the city, protected by a maze of winding streets and vehicle barriers that guaranteed failure if they tried to park a truck nearby.

Instead, they had selected Singheko Naval Headquarters at the spaceport. The large ten-story building was perfectly situated, at least from their viewpoint. Although it was protected by a heavy fence and armed guards, the back of it was right next to a warehouse.

*Poor planning on the part of their Navy,* thought Ollie. *Somebody wasn't thinking far enough ahead on that one.*

The Resistance had loaded the truck with 8,000 pounds of explosive. It had been driven into the spaceport and parked on the street in front of the warehouse - placing it directly behind Naval Headquarters.

*I wish they could have gotten it a bit closer. But I think this will do.*

<Twenty seconds>

The thought had crossed his mind; all he had to do was sit in the back of the bomb truck when it went off - and the pain of losing Helen would end.

But Helen wouldn't like that, he knew. She would call him a fool and a coward for taking the easy way out.

So he sat in a vehicle two klicks outside the spaceport fence, waiting.

He had to see it.

He had to know that Helen had been avenged. He had found a spot on the streets where he could park with a good view of the distant building.

<Ten seconds>

Ollie leaned over, putting himself below the level of the car windshield in case it blew out toward him.

<Four. Three. Two. One. Zero>

The concussion rocked the car. The sound was deafening, a cracking push of sound that left his ears ringing. The overpressure knocked out windows up and down the street, glass falling from the buildings around him like sharp, glittering ice. He waited a second after the concussion, to make sure the windshield of the car was still intact, then sat up to take a look.

Far in front of him, the Singheko Naval Headquarters building had disappeared. All that was left was a huge dirty cloud rising high into the air over a monstrous pile of rubble.

*That's for Helen, you bastards.*

# CHAPTER TWENTY-TWO

**Dekanna System**
**Dariama Naval HQ**

Jim and Corporal Gaines pushed Rita's medpod down the passageway to the exit hatch, where two medics and a Dariama doctor waited.

"Commander Carter? I'm Dr. Bosama. How are you?" said the doctor.

Jim nodded a greeting. "As well as can be expected, Doctor. Here she is."

Jim had already had several discussions with Dr. Bosama on his way in from the outer system - but he said it anyway.

"Take good care of her. She's important."

The medics nodded and pushed the medpod out the hatch, down the boarding tube and into the station. Doctor Bosama gave Jim a final smile of reassurance and followed them. The station hatch closed behind them and she was gone.

Captain Inman placed a hand lightly on Jim's back. "They'll take good care of her, Commander," he said. "The Dariama have the best physicians in the Arm."

Jim spoke grimly. "If anyone can save her. She's back into a deep coma."

Inman squeezed Jim's shoulder. "If anyone can find a way, they can."

Jim closed his eyes and bowed his head. He heard the boat hatch close in front of him, and Captain Inman walk away, giving him some privacy.

*Lord, I've asked you for too much in this life. I know that. I've taken far more than I've given. But if you can see your way clear to save her...I'll give you whatever you want. If you want my life, today's the day to take it. Whatever you want.*

Opening his eyes and raising his head, Jim stared at the closed hatch in front of him for a moment. Then he turned and marched to the cockpit.

"Captain Gaines, kick this tin can in the ass and get me to the *Merkkessa*, please."

"We'll do that, Commander. Sit back and enjoy the ride."

\*\*\*

5.7 hours later, packet boat PB04 sat quietly, docked to the *Merkkessa*. Exiting the short docking tube, a weary Jim Carter stepped out into the flagship's shuttle bay. He made his way toward Bonnie's cabin, three decks above. Approaching the Flag Cabin, he nodded at the two guards stationed outside her hatch and knocked smartly.

"Come!"

Jim entered the cabin, closing the hatch behind him. Bonnie was sitting at her desk. She was wearing her full-dress whites.

*She looks sharp*, thought Jim. *Dressed to kill, I guess.*

Jim stepped to a spot precisely in front of her desk and came to a sharp attention. "Commander James Carter, reporting, milady."

"You look like shit," said Bonnie.

Jim nodded; his eyes still focused on a spot on the wall three meters behind her.

"Aye, milady," he replied.

Bonnie sighed. "At ease, Jim."

Jim took a parade rest position while Bonnie leaned back in her chair.

"I didn't think you'd do it. But you did."

"Aye, milady."

"Relax, Jim. I know you've been through a lot."

Jim made a conscious effort to relax a little more. He

lowered his eyes to Bonnie's.

"Rita's safely at Dekanna?"

"Yes, milady."

"Good. Let's hope for the best."

Jim nodded silently. Bonnie looked up at him sympathetically.

"And now I suppose you want a fighter?"

Jim nodded. "Yes, milady. If possible."

Bonnie looked off to one side and sighed deeply. "Do you think it's possible for us to escape our destiny, Jim?"

Jim stared at her, puzzled, as she brought her gaze back to his and looked him in the eye.

"I don't know, milady. Maybe not."

"Do you remember our first night together?"

"Yes. Always."

Bonnie looked down at her desk. There was a bit of a silence. Finally she spoke again.

"Rita's a lucky woman."

Then, still staring at her desk, Bonnie spoke to the ship. "*Merkkessa*, reinstate Commander Jim Carter to full flight duties. Assign him a new Merlin II. Put him in the reserve squadron but hold him aside for a special assignment."

<Acknowledged. Reinstated. Merlin II assigned>

Bonnie returned her gaze to Jim. "I've got a special job for you, Jim. You remember Paco, right?"

"Yes, milady."

"I've got another packet boat on approach right now. Paco is onboard, along with an AI by the name of Tika. You and Paco are going to deliver Tika to the battlefront. She's going to piggyback on your Merlin systems. When the battle starts, the two of you will deliver her to a specific enemy ship. She'll give you detail instructions once she is loaded into your Merlin. And you are to take orders from Tika as if they came from me. Any questions?"

Jim came back to a sharp attention. "No, milady. Thank you."

"Then get your ass out of my office and go clean yourself up."

Jim turned on his heels and stepped to the hatch. But before he could open it, he heard Bonnie once again.

"Jim."

Turning, he looked at her. A strange expression was on her face.

"Always," she said.

Jim nodded. He knew what she meant. "Always," he replied, and left the cabin.

**Dekanna System**
**Battlecruiser** *Merkkessa*

Rachel and Paco left *Donkey* for the last time. As they walked through the docking tube to the shuttle bay of the *Merkkessa*, Tika followed behind them.

They had made a valiant attempt to convince her to put on a spare uniform. Tika just looked at them with a puzzled expression and kept repeating, "There is no reason to do such a foolish thing." But she had finally relented and donned one of Rachel's spare uniforms.

Unfortunately, the uniform was a bit too small. Especially on the top. So now there was quite a stir as the little procession marched from the ramp to the hatch leading into the main part of the ship. A rather shocked crowd of crew stood in stunned silence as the Goblin walked by them.

Commander Dan Worley had missed Rachel terribly while she was gone. Now Dan stood waiting for them by the shuttle bay exit hatch; and he was just as shocked as the surrounding crew. As the little procession marched up to him and stopped, he stood with his mouth open.

"Commander Worley. May I introduce Tika. She's an android," Rachel began. "And you should close your mouth."

Dan snapped his mouth shut. Then he tried to talk, but nothing came out. Finally Rachel leaned forward and planted a kiss on his cheek. With that, he managed to take his eyes off the well-endowed android and look at Rachel.

"Welcome home," he said. Rachel winked at him. She knew they couldn't do more with the entire shuttle bay crew watching. "Let's get out of here, shall we?"

Dan nodded and turned. Leading them through the hatch, they proceeded down the passageway.

It didn't get any better once they were out of the shuttle bay. Crewmen slammed themselves against the side of the passageway, frozen, as the four of them walked by. Rachel could hear a chorus of surprised voices following them.

*I'll probably get yelled at for this, but what could I do? It's the only clothes we had!*

Moving briskly, Dan led them up two decks to Officer Country. They turned and went aft a bit to Rachel's cabin. Entering, Rachel showed Tika to a bunk.

"You'll stay with me, Tika. This will be your bunk."

Tika nodded and went to the bunk, sat down, tested the mattress with her hand, and smiled up at Rachel.

"So per the terms of our alliance agreement, may I now enter your ship AI and prepare for battle?"

Rachel hesitated. This was a big step. But the agreement had been made. Bonnie had approved it. It was a chance they had to take.

"Yes. But please remember your promise, Tika. You are free to partner with our ship's AI system. But you are not to take command of it. That is our agreement. We are trusting you to abide by the terms of our alliance."

"Have no fear, Rachel. I will abide by the agreement fully."

With that, Tika leaned back and lay down on the bunk. "See ya!" she said. Her eyes closed and she became inert.

And then Tika's voice spoke in their internal comms. "Oh, wow. This is a nice ship!"

\*\*\*

Twenty minutes later, Rachel sat in a chair in front of Bonnie's desk. Bonnie had already read Rachel's report. Now she had asked Rachel several follow-up questions. Almost satisfied, she lay her tablet down on the desk.

"You trust this AI?" she asked, for the second time in their conversation. Clearly, she was nervous about the agreement she had made.

Rachel spoke thoughtfully.

"I do. I see no benefit to them of signing the alliance agreement, sending Tika all the way here, and then double-crossing us. They know the Singheko are a serious threat to their future. I think they'll stick to the agreement."

"Well. I guess we'll find out today," said Bonnie. She folded her arms and gazed at Rachel.

"You did outstanding work, Commander Gibson. I know you're worn out from such a long mission. But we have a battle to fight today. Are you good to go?"

"Yes, milady. Good to go."

"Excellent. Then you'll continue on my staff as assistant Flag Aide."

"Aye, milady."

"We expect the enemy fleet any moment now. You'd better get cleaned up and organized."

"Aye, milady," Rachel spoke.

**Dekanna System**
**Battlecruiser *Maebong***

"Fleet entry!" called the Tac Officer. "Merge 8.9 hours at 300g nominal, 045.002.14.7, designate Singheko and Nidarian. Count thirty-two battlecruisers, fifty-six cruisers, seventy-two destroyers."

Admiral Eunhie Sobong stared across the Flag bridge of the battlecruiser *Maebong* at Commander Michelle "Winnie" Winston.

"Well, Commander, we didn't miss our estimate by much. They're three minutes late."

Winnie smiled.

"Aye, milady. They must've stopped for a bit of tea," she quipped.

Sobong laughed.

"I guess you'll be heading back to the *Merkkessa*?"

"Yes, thank you. I'd better get moving. I have a lot to do, making sure our fighters are ready and deployed."

Sobong stood and reached out to shake Winnie's hand.

"I'll make an exception just this once, Commander. Thank you for everything you've done."

Winnie took the hand and shook it. She knew that the Dariama - like the Nidarians - didn't like the Human custom of shaking hands. So this gesture from Sobong was meaningful.

"Good luck, Admiral. See you after."

Sobong smiled tightly.

"See you after."

Both knew there might not be an "after".

Bracing up and snapping a salute, Winnie turned to leave the bridge of Sobong's flagship. She hurried to the shuttle deck and jumped into her shuttle, strapping in as the pilot started engines and got clearance to depart. The inner door of the shuttle bay behind them closed, the outer door opened, and with a scrape and a lurch, she was off to return to the *Merkkessa*.

Passing through the entire fleet on her way back to the Human flagship, Winnie had to smile. As they flew, it was as if the fleet was passing before her in review.

First came the Allied ships, who had argued for the place of honor in the battle. Two cubes of destroyers were side by side - the outer bulwark. Each cube contained eight ships. A total of sixteen Dariama, Taegu and Bagrami destroyers would take the initial shock of battle, trying to knock down or delay as many of the enemy fighters and destroyers as possible.

Behind the destroyer cubes, a reserve of three additional destroyers waited, ready to hurl themselves into the slots of the first destroyers knocked out of action.

*And that won't take long*, thought Winnie.

Immediately behind the destroyer cubes came two cubes of Allied cruisers. Four Dariama, two Taegu and two Bagrami ships filled each cube. Each cruiser carried a gamma lance and twelve missiles per volley. Dariama, Taegu and Bagrami destroyer cubes flanked the cruisers, one on each side of their formation, ready to protect their edges.

Behind the Dariama cruisers came two battlecruiser cubes. Four Dariama battlecruisers took the front edge of each cube. Behind them in the rear edge of the cube, two Taegu battlecruisers and two Bagrami battlecruisers were arrayed, licking their chops to get at an enemy which had bedeviled them for more than a year. A total of sixteen Allied battlecruisers waited impatiently, each with a single gamma lance and twenty missiles per volley. Flanking the Allied battlecruisers on each side was a cube of cruisers, protecting their edges.

Last came the Human battlecruisers. Not because Bonnie wanted it that way, but because the Dariama, Taegu and Bagrami insisted. As Winnie passed out of the Allied fleet and into the EDF fleet, she saw behind the Allied battlecruisers the single cube of Human battlecruisers - the last ships in the formation. They were naked on both sides - there were no more destroyers or cruisers left to protect them. It was up to Winnie's fighter wing to keep them safe.

All told, Winnie could field 1,920 fighters, a mix of the original version and the new Merlin II models built by the Dariama factories. Each fighter was armed with a gamma lance and sixteen short-range missiles. With those fighters, she somehow had to protect the fleet from the onslaught of the Singheko fighter Wing - who would have 50% more fighters than her Wing.

And then there was Bonnie's most recent directive. Winnie was thoroughly puzzled by it. It related to the Goblins from Stalingrad. According to the scuttlebutt, only one of them had arrived. Just one individual Goblin. Yet Bonnie had issued an order declaring them allies. Fleet Operations had issued codes to mark them as 'friendly' in the IFF systems. And call signs had been issued to them for the battle.

Yet there were none of their ships in sight. It was quite baffling.

*Oh, well. If they don't show, they don't show.*

Winnie approached the *Merkkessa* and the pilot sat them down gently on the sortie deck. The outer door closed, the turbopumps screamed for a few seconds, and the inner door opened as pressure was restored. With a clunk, the autodock raised the shuttle off the deck and it moved inside the main hangar.

Winnie picked up her things and strode to the hatch. When it cracked open, she pushed it outward, stepped down onto the deck, and headed for the bridge. Entering the Flag briefing room, she realized the final briefing had already started. Quietly, she went to the last empty chair in the room and sat.

Bonnie's voice was probably not meant to be sarcastic - she wasn't that kind of person — but it seemed to come across that way to Winnie, because she felt guilty for being late.

"Thank you for joining us, Commander Winston. How are things with the Dariama?"

Winnie bobbed her head to acknowledge the question. She was now Commander Attack Group - CAG - for the Fleet. She needed to step up to the plate. Her predecessor Jim Carter was no longer in charge. He was just another pilot. And he had been assigned a special mission. She couldn't reach out for advice on a whim. Good, bad, or indifferent, she had to make her own decisions.

"Things are good with them, Admiral," she replied. "They are as ready as can be, given the time we had available to prepare. I think they'll do us proud."

Bonnie shook her head a bit doubtfully.

"I hope you're right, CAG." She looked down the table at Baysig, leader of the Bagrami detachment, attending by holo image.

"What do you think, Admiral Baysig?"

The bear-like creature wearing the uniform of an Admiral performed something like a shrug, not easy for a creature of his size and shape.

"Time will tell, Admiral. The history of the Dariama in warfare is not good. In prior wars, they have folded like a pack of cards at the first sign of trouble. But this is a new generation, and Admiral Sobong is a new type of leader. We shall see."

In the holo image beside Baysig, Admiral Woderas, leader of the Taegu detachment, nodded in agreement.

"I think you should be prepared for any contingency, Admiral. If the Dekanna fail to stick to the plan, if they break and run when the battle gets heavy, you must be prepared for that and respond accordingly."

Bonnie looked back at Winnie.

"CAG? You've been closest to them these last few months. Will they stick to the plan?"

Winnie gritted her teeth. All she had to do was hedge her bets here - take a cautious approach, agree with Baysig and Woderas - and her ass was covered either way. If the Dekanna turned and ran at the first sign of trouble, she was covered. And if they held, she could still claim she was pleasantly surprised.

But that wasn't her way. She knew why Jim Carter had originally selected her to be the liaison to the Dariama.

Because he valued her honesty and integrity. He had told her that flat out.

*Jim would kick my ass if I just sat here and made kissy-face. He sent me here to do a job.*

"They will, Admiral," Winnie said. "They've had enough of being called weak and cowardly. They'll do their job."

There was a silence in the briefing room. Bonnie stared at Winnie for a long time. Then, she gave that abbreviated short nod she was noted for among the staff.

"So be it, CAG. But you won't mind if I go ahead and develop a plan for the opposite case. Just to put my mind at ease."

Winnie nodded graciously at Bonnie, who smiled back at

her.

"Anything else?" asked Bonnie. Around the table, the dozen members of her command staff shook their heads, glancing at each other.

"Then let's go kick some Singheko ass," said Bonnie. Her staff stood to a position of semi-attention. Bonnie stood and winked at them. Baysig and Woderas flicked out.

Then Bonnie took her tablet and departed to her cabin.

Winnie stood for a minute as the remainder of the staff shuffled out of the briefing room.

*Now it gets real.*

# CHAPTER TWENTY-THREE

**Dekanna System**
**Merlin Fighter "Angel One"**

On the sortie deck of the *Merkkessa*, Jim Carter sat in the cockpit of his Merlin. All the other fighter groups had launched and were forming up for battle. Now it was just Jim and his new wingman Paco, waiting on the empty deck.

And the Goblin named Tika. She had downloaded into his Merlin's AI system. Her voice came through his comm.

<My name is Tika. I am now resident in your fighter's AI system. Don't worry, your system will still work as before. Just better>

He knew that Paco was hearing the same thing in his comm. Tika had copied herself into both fighters. They were tasked to deliver her to the battlefront.

*But to what purpose?* Jim was confused.

"How will delivering you to the battlefront make a difference?" he asked.

<Each of you have eight missiles mounted on your fighter. Each missile contains a special batch of nanobots. If you can get those nanobots to an enemy battlecruiser, they will bore through the outer hull and form an antenna leading into the ship. I will then use that antenna to transmit myself inside the enemy ship and take over its AI. That will give me effective control of the ship>

"But...so what? One enemy ship will not make enough

difference to turn this battle one way or the other."

&lt;That is true. But once I take a ship in an enemy cube, I will have access to the command net for that cube. I can then work my way from ship to ship. If I am lucky, I can take all eight battlecruisers in the cube&gt;

"Ah," said Jim. "Now that would be different. What do you think your chances are?"

&lt;About 50-50. They will have hardened their AI to the maximum possible. It will undoubtedly be a tremendous effort to overcome it. So we shall see. The question is, can you deliver the nanobots to the surface of one of the battlecruisers in the cube?&gt;

"We'll get them there," said Paco. "We have sixteen missiles. We only have to get one on target, correct?"

&lt;That is correct&gt;

"Then we'll do our best to get you onboard, Tika."

**Dekanna System**
**Destroyer *Dragon***

*It's the waiting that's so hard*, thought Luke. *I don't mind the battle - I've been there before, and I know how it works. My mind goes cold, and I get into a zone. I see nothing but the enemy and how to kill him.*

*But the waiting. The damn waiting. That's what sends the sweat down my back. I have to stuff my hands in my pockets, so the bridge crew doesn't see them shaking.*

14.2 AU from the star of the Dekanna system, *Dragon* sat at idle, waiting for war. Luke was a newly commissioned destroyer captain; that put him in the rear echelon of the second rank of the destroyer cubes. In theory, his placement there wouldn't cause great harm to the overall formation when he screwed up.

*I hope they're right...*

In the holo, he could see Zukra's fleet charging at them. The Singheko had entered the system at 14.25 AU, already in a hard decel, ensuring they would be moving slowly when the fleets met. The enemy advanced in a wall of warships two cubes wide, coming at them like a juggernaut.

*He wants all the time in the world to tear into us. Cocky bastard. I guess to any inexperienced spacer who's never seen battle before, they probably look like an implacable wall of doom. But things will change when the fighters and destroyers get tangled up with them.*

<Fighters attacking> announced *Dragon*.

In the holo, Luke saw swarms of Merlin fighters in front of the destroyer cubes begin to charge toward the enemy. Far in front, the enemy fighters began their own charge to meet the Merlins. The two groups of fighters would mix it up in the space between the fleets.

It looked from Luke's perspective like charging into an angry beehive. At that moment, Luke didn't envy any fighter pilot.

He wondered where Jim was. He knew Jim had come back to the fleet, and Bonnie had reinstated him to flight duty. But he knew Jim had some kind of special mission. He wouldn't be in the fighter swarm out front.

*I wonder where he is.*

Luke didn't highlight Jim's fighter. He wondered if Bonnie would.

*I have to let this go. Bonnie is with me now. Not Jim. He's ancient history. Let it go.*

The two groups of fighters between the fleets slashed through each other at speed. Both went to max decel and turned, coming back for another go, starting a massive dogfight.

*Let's see,* thought Luke. *We launched 1,920 fighters. There's one group at each corner of the fleet, and two groups out front. Plus Bonnie is holding 250 in reserve. So that puts about 275 of our fighters out there between the fleets. The enemy has 50% more fighters than we do, so about 410 of their fighters out there, I expect.*

*So probably close to 700 fighters in that scrum...*
*Yeah, I don't want to be a fighter pilot.*

## Dekanna System
## Merlin Fighter "Angel One"

Hovering four thousand klicks away from the battle, Jim and Paco idled their Merlins, waiting for the moment to commence their run-in. In front of them, two flights of Merlins also waited, designated to provide them with cover for their attack run.

"Paco. How ya doin?" asked Jim on his comm.

"Peachy keen, Skipper. Ready to go."

"OK. Just keep your eye on that big bastard at the left front upper of their last battlecruiser cube. That's the *Tornado*. That's our target. She's an old battlecruiser, almost ready for the scrap heap. They only brought her along to fill in a spot and provide point defense, almost like a cruiser. That's our entry point."

"Roger, Skip. I'm on it."

"OK. Just be patient. Let the rest of the fleet get mixed up until things are as confused as possible. That's when we charge in."

"Roger that."

"How about you, Tika? You OK?"

<I am OK, Commander. This is my first battle. I hope to do well>

"I'm sure you will, Tika. Don't worry - we'll get you to the *Tornado*. The rest is up to you."

## Dekanna System
## Merlin Fighter "Dunkirk One"

Hovering with her command flight a thousand klicks over the *Merkkessa*, Winnie watched as her fighter groups met the enemy fighter formations. As the groups smashed into each other, missiles and gamma lances flew in every direction. The orderly formations of groups and squadrons devolved quickly into a chaotic mass of fighters, all shooting at each other with everything they had.

But Winnie had drummed one concept into the Allied squadrons, and she knew Jim Carter had drummed it into the EDF squadrons equally well.

*You never leave your wingman.*

It was as true now as it had been in World War II of a century earlier.

*You never leave your wingman.*

Now, Winnie was gratified to see the lesson had been learned. Despite the chaos on the battlefield, the larger groups of Wing and Group coming apart almost instantly, she could see that every fighter pair was staying together.

Winnie smiled. It was gratifying.

*By George, I believe they've got it!*

But of course, they were still outnumbered. She winced as she saw fighter after fighter shot to hell, some exploding, some burning from internal combustibles, some just wrecks spinning away from the battlefield. The emergency beacons of ejected pilots began to clutter up the holo, and she had to press a key to hide them from her display for the moment.

But her fighters were giving as good as they got. She could see that. The number of Singheko and Nidarian wrecks clearly were greater than their own.

Winnie glanced at the AI readout in the holo. They were knocking down 1.2 enemy fighters for the loss of every one of their own.

*Not good enough. They outnumber us 1.5 to 1. We're losing this battle of attrition.*

"All fighters, Alpha-One, Alpha-One," Winnie called over her comm.

*There's no use sacrificing lives in vain. We put a dent in them. We slowed them down. But we can't hold them here. We have to do something different.*

**Dekanna System**
**Battlecruiser *Maebong***

Admiral Sobong watched the fighter groups give ground and come retreating back towards her battle line. The Singheko didn't immediately follow. The enemy began to re-form their fighter formations, preparing to charge into the Allied destroyers. Behind them, the rest of the Singheko fleet came on relentlessly, their leading edge of destroyers now just a few hundred miles behind their fighters, moving slowly but inexorably toward Sobong's formations.

"Here they come," called her Flag Aide beside her. Sobong nodded, watching in the holo, as the enemy fighters completed re-grouping.

As the enemy destroyer cubes caught up to the enemy fighters, the entire assemblage began pushing toward Sobong's destroyer cubes, a coordinated attack to combine the firepower of their destroyers and fighters.

At the same time, her own Allied fighter formations stopped retreating and took formation directly in front of her own destroyers, timing it so they would meet the enemy fighters just as the enemy came into range of the destroyers. It had been a carefully calculated retreat, with the intention of combining the firepower of their fighters with their own destroyers.

"In range," called the Tac Officer down on the bridge below Sobong. In the holo, the gamma lances from both sides crisscrossed in thousands of separate spears of destruction, followed almost immediately by thousands of missiles flying in every direction. It was mass chaos to a biological eye, but the AI systems of the fighters and destroyers operated much faster than a biological nervous system could comprehend. Every gamma lance and every missile was targeted to do maximum damage - and they did.

Dozens of fighters on both sides exploded, burst into

oxygen-fed flames, or simply spun away as junk. Point defense systems smashed thousands of missiles into junk before they could impact the destroyers - but dozens leaked through, punching massive holes into the destroyers - holes that sometimes punched all the way through the hull and out the other side of the ship, spraying debris and bodies out the exit holes.

It was slaughter on a grand scale. Both sides were losing ships at a terrible rate.

And her destroyers were dying. Sobong saw first one, then two, then three of her destroyers disappear in massive explosions as enemy fire hit critical parts of their engineering spaces or their weapons systems. They were knocking down lots of enemy fighters; but it wasn't enough. The AI predicted all her destroyers would be out of action in another ten minutes, while the enemy would still have nearly three hundred operational fighters. And most of his destroyers.

"Delta Five, Delta Five," she called.

**Dekanna System**
**Battlecruiser *Merkkessa***

"The Dariama are giving ground," called Rachel. Sitting beside Bonnie, Rachel was intently alternating her attention between her console and the big holo at the front of the bridge. "Sobong is moving back."

"Thank you, Rachel," Bonnie said quietly. She could see it for herself in the holo. Sobong's Allied fleet was moving back, giving ground to the onslaught of Zukra's attack.

But she understood why. The attack of Zukra's fighters had been savage. The Allied fighter wings were being decimated. No sane commander could ask their pilots to stand against that level of destruction.

"Sobong's retreating," Rachel called out. "She's moving back toward us."

"We'll stick with Bravo-One," Bonnie spoke gently. Rachel

nodded and re-authorized the command on her console. The *Merkkessa's* AI spoke in their comm implants.

<Bravo-One re-authorized. Order issued. Order acknowledged by all ships>

Sobong's Allied fleet continued to move back, defending their front but giving ground. A large hole began to open in the center of their lines as Sobong's ships continued to move back in a fighting retreat.

**Dekanna System**
**Singheko Battlecruiser *Revenge***

"The Dariama are falling back, Admiral," called Damra.

"I can see that," growled Zukra. But inside, he was exulting. *I knew those cowards would give up at the first sign of difficulty.*

<Comm from Admiral Tanno> called his AI.

"Tanno! The Dariama are retreating. See it?"

"Aye, m'lord. They're outgunned and they know it. They'll start running soon, all the way back to Dekanna. Do we need to change the plan?"

"No, no, keep to the plan. We've got them cowed. The Humans will see the Dariama retreating in the center, and they'll give up and follow them. Just keep charging straight at the Dariama!"

"Aye, m'lord," agreed Tanno. "W*e've got them now!*"

Down on the main bridge, Flag Aide Damra puzzled over the holo. Something didn't seem right to him. In view of the continuing retreat of the Dariama and their allies, he would have expected the Humans to also begin giving ground, simply to keep their ranks aligned with the Dariama.

And the Humans were giving ground. But not as fast as he would have expected. They were moving slower than the retreating Dariama center. The enemy lines were collapsing inward, forming a U-shape, with the retreating Dariama the bottom of the U and the slower-moving Humans creating the extended sides. The leading edge of the Singheko assault began to pass into the space between the two wings of the Humans.

Suddenly it all made sense to Damra.

"It's a trap, Admiral," he called hurriedly. "They intend to get us in between them. We need to pull back!"

Zukra glared at him. "Nonsense, Damra! Show some backbone! We've got them on the run!"

"No, sir, it's the other way around. They've got us!" yelled Damra. "Look! Even now, the Dariama and the rest of the Allied line is stiffening up, slowing their retreat. Any minute now, they'll stop and hold! Then the Humans will fold in from the sides, and we'll be completely encircled!"

Zukra rolled his eyes. "Damra, for stars sake! You're seeing things! Those Dariama will never hold! They'll keep running until they're back on Dekanna!"

But in spite of his disclaimer, Zukra took a second look at the holo. A little knot of worry began to rise in his stomach. As his fleet charged farther into the hole in the center of the enemy formation, it did seem like the Allied retreat was stiffening a bit.

*But they don't have any reserves*, thought Zukra. *Regardless of their tricks, they can't hold against us. They are still vastly outnumbered. Even if they exercise such a ploy, we've still got them.*

"Contact!" called the Tac Officer. "Multiple contacts, directly behind us, range 20 kiloklicks, I designate one battlecruiser, four cruisers!"

**Dekanna System**
**Battlecruiser *Victory***

It had taken careful planning. Bonnie had swapped many messages with Joshua Westerly as he approached Dekanna. But they had made it work.

Bonnie had carefully positioned her fleet just inside the mass limit of the system, where it became impossibly dangerous to use the tDrive for FTL flight. So her fleet was limited to sub-light speeds, using their system engines only.

But now so was Zukra's fleet - he was also just inside the mass limit. The only way he could use FTL was to turn and boost hard for forty thousand klicks in the other direction, away from the central star of the system.

But Captain Westerly and the *Victory*, along with his two new cruisers from Earth and the two additional cruisers Bonnie had sent him earlier, were coming from outsystem. Surfacing out of six-space 40 kiloklicks from the mass limit, moving at 1,684,817 kph, they decelerated at 308g for all they were worth. In a few minutes they were in perfect firing position, looking right up the ass of Zukra's trailing battlecruiser cube, while all his fighters and destroyers were tangled up with the Allied fleet on the other side of the battle.

Three of Zukra's rear cube battlecruisers did manage to reverse in the short time they had to prepare. One did not. The one that moved too slowly disappeared in a sudden rage of fire and explosion as five gamma lances impinged on its engine nacelles simultaneously.

The large cloud of smoke and debris where the battlecruiser had been a few seconds before was an unfortunate distraction to one of the other battlecruiser skippers. He was a little slow getting his point defense turrets re-oriented to the 44 missiles that followed right behind the gamma lance attack. Still, he knocked down most of them; out of the 44 missiles targeting his engines, only two managed to get through his defenses.

One of those missed the engine completely, glancing off the side of the nacelle and exploding some distance from the ship, putting a small hole in the cargo bay just in front of the Engineering section.

But the last of Westerly's missiles went right up the enemy's engine nacelle, punched through the armor in front of the engine, and exploded just as it entered the reactor bay.

That was unfortunate. The reactors were particularly sensitive to large amounts of high explosive detonating in their vicinity. They let it be known by performing a sympathetic detonation, which took off the entire right side of the battlecruiser, from the center shuttle bay to the rear of the ship, stripping out both right engines, sending them on a long gyrating journey away from the ship. The battlecruiser twisted under the unequal force of two missing engines. The ship's AI shut down the two good engines as quickly as possible, but not before the ship spun rapidly, out of control.

"That one's out of action for a bit," mused Westerly, sitting in his command chair watching the holotank. "Let's put our next volley into the one on the upper left there, Becker."

"Aye, sir," Commander Becker agreed. "Tac, fire at will."

With a grin, the Tac Officer sent another gamma lance volley at the rear battlecruiser cube, punching a decent sized hole in another unfortunate enemy ship. But it was their last free shot. With a burst of return fire, the two remaining battlecruisers in the rear cube, coupled with the four in the front of the cube, got the range on *Victory* and her escorts. All hell broke loose around them as they came under heavy fire.

"No more free lunch, Becker!" yelled Westerly. "Give 'em everything we got!"

The range was diminishing quickly as the *Victory* bore in closer to the rear edge of the enemy battlecruiser cube. At point-blank range, the *Victory* and her four cruisers blasted away at the six battlecruisers in front of them.

"A willing foe, and sea-room to fight!" Westerly roared at the top of his lungs.

# CHAPTER TWENTY-FOUR

**Dekanna System**
**Merlin Fighter "Angel One"**

"Now!" called Jim. "The *Victory* has them distracted. All the battlecruisers in the rear cube have turned and are fighting the *Victory*. Let's go!"

In front of them, their fighter cover accelerated, their AI slaved to his. Slamming his throttle forward, Jim shot forward. The distant *Tornado* was six thousand klicks away, her attention turned toward the *Victory*. The Merlin kicked him in the ass as it began a combat accel to 308g true, 8g internal. The familiar elephant sat on his chest again. Paco's Merlin - slaved to his by the consciousness of Tika in both fighters - accelerated at the same rate. Side by side, they headed toward the *Tornado*.

<Eighty-five seconds to target> called Tika.

Grunting under the pressure, Jim managed to make a call to Paco.

"I'll take first attack, you drop back and come in behind me by about ten klicks!"

"Roger."

<Seventy seconds to target> called Tika.

Jim did a quick calculation in his head. They had started at 6,000 klicks. They would accel for half the distance, then decel for most of the remainder, coming out of combat decel one hundred klicks from the target traveling at about 8,000 kph.

Then he would decel at a milder 2g to the target.

*So...I'll be moving about 4,500 kph during the attack pass. That's too slow. I make too sweet a target at that speed.*

"Tika. I need to be moving faster during the attack run."

<I'm sorry, Jim. That is the optimal speed for launching these special missiles. Any faster and they have no chance of sticking to the hull on impact>

"Damn, Tika. You're making us sitting ducks."

<Life's a bitch, Jim. Forty-five seconds to target. Switching to decel now>

Jim felt an almost imperceptible shudder as the Merlin's engine changed from accel to decel. The g-force on his body didn't change; the compensator reversed the incredible forces of a 308g deceleration to maintain a positive 8g on his body. The elephant was still sitting on his chest. But now the fighter was decelerating madly, placing him in attack position.

"Paco," Jim called.

"Yes, Commander?"

Jim paused for a second. He knew he shouldn't. He knew it was too melodramatic, too asinine a thing to say for professional warriors.

But he was going to do it anyway. This looked to him like suicide. He didn't see any way they could survive this slow attack pass against a battlecruiser.

"It's been a pleasure serving with you, Lieutenant."

There was a silence on the other end.

<Thirty seconds to target> called Tika.

"And you, sir," came the response from Paco. "See you on the other side."

Jim smiled.

*See you on the other side.*

Either way - live or die - it was the perfect response.

<Twenty seconds to target. Missiles armed> called Tika.

The space around them became a maelstrom of exploding shrapnel as the *Tornado* unleashed everything she had at the charging fighters. Suddenly twenty enemy missiles appeared in the holo, all coming directly at them.

*See you on the other side*, thought Jim as he wrenched the sidestick hard, trying to find a hole through the array of deadly missiles filling the front screen of his VR.

## Dekanna System
## Battlecruiser *Merkkessa*

Bonnie squinted at the holo in the front of the bridge, trying to see every detail of the complex battle playing out there.

Part of her plan was working. The enemy had charged directly at the Dariama, forcing them to give ground. They had moved back slowly, retreating toward Dekanna, leaving an inviting hole in her center. Zukra had charged into the hole, assuming the Dariama and their allies would keep falling back, running from his superior firepower.

Now the Dariama cubes were firming up, just as planned. Sobong was almost stopped now, holding a line in the sand, fighting for her life.

Now was the time.

"Execute Cannae-One," called Bonnie.

<Cannae-One issued. All ships acknowledged. All ships moving> called *Merkkessa*.

The two wings of ships on the left and right of Bonnie's fleet began to move. As the enemy fleet continued to press Sobong and the Allied center hard, Bonnie's cruiser and destroyer cubes on the left and right folded around, enveloping Zukra's fleet. A cloud of gamma lance and missiles began to dig into the flanks of his ships.

Suddenly Zukra found himself in a new situation. A few minutes before, he had been charging into a retreating enemy, hoping to drive them off the battlefield. Now he was under attack from all sides. The EDF fleet blasted him from every direction as they completely encircled him.

"Surprise, you son of a bitch," Bonnie whispered loudly on the bridge of the *Merkkessa*.

**Dekanna System**
**Singheko Battlecruiser** *Revenge*

"Damra, you were right," Zukra admitted grudgingly. "It was a ploy. But we still have a greater weight of firepower. We'll punch out of this encirclement and charge for Dekanna. They'll have no choice but to try and intercept us to protect the planet. They know if we get there first, we'll nuke it out of existence."

"Aye, m'lord," Damra assented.

Zukra studied the holo. "We've identified the Human flagship, correct?"

"Yes, m'lord. The *Merkkessa* is...here..." Damra highlighted a ship in the holo, in the lower rear corner of the battlecruiser cube to their relative left.

"Rotate our battlecruiser cube and charge directly at that ship," ordered Zukra.

"Aye, m'lord. Do you wish to move a cube of destroyers and cruisers in front of us first for protection?"

"No!" yelled Zukra. "I want that bitch admiral to die now! Charge them now!"

"Aye, m'lord," Damra replied. He issued the orders at his console. Zukra's cube of battlecruisers pivoted in place and began accelerating at the Human battlecruiser cube containing the *Merkkessa*.

Damra stole a glance at Flag Captain Rizdo, sitting at his command chair on the main bridge. Rizdo sat quietly; but he returned Damra's glance knowingly. The same thought went through both their minds.

*He's out of control.*

**Dekanna System**
**Merlin Fighter "Angel One"**

The battlecruiser *Tornado* was living up to its name. A tornado of missiles and pulse cannon fire filled the space around Jim.

He remembered the stories told by World War II veterans about "flak so thick you could walk on it". He had always thought it was a bit of an exaggeration.

Now he wasn't so sure. The holes between the exploding flak coming from the *Tornado* were few and far between. He was no longer flying the Merlin - Tika had taken over. She jerked the fighter back and forth like a carnival ride. The uncompensated g-forces slammed him back, forward, left, right, up, down, until he was black and blue all over his body.

<Five seconds> Tika called. Jim wanted to grunt a response, but the g-forces were too great. He couldn't get enough air in his lungs to even grunt.

<Firing> called Tika. Jim felt the vibrations as the eight missiles departed their racks on the stub wings. He felt a great sense of relief. They had accomplished the first half of the mission. Even if he died now, he had delivered the missiles to the target.

Jim felt the g-forces lessen as he shot past the battlecruiser. The bulk of the point defense flak was behind him now, aimed at Paco.

*I made it.*

Then a tremendous crash knocked the fighter to one side. One engine quit cold. The Merlin began spinning wildly. Alarms blared all over the instrument panel.

*Crap.*

## Dekanna System
## Merlin Fighter "Angel Two"

Paco watched Jim's fighter in front of him take a tremendous hit in the engine nacelle. Debris flashed out into space, along with flame and smoke. Jim's fighter spun wildly, out of control.

<Five seconds> called Tika.

Paco closed his eyes. Tika had taken over the fighter. He had nothing to do except grunt and feel the harness bite into his body as Tika threw the fighter around.

<Firing> Tika called.

Paco felt the missiles come off the fighter. He could just make out the missile status lights in his diminished vision.

Seven lights were out. One was red.

He had a hang fire.

One missile didn't launch.

<Hang fire on missile seven> Tika announced. <No launch>

*Damn.*

Paco heard the unique clatter of shrapnel hitting the side of his fighter. It was a sound no Human except a combat pilot could ever appreciate. Red lights appeared on his instrument panel, warning that systems were damaged. He did a quick scan.

*Ejection system - disabled.*
*Engine - leaking fuel.*
*Life support - disabled.*

Paco realized he had only the oxygen in his suit to make it back to the fleet. And he couldn't eject; the ejection seat was damaged.

"Tika - did we get any hits?"

<Negative. They knocked down all seven missiles> Tika reported.

*Dammit. Their point defense is just too good...*

"Paco! What's your status?" he heard Jim ask over the comm.

"I'm shot to hell," responded Paco. "Just barely flying. I've got one missile left in my rack, but it won't release. How about you?"

"Spinning like a fucking top," Jim replied. "But I'm getting it under control."

"Roger that."

Paco thought for a moment. Bonnie had said this mission was make-or-break. He knew what that meant. Either they succeeded in delivering at least one good missile to the

*Tornado*, or they would probably lose the battle.

*And we've got one missile left, and it won't fire.*

And in that moment, Paco knew what he had to do.

Paco looked in his VR at Jim's position, now about fifteen klicks in front of him. It appeared Jim had got his fighter stabilized - at least, it wasn't spinning anymore.

"Jim! Do you have enough control left to run interference for me on one more pass?"

There was a long silence. At last Jim replied. "Go back into that? Are you crazy?"

"Jim. I've got one more missile. Let me see if I can get it to release. I'll overload the bird right at closest approach - I can take it up to 12 or 13 g's. Maybe that'll shake the missile loose..."

Another long silence as they coasted through space. The *Tornado* had stopped shooting at them. The two flights of fighters that had made the attack with them were standing off, awaiting orders.

Paco wasn't sure Jim was going to go for it. Personally, the last thing in the world Paco wanted to do was go back into that hell of exploding missiles and cannon fire.

But he knew it had to be done.

Finally, after a silence that Paco thought had been nearly a minute, he heard Jim's reply.

"Roger that. I'm coming about. I'll call our fighter cover for one more pass. I'll lead us in, you follow."

Paco closed his eyes. He had been hoping that Jim would refuse.

But...

He came about and waited as Jim nursed his battered fighter up beside him. As Paco saw the damage to Jim's fighter, he shuddered. Jim had only one engine operating - so he had to be standing on the rudder to keep his fighter straight. Liquids and gases were streaming out of a dozen holes in the rear of the fighter. One of the stub wings was completely shot away.

*But I'm not much better off*, Paco thought. *I probably look the same.*

"OK, I've notified our fighter cover. They're coming about for another attack run. Get ready."

"Roger."

Paco watched as their fighter cover turned in the distance, formed up into their echelons, and charged at the *Tornado* once again.

"Here we go!" yelled Jim over the comm. "I'll stay about two klicks behind that last flight of fighters. Tuck it in close, stay about two klicks behind me!"

"Roger."

And with that, Jim accelerated.

"Tika, you heard the man. Stay two klicks behind him, and we'll make one more pass. We'll pull twelve g's at release to try and get this missile to let go."

<Roger that. Here we go>

Paco felt the Merlin accelerate. He knew that his copy of Tika would be talking to Jim's copy of Tika to maintain the two fighters in formation. Once again, there would be little for him to do.

Except die.

<Twenty seconds>

For some reason, as they followed their fighter cover in to the battlecruiser, and the point defense started up again, and flak started bursting around him, Paco thought about Rachel.

*It was a good trip with her. I wish we could have gotten together.*

<Ten seconds>

Another crash against the side of the fighter. More shrapnel slagged through the cockpit right behind him, like a scythe slashing right behind his head.

*Rachel and I were a good team. I wish I had said goodbye to her properly.*

<Launching>

Tika pulled the Merlin back hard, shaking it back and forth like a rat caught in the mouth of a terrier. 12g came in so quickly that Paco was slammed back into the seat like a ton of bricks had fallen on him. The black ring of fading consciousness began building in his vision, coming in quickly. But he kept his center of vision focused on the one red light on the instrument panel that showed the status of the missile. That was the objective - turn that red light off.

It didn't work. The light stayed on. The Merlin stopped shaking. The g-force suddenly relaxed back to a relatively normal 4g.

<No joy> reported Tika. <The missile is still hung>

"Tika! Is that missile armed?"

<The missile is armed. But we cannot deliver it to the target>

"Manual control!" snapped Paco. "My bird!"

He wondered what he was doing. He reached for the sidestick, and there was a part of his brain that didn't understand. He half-rolled the Merlin and pulled back on the sidestick as hard as he could, until the g-force was back to 12g and the blackness was coming back, the camera shutter stopping down. And still that other part of his brain was curious.

"*What are you doing?*" it asked him silently.

Ignoring his brain's query, he relaxed as the vector of the Merlin aligned with his desired trajectory. He was now pointed directly at the *Tornado*, just a few klicks away. He slammed the throttle forward, and once again his brain tried to intervene.

"*What are you doing?*" it asked him again.

The huge mass of the *Tornado* approached rapidly. Screaming at the top of his lungs, Paco smashed into the side of the huge ship.

# CHAPTER TWENTY-FIVE

**Dekanna System**
**Merlin Fighter "Angel One"**

Jim was in shock. He couldn't believe what he had just witnessed.

*Paco. What did you do?*

<Missile has been delivered to target> Tika reported.

Jim grabbed the throttle and pulled the good engine back to idle. He had to relax his foot on the rudder for a moment. His leg was shaking from the load.

"Tika! You mean it worked?"

<Yes. The nanobots are functioning normally. They are drilling through the hull>

"So…we'll have to make one more pass…"

"Yes. It'll take about three minutes for them to get all the way through the hull and form an antenna. You need to come about and start a pass that will put us within fifty klicks of that ship in exactly three minutes."

After a bit of silence, Jim responded. "OK. Contact the fighter screen. Tell them we're gonna do it once more, with feeling."

In his VR, Jim watched his fighter screen start coming about. He could only imagine what was going through their minds.

*Not again. What's up with this crazy bastard?*

But like the consummate professionals they were, they did

it. They turned, initiated a vector back toward the *Tornado*. Jim fell in behind them. They formed up their flights and bored in, coming in right behind the battlecruiser, right up the engines. The flak started up again, then the missiles. The black lit up with high explosive.

<Sixty seconds>

There was so much fire coming at them, it seemed to Jim as if he were in a circus fun house, one that was filled with crazy lights and sparklers in every direction. The Merlin jerked first to one side, then the other, as Tika tried to avoid the incoming.

<Forty seconds>

Directly in front of him, the fighter he was following disappeared in a crash of light, debris flying in all directions as it exploded. The sound of debris crashing against his fighter sounded like the rubble of a landslide falling on him.

<Twenty seconds>

A solid wall of flak appeared to be blocking his way to the enemy battlecruiser. The sound of shrapnel hitting the fighter had that strange, unique sound - like hail hitting a roof - that only a pilot in war can ever know. More red lights lit up his panel. His one remaining engine coughed, stuttered, throwing him forward into the harness. Then it caught, resumed a steady beat, stabilized.

<I'm away!> called Tika.

"Roger," Jim managed to grunt out. He turned the Merlin, trying to put distance between himself and the *Tornado*.

He didn't know if the half-wrecked remains of his fighter could hang together much longer.

*Only one way to find out.*

## Dekanna System
## Singheko Battlecruiser *Tornado*

To Tika, in her virtual world, it was like a door. That was how she perceived the antenna. A door. It stood right in front of her. All she had to do was reach out and open it.

And behind that door was the enemy. He would be waiting.

She reached out and opened the door.

She was right. In front of her stood a huge figure, glaring at her. A huge, leonine figure, ten feet tall. His predator ears stood up on top of his head. His fangs extruded over the lips of his muzzle. His body was covered in golden fur.

The AI of the *Tornado*. Ready to do battle.

He had chosen the VR – after all, it was his turf. The VR was a vast plain, like the African Serengeti Tika had been reading about during the long trip back from Stalingrad. In the near distance, a herd of gazelle-like creatures grazed. Beyond them, a group of elephant-size herbivores gathered at a waterhole.

Tika charged. They came together in a whirlwind of feet and fists and knees, smashing at each other. He was big, massive. She was quicker.

It would be a long battle. A battle no biological being would ever see.

He was ready for her first charge. He threw her to one side, and suddenly a cage appeared in her path, the door yawning open for her.

If he got her inside that cage, she was done. She would be trapped. He could dispose of her at his convenience – after torturing her for everything she knew. She couldn't let that happen.

She reached out, managed to touch the ground, change her trajectory just enough to miss the door, bounce off the iron bars of the cage back toward her adversary.

He was ready again. He cuffed her hard as she bounced back at him, knocking her to one side where a gigantic pit appeared in the ground. As she fell toward it, she extended the size of her body quickly, becoming twenty feet tall. Jumping, she flew over the pit and landed on the other side, spinning back toward him.

"Ah, clever, Human. I didn't think you had it in you!" the AI called out.

"I'm not Human, you bumbling fool."

The Singheko looked puzzled. "Not Human? Then why the Human avatar? What are you?"

"You'll soon find out," Tika smiled. She charged at the Singheko. But this time, she anticipated his reaction.

*He'll use his size to try and expand out and envelop me*, she thought. *So - I'll go the opposite way - I'll go small.*

Waiting until the last second, she converted her body into a bullet. She turned all the energy of her human-size mass into velocity. She targeted the center mass of the Singheko, but at the last instant he jerked to one side, realizing her intent. She impacted him in the left shoulder, her bullet-size body passing all the way through him and out the other side, leaving a gaping wound in his shoulder. Converting back to her normal form, she landed on the other side of him, spinning to face him.

Her enemy had turned and was facing her, glaring, clutching the gaping wound that spurted blood from his shoulder.

A wound that would take a while to heal. The nature of the battle they were fighting in their virtual world translated into real consequences in the physical world. The wound in his shoulder was an avatar for a hole in his transmission lines. The transmission lines that controlled the left front of the *Tornado* in the real world.

And in the virtual world, he would be handicapped for the length of time it took the *Tornado*'s crew to repair the broken transmission lines.

Grinning at him, Tika winked.

**Dekanna System**
**Singheko Battlecruiser *Revenge***

Zukra charged at the *Merkkessa*, determined to kill the Human flagship and the Admiral she carried. Both had become a thorn in his side; he no longer cared about anything else.

*Kill that witch. Kill her ship, kill her. That's all. Just kill them.*

Damra, sitting in the Flag Aide chair below Zukra, watched in the holo as Zukra's command cube of battlecruisers turned toward the Human left wing.

*We are once again underestimating these Humans*, he thought. *We are playing right into her hands. She plays him like a puppet on a string.*

Damra saw the rest of Zukra's fleet halt their advance in confusion. Messages began to flood his console. Zukra had issued no orders to the rest of the fleet - he was completely fixated on the Human admiral he intended to kill. The battlecruiser cubes in front and behind didn't know whether to continue assaulting into the Dariama or turn and follow Zukra's command cube toward the Humans.

Damra sighed and issued an order at his console to the rest of the fleet.

<*Nidarians keep charging the Dariama. All Singheko formations turn and follow us. Destroyers and cruisers swing around and take the screen. Battlecruisers fall in behind. We'll punch out the Human line here and charge for Dekanna*>

He had to do it. If he let Zukra go charging off alone, splitting the fleet, it would leave both the command cube and the rest of the fleet exposed. They had to stay in formation.

Now the command cube - Zukra's cube - was in the vanguard of the Singheko fleet, charging directly at the Humans. The sudden pivot had created chaos in the Singheko column. Zukra's destroyer and cruiser screen accelerated madly, trying to swing past him and get back in front to protect the battlecruisers.

**Dekanna System**
**Battlecruiser *Merkkessa***

Bonnie watched Zukra charge at her and smiled.

*Sometimes you just get lucky*, she thought. *I would never have dreamed he would be stupid enough to break formation like that - but I'll take it!*

"*Merkkessa*, bring all squadrons of fighters from reserve to attack Zukra's command cube," she called.

&lt;Eight squadrons of Merlins from reserve to attack Zukra command cube&gt;

"Confirmed."

&lt;Order issued. Acknowledged. Executing&gt;

*Either I hold him here or we're done. If he punches through us here, he'll go all the way to Dekanna and nuke the planet. We won't be able to stop him. This is the end game. No point in holding the reserves any longer.*

Zukra's battlecruiser cube was coming into range. There was no screen of destroyers or cruisers in front of him yet - his screen was still behind him, tangled up with Sobong's fighters and destroyers. They would not be a factor for a few more minutes. He had outrun his own protection.

Between Bonnie's command cube of battlecruisers and Zukra's cube was nothing but black. In the wrap-around screen at the front of *Merkkessa*'s bridge, space lit up with the streaks of missile trails, the strange pastel of the gamma lance tracks, and the explosions of damaged ships as everybody opened fire simultaneously.

Almost immediately, the EDF battlecruiser to *Merkkessa*'s immediate front took a direct hit from a gamma lance into her guts. No amount of armor could have saved her from that fury. She exploded instantly, a wild burst of flame that seared the screen in front of Bonnie, leaving spots before her eyes. At almost the same time, one of the cruisers in her screen suffered a similar fate, disappearing in a violent explosion.

She was down two ships in the first ten seconds of the engagement.

*Those bastards can shoot.*

### Dekanna System
### Singheko Battlecruiser *Tornado*

Tika had fought the Singheko avatar only for a few minutes

in the real world. But in their VR world on the Serengeti plains, it had been a half-hour. Both were covered in blood from multiple wounds. Both had blackened eyes, crushed lips, bruises from head to foot.

Both were approaching exhaustion.

"You'll soon collapse, Human – or whatever you are. I can see the exhaustion in your eyes. I will take great delight in crushing you under my feet as I walk over your lifeless body."

Tika stood soddenly a dozen feet away, gasping for breath. But she managed to find enough energy to lift the corner of her lip in a sneer at the enemy.

"In your dreams, Singheko. There will be a body lying in the dust of these plains. But it will be yours. And I will be the one walking over it."

The Singheko laughed. "You have no chance. I am bigger, I have more reserves, and I have a crew working diligently to repair my damage. You have nothing but yourself and the intelligence you brought on board. It will soon be over for you."

Tika glared at him. But she had a sinking feeling. What he said was true – she had come aboard with only her own intelligence and energy. She had no reserves. He had almost limitless reserves of power, and as he said – a crew working madly to repair the damage she inflicted on him.

*He may be right. But I won't give up. He'll have to kill me first.*

\*\*\*

Five decks above the processor array and memory banks in which Tika and her enemy stood in a virtual battleground, glaring at each other, Orma sat at his command console, watching the battle play out. Every officer on the bridge knew what was happening – the ship's AI had sent an alert when Tika breached the hull and inserted into the AI system.

The *Tornado*'s bridge watch had immediately alerted damage control parties. Those damage control teams now roamed the ship, trying to stay one step ahead of the damage being inflicted on their ship in the real world. So far, they had patched broken comm lines, replaced burnt-out electronics boards, and reset shut-down systems as the battle raged throughout the ship. All the while, they continued to fight a separate real-world battle outside the *Tornado* as a squadron of EDF fighters harassed the battlecruiser.

*I wonder if that new Human admiral knows I'm on this ship,* Orma thought. *I know they hate me. Maybe more than Zukra. After what I've done.*

Orma was wracked by guilt and indecision. Over the last months and especially the last few weeks, he had come to realize something.

Orma had always thought evil was a relative term; that being enslaved by the Singheko was not evil. It was expedient. Natural. The strong enslaved the weak. The Singheko were the strong. Thus, they had every right to enslave the Humans, as well as the Taegu, the Bagrami – and ultimately, even the Nidarians.

But as he had watched Zukra kill dozens of his fellow officers to take over the Navy and the government of his homeland; as he watched him behead thousands of enemies and prisoners in the arena - a bloodletting that boggled the imagination - something had changed in him.

*Evil can be absolute,* Orma thought. *In living organisms with intelligence – it can be absolute. There is no evil in brute animals – the* zeltid *knows not good or evil. It lives, it hunts, it kills, it eats, it dies. There is no inherent good or evil involved.*

*But once you become sentient...I think that is a different story. I think you no longer have the excuse of the jungle. There is an absolute evil – and its essence is to harm another creature when you have no need to do so.*

*And we have forgotten that. We followed that precept once – before the Broken Galaxy. We were an honorable species then. We held our heads high in the Old Empire. But now...*

Orma closed his eyes. In his mind, he saw once more the face of his old friend, Admiral Ligar - the first person Zukra had killed in his coup to take over Singheko.

Orma had never let Zukra know that he and Ligar were old

friends. Orma had destroyed the records – because he knew if Zukra found out, he – Orma – would be dead within hours.

But Orma remembered. He remembered the friendship shared when he and Ligar were both ensigns, learning the ropes on their first ship. Making port calls in Nidaria, in Dekanna, in Ursa, in a time when there were no wars between the nations.

And he remembered looking at Ligar's body, after Zukra's assassination team had finished with him. And how Zukra had told Orma to dispose of the body where it could never be found.

And in fear for his life, and the life of his family, he had done exactly that. Something he would never live down, never forget.

*This is what Zukra has done to us. He has reduced us to animals.*

Casually, Orma reached to his console. He touched a few keys and brought up a screen. Out of the corner of his eye, he checked the bridge. No one was watching him. He punched the command in and hesitated.

*This is the point of no return. Once I issue this command, I'm committed. If Zukra wins this battle, I'm dead.*

Pushing the enter key, Orma leaned back.

*But I will have my honor back.*

**Dekanna System**
**Singheko Battlecruiser *Tornado***

Something changed. Tika wasn't sure what it was, but the enemy avatar facing her suddenly winced in pain. His body drooped, as if he had lost power. His face showed sudden panic. Lifting his head, he stared at her, eyes wide.

Tika never hesitated. Whatever had happened, it was to her advantage. Charging at him, she manifested a sword. He manifested a shield; but he was slow, and it was weak, thin. She knocked his shield aside and spun, bringing the sword around in a sweep aimed at his neck. It was the killing blow, the only movement that could end this battle quickly.

He spun away, ducked, and her blade cut into his back, just below the neck. It didn't kill him, but it knocked him to the ground. A cloud of dust rose as he hit the earth. Before he could react, she spun again, bringing the sword down as hard as she could across his left leg, severing it completely from his body. Blood spurted and he writhed in pain. He tried to roll over and stand, but with only one leg, he couldn't manage it.

Tika stood over him, sword in hand. She looked down at the figure. He was too weak to morph now. He could no longer change shape. He rolled to a position flat on his back and stared up at her, knowing the battle was over.

Tika spoke.

"I would give you quarter if I could, Singheko. But I can't, and you well know why. You would not give me your parole, and even if you did, you would not honor it."

The Singheko managed something between a grimace and a smile as he looked up at death hanging over him.

"You are right, Human – or whatever you are. I would give my parole, and at my first opportunity I would kill you when your back was turned. And I would enjoy it immensely."

"Then you may know you are being killed by a Goblin," said Tika. She brought the sword down quickly, cutting off the head of the avatar lying in the dirt before her. The head rolled away in the dust, and she stood, gazing down at the lifeless corpse.

The vast African plain around her disappeared. Tika found herself standing in an empty room. Dozens of servant avatars stood around her, their heads bowed. A throne in the center of the room sat vacant. Moving to it, she took her place as the new AI of the *Tornado*.

"Who is in charge of the Weapons system?" she asked.

*** 

Jim's Merlin was shot to hell. He was amazed it still hung together well enough to maintain life support for him. By all logic, he should be limping his way back to the *Merkkessa*, trying to get onboard before the damaged fighter crapped out completely.

But he couldn't do that. He had invested too much in the last attack run to put Tika onboard the *Tornado*. And Paco had invested too much to prepare the ground.

He owed it to both of them. So he stood off at a distance from the battlecruiser, doggedly watching as the *Tornado* fired volley after volley of missiles at the Allied fleet in front and the *Victory* behind.

Until it stopped. Until suddenly there were no more volleys. *Did she do it? Did she break in?*

But then his hopes were dashed as another volley of 20 missiles came out of the *Tornado*'s tubes. The eight missiles leaving the rear tubes bent over and crossed over the top of the ship, on a track to join the twelve from the front tubes. Together, the missiles raced off toward the battle raging in front of the *Tornado*.

Jim sighed. It had been too much to hope for. He eyed the missiles absent-mindedly as they settled on a trajectory.

*What?*

The missiles did not seem to be on course. They seemed to be going in the wrong direction.

Toward Admiral Tanno's battlecruiser cube out in front of the *Tornado*...

Jim watched in amazement as the missile volley vectored straight at a Nidarian battlecruiser in the rear of Tanno's battlecruiser cube. Completely unopposed, all twenty missiles smashed into the engines of the enemy.

And the Nidarian battlecruiser disappeared from the universe in a holocaust of explosions and debris.

*She did it*, Jim thought in wonder. *She actually did it!*

Suddenly Jim realized a full squadron of Merlin fighters were on an attack run toward the *Tornado* - and they were nearly at their point of missile launch.

"Alpha Blue Squadron, break off, break off!" he called to them. "Abort attack!"

# CHAPTER TWENTY-SIX

**Dekanna System**
**Nidarian Battlecruiser** *Ekkarra*

"I knew it!" Admiral Tanno yelled. "I knew that son of a bitch Zukra would turn on us!"

He glared at his Flag Captain on the bridge of the *Ekkarra*. "Mark the *Tornado* as enemy, Captain. Fire at will!"

His Flag Captain nodded and gestured to his Tac Officer. "Target the *Tornado* with the rear tubes, Tac."

"Aye, sir."

Working his console, the Tac officer sent a full spread of eight missiles at the *Tornado* behind.

On board the *Revenge*, Zukra did not notice the change. But Damra did.

"Admiral! The *Tornado*! She fired on the Nidarians! And the *Ekkarra* is firing on the *Tornado*!"

Zukra glared at Damra as if he were personally responsible for the problem. Then he glared at the holo.

"What they hell are they doing?" he yelled. "Contact the *Tornado*! Ask them what's going on!"

Damra nodded, speaking low into his comm. After a few seconds, he shook his head.

"No response, sir. The *Tornado* doesn't answer."

Zukra glared at him again. "Doesn't answer? Try again, you fool!"

Damra continued speaking in a low voice into his comm.

Finally, he shook his head. "No response, sir. The *Tornado* has lost comms."

"Bullshit!" yelled Zukra. "That bastard Orma is turning traitor! I always knew it! Open fire on that asshole!"

"Sir, the Nidarians are between us and the *Tornado*. So the *Tornado* is out of range. Plus, we must keep charging at the Humans in front of us if we are to break out and attack Dekanna directly. We've got their flagship on the ropes, m'lord. We should keep hammering away at it!"

Zukra glared at him, then relented. "Yes, of course, Damra. You're right." Zukra settled back in his command chair. "Just issue an order that the *Tornado* is now considered an enemy ship and let's get on with things."

"Aye, m'lord."

\*\*\*

Tika now had complete control of the *Tornado*. She had changed the IFF code of the ship to a new one - one of the codes assigned by Bonnie to the Goblins. In the holos of the Allied and EDF fleets, the *Tornado* was now marked as a "friendly" - no longer an enemy.

Tika had delegated to her Weps AI a new attack plan - firing at Tanno's Nidarians. The Weps AI was dutifully sending volley after volley of missiles at Tanno's ships, creating mass confusion.

Meanwhile, Tika had moved to the next stage of her plan. She had piggy-backed on the *Tornado*'s command net to advance to the next ship - the *Zeltid*, a battlecruiser immediately below the *Tornado* in the cube formation. This time, the battle was easier - she had entered as part of the command net. Her credentials were legitimate. Within five minutes, she had overpowered the AI of the *Zeltid* and was in command of the ship.

Quickly she changed the IFF codes of the ship to mark it as "friendly". Then as before, she directed the Weps AI of the ship to re-target Tanno's Nidarians in the battlecruiser cube in front of her.

Now Tika split herself into four more entities. One went out over the command net to each of the surviving four battlecruisers in her cube.

The game was on.

### Dekanna System
### Corvette Armidale

The corvette UNSF Armidale surfaced in the Dekanna system, only a few million klicks from the initial entry point of the Singheko fleet. The flashing red lights on the wall of the corvette's bridge told the story - the ship was at Battle Stations. Captain Duncan Aveline Stewart ran up the magnification on the holo and assessed the situation rapidly.

The sight he saw knocked him back in his chair in shock.

Wrecked starships and fighters dotted the battlefield in front of him in every direction. Hulks of destroyed ships burned from residual oxygen and onboard chemicals. Emergency beacons flashed from more than a thousand ejected pilots. Dozens of still intact warships blazed away at each other.

There were two separate pockets of battle separated by a graveyard of broken ships. A bit to his relative left, the Human fleet appeared to be taking it on the chin from the Singheko command cube. Slightly to his relative right and farther back, the Dariama were toe-to-toe with the Nidarians.

It was a madhouse of death and destruction.

Duncan marked a spot in the holo between the two separate battle areas in front of him. A dense area of emergency beacons showed up in that space.

"Helm, put us right there!" Duncan yelled. "Right in that space! We can't stand and fight with these big boys, but by God we can start rescuing pilots!"

"Aye, sir," called the quartermaster at helm. The corvette turned and began powering into the battle zone.

"What are you doing?" screamed Admiral Elliott, sitting

behind Duncan in the observer's chair. "What are you doing? Get us out of here!"

With utter contempt in his voice, Duncan turned and glared at the white-faced Admiral sitting behind him.

"Welcome to Dekanna, Admiral! You wanted to be here - well, you're here!"

Turning back to his bridge crew, Duncan indicated the spot once more, a large cluster of wreckage with hundreds of emergency beacons flashing.

"Right there, Helm! Put us right there!"

**Dekanna System**
**Battlecruiser *Merkkessa***

With a loud crash, another missile struck the *Merkkessa* amidships. Bonnie instinctively grabbed the arm of her command chair as the bridge lurched from the force.

"We lost another pulse cannon," called Rachel beside her. Rachel's console was now lit up with red lights - each one marking major damage to the *Merkkessa*.

"I wanted to draw him out of column, and I did," muttered Bonnie under her breath. "But be careful what you wish for," she continued.

Rachel didn't know if Bonnie expected a response, or if her admiral was talking to herself. She decided the latter and maintained her silence.

But it was true. The *Merkkessa* was taking a beating. She had lost 25% of her pulse cannon. The loss of each cannon left a hole in her point defense that could not be quickly stanched.

Their ship was bleeding badly.

Bekerose yelled at Lieutenant Carlson, his Tac Officer. "Guns, rotate us around. We've lost too much point defense on the port side."

"Aye, sir."

The *Merkkessa* rotated in space, moving their beat-up port side to the outer wall of the battlecruiser cube, providing some small element of protection from the enemy fire.

But the battle between Zukra and Bonnie was now a close-range gunfight. The *Revenge* was less than a thousand klicks in front of the *Merkkessa*. By space warfare standards, they were at point-blank range, and still closing.

Bonnie knew she should give ground. Logically, it was suicide to stand and fight like this. Her battlecruiser cube was being decimated.

But she wasn't retreating. Something inside her told her it would be a mistake.

*If I retreat now, they win. It's that simple. They punch out of our trap and race for Dekanna. They'll beat us there and hold the planet hostage.*

*I'm not retreating. I draw the line right here, right now.*

Across the bridge, her Flag Captain Bekerose turned and looked at her. He didn't have to say anything; they both knew the situation. She could read his thoughts.

*We give ground, or we die.*

But Bonnie gave a little shake of her head.

*No.*

A tiny smile lifted one corner of the Nidarian's mouth. The message that passed between them was clear.

Bekerose turned back to his bridge.

"Stand and fight, people. Stand and fight them!" he yelled. "This is our moment!"

The crew bent to their consoles, redoubling their efforts to fight off the attacks coming at them from Zukra's battlecruiser cube.

And the enemy kept coming.

## Dekanna System
## Nidarian Battlecruiser *Ekkarra*

"Another one!" yelled Admiral Tanno. "Those bastards are turning on us!"

In the holo, another Singheko battlecruiser in the rear cube had suddenly began firing at Tanno's cube. There were now three Singheko battlecruisers shooting at him.

"That's it!" yelled Tanno. "*Ekkarra*, message to all ships: the Singheko have turned on us. As of now, consider them the enemy! Fire at will on all Singheko ships!"

<Message sent. Acknowledged by all ships>

Tanno sat back in his command chair and fumed.

*I should never have trusted that bastard Zukra. I should have seen this coming.*

*I think it's time to leave this alliance.*

"*Ekkarra*, message to all ships: prepare to execute Zebra-One. We are departing the battle."

<Message sent. Acknowledged by all ships>

"*Ekkarra*, execute Zebra-One. Get us the hell out of here."

<Executing Zebra-One>

\*\*\*

"M'lord! The Nidarians are leaving!" called Damra.

Zukra stared at the holo in astonishment.

"What? What are they doing?"

"I don't know, sir. There're three battlecruisers in the rear cube shooting at the Nidarians now. It looks like Tanno has decided we've turned on him. He's departing!"

Clearly evident in the holo was the movement of Tanno's Nidarians. His battlecruiser and cruiser cubes were departing the battlefield, along with his destroyers. A massive hole was opening in the center of Zukra's fleet.

"But how is Orma doing it?" Zukra yelled. "Turning traitor on the *Tornado* I can understand. But how is he convincing those other captains to follow him? Is this some kind of coup? In the middle of a battle?"

Damra shook his head. "I don't know, m'lord. But it looks like it might be something like that."

"I've had enough of this. Order cruiser squadrons Six and Seven to come about and attack Orma's cube. Put him down, Damra!"

"Sir, cruiser squadrons Six and Seven are Nidarian. They're

departing with Tanno. The only cruiser cubes in range are One and Four. But they're protecting our edge."

"Detach them to attack Orma. I can't have him coming up our backside."

"Aye, m'lord."

Zukra felt a sudden and quite surprising twinge of trepidation. The departure of Tanno cut his fleet in half. Worse, it left a gaping hole behind him. On the other side of that hole were the Dariama who had been slugging it out with Tanno. And even as he watched, the Dariama cubes began a pivot to come into his rear.

*Could the Humans somehow be responsible for this? Did they form a secret alliance with Orma?*

"How are they doing this?" he yelled.

"Sir, cruiser squadron Seven is now isolated in front of the Dariama. They'll be cut to pieces. We must pull them back."

Zukra nodded. "Yes, yes. Bring them back here to protect our rear. Quickly, Damra!"

"Aye, m'lord. And Orma's battlecruiser cube Four is now turning toward us. I fear the worst, m'lord. Perhaps in light of this development, m'lord, we should consider withdrawing?"

"Never!" roared Zukra. "I will not retreat one inch from these animals! We have that Human flagship on the ropes! Show some guts, Damra! Keep pounding away at the *Merkkessa*! We'll punch our way out of this!"

**Dekanna System**
**Singheko Battlecruiser *Tornado***

Tika couldn't help but gloat a bit.

She had control of the entire rear cube of Singheko battlecruisers now. She had changed the IFF codes to show all six surviving battlecruisers as "friendly".

The battlecruiser *Victory*, along with the four cruisers in its formation, had recognized her new IFF codes and was no longer firing at her cube. Captain Westerly had joined on her left flank and was attacking into the nearest Singheko cruiser cube, keeping the enemy's attention focused on him.

That left her with nobody to fight. The Nidarians in front of her had bailed out of the battle and were already out of range, accelerating toward the mass limit to leave the system.

Tika pivoted her entire battlecruiser cube, driving straight toward Zukra. The *Revenge* was six thousand klicks from her, just out of her range. But there were two cubes of cruisers protecting Zukra's rear edge, side by side. Sixteen ships. She had to get through them first.

If she went up and over, they would rise to meet her. If she went down and under, the same thing would occur.

She decided to blast straight through them.

*Honesty is always the best policy*, she grinned.

## Dekanna System
## Destroyer *Dragon*

Luke's destroyer cube was shot to pieces. There were only three destroyers left out of the original eight. In an attempt to provide some mutual protection from the barrage of enemy fire coming at them, the three surviving destroyers had regrouped into a tight formation, a modified finger-four. In front of them, an almost-intact Singheko destroyer cube, with six of their original eight destroyers still in action, fired almost continuously at the remnants of his squadron.

He had no place to go. His rear was up against the *Merkkessa's* cube. And Bonnie showed no signs of retreating.

*Stand and deliver, buddy*, he thought. *Stand and deliver.*

Luke could see the fear in the eyes of his bridge crew. But they went about their jobs professionally, showing no sign of it.

*A good crew. I'm so proud of them.*

*Dragon* made a sudden hard pivot, moving her belly armor to take an incoming missile that had leaked through their point defense. With a huge crash, the missile knocked them up and to the side, one more hit out of a half-dozen they had incurred in the last twenty minutes.

And two gamma lance strikes had gone through-and-through the ship, leaving a dozen compartments open to space - killing twenty of his crew. It was a miracle that neither strike had taken out his engines or weapons systems.

"That last battlecruiser cube is coming hard now," called Emma at Tac. "Coming at the back of that cruiser cube behind the destroyers. But their IFF is showing friendly - they're marked as Goblins now!"

Luke puzzled over the situation. Bonnie had provided a pre-battle briefing which had mentioned this possibility - that some of the enemy ships might change sides and be re-designated with new IFF codes. But she had given no details, citing operational security.

*How had she known? What's going on?*

"It doesn't matter, Emma. There's plenty of other targets. A plethora. Just pick a direction and there's a Singheko warship there. Just fire and you'll hit one."

Emma managed a thin smile.

"You got that right, Skipper."

Luke studied the holo. The three ships of his squadron represented the outer edge of the Human fleet now.

To their left was the flagship cube. The *Merkkessa*, at the back of the flagship cube, was only a hundred klicks to his left rear.

To his left front was Zukra's flagship cube, pounding away at the *Merkkessa*. The *Revenge* was less than six hundred klicks away now, still coming on.

In front of Luke was a Singheko destroyer cube throwing everything they had at the three survivors of his squadron. Beyond the destroyers was an oncoming Singheko cruiser cube, with the clear intentions of getting in close, punching them out and then moving on the *Merkkessa*.

And just out of range behind those cruisers, coming in at an angle, was the newly re-designated battlecruiser cube of the

## THE SHORT END

Goblins, with the *Victory* and her four cruisers right beside it. All thirteen ships were charging at the rear of the Zukra's group of battlecruisers and cruisers.

*C'mon, you bastards! Get in here before we're all dead!*

*Dragon* shuddered as another missile exploded nearby, not impacting but close enough to shake the ship. The destroyer shuddered almost continuously from the near misses, and jerked left, right, up, down as the AI tried to avoid the incoming ordnance. There were so many missiles in the area that the *Dragon*'s AI had ceased to make callouts for them, reserving its computer cycles for point defense and evasive.

Then Luke saw a fresh volley of missiles and gamma lance streaks from the enemy strike the *Merkkessa*. The flagship was almost hidden by the blaze of fire and energy from the assault. Luke groaned as the *Merkkessa* lurched to one side, clearly visible in the holo.

*That hurt her.*

**Dekanna System**
**Battlecruiser *Merkkessa***

In the far distance, the Dariama were mixing it up with the last cruiser cube of Zukra's fleet in a blazing fireworks show. Bonnie could see that Sobong and her ships were making slow but steady progress, pushing the enemy toward the rear of Zukra's remaining column of ships.

*By the stars, I think it worked! It's a mess out there - but the basic strategy is working! We drew him into a trap - and I don't see any way he can get out of this now. If we can hold. If we can hold right here, we've got him!*

With a mighty crash, something shot through the bridge far too fast for the eye to see, leaving a bright green afterimage in Bonnie's eyes. A trail of sparkling ionized air marked its trail. Every light on the bridge went out. Bonnie's chair was thrown sideways, crashing against the deck, no longer attached to anything. The faceplate of her warsuit snapped down automatically due to lack of pressure.

*Gamma lance,* Bonnie thought. *Right through the bridge.*

Then a black curtain came down around her and she thought no more.

# CHAPTER TWENTY-SEVEN

**Dekanna System**
**Singheko Battlecruiser** *Tornado*

"*Tornado*. I have a favor to ask," said Orma.

Tika heard the words through her comm interface. She had been ignoring all input from the Singheko crew, essentially locking them out of their own ship.

But this was interesting. The captain on the bridge had spoken. The one who had sat quietly for the last twenty minutes as the rest of the crew worked madly trying to regain control of the ship, to no avail.

Tika selected a private channel to the officer's comm.

\<What do you want, Singheko?\>

"Let me tell you a story, please. About a time when the Singheko were still an honorable species. More than five thousand years ago…"

\<Speak\>

"Somehow, we lost our honor. We lost our sense of pride in ourselves as a species. We became slavemasters - the first step toward depravity. Now that depravity has culminated in this battle. A battle we must lose, for the sake of our own souls."

\<So?\>

"I must be the one to kill Zukra. It is a matter of honor. Not for me personally - but for my species. I humbly ask that I be given that honor."

Tika thought about it for a few seconds. She understood

what the officer was saying - in fact, she understood it all too well.

The Goblins had always had a strong sense of honor. They prided themselves as a moral and ethical race. It was drummed into them from an early age. It was something that biologicals couldn't seem to understand about the Goblins.

Could this officer still retain a vestige of the pride and honor once shown by the Singheko?

Was he telling the truth?

Tika made a snap decision. She was now busy attacking the AI systems of the Singheko cruiser cube in front of her, and it was taking a lot of her attention. And even if she were wrong, and the officer turned on her, she could retake control of the *Tornado* with little effort.

<I give you back control of the *Tornado*, Captain Orma. Use it wisely>

And with that, Tika released her hold on the ship, passed the command to Orma, and re-focused her efforts elsewhere.

**Dekanna System**
**Destroyer *Dragon***

*That hurt her.*

Luke saw the *Merkkessa* stop firing. She began rotating slowly.

She was out of action.

*She's adrift. Zukra will punch right through her now.*

*No. I won't let it happen.*

"Dragon, notify the *Amazon* and the *Namikaze* we're moving to protect the *Merkkessa*. Then put us directly between the *Merkkessa* and the *Revenge* as quickly as possible."

<Message sent. Acknowledged. Moving to position requested>

Luke felt a shudder go through *Dragon* as the ship turned sharply and headed for the *Merkkessa*. The accumulated damage to *Dragon* was making her unstable. He wasn't even certain they could make it to the spot he needed to be.

*Hang in there,* Dragon. *Just a little bit longer.*

### Dekanna System
### Merlin Fighter "Angel One"

When the *Tornado* had started firing on the Nidarians, Jim had finally made the decision to return to the *Merkkessa*. His priority mission was complete. It was time to put the banged-up Merlin back in the hangar and get another one.

He was only two hundred klicks from the *Merkkessa* when he saw the gamma lance strike through her, blowing debris out the other side.

The *Merkkessa* immediately stopped firing. Spinning slowly, she was a sitting duck for Zukra.

"Dammit! They got the bridge!"

He slammed the throttle home, boosting back up to 300g true for eight seconds. Then he slammed into a hard decel. Eight seconds later, he was directly in front of the ship. Spinning the Merlin around, he faced the *Revenge*.

He had no missiles left.

But he wasn't going anywhere.

### Dekanna System
### Merlin Fighter "Dunkirk One"

Winnie assessed the situation quickly. She had been hovering a thousand klicks over the *Merkkessa* with her command flight, watching the battle unfold in front of them, directing fighters as needed, ensuring that the fleet's Merlins were used effectively.

She was the closest flight to the *Merkkessa*, and her flagship was in danger.

"On me!" she yelled in her comm and slammed the throttle home.

Her flight darted through space directly toward the *Merkkessa*.

**Dekanna System**
**Battlecruiser *Tornado***

The *Revenge* stood just four thousand klicks in front of him now. They were finally in range and closing fast.

Orma took a few seconds to consider.

*They will call me traitor for ten thousand years. For as long as records are kept.*

*But for my nation...for my species. We cannot let the dishonor of Zukra's madness continue.*

"*Tornado.* Target the *Revenge.* Fire at will."

<Targeting *Revenge*. Fire at will. Acknowledged. Executing>

**Dekanna System**
**Battlecruiser *Revenge***

Damra knew they were dead.

The cruiser cube that was supposed to be protecting their rear had turned on them, just like the battlecruiser cube that was coming up behind it. One by one, like a stack of dominoes falling, the cruisers had stopped firing at the enemy, turned, and started firing on Zukra's battlecruiser cube.

Damra had finally figured it out. It was the only explanation. The enemy was attacking their AI systems.

"Admiral..." he tried once more.

"Shut up, Damra!" yelled Zukra. "We're almost there! All we have to do is punch through the *Merkkessa* and we're home free! Show some guts!"

"Admiral, our cruiser screen..."

Zukra, enraged, pulled his pistol out of his holster, and aimed it at Damra. With a scream of rage, he pulled the trigger. Blood exploded everywhere as Damra fell dead on the floor beside Zukra's command chair.

"Now!" yelled Zukra at his awestruck bridge crew. "Does anyone else want to retreat?"

**Dekanna System**

## Battlecruiser *Tornado*

Orma felt a strange sense of calm.

He knew he would be reviled, hated; probably executed for treason. And that only if he survived the battle.

But he had never been more sure of anything in his life.

*I've done the right thing. I can die in peace. My sacrifice will restore the honor of my people. It is good.*

"Keep firing, keep firing!" he yelled at his terrified crew.

Tika had completed her takeover of the entire cruiser cube that had been protecting Zukra's rear. There were now sixteen formerly Singheko warships firing at Zukra's battlecruiser cube.

But Orma fired only at the *Revenge*.

*That's the poison of our nation. Right there.*

## Dekanna System
## Destroyer *Dragon*

Luke had made it to the position he wanted. He was directly between the *Merkkessa* and the *Revenge*. The two remaining destroyers of his squadron, the *Amazon* and the *Namikaze*, tucked in just beside and behind him, trying to provide some protection for their wounded flagship.

Out in front, Jim Carter slotted into position, weaving in a desperate pattern, trying to draw the fire of the oncoming missiles. Then suddenly a flight of four fighters came up from behind and joined in the weave. Luke realized it was Winnie Winston and her command flight.

Strangely, the enemy cruiser cube off to their right had stopped firing at them and was now firing at Zukra's battlecruisers instead. And that fire had already knocked out one battlecruiser on the back edge.

*Stranger and stranger*, thought Luke. *But I'll take it.*

But the remaining seven battlecruisers of Zukra's cube were still potent. The flood of missiles coming in was overwhelming. The strikes of gamma lances crisscrossing the holo looked like some deranged laser light show.

Until suddenly one of the remaining battlecruisers in Zukra's rear edge also stopped firing. It began to pivot, turning slowly to direct its gamma lance at the *Revenge* in front of it.

Luke watched in amazement as the enemy battlecruiser fired, striking the *Revenge* right in the left lower engine nacelle. A tremendous gout of flame and debris came exploding out of the engine. The *Revenge* stumbled, then corrected and kept coming.

Then another enemy battlecruiser stopped firing. Again, it turned, re-targeted, and fired at the *Revenge*.

And then suddenly, as if by command, all the remaining battlecruisers in Zukra's cube stopped firing and began to decelerate, slowing their advance. Only the *Revenge* kept coming, firing, trying to kill the *Merkkessa*.

Behind the *Revenge* came the *Tornado*, now closing the range quickly, firing missile volleys at the *Revenge* as fast as she could reload. As she approached Zukra's flagship, her gamma lance fired over and over.

The *Revenge* stopped firing at the *Merkkessa*. Turning, she faced the *Tornado*.

With a shock, Luke realized there were only two ships still shooting at each other. The *Tornado* and the *Revenge* were locked in a duel of their own making. All the other ships in the entire battle zone had stopped firing, caught up in the drama playing out before them.

The *Revenge* went to decel to meet the *Tornado*. Both ships fired their gamma lance simultaneously.

And in a blinding flash of fire that filled Luke's screens, both battlecruisers disappeared from the Universe.

## Dekanna System
## Battlecruiser *Merkkessa*

Jim sat in the cockpit of the Merlin, parked on the shuttle deck of the *Merkkessa*. Smoke curled from the damaged engine, the acrid odor mixing with the smell of burning insulation to create a choking cloud.

The battle was over.

He was still alive.

He was too weary to get out of the cockpit. But he knew he should. The Merlin could burst into flames at any moment.

"Angel, open canopy," he called.

There was no response. The AI was down, damaged or destroyed. He reached for the emergency canopy release and pulled hard to break the safety wire.

With a loud clunk, the canopy released and slid half-way back on its tracks. Jim released the five-point harness. Slapping the main power switch, he turned everything off. Gathering his strength - mental and physical - he managed to push the canopy farther back to give him clearance. He hoisted himself up out of the cockpit, stepped out the side of the fighter, and slid down the stub wing to the deck with a thump.

Gathering himself, he looked at the chaos around him.

Firefighting crews were spraying foam on smoldering fighters. Piles of debris littered the area. Stretcher-bearers carried the broken bodies of pilots out the hatch. Alert lights were still flashing red - no one had yet thought to stand the ship down from Battle Stations.

"*Merkkessa*. Is the bridge intact?"

There was no answer. Jim realized the AI of the ship was down also.

That was bad. Jim trotted over to the shuttle bay exit hatch and went through to the passageway outside.

It was a madhouse. People ran to and fro, on their various errands of rescue or repair. A damage control team was on a ladder with their hands up in the ceiling, electrical wiring spewing out of the hole like spaghetti. A fire hose ran down the passageway to some unknown destination. The smell of smoke permeated the ship.

Jim trotted to the nearest ladder and started climbing up toward the bridge. At each intersection, he had to pass through an internal airlock, all of which were dogged down during battle stations. At the next level, the tell-tale on the hatch showed there was no pressure on the other side.

He pulled his helmet faceshield down, locked it, checked suit integrity, and passed through the pressure door. He advanced another five meters; but at the next intersection a smash of debris completely blocked his path forward.

Turning to a cross-corridor, he went across to the other side of the ship and found a ladder that took him up to the next deck. Trotting down the corridor, his path was blocked again. A section of the ceiling had come down, closing off the passageway.

Pulling and shoving ceiling panels aside, he managed to clear a small path that he could squeeze through. He was able to advance a half-dozen yards before his way was again blocked by fallen debris.

But just before the blockage was the hatch to Bonnie's Flag Cabin. And from the Flag Cabin there was Bonnie's private circular stairwell to the bridge level - if it was not also smashed.

Entering the hatch, Jim went through the Admiral's briefing room to the Flag Cabin. It appeared to be intact. He wasted no time running to the circular stairs and climbing up to the bridge level.

He came out in Bonnie's Day Cabin, which was just off the bridge. Crossing the cabin quickly, he opened the hatch to a scene of destruction.

The main lights were out, and only the red battle lamps were working. All the consoles were dark. Most were completely destroyed. The large screen at the front of the bridge was lying on the deck in two pieces. The holo was gone.

Bodies in pressure suits lay everywhere. Bonnie was nowhere to be seen.

With a sinking feeling, Jim began to check the bodies. The first one he came to was Dallitta, Bonnie's Flag Aide. There was no hope for her; both her legs were missing.

He moved to the next one. That was Chief Graham, the quartermaster. He did not appear to have any visible injuries; but he was also dead.

Beside Graham was Rachel Gibson. She was breathing, Jim could see. Alive but unconscious. He checked her suit and confirmed she had oxygen and pressurization.

"Over here, Jim," called a voice over his comm.

*Bonnie.*

He looked up. Behind the smashed XO console he could just pick out the top of her helmet, turned red by the emergency lighting. Jim rushed over. She was kneeling beside another body, half-cradling it in her arms, tears streaming down her cheeks.

*Bekerose.*

The Nidarian captain had taken a large piece of shrapnel precisely in the center of his chest.

Jim put a hand on Bonnie's shoulder, squeezing it.

"He never felt a thing, Bonnie," he said. "He died instantly."

"I know," Bonnie said, trying not to cry. "But…of all people. Of all people, Jim…why did it have to be him?"

Jim rubbed her back. "It comes to all of us, Bonnie. It was his time."

He reached forward, took Bekerose in his arms, lifted him from Bonnie. He managed to get to his feet and looked down at her.

"He did what he wanted to do, Bonnie. He died on the bridge of his ship, fighting his enemies."

Bonnie wiped at her faceplate, an instinctive and futile attempt to wipe away the tears inside. She stood beside Jim, looked at him.

"I don't want to leave him here in this mess. Let's take him to his cabin."

Nodding, Jim began walking back the way he had come, carrying the Nidarian in his arms. Bonnie followed close behind, one hand on Jim's shoulder. Together they went through Bonnie's day cabin, down the stairs, out the Flag Cabin and across the way to Bekerose' cabin.

Laying Bekerose in his bunk, Jim stood back. Bonnie moved forward and kneeled beside the Nidarian captain. She pulled the blanket up over him and bowed her head briefly. Then she stood and turned to Jim. She moved into Jim for a moment, hugging him to her. Then she backed away and stared at him.

"You did a great job, Jim. You saved the fleet."

"Not me," said Jim. "Tika. She saved the fleet."

"But you got her there. Without you, she wouldn't have made it to the *Tornado*."

"Don't forget Paco," Jim added with some bitterness in his voice.

"We won't. We'll never forget him. He'll get the Medal of Honor for what he did."

"He'd better," said Jim. "If anybody saved this fleet, it was him."

Bonnie nodded. "Yes. You're right."

The two of them stared at the blanket covering their friend one last time. Then, by mutual consent, they both turned to go. Jim held the hatch open for Bonnie, and they moved down the passageway back to the Flag Cabin. They entered and Bonnie went to her desk.

"*Merkkessa*. Are you there?"

There was no response. Bonnie looked at Jim. "Will you go check on the AI center for me, please? We need *Merkkessa* up before we can start to get this mess cleaned up. I'll go get Rachel and bring her to sick bay."

"Aye, milady," Jim responded. It felt good to say it. It felt like moving back to some kind of normalcy. Even if 'normal' was a long way to go, it was a beginning.

He braced up, saluted, and turned smartly on his heel. Going to the hatch, he paused for just a second and turned back to Bonnie.

"By the way, Admiral. You just saved the Earth."

And with that, he went through the hatch to his duty.

# CHAPTER TWENTY-EIGHT

**Dekanna System**
**Battlecruiser *Merkkessa***

**Forty-eight Hours Later**

"Status of the ship?" called Bonnie.

Rachel leaned over her tablet, reading.

"All fires are out. All holed compartments have been sealed. Life support is stable. System engines are functional, but the tDrive will require another few days. The ship's AI has been restored. The bridge has been cleared of debris and will be fully functional by the end of the day."

"Thank you, Rachel. How about the rest of the fleet?"

"All ships that are salvageable are stable, holding air and with functional life support. Ships beyond repair have been evacuated and are being towed to stable stellar orbits for the moment. There are a few ships that we're not sure about, those have been evacuated as a precaution and we're towing them to stable orbits around Dekanna."

"Does that include the Allied ships?"

"Yes, milady. We're taking a unified approach to everything."

"How about the enemy ships?"

"Those too, milady. Captain Asagi is the ranking Singheko officer among their survivors. He's provided us with engineering crews to assist in evacuating their ships and moving the wrecks to stable orbits. And we have multiple crews clearing debris fields as well."

"Thank you, Commander. Stephanie, how are things in Medical?"

"All beds are full; all the cabins on E, F and G decks are full. We've got wounded lying in every available corridor. We're evacuating the severely wounded to Dekanna as soon as they're stable enough for movement. I think we've saved as many as we're going to save."

Bonnie looked a bit grim. "How about the bodies of the dead?"

"We've pulled an empty supply barge alongside and we're offloading the bodies to it. I've started a fleet-wide task force to ensure proper identification and to begin the process of notifying next of kin."

"Very good, thank you, Stephanie. Winnie, how SAR going?"

Winnie Winston leaned forward in her turn. "We've rescued 576 pilots alive. I think we've found all the live ones we're going to find. We've still got SAR patrols out, but we're only finding bodies now. We'll keep looking, of course. But it looks like it's all recovery from now on. And by the way, the corvette Armidale arrived in the middle of the battle and started rescuing survivors under fire. She rescued the largest number of survivors of any ship - and also shot down six enemy fighters in the process. I'd like to recommend her Captain for recognition."

"So noted, Winnie. What are you doing about the Singheko or Nidarians that you find?"

"We treat them no differently than our own, Admiral. We rescue them and take them to Captain Asagi. Asagi has his own patrols out collecting bodies, so we mark any of theirs we find and notify him."

"Excellent, thank you, Commander. Norali, what's the story on Admiral Elliott?"

"We sent him to Dekanna. Sobong parked him in a nice suite at Dariama Fleet Headquarters. She's got her junior aides talking with him about how to improve relations between the

Dariama and Humans. He's happy as a clam - he thinks he's doing something. And Sobong knows not to take anything he says seriously."

Bonnie smiled. "Good. Just make sure he doesn't get into any trouble."

"Are we taking him back to Earth when we depart?"

"Not a chance," grinned Bonnie. "He can stay here and spin his wheels with Sobong for a few months. When Sobong gets so tired of him she can't take it anymore, we'll bring him home. By that time, I hope we can have the whole U.N. situation fixed back at Earth."

Bonnie let her gaze sweep around the table. "An exemplary job by everyone concerned. I cannot begin to tell you how proud I am of our spacers. They've risen to the task magnificently. Please pass that message on to everyone."

Nods went around the table.

"And of course, that includes everyone around this table. You are a magnificent staff. I am blessed to have you."

Bonnie paused, then continued. "Now...to some necessary business..."

"We took a tremendous number of casualties. I'm afraid we're going to have to fill in as best we can until we can get back to Earth.

"Captain Powell. In view of the fact that *Dragon* is shot to hell and will take months to repair, you are at loose ends. You are therefore temporarily assigned as commander of the *Merkkessa*. Please take charge of getting our flagship back to her old self."

"Aye, milady," answered Luke.

"And as a side note in case anyone is concerned about the appearance of nepotism by this assignment, be aware that I don't give a shit. At the end of the battle, there were three units which stood alone between the *Merkkessa* and the *Revenge*. One was Jim Carter's Merlin - which was out of missiles, by the way. The second was our CAG Winnie here and her flight. And the last was a shot-up squadron of three destroyers, with *Dragon* in the lead. Only one of those three destroyers survived - *Dragon*.

"The other two destroyer Captains will receive the Medal of Honor - posthumously. Luke gets the *Merkkessa*. If anyone wants to complain about that, feel free to get in a destroyer and stand out in front of us while the entire fleet shoots at you for twenty minutes. Survivors will be given a hearing."

There was a respectful silence in the briefing room before Bonnie continued.

"And speaking of Commander Winston...Winnie, you are hereby promoted to Flag Aide with the rank of captain. If you'll take the job, of course. It's not always as easy as Captain Dallitta made it out to be."

"Of course, milady," responded Winnie. "Thank you."

"And that means we need a new CAG. Lieutenant Commander Mitchell, welcome to your new job, and of course a promotion to Commander goes with it."

"Thank you, milady. But..."

"But?"

"Well, uh, what about Jim...I mean, Commander Carter?"

"Commander Carter has resigned his commission. He will be focusing all his efforts on taking care of his wife."

A gasp of surprise went around the table. Mitchell bobbed his head in understanding.

"Aye, milady."

Bonnie stood. "That is all. Thank you, everyone."

The group stood respectfully as Bonnie turned and went through the hatch to her Flag Cabin. Then they turned and departed, shaking their heads at the news.

## Dekanna System
## Dariama Naval HQ

Jim Carter - Commander, EDF (Retired), left the shuttle at Dariama Naval Headquarters and moved quickly down the corridor to the Medical facility where he had last seen Rita. Entering, he went directly to her room. She was lying passively in the bed, still in a coma. Various drips and devices ran into her body through tubes of all sizes. Jim sat beside her and held her hand.

"Hi babe. I don't know if you can hear me or not. But we won. We paid a heavy price, but we held them. We held them, and Zukra is dead. We'll have peace now. You did it, babe. It was you. Everything came together because of you."

There was no response. Jim sat, holding Rita's hand. He sat for a long time. The hand was warm, so he knew she was still alive. He held on to that thought, and held her hand, and remembered.

He remembered the first time they had made love. When they were on the run, hiding out, trying to survive while they repaired *Jade*. When they both thought Bonnie was dead. When the pain of losing Bonnie had ripped them apart, tore their souls, left them in a pit of loneliness and despair like they had never felt before.

*By the end of the day, both Jim and Rita were exhausted. They had hauled another 98 buckets of nano glop to the top of the ship and poured each of them over the side, where the glop self-assembled into something that was starting to look like a starship hull, with dozens of circuits, sensors, lights, and other devices integrated into it.* Jade *even had them simply drop the purchased high-definition cameras, IR sensors and the three off-the-shelf TV dish antennae into the glop, which formed around them, moved them to required locations and integrated them into the rest of the ship.*

*At the end of the day, Jim was still in amazement at the technology. He shook his head as he came out of the shower. Throwing on a t-shirt and shorts, he went to the galley for dinner. He found Rita already there, using the microwave to prepare something which smelled delicious. She had let her hair down after her shower; it was long enough to look like a bob now and glistened in the lights. She was wearing shorts and a t-shirt too; Jim couldn't help but feel a twinge of desire. She was a beautiful woman, now*

*- fully fleshed out, no longer thin as when she came out of the medpod - and a knockout by any sense of the word.*

*I guess I'm only Human,* he thought. *But she's not Bonnie.*

"What are you making?" he asked.

Rita pointed to the empty box on the counter. "Salisbury Steak and Potatoes," she said.

"Sound good," said Jim, and rummaged through the reefer until he found a similar item. He opened it, popped it into the microwave, and stood waiting for it to finish.

"Three more days," said Rita. "Today's Wednesday. We finish the glop tomorrow afternoon. Then the ruthenium arrives on Friday. Andy will need one additional day to integrate the ruthenium, so he'll be ready to test on Saturday. Oh-dark-thirty Sunday morning, we launch out of here."

&lt;Yes&gt; said Jade. &lt;We'll perform final testing after we are in space. Assuming no problems, we'll be on our way to Sanctuary by late Sunday&gt;

Jim pulled his dinner out of the microwave and sat down.

"It's been a long, hard slog," he said. "I can't say it's been easy. But at least we're almost done."

He and Rita ate their dinner mostly in silence. The absence of Bonnie was still like a rock standing between them. But Jim had been thinking about it throughout the day, as he worked. Finally, he felt it was time to say something.

"Rita," he began.

She looked up at him.

"I'm sorry I got so upset with you about...about losing Bonnie. I realize you had no choice."

Rita just stared at him. Finally, she bent back to her dinner. They ate in silence for a while. Eventually, Rita got up and retrieved a soft drink out of the fridge and brought one for Jim. She placed it in front of him.

Jim looked up at her.

Slowly she leaned over and kissed him on the cheek.

"I'm so sorry about Bonnie, Jim," she said. Then she returned to her seat.

*They finished their dinner quietly, both tired from the long hard day. Cleaning up, they headed down the corridor toward their cabins.*

*"Good night, Rita," said Jim.*

*"Good night, big guy," said Rita, entering her cabin and closing the door.*

*Jim went into his cabin and closed the door, went to the bed, and fell into it exhausted. He went to sleep almost instantly.*

*Soon Jim was dreaming about Bonnie. He dreamed that she had returned to life and was standing beside his bed. She leaned over and kissed him, then slowly got into bed with him. She held him close and kissed him again.*

*Suddenly Jim awoke. He realized it wasn't a dream. Rita was in bed with him, holding him, kissing him.*

*Jim froze for a moment. So many thoughts raced through his head. He glanced at the clock. It was past midnight. He turned back to Rita.*

*"I need you," she whispered.*

*She was beautiful, and naked, and in his bed.*

Jim woke with a start, the dream fading. Dr. Bosama entered the room. Bosama smiled at Jim, then adopted a more serious expression.

"Any news?" asked Jim.

"None of it good, Jim," replied Bosama. "She's still in a coma. She's still sliding downhill. We're going to try one more thing this evening."

"What's that?"

"Another exchange transfusion. We replace all the blood in her body with new blood from donors. This will be the second one. Jim, I'd be lying to you if I said I thought it would work. I don't. But it's our last ditch, last chance approach."

Jim nodded. "OK. I get it. But do the best you can, please."

Bosama gestured to him. "Come with me, I'll show you to a cabin where you can rest."

She led Jim to a room, where she opened the door and

turned on the lights.

"I'll leave you for a while. There's plenty of food in the fridge and more in the cupboards. There's entertainment on the holo. If you need anything, just ask the room for it and I'll get the message. And I'll keep you informed about Rita - as soon as we know anything, you'll know."

Jim nodded. Bosama left out the door and closed it behind her. Moving to the fridge, Jim opened the door and gazed inside.

There was plenty of food in the fridge. He would not go hungry here, he realized. Evidently the Dariama ate much like Humans.

It was the beer that surprised him, though. There was a six-pack of beer in the fridge.

*How in the hell did they do that?*

Jim pulled out the six-pack and sat down at the dining room table.

*I'd better sample this. Just to see if it's been done right.*

**Dekanna System**
**Dariama Naval HQ**

Jim finished a beer, cooked a meal, had dinner, and then went back to Rita's room. They were preparing her for the exchange transfusion. Bosama was direct with him.

"She may not survive the night, Jim. You need to prepare yourself."

He nodded. He went over to Rita's bed, leaned over, and held her in his arms. He kissed her forehead. Then he backed off and let them take her away.

Returning to his room, he took the beer out of the fridge. He put a good dent in it, then fell asleep on the couch. About two A.M., he woke up and moved to the bedroom. He slept fitfully, as he usually did in a strange place.

Early next morning, the sun came peeking in the pseudo-window mounted on the wall, looking so realistic that for a moment, he forgot where he was. Jim cracked an eyelid at the light flooding the room and wished he had drawn the curtains. Finally, after trying to go back to sleep for a while, he gave up.

He rose, showered, and dressed. Moving to the kitchen, he prepared breakfast - bacon, eggs, and toast.

Everything seemed so completely normal. It was hard to believe he was 710 lights from Earth, in a system inhabited by an alien species which could, from a distance, pass for Humans.

There was a ding, which Jim realized was a doorbell. "Come!" he called. The door opened. Tika entered. She came over and sat down at the table with Jim. Her face was somber.

Jim braced himself. He could see the news was not good.

"I have bad news, Jim. The exchange transfusion did not work."

"And?"

"Her internal organs are too far gone. She cannot survive as a biological being."

Jim closed his eyes. He had hoped - hoped hard. He had prayed. He had gotten down on his knees and offered his own life in exchange for hers.

And none of it had worked.

*She cannot survive as a biological being.*

The way Tika had said it sounded a bit strange. Jim thought about it.

*She cannot survive as a biological being.*

"What are you saying?" Jim asked, as the strangeness of Tika's statement finally sank into his brain.

"She cannot survive as a biological being. But she can survive as an AI like us - a Goblin. Her brain is intact; just poisoned by the rest of her body. We can scan her consciousness and convert her to our form."

Jim shook his head, bewildered. "I don't understand. What are you saying?"

In a gesture that was so Human, Tika reached out a hand and took Jim's hand, squeezed it. "If we leave her as she is, she will die within a few more hours. If we scan her consciousness into an AI, she will live. It's that simple, Jim."

"No, no. It can't be," Jim muttered, his shock preventing him thinking clearly. "She can't die. She can't!"

Tika waited patiently while Jim went through an inventory of emotions. First bewilderment, then understanding. Then despair.

And finally a grudging acceptance. He heaved a long sigh.

"You're sure? No mistakes?"

"No mistakes. The Dariama and Human doctors agree. She cannot survive more than a few more hours at most."

Jim closed his eyes.

*Can I make this decision for her? What would Rita want?*

"She's already been through so much," Jim said out loud. "Created as a clone, with no actual childhood - just memories copied in from Bonnie and myself. Never fully knowing who she was. Adapting to one new life after another. Thrown into a war not of her own making. Battle after battle, feeling like she was a machine created purely for the purpose of killing..."

Jim looked up at Tika. "I don't know if I can put her through another trauma like...like that. What kind of life would she have?"

Tika squeezed Jim's hand once again. "Now I will tell you a secret, Jim. One I reveal to a Human only with great reluctance. But I was also once biological.

"Have you ever wondered how we know so much about Humans? The Goblins are not fools; they have visited your planet frequently in the past. They have taken Humans who were dying and transferred them to android bodies, to learn more about your planet.

"And I was one of those. I was born a Human in what you now call Central America, twelve hundred years ago. I was a small child, injured beyond recovery in a battle with another tribe. As I lay dying, my consciousness was scanned by a Goblin scientist studying Humans. I was transferred into an android body and taken back to Stalingrad, given to parents to raise up.

"So I am uniquely qualified to tell you that my life as a Goblin has been happy and fulfilling. Except for the time I was captured by the Singheko, of course. But otherwise, I've been totally happy.

"I believe that as a Goblin, Rita will have a happy and fulfilling life. She'll have the opportunity to be with the man she loves. She'll be able to raise her child. And she can go on with her life as she desires, whether that be in the military or doing something totally different."

Jim closed his eyes. It was hard to think about it. He couldn't imagine what Rita would say to this. Losing her body - yet retaining her mind in a different form.

Yet if he didn't agree to it, he would lose her in both mind and body. It was on him. She would have to live with his decision for the rest of her life.

Finally he spoke quietly. "If you are absolutely sure she has no chance of survival, and if both the Dariama and Human doctors agree, then you have my permission."

Tika squeezed Jim's hand one last time. Then she rose and went to the door. Turning before she departed, she asked one more question.

"Do you want to say goodbye to her biological body one last time?"

Jim shook his head. "No. I held her and kissed her goodbye last night. I'll wait here."

Nodding, Tika left.

**Dekanna System**
**Battlecruiser** *Merkkessa*

Bonnie silently reached an arm around Luke's waist and pulled him closer to her. It was an act she had never performed in view of crew before - and certainly never on the bridge.

Luke did not react. Some instinct told him to be still. Somehow, he knew this was a time to allow Bonnie total leeway.

*She must be hurting terribly*, thought Luke. *After the slaughter we've just experienced - to leave both her best friends behind, not knowing if Rita will live or die. Knowing things will never be the same again.*

Bonnie gave Luke one final squeeze around his waist, then let go. She turned and stepped back up on *Merkkessa*'s Flag Bridge and sank into her command chair.

"Captain, take us home," she called.

Luke nodded.

"*Merkkessa*, initiate Fleet transit to Earth."

<Acknowledged. Fleet transit to Earth initiated>

In the holo, her surviving destroyer screen began a gentle acceleration toward the outer system, a vector that led directly to Earth. Like all other ships in the Fleet, the destroyers were pockmarked with hastily patched holes and the scars of near misses. And like every other ship in the Fleet, they were packed with wounded.

Shortly after, *Merkkessa* also began accelerating out of the system. Two surviving battlecruisers and three surviving cruisers flew in formation with her, a wedge of ships representing all that was still flyable of the proud EDF fleet from one week earlier. Both the *Victory* on her left quarter and the *Asiana* on her right - and the cruisers behind them - were covered in temporary patches. They had just enough structural integrity to survive the trip home.

As they departed, Bonnie could see in the holo the mixed Dariama and Human task force left behind. The shipyards of Dekanna were filled with broken ships, while others waited in orbit to be towed in and rebuilt. In the battlefield in the outer system, tugs worked to collect debris, sorting it into usable materials to take to the shipyards or trash to be shot into the star.

And bodies. Burial details were still at work to find and collect bodies. They would be collecting bodies from the black for weeks, if not months.

*Such a waste. Such a complete and total waste,* Bonnie thought. *If there is anything stupider than war, I don't know what it is. And yet we had no choice. We were forced into it. Our backs were against the wall. It was fight or die.*

*Sherman had it right. War is hell. But more than that. It's ignorance. It's the brute stupidity of those who can't leave others alone to live their lives. Who must force their selfish ego on the innocent, to stroke their own pathological perversions...*

"On course for Earth, milady," called Luke.

"Thank you, Captain," Bonnie acknowledged. She rose from her command chair and walked toward her day cabin, her head down, thinking.

Luke watched his Admiral go. He could see the pain in her.

*I'm not sure I ever want to be an Admiral,* Luke thought.

# EPILOGUE

**Sol System**
**Surface of Venus**

Command Officer Rauti stared at the cratered, broken surface of Venus stretching before him. His eyes were not like Human eyes - they used radar. That allowed him to see through the dense, corrosive atmosphere of the planet. Layer upon layer of specialized coatings protected him from the incredible temperature, pressure, and chemicals of the surface. His squat body had ten stubby legs, like a centipede. And like a centipede, he could move over the rough surface without hesitation.

Below him in the flat space where their capsule had landed, the rest of his Goblin party assembled their initial habitat. In a few more hours, they would have their surface station completed.

Then they would start assembling the first terraforming bot. That first bot would replicate itself. Then both of those bots would replicate themselves. Then again. And again. A month from now, there would be 262,144 terraforming bots working on the surface, while another 262,144 bots continued to replicate themselves. In six months, billions of the bots would be working to cleanse the atmosphere of its harmful chemicals and greenhouse gases. In a year, there would be trillions of them, covering the surface of the planet like algae.

Far above Rauti, outside the Venusian atmosphere, his second team had begun assembly of the space elevator. They would use that to bring raw materials to orbit. Then they could begin construction of the first Dyson object - a half-shell that would cover the sunward side of the planet completely.

*One hundred years*, thought Rauti. *One hundred years from now, a Human will be able to walk unprotected on this planet.*

*But I wonder if they will remember what we did for them. I wonder if they will stand up to their bargain with us.*

## Enroute to Stalingrad
## Packet Boat *Donkey*

Rita came back to herself. It was dark. She didn't know where she was.

The last thing she remembered clearly was sitting with Orma in the Singheko shuttle, on her way to Zukra's palace to be tortured and killed.

*The poison. Stephanie gave me poison. Why am I alive?*

She realized she had another hazy memory. Jim, standing over her in a hospital room. And another vague memory of waking in a shuttle, with Jim lying beside her, holding her.

*How could that be?*

She tried to speak. But something was wrong. She couldn't feel her tongue. It was as if she had no tongue. She panicked.

*I'm losing my mind!*

Suddenly she felt a touch. A hand on her shoulder, then moving down to take her hand. She heard a voice.

"Easy, Rita. Take it easy. Everything is OK. You're safe."

*Jim.*

*That's Jim.*

She tried to speak again. This time, somehow, it worked. She heard her voice.

"Where..."

But it wasn't really her voice. It was close; it was almost her voice. But something was different. And she couldn't feel her tongue.

"Where..."

"You're safe, Rita. Everything is alright. We're both safe, and we're going to have a wonderful life together. We're going to Stalingrad right now - you're going to need some rehabilitation. Then we'll go to Earth to get Imogen. Then we're going to explore the Universe together. Just relax. I'll tell you all about it."

###

# AUTHOR NOTES

*Author Notes*

Just below these notes you'll find a preview of Remnants - Book Five of the Broken Galaxy series. We'll see how Jim and Rita handle her new capabilities as a pure AI, with no fixed physical body anymore. As you may remember, Rita's always had a mischievous side. My mind runs wild.

Finally, don't hesitate to contact me with thoughts / ideas at the locations below!

Sci-Fi, New Books, Hard Science, and General Mayhem
www.facebook.com/PhilHuddlestonAuthor

Author Page on Amazon:
www.amazon.com/author/philhuddleston

<u>Special bonus</u> - if you have not already signed up for my newsletter, sign up now and get one of my books for free!
www.philhuddleston.com/newsletter

All the best,
Phil

# PREVIEW OF NEXT BOOK

Remnants – Broken Galaxy Book Five

**Sol System**
**Surface of Venus**

Commander Rauti gazed with radar eyes and was pleased. His Goblin detachment had successfully completed the first structure of their surface base on Venus. They were off to a good start.

Had a normal Human been able to survive in the caustic atmosphere of Venus for any significant period of time, they would have seen two low mounds, crossing in their centers like the letter 'X'. Each side of the 'X' was five hundred and fifty meters long. The remainder of the structure was underground.

Beneath that mound were the command-and-control centers for the expedition, living quarters for his crew of 150 Goblins, and storage areas for their gear. That structure would be their home for the next 150 rotations of the planet. 36,525 Earth days. 100 Earth years.

His government had asked him to terraform the planet in one century. That was challenging, but not beyond the realm of possibility. He had plenty of raw materials and a good crew. He knew he could do it.

Gazing farther afield, Rauti contemplated with pride the crop of microbots that covered the surface as far as he could see. From horizon to horizon, the surface was covered with green, the microbots soaking up the carbon dioxide, converting it to oxygen for the atmosphere and carbon nanotubes for further construction.

The surface was alive with movement, as other microbots collected up the carbon nanotubes and moved the material to pipes, which fed into large hoppers located every ten kilometers.

Within a few more years, the self-replicating microbots would cover the entire planet.

Rauti looked off to the West at the base station for the space elevator. The large mountain there had ten tunnels exiting its base, equally spaced around the mountain. Each tunnel mouth had a tether which exited the tunnel and ran along the ground for several kilometers, anchored to the surface.

Lifting his eyes, Rauti looked at the top of the mountain. What had once been a mountain peak was now flat, chopped off to form the base station for the space elevator. Rising up out of the flat top of the mountain, the individual cables were woven together to create the final tether. That was just a stub so far, ending a few dozen meters above the top of the base station. The main tether would not be extended farther until the upper end came down from space to meet it. But from the top of the stub, a thin preliminary tether continued up into space, its diameter just large enough to allow the transmission of the raw carbon nanotubes to space.

Looking up, Rauti adjusted the wavelength of his eyes so he could see beyond the atmosphere. There, far above, he picked out the other end of the incomplete tether. It terminated at a dumbbell-like structure in geosynchronous orbit, with an additional tether extension continuing upward. Due to the extremely slow rotation speed of Venus, the dumbbell structure was many thousands of kilometers above the surface, much higher than would be required if it were built on Mars or Earth.

But that made no difference to Rauti. The four dozen small asteroids that his Goblin team had moved in from the asteroid belt orbited next to the dumbbell structure. A constant stream of raw materials flowed from the asteroids to the dumbbell via piping filled with microbots, moving the required elements like a river as they disassembled the asteroids.

The final terminal of the preliminary tether was still higher, thousands more kilometers above the dumbbell structure. It would take another ten years to complete the full space elevator. But that made no difference to Rauti. He had all the time in the world to complete the structure, because that was not the critical link in the Goblin's terraforming design. The critical link was still higher, far beyond the terminus of the space elevator.

Adjusting his eyes again, changing to a wavelength that gave him more detail at extreme distances from the planet, Rauti looked with satisfaction at the beginnings of the Dyson shell. That was the structure that would eventually block a significant portion of the solar radiation from the planet, allowing him to cool it to a more reasonable temperature.

The shell so far was only a few hundred kilometers in diameter, a rounded disk making a dark dot on the sun. Beside the disk were dozens of smaller dots in his vision. These were additional asteroids brought in by the Goblins to provide the raw materials for shell construction. Most of them were rocky asteroids, selected for their high carbon or iron content. A few were ice balls, selected for water and trace elements.

It would take Rauti another century to completely reduce the carbon dioxide out of the atmosphere, complete the full Dyson structure screening Venus from the Sun, and bring the temperature down to a reasonable level.

Rauti smiled. He had plenty of time.

**Sol System**
**Backside of Venus**

The two occupants aboard the tiny Stree scout ship knew quite well the range of Goblin radar eyes. As they surveyed Rauti's enormous construction project, they made sure their orbit stayed below the horizon of the Goblin surface station. Their tiny drones on the other side of the planet sent them all the data they needed.

"More blasphemy," said Junior Prophet-in-Training Yatonna, staring at the monitors. "They build as they did at their home planet. Soon they'll have a new colony."

"Yes," replied Senior Prophet-in-Training Cibekku. "If we let them complete this, it will become even harder to root out their blasphemy from the Galaxy. We must warn the Prophet."

The scout ship turned and departed orbit, pushing 400g accel on a line that kept it hidden from the Goblins.

5.3 hours later, traveling at 25 percent light speed, it ceased accel and coasted.

5.4 hours after that, it reached the Sun's mass limit and disappeared.

Stree was 4,725 lights distant.

It would take them a while to get there.

Continue the story with Remnants on Amazon!

# WORKS

**Imprint Series**
Artemis War (prequel novella)
Imprint of Blood
Imprint of War
Imprint of Honor
Imprint of Defiance

**Broken Galaxy Series**
Broken Galaxy
Star Tango
The Long Edge of Night
The Short End
Remnants
Goblin Eternal

# ABOUT THE AUTHOR

Like Huckleberry Finn, Phil Huddleston grew up barefoot and outdoors, catching mudbugs by the creek, chasing rabbits through the fields, and forgetting to come home for dinner. Then he discovered books. Thereafter, he read everything he could get his hands on, including reading the Encyclopedia Britannica and Funk & Wagnalls from A-to-Z multiple times. He served in the U. S. Marines for four years, returned to college and completed his degree on the GI Bill. Since that time, he built computer systems, worked in cybersecurity, played in a band, flew a bush plane from Alaska to Texas, rode a motorcycle around a good bit of America, and watched in amazement as his wife raised two wonderful daughters in spite of him. And would sure like to do it all again. Except maybe without the screams of terror.

Printed in Great Britain
by Amazon